THE ALCHEMY OF SECRETS

Priya Balasubramanian graduated from Christian Medical College, Vellore and is a gastroenterologist and transplant hepatologist in Sacramento, California. Her non-fiction has appeared on NPR, *Scoundrel Time* and ROAR, and her fiction has been featured on *Litro* in the UK.

The Alchemy of Secrets is her debut novel.

www.priyabalasubramanian.com

PRIYA
BALASUBRAMANIAN

THE ALCHEMY OF SECRETS

First published by Tranquebar, an imprint of Westland Publications Private Limited, in 2019

Published by Westland Books, a division of Nasadiya Technologies Private Limited, in 2023

No. 269/2B, First Floor, 'Irai Arul', Vimalraj Street, Nethaji Nagar, Allappakkam Main Road, Maduravoyal, Chennai 600095

ISBN: 9789357761536

10 9 8 7 6 5 4 3 2 1

This is a work of fiction. Names, characters, organisations, places, events and incidents are either products of the author's imagination or used fictitiously.

Typeset by SÜRYA, New Delhi

Printed at : Manipal Technologies Limited, Manipal

For Nanda

1
Mira

It is a late evening in 1979, in a Bangalore that now exists only in faded newsprint and memory.

The sky darkens overhead while the vegetable vendors on the street fire up their kerosene lamps in anticipation. The evening pooja at the temple has ended and supplicants straggle homeward, stopping for vegetables or gossip. A game of street cricket continues in defiance of impending demise, for streetlights will flare momentarily to announce dinner for the players. Tiny brown and white sparrows take flight, squawking at wayward balls that interrupt their pecking. Bird sounds, wheels bumping along on potholed road, shouted conversations across the street and the thump of ball on bat, all melt into the evening breeze that arrives from some cooler clime, making it hum as it dusts off the street.

My grandmother stops at the flower-seller's stall. It is halfway along the steps to Ganesha's temple on the hill. We are on our way back after the evening pooja and Ajji has a basket to return. She adjusts her white saree over her head as we wait. I am almost four years old, wearing a favourite striped green frock and clutching a photograph in one hand. I stand on tiptoe and strain to see over the wooden platform that Lakshmi, the flower-seller, sits on with her son, Vinay, who is just a little older than I am. I lean in and the tobacco-laced betel that she chews and the jasmine strands that she sells all day long envelop me, in smells pungent and delicate all at once.

Lakshmi sits cross-legged, surrounded by reams of white jasmine, orange kankambara and yellow marigolds. She measures them fingertip to elbow and sells them to hurried housewives and white-sareed widows with motherless girls in tow. She talks incessantly. Of drunken husbands and lazy wives, negligent mothers and barren women. Mothers who die early to leave their children orphaned.

She questions Ajji with nonchalance, as if it is the weather she enquires about.

'Amma,' she says, 'what a beautiful child. They told me she is your granddaughter?'

'Yes,' Ajji says, returning her basket.

'Your son's daughter? Or your daughter's? Such sadness in the world, when mothers die so young—'

'My son's daughter, he's the one who has gone to America. Her name is Mira,' Ajji says, and adds, 'We need to be going home, it was a long pooja.'

She starts to turn, but Lakshmi presses on, 'Was it childbirth, Amma? That was how my cousin's wife died, taking the baby with her. He would have been twelve today if she had left him behind.'

Ajji stops mid-turn. 'Lakshmamma, we are an old family, even if we are from a small town. We do not speak of these things on the street. But since you ask, she died in an accident.'

Lakshmi waits for more information, but none is forthcoming.

Lakshmi knows people by the depths of their desperation, which stops them at her stall for flowers on their way up the hill and unburdening on the way down. She collects these nuggets to share with her other customers, ending her tales with little homilies, 'Everyone has troubles, don't you see? You should be grateful to Ganesha yours are not as big as theirs.' But she is no wiser at the end of this short exchange than she was before, and she sighs to Ajji in defeat, 'Some people talk about their troubles, Amma, some hug them to their chest like treasure. Here is your change.'

I have been entranced, through this conversation, by Lakshmi's fingers. They loop, bend, slip, knot and pull string over the frail jasmine stems pinched together in two-headed clumps, even as Lakshmi is busy at her gossip, making evenly spaced garlands of white fragrance. She has noticed my fascination. She holds a small length of flowers out to me as we turn to leave, as she will many times in the years to come. Ajji tries to pay for the flowers, and Lakshmi refuses. 'My gift, Amma, for this motherless child.'

Lakshmi turns away from us. Perhaps a corner of her pity for me has been assuaged by the gift. She returns to weaving hope and devotion, measured finger-tip to elbow, four lengths to a rupee. Ajji turns away as well, looking mildly irritated at this suggestion of charity that her granddaughter has brought on.

We walk home through the winding tree-lined streets. Ajji strides ahead, saree pulled close against the faint evening breeze. I hang on to her little finger. My whole hand is curled around it. In my other hand, carefully clutched, are my flowers and the photograph. My short frock tickles my legs in the breeze as I take three steps to one of hers. She hurries me along the way because I let go of her hand often, to pick up leaves and stones or stop and peer at insects in the dirt. There is a gentleness in Ajji's gestures to me that is absent in her other actions or her straight-backed efficient stride, a patience that I sense is not usual for her, and the smile she cannot hide when she scolds me for picking up stones off the street. All of it adds up to a love that proclaims itself so quietly, it cannot be denied.

We hurry past the boys now pulling up the branches-that-are-cricket-stumps and debating winners and losers to the day's game. We walk by a busy ration shop that will be abandoned in the years to come, because the shop keeper is going to hang himself from its ceiling over a bad debt and be rumoured to come back nightly after. We go by a movie theatre that will one day be destroyed. By the new and empty block of apartments that will soon house Anisa, my constant childhood companion, and her family. The path takes us to the winding street that ends on Sampige Road, where, in a flat roofed, squat and spread out home, my childhood will be lived.

A black Ambassador sedan with government licence plates leaves our street as we turn into it. Ajji stops mid-stride as if she suspects who might be sitting behind the opaque windows of the back seat. She does not say anything just then, but I feel her anger, sharp and sudden.

Girish uncle, my father's older brother, sits at the veranda in our house. He is young, and his full head of hair, black. His prodigious future paunch is still an incipient roundness. He fans himself with the day's newspaper, while others lie at his feet, crumpled and read. He has had visitors and their empty cups of coffee lie scattered on the floor, attended by a lone housefly. He smiles and holds his arms out to me.

But then his eyes narrow on the photograph that I have been clutching all day, along with the jasmine Lakshmi just gave me.

It is the photograph I found the day before, rummaging through the things my father left behind when he went off to America. The woman in the picture is wearing a deeply blue saree with sequins like stars. There is elegance to the tilt of her head, a playful curve to her smile. There is laughter in her eyes, maybe love, even. I had carried the picture into the kitchen, laughing, waving it so Ajji would see. Ajji and my aunt, Vimala, had looked at each other, and Ajji said, as if she thought I could not understand, 'Children forget quickly, she will not remember tomorrow. I don't know how she managed to find the one picture of her that we have.'

It is already the day after, and I have not let the picture out of my sight or grasp, waking or asleep.

Ajji notices the narrowing of my uncle's eyes, as I do.

'You let her carry *this* around?' he asks Ajji, as if it is proof of some greater wrongdoing. 'Out into the street so everybody can see her face?'

'Time for dinner,' Ajji says to no one in particular, scooping me up in her arms and stepping past him.

Girish uncle refuses to be deflected. 'As if you are proud of all the things her mother did. This is what you teach your granddaughter? Think of what my father would say.'

He says the last under the picture of my grandfather in the hall that Ajji has garlanded with fresh flowers just that morning. It is a formal picture of my grandfather taken a few years before he died, in which the stiffness of his posture is belied by his youth and the smile in his eyes.

Ajji stops. It is as if my uncle has crossed some invisible line. 'I know what my husband would want, better than some young fool who barely knew him.'

My uncle continues to mutter, pacing the hall, but it is useless. Ajji steps into the kitchen, and her domain.

I see my uncle from the kitchen, as I do my grandfather. Girish uncle has my grandfather's sharply angular cheekbones, his bony nose and deep-set eyes that draw attention. But his petulance, and the comfortable padding of fat that stoops his shoulders and rounds his cheek and chin, make him, in balance, completely different in appearance.

Ajji is angry. There is just a little extra force to the plate she sets on the floor and in the thud of the steel tumbler of water alongside next.

'Who came to the house, Vimala?' she asks my aunt, Girish uncle's wife. Vimala aunty stands at the stove, in her creased saree and flyaway unruly hair that she attempts to subdue in a knot at her neck, making neer dosa, a special treat for me. The batter sizzles, and it is almost louder than my aunt's mumbled answer, 'Surendra.'

My aunt drops the first neer dosa on my plate, careful not to let the serving spoon touch the plate. They will sit down to dinner later, together or separately, and eat the more traditional rice and vegetables. But they indulge me in this treat for dinner, and with such lack of fanfare, I recognise it for the everyday occurrence it is.

As she feeds me, Ajji tells me a story. In a carrying voice doubtless meant to reach my uncle in the hall, Ajji tells the story of Shravana. Between bites of buttered neer dosa that are wrapped around morsels of jaggery and coconut, I listen.

Shravana is a boy who carries his blind father and mother in baskets hung on either side of a bamboo stick that he bears on his shoulders. He puts duty to family above all else and goes to heaven because of it. It is a part of some larger story, and Ajji picks this dreary tale for her own reasons. It leaves a sinking feeling in my chest. The weighing-down worry that if Ajji, Girish uncle and Vimala aunty became old, it will be my lot to carry them, in wicker chairs like the ones in the veranda, strapped to a bamboo stick on my shoulders.

~

Ajji's stories are like that. I see them better in hindsight twenty years later, standing at my kitchen counter in my pyjamas, than I have ever done before.

Ajji shifted details and blurred story lines, and thought she controlled all they contained. But the stories were older and wilier than she was. They hit eardrums and minds other than the ones she intended, with messages she could not anticipate. It was Girish uncle she was angry with, either for his reaction to the picture, or the visitor that he had. But the tale delivered its burden to the child I was that evening instead.

Outside, a dark California predawn shrouds my windows and the homes of my neighbours. A tap drips, indoors somewhere. Cold air seeps in under the kitchen window of my second-floor apartment, and I stand, still holding on to the phone. Soldier, my little affenpinscher, rubs up against my legs.

My father has just called me to say that Ajji is dying.

I turn on the lights, find the tap that is dripping, scoop coffee out of a jar for the machine and try to process the fact that seems so improbable. Ajji, dying. It shouldn't be the surprise it is; she is not young. But Ajji's presence in my life—loving, annoying, stubborn and completely maddening—is one I have not imagined being without.

When the coffee maker gurgles and spits behind me, Soldier barks alongside. He's excited by our changed routine. I worry about the thin walls, and the neighbours. I shush him, and call my father back. Just how sick did they say she was, I intend to ask, and how can they be sure she is dying? But when I hear his voice, I remember that he is Ajji's favourite son, and I, her only granddaughter. I find myself saying instead that I'll go with him to Bangalore after all, even though I have spent years thinking I never would.

The world outside softens and greys as I make preparations to leave. I water my collection of potted plants, and gather them together by the door. They, like Soldier, will have to be handed off to other people's care. I turn up blinds, find sheets to cover furniture and empty out the fridge, a task made easy by the fact that I can, but almost never, cook. There's a half empty carton of milk and wilted salad greens among an assortment of take out containers. I contemplate my wardrobe for clothes that will pass muster in India, and realise my defiance has been limited. There is nothing in it that would be scandalous or inappropriate. I pull out at random and pack away long-sleeved blouses in shades of grey and black, loose fitting jeans and sweat pants. Longish skirts.

There are calls to make. To my boss, who's sympathetic despite the early hour. To friends with whom I've made plans for the week. Then the man I was supposed to meet for lunch today. It was a date I'd accepted in annoyance over Ajji's long-distance meddling, her insistence on marriage and the suitable sons of distant relatives she'd sent my way. He only half believes this story of a family emergency, though I assure him it's true. He laughs the easy laugh he had when I first confused his name, Yohannes, for Your Highness. I'd stared a bit and wondered if he were joking. He'd asked me out almost immediately after. He's tall, good looking and Ethiopian. I'd accepted for once, an impulse based on all that, and more: a sneaky delight at Ajji's possible reaction to him. This stops me in my tracks again; how can she be dying?

Then, behind my passport, in the drawer with valuables, I find the picture. A young woman smiles into the camera. My mother's glance is at once intimate and enigmatic, sequins bright in her blue saree like the stars in her eyes. In the moment before I slide her picture into my purse with the passport, I think: I once wanted to look just like her. I don't, not now. My hair is short and permed where hers was long, silky and coiled. My clothes loose and dark, where I know hers were probably fitted close, bright and elegant. I scan anxiously in the mirror now and then for differences, not similarities.

I *am* different from her, I tell myself even as a small voice of honesty adds, *at least on the outside.*

Soldier jumps up into my arms with the way he has of knowing my moods and passing clouds. Together, we watch my neighbours' carefully tended lawns and hedges being unveiled, along with the fine frost that dusts them into beauty. We wait for my father. Suddenly, I want nothing more than to be able to see Ajji, alive and impossible as always, for one last time. The price, of course, is to face all that remains in Bangalore, all that I thought, until this morning, was left safely behind. Ajji might smile at my predicament, even under the circumstances. Her stories of Fate and comeuppance are ones I remember, even if I no longer believe. There are people I've hurt and mistakes I've made. A sorrow of my doing that I ran from seven years before.

I set Soldier down gently by the plants. I have promised Appa and made my preparations. There is no turning back now. I cannot afford to wonder if I am strong enough. I have to be, and it is time.

2

Vimala

It was late evening and Vimala was cooking to a haze of aerosolised rice flour in her windowless kitchen when the phone call arrived. It was her husband, Girish, and a short conversation. Ajji had collapsed on the street, and passers-by had sent her to the new hospital in town, Lakhotia's. Vimala turned off the stove under her simmering lentils. She covered the rice dough she had been working on with a wet towel, locked the front door, and left. She did not wait to change her flour-dusted saree or run a comb through her hair or stop to greet the neighbour who came out into the street as she closed the gate behind her.

It's probably the heat, she told herself, or the fasts she keeps. Once she's better, she'll have to stop. Somebody has to make her stop.

When the auto rickshaw she took deposited her at the hospital, the watchman waved her through without the customary crisp salute. Vimala was suddenly conscious of her flyaway hair and old saree, and a realisation that she must seem like someone's maid. She made her way to the imposing reception area with gleaming dark wood at the north end of the marble foyer.

'I'm looking for Mrs Meenakshi Murthy,' she said to the receptionist, who looked surprised for an instant, before saying smoothly, 'Of course, Madam, and you are a relative?'

Vimala was momentarily amused. She imagined the girl would have pointed to the service elevator in the back, had she asked the question in Kannada instead of English.

Vimala was not allowed to enter Ajji's room, despite being escorted to the door. Ajji was in the ICU. No visitors were allowed. When Girish arrived two hours later, Shyamal Lakhotia, the owner of Lakhotia Hospital, came down himself to welcome him, positively beaming at the opportunity to have Girish Murthy in his debt. Vimala supposed there was always a likelihood that he would need permits or leave for the odd transgression from the Public Works Department, where Girish had risen through the years.

The senior ICU specialist, Dr Jayant Shenoy, was summoned quickly after. 'She's quite sick, critical really—but some of her problems may be reversible,' he said. 'We'll have to wait and see. Another two to four days, and things will be clearer.'

Vimala wondered if this was his standard response to the better-heeled patients and their families, especially when there were empty beds in the ICU to be filled and quotas for the month to be met. Assurances regarding Ajji's care were given and received, however, and Girish remembered that he had an appointment at the club that could not be missed.

'I'll send someone with a change of clothes,' he told Vimala as he left. 'Maybe some food from the canteen downstairs?' he asked of Shyamal, who said, beaming some more, 'Of course, of course, I'll make sure some is brought up for Madam, for as long as your good mother is with us. You are both our guests, of course.'

The rules were bent a little, just enough to let Vimala slip between them and behind the frosted glass doors of the ICU, where a chair was found for her to sit by Ajji's bed.

Ajji looked grey and drawn. Vimala began to worry again. She had watched Ajji's fasts begin that final morning when

Mira left, when her niece had seemed a shadow in the clothes of a girl they had known and loved.

Ajji's fasts had intensified in the years of Mira's absence, and Vimala had known that they drained Ajji's body even as they fortified her resolve. But she had not expected this, where her mother-in-law lost herself in increments to become this gaunt and birdlike woman who might be on her deathbed. Vimala sat by her, watchful and awake, until the early hours of dawn with the faint red haze of the sun in the window behind Ajji's bed. That was when she walked to the window, craning her neck, only to see empty streets and shuttered storefronts that were still lit by orange street lamps.

What happens, happens, she thought as she often did when faced with problems that seemed insurmountable; what is the point of running around like a chicken in a farmyard? We do the little we can and think we change the world—but all we do is run inside a train that has left the station and is on its way somewhere. We get there whether we want to or not, whether we run to or away from that station.

But this calming mantra that she summoned up did not work as it usually did. This moment seemed a major change from all that had passed in her life, a decision point of sorts. If Ajji lived, life could go on as before. If Ajji died, she thought, as the guilt rose up in her throat fast and hot at the implied disloyalty of that thought, all of the things that she had held as constant all of her adult life would change.

The first signs of life appeared on the street below. Workers who began their day early could be seen walking up the street to the bus-stop right under Ajji's window, lighting cigarettes, rubbing their arms in the coolness of dawn, talking. Soon there will be milkmen, she thought, or newspaper boys on their bicycles. Or women with produce and flowers in wicker baskets on their heads, fresh from the wholesalers at City

Market, singsong voices announcing their wares to waking housewives.

But before that, just around now, she thought, her husband would be leaving his mistress. The driver was probably hurrying his car to the gate of her apartment building for him to sneak into, before he could be spotted in the morning light. Then he would be on his way home from the discreet apartment in Benson Town where he had most likely entertained last night, his deal-making facilitated by imported liquor and spicy tandoori food served by his glamorous mistress. She knew her, of course. Despite Girish Murthy's discretion and his vast network of favours given and received, loyalties bought and bartered, Vimala knew. Girish's driver was Vinay, Lakshmi the flower-seller's son. Lakshmi had ferreted the truth from her son in her demands to know how and where he spent his hours when he came home so late and left so early. And she had told Vimala, in a whispered conversation on one of Vimala's rare visits to the temple.

The next time Vimala saw Sitara, the starlet who was her husband's mistress, it was in a rerun on television. She noted especially the slippery chiffon saree over her plump roundness, the simpering overstated sexuality that, she supposed, older men like Girish found irresistible. She shrugged. The movie career must have ended, poor thing, she told herself, and designed a Technicolor dream where the slightly-beyond-her-prime-starlet and her husband had a blazing row over his inability to satisfy her many needs, primarily her sexual ones.

After that, the mistress no longer bothered Vimala, or so she told herself. She read letters from other women who shared her plight in the advice sections of *Eve's Weekly* and *Women's Era*, and thought, more chickens running around in a farmyard. As if their advice will change anything. Divorce, hmpf. Don't they get tired of printing these letters? She pretended these letters had no relation to the tension headaches and the cramps in her abdomen that came so suddenly, out of the blue, soon after. It was the heat, something I ate—she would stubbornly rationalise, prostrated in pain.

No, Vimala liked to think that Girish's mistress bothered her slightly less than the fact that the lentils were slowly spoiling on the stove in her kitchen. It certainly could not compare to the bitter green bile of guilt and fear that she tasted in her mouth when she thought that Ajji might die. She did not feel that way because Ajji had agreed that she, the daughter of a poor relative, could be her older son's wife so many years ago, without a grand wedding or a dowry. She did not think it because Ajji had been, despite her overbearing manner and her histrionics, the only mother that she now remembered. It was because Ajji bore the blame and the secrets of things greater than Girish's infidelities.

I'll go back to Malehalli, she decided, I'll have to find someone who will give me a job, to look after a baby or an invalid parent, for food and a roof above my head.

Vimala watched the sun declare itself in the glistening of leaves on trees outside her window, thinking of the phone call her husband had no doubt made. Girish telling his younger brother Kishore, Mira's father, in America, 'She is sinking, there are no guarantees. The doctor wanted us to let all her close relatives know.'

The first vehicles interrupted the solitude of the street, empty buses that stopped to pick up the day labourers and office-goers outside her window, and she allowed herself to wonder about the aftermath of the phone call. There would be more hurried phone calls, she thought, her brother-in-law would have to call Mira and find those emergency quota tickets again, many layovered and roundabout ones that would bring him and Mira back. His new wife, Celia, would probably stay behind. It has been years since they were married, she thought in surprise, but Celia was still the new wife, and maybe she would always be. Perhaps she would kiss them both, outside the airport. Women did that in America, Vimala knew, kissed their husbands in public. Still, she could not avoid the polite embarrassment she felt at the image of her brother-in-law, now middle-aged, being kissed in plain view of all who cared to look.

But Mira, she thought, as the noises in the street grew under her, Mira. She was a young woman and, now, probably the very image of her mother. Radhika Murthy, the woman she had been careful to avoid in her thoughts for all these years.

Vimala turned away from the window and her meandering imaginings to Ajji. Ajji could not die. She could not leave her to bear the burden of Radhika and their silence, alone. Vimala reached for her mother-in-law's hand with a new urgency, hoping the strength of her desperation would transmit itself to her, and wake her to life and responsibility.

3

Mira

When the doorbell rings, the sky outside has lightened to the pale blue of a genteel dawn. Appa stands outside in his usual attire—dark pants, striped shirt and the customary air of a man who has misplaced something vital and does not know quite what it is yet.

He draws me into a one-armed embrace and relieves me of my bag. I'm almost as tall as he is, and his arm rests easy on my shoulders.

'Oh good, you're packed and ready,' he says. 'We were lucky. The tickets were easy to get.'

Downstairs by the car, Celia gathers me into her arms the way she did when I first arrived, as Soldier leaps and yaps alongside. There are dark smudges around her eyes, faint crow's feet now more apparent, her auburn curls listless and lacking in their usual fire. My own curls are an homage to Celia's, though she doesn't know. I wonder when the phone call arrived. She looks as if she has stayed up all night.

'Are you sure?' she asks, looking hard into my face. 'Do you really want to go?'

'I have to. It's Ajji.'

'Yes, of course,' she says, patting me on the shoulder and sighing. 'You have to.'

We drive up through the quiet streets in a silence punctuated by Soldier's barking, and Appa and Celia murmuring incessantly to each other in the front seat. It is mostly details of shared domesticity—of bills and gradings of assignments due, of lawns that need mowing and a car scheduled to be serviced. From time to time one of them turns around to me—did I remember my passport, have I let the people at work know?

It feels quick, this journey. My adopted home rushes by my window in empty sidewalks and still-sleeping neighbours. It stretches outside our sparsely populated freeway in dense orange groves and fallow land, fast food signs and familiar cities, bushes of oleander growing thick and wild alongside through them all. When the road hugs the coastline close to San Francisco, it is only a little more than an hour later. My first glimpse of the familiar skyline, for once and like some gentle omen, is unobscured by fog.

At the airport, Celia worries that we have cut it too close. The tickets Appa found are for a flight that leaves soon. A flurry of activity ensues, with baggage, carts, boarding passes that a determinedly cheerful gate assistant prints up, and we are finally at the security check where the lines seem short.

Celia hugs me again, and whispers, 'Be strong,' as if it is a talisman. I can feel her unspoken worry. When I first arrived from Bangalore, distraught and lost, Appa was too overwhelmed to do anything but watch me from across the dinner table in a bewildered silence. It was Celia who drove me to school and doctors' appointments, short-lived and futile counselling sessions, even a discourse that a saffron-clad monk gave a hundred miles away, once. It was Celia who found Soldier, my ironically named little toy of a dog. Perfect, someone had told her, for girls that needed therapy, and love.

It *will* get better, she'd say, often and without prompting. It was her belief, and Soldier, that I clung to during the years I graduated from college, found a job, and moved out of their home to my tiny apartment, all the steps to building my American life anew. Her worry now gives me pause, but it is only a momentary weakness.

'I'm going to be fine,' I tell her, and believe it a bit more for saying it.

'Come back soon,' she says, unconvinced.

I give Soldier one final, good-for-weeks hug. 'Be good for Celia,' I tell him as I set him down, and he runs merry oblivious circles around the three of us.

Appa and I make it to the gate with plenty of time, after all. We settle into plastic chairs and wait to board. There are businessmen and students, grandparents and young families with infants.

'I should have gone back sooner to see her,' Appa says, presently. He looks a bit haggard, as if we are at journey's end and not the beginning.

'She will be fine until we get there,' I say, reaching over to pat Appa's arm. I am not sure I believe that, but I have an urge as always, to comfort Appa. I suspect that this is something that other people feel, too. He looks, some days, like a man lost in some personal quagmire.

I don't ask him why he did not go sooner. His relationship with Ajji has been fraught. I don't know the details, but I do know my mother was a big part of it. Years ago, before Soldier, making my way out of a fog of antidepressants and therapists, I had asked him about it. It had gone badly.

When I had mustered up the courage to ask, the question came out brash, and bald. 'Is it true what they say about her,' I'd asked him, meaning my mother, 'that she abandoned me? That there was a lover?'

Even as I'd heard the words leave my mouth and begun to wonder at my daring, Appa had erupted in fury. 'How dare you?' he'd said, over and over. 'And you are her daughter.

You!' It was a tirade that told me little, and ended with him dragging me over to the kitchen sink. 'Wash your mouth out with soap, stupid girl.'

I had never seen Appa angry. Not even mildly, the way parents are at a report card, or a crazed driver on the street. And perhaps he had never lost control so completely before. I remember staring at him for what seemed a long time, until we heard the garage door open, and Celia return with groceries.

It seemed to bring him back, the sounds of Celia in the hallway just beyond.

'People talk,' he said, removing the fingers that had been digging into my shoulder and retreating into the mild-mannered man he was, 'but you know that's not true. You, of all people, should know. You know the things they said about you.'

Which is the thing, really: the things people said about me were true.

~

In that Bangalore of seven years ago, a summer holiday is close to its end. Soon we will be back at school, in twelfth standard. We are seventeen. Anisa is fair and petite, a younger and prettier version of her mother, with dimples she flashes at will and to good advantage. I am dark-skinned, angular and tall, given to comparing my face anxiously and frequently to my mother's in the one picture I have of her. Anisa and I met in kindergarten, and have been inseparable since.

Anisa's mother, Rehana aunty, mixes up batter and slices onions. She is making pakodas.

Anisa is my sister, more than friend. There is not much that we own alone. She explores my pantheistic idol-worshipping religion, insisting on knowing the lesser-known details of minor Hindu tales, while I pretend in secret guilt that her parents are also mine. I do not yet suspect that I will eat her mother's famous mutton biryani one day, leaving the meat untouched in little piles on my plate, or that the forbidden food will flavour my mouth with the promise of another, more forbidden happiness. We are ignorant that it is our last summer together.

Anisa and I are bored. We have listened to the same top ten Bollywood songs one too many times. We can recite their inane lyrics in entirety. '*Kaboothar Jaa Jaa Jaa*,' we have sung, and then giggled through, 'Pigeon, go, go, go,' in an unnecessarily literal translation, swooning like the teenaged heroine does in the throes of her first love. 'How silly, how totally silly,' we've gasped between laughs, confident that we will never be so overcome.

The books we've borrowed from the library have been exhausted. There isn't one among them that bears a second read. The movie being re-run on the only channel other than Doordarshan is insufferable, melodramatic. So we venture out on to the balcony, which is baking in the heat. We lean over the rails. The air settles like a blanket. Pedestrians dwindle in defeat.

There are boys playing cricket on the road below us, and they do so resignedly, walking instead of running between the makeshift wickets, or behind the balls they knock between parked vehicles. We ignore them, and the fact that from time to time one of them looks up in our direction.

It is not that we know them, except for Vinay, who is Lakshmi the flower-seller's son. Vinay was our playmate on the street for several years when we were too young to know any better. Now we ignore Vinay along with the rest of them. It has been years since we have talked to him, anyway. We saw him smoking behind the movie theatre once, with the tonga drivers. So it seems natural, the way it happened, the way we stopped smiling at him in the street, and the way our eyes slid right by him for the first time as he played cricket with his friends. Besides, it is not proper, we've told ourselves, for girls our age to be seen talking in the street to someone like him.

'I wish it would rain,' Anisa says, without much hope that it will.

'It's still too early for rain,' Rehana aunty calls out to us over the half-hearted sizzle of the first pakoda that goes in too early. 'Why don't you sit inside under the fan, instead of complaining?'

The fan seems irresistible. Yet we linger, and suddenly, improbably, the first few raindrops arrive out of nowhere. Anisa calls out to her mother, 'It's starting to rain. Are there clothes drying on the terrace?'

Before we hear Rehana aunty's reply, we hear the thunder rumble. Gusts of wind arrive, whipping up mud and leaf, clothing hung out to dry, all into the street. They knock tree branch against window, rattle panes left open in what might have been vain hope only moments before. As Rehana aunty says, 'Thank goodness, no,' leaving the pakodas on the stove to rush out on to the balcony, the giant black clouds arrive, blotting out the sun in sudden swift revenge. All around us, the world is jolted into activity.

Pedestrians dive for cover under awnings and porticoes. Housewives rush out to rescue their washing, green mangoes left to dry in the sun for pickling and their wayward toddlers drawn outside by the commotion. The boys playing cricket outside pull up their wickets. Instead of rushing inside like everyone else, they begin to run around the street waving bats, wickets and shirts through the mud-flecked air, shouting and laughing. Grandmothers and grandchildren gather on doorsteps and at windows, calling out to neighbours they had ignored just that morning. We stretch our hands out into the cooling air, through the air flecked with leaves and the gritty dust it swirls up, in anticipation.

In moments, a giant shower darkens the sky.

Only minutes into it, a motorbike slices neatly through the sheets of rain to stop in the courtyard of Anisa's apartment building. The driver is lanky and helmeted, his blue jeans darkened on the sides by wetness, shirt plastered to his back. Before I see his face, I count the nubs of bones that stand out under his shirt. Two scapulae and three vertebrae, just a hint of ribs, maybe. It is a triumph of Mrs Singh's biology lessons that she will never know about.

He gets off and swings a long length of rain-splattered blue-jeaned leg off the seat. Then he takes off his helmet and unfastens the black bag secured to the back of the motorbike, and loops it over his head onto his shoulder. It is a single fluid movement. There is rain still falling on his exposed hair and back, which is turned to us. He doesn't lift a hand to shield himself. Instead he turns around and looks up, through the still falling rain. Directly at me. It is as if my scrutiny draws his eyes, even though there must be at least a dozen different pairs of eyes on him from the minute he roared into our street. For a moment, like in the most tawdry of potboilers, we both freeze.

Rehana aunty says, 'Oh look, Adil's here,' and waves from the balcony, as does Anisa. When he finally looks away at them, I see the rest of his face. The small rectangle of forehead over which his hair strays. Rain-splattered eyebrows, both broad, one slightly bigger than the other, and thick, stubby eyelashes, just above a slender nose and a wide mouth, thin lips framing even teeth. And finally, like a surprise for last, a wide chin with a perfect mid-line cleft. A hint of stubble shades cheek and clefted chin. Is he handsome? I cannot say. I haven't had time enough to look at that face properly, as a whole instead of its parts. But perfect, it is. Of that, there can be no doubt.

For a moment he stands there, smiling and waving in the rain, and the next, he has walked on towards the entrance of the building, out of sight. Rehana aunty remembers her burnt pakodas blackening in the hot oil while she watched the rain. She tch-tch-es her annoyance as she runs to turn off the stove.

'Anisa, can you go find a towel for Adil?' she says, as she fishes out the ruined fritters. 'Mira, can you open the door?'

It is only a short walk to the door, but one I wish were longer. I need the time to summon up the homilies that Sister Lalitha launched into at school, in the middle of her integrated math lessons. Unexpected speeches that began with, 'Boys want only one thing,' in the middle of solving quadratic equations, or, 'Good girls need to be careful,' while we pondered trigonometry, sine-cos-tan, as if she saw in our short-skirted uniforms and folded-down socks an invitation that we intended. Be-careful-be-careful, I mutter under my breath, trying to slow down my steps to the door. But the words slide, heedless, just as they did when Anisa and I first heard them, giggling together under raised textbooks.

He stands there, arm still raised over the doorbell, when I open the door. I feel his eyes focus and narrow down on my face. It is an odd, wordless moment before Anisa comes up with the towel, saying, 'Adil, why are you still standing outside?' and Rehana aunty follows, clucking her tongue over his wet hair and clothes. 'Why didn't you wait somewhere for the rain to stop, you will catch a cold.'

I step aside. I am being fanciful, I tell myself. The air does not crackle between us when he steps past me into the drawing room. This is Adil, Rehana aunty's youngest brother. Anisa's youngest uncle, only four years older than us, and one she treats like a cousin. A boy I have seen so many times before, and ignored almost as often. He is here for a summer project at the Indian Institute of Science, where Farid uncle, Anisa's father, works. This is silly. In a minute we will talk, and this strangeness will be gone.

'Adil, remember Mira?' Anisa says, sending an apologetic glance my way. 'You haven't even said hello.'

'But he did,' I lie, almost automatically, as he turns around to look at me. As if he's been waiting for an excuse to do just that.

'Mira,' he says. 'Of course I remember Mira. But she looks so different, all grown up.'

I can feel the blood rush into my cheeks.

'Well, you haven't visited us for four years,' Rehana aunty says, taking his towel from him to do a better job with drying his hair. Adil was born when Rehana aunty was in college, and he will always be more son than brother to her.

'I can do that,' Adil says, escaping inside to change. I tell Anisa that I have to go home.

'Ajji wants me to go to the temple with her today,' I improvise. 'It is a festival.'

'What festival?' Anisa asks; as if there could not be one that she did not know about.

'You haven't had any pakodas,' Rehana aunty says. 'At least wait until I can make some for you to take with you.'

'But I just ate lunch, aunty.'

It is useless, of course. Adil emerges, bathed, dry, hair tousled and spiky, before I have been able to leave. We are careful to avoid each other's eyes that evening, careful to avoid the slightest brush of a finger as we pass plates of pakodas around the table, our backs to the cool, sated air that rushes in through the open windows.

Anisa walks home with me when I finally manage to leave, with pakodas wrapped in the morning's newspaper that

Rehana aunty forces on me. We are silent as we walk down the stairs, and as we walk on to the street.

Suddenly, Anisa says, 'It's okay, you know, people have crushes.'

'Oh my God!' I say, too embarrassed to disagree with her. And then, 'Do you think Ammi noticed?'

'Don't worry,' Anisa laughs, delighted to catch me out. 'It probably wouldn't even occur to her. She thinks Adil's ten years old, usually.'

Girish uncle is outside on the veranda, and Anisa stops to say good evening, while I rush indoors to leave the pakodas in the kitchen.

'We're going to take a walk,' I tell Vimala aunty, who is happy not to have to deal with us until dinner time, argumentative as we've been of late.

'Take an umbrella,' my uncle calls after us, but we've already left, skipping over puddles in our haste to find some privacy. We walk along the side of our street towards Sampige Road, stepping over fallen branches and windswept flowers. The fallen leaves still swirl in half-hearted dances. Passing vehicles churn up sprays of muddy water collected in the potholed road. Dusk approaches, and the roadside vendors along our street are just starting to light up their lanterns under feeble tube lights. It feels festive. There is an undercurrent of laughter in the conversations around us, and relief underlines the mock complaints of wet streets and too early monsoons.

We turn on the side street past the magazine stall, behind the movie theatre. It is a narrow alley that bisects the theatre's parking lot, motorbikes and scooters on one side, a few cars on the other. The attendant ignores us as we walk past. It is between shows, so there is no one else in sight. The streetlights stop at the edge of the parking lot, and begin again where the side street curves around between the movie theatre and the tonga stand to work its way up to Sampige Road. We stop somewhere in the middle of the unlit private stretch, and look for a place to sit. Everything is wet, even the parked vehicles. So we walk back and forth instead, cocooned in the half lit dusk. Ajji would not approve, nor would Rehana aunty, both united in their irrational fear of being outside after dark. But since neither of them is likely to walk this way, it is perfect.

There is an exhilaration that sings in my ears that evening, of strange unexplored worlds. It is as if a private new space has opened up, one that includes no one else, not even Anisa. Anisa smiles at me.

'Of all the people,' she says, smile turning into laugh, 'you had to have a crush on Adil? He is going to end up with such a swollen head.'

'Maybe I'll wake up tomorrow morning and it will be gone,' I say, in either hope or regret. 'Do you think he noticed?'

'I'm not sure,' Anisa says after a beat, and I notice her tone is careful, the one she usually uses when she wants to shield me from something. 'He was much more formal with you today, that's for sure.'

The faraway lights on Sampige Road twinkle between its arching trees, like strings of coloured lights ostentatious neighbours hang up at Diwali, or weddings. The cool air on my skin feels laden with sweetness, delicious like my thoughts. It is both an ache and a relief to be away from Adil, I realise with surprise, and it is easy enough to ignore Anisa's tone. I know it is silly to have a crush. There are the warnings the Sisters at school have for us. And Ajji has always talked about how women's hearts are given only once. That is our way, not the world of crushes and infatuations. And yet, Adil.

I sigh.

'Mira,' Anisa begins again, hesitantly, and then, as if she has changed her mind, she says, 'You'll get over this soon enough. It's probably like the Sisters say at school. Perfectly natural, and as long as you don't do anything stupid, it'll pass.'

We talk of other things for a while as we walk back and forth on the street and dusk coalesces around us, but Anisa can tell my thoughts are far away. 'Maybe you're going to break into song any minute,' Anisa says, finally, 'something about pigeons and messages.' We laugh together.

'Show *mugiyo* time,' the attendant calls to us as vehicles start to trickle in for the next show. Soon the place will be chaotic, with everyone trying to leave and come in at once through the ends of the narrow side street. We are closer to the end with the tonga stand when he calls out to us. So we continue walking past the parked tongas and the chewing horses, intending to follow the loop around to Sampige Road before the walk back home.

Beyond the tonga stand, the road bends around the theatre's back wall. Further ahead there are vacant sites on either side overgrown with weeds, bordered by the back walls of houses with open windows, cooking smells and television sounds. This is not a stretch we have been on many times. The last time we were there, we caught Vinay smoking with the tonga drivers. And we see him again today, as he stands under a spreading gulmohar tree, with the other street boys he plays cricket with. We bend our heads and look at the ground as we walk past them, like the well brought up girls we are. We can hear one of the boys say something loudly to Vinay in Kannada as we go past, and they all laugh, even as Vinay says something that sounds angry, the words indistinct. Their laughter follows us after we have crossed their tiny stretch, where it is safe to look up and talk again. The darkness of the street makes the laughter seem just a bit more raucous, and I think of what Ajji would say if she knew.

'Maybe we should walk by the temple,' Anisa says, as if she has remembered Ajji at that very minute. 'It has been a while since we did that.'

There are no side streets that open into this alley, which is apparently an afterthought, quite separate from the maze of main roads and cross streets just outside. So we hurry on the deserted road until we reach Sampige Road and the refuge of its evening crowd. A short walk up Sampige Road takes us to the cross street with the Ganesha temple on the hill, and the market opposite. People are pouring out into the street already, holding flowers and fruit that have been blessed. The evening pooja must have ended. We cross the market that is winding down, weaving between families and friends calling loudly to one another as we climb the steps up the hill.

We pass Lakshmi the flower-seller, too deep in conversation with a middle-aged couple to notice us. Past her on the steps up the hill there are newcomers—saffron-clad young men standing in uncertain clumps. There are ten, maybe fifteen of them. They stand out because of the bright colours they wear, and the novelty of their presence. Just beyond the steps, on the vacant spot of land that belongs to the temple, is a dance troupe in a makeshift theatre. It is a yakshagana performance. The masked actors step and prance around the stage to the music of cymbals and drums. From the steps, we can see into the stage and the crowd gathered in front of them. I think I catch a glimpse of a white saree in the crowd, but it is too dark to be sure. The performance seems to be at a climactic moment, by the loudness and urgency of the music rising up from the ground below us. An arrow arcs in the air on stage momentarily, and with a thundering clap of drums, an actor tumbles to the floor.

Anisa and I walk towards the edge of the steps to get a better look. And somehow, as we make our way over there,

Anisa collides with one of the young men at the edge of the saffron crowd. He apologises. Anisa steps back, and then we move past him. It is innocuous enough.

But behind us, just after, comes the sound of an open-faced slap on cheek, and we turn around. A tall man, middle-aged and balding, also in saffron and perhaps a leader of some sort, has walked over and slapped the boy.

'*Maryade illva*?' he asks the boy. Have you no respect?

All around us, people turn around to look.

He glares at us. 'If you come to the temple, you need to go inside and pray, not parade yourselves outside to distract the boys.' He says something else after which we either can't hear clearly or don't understand, but the contempt the words contain is clear.

I notice that one of the faces turned to us belongs to Gautham uncle, our neighbour, when he takes a step forward. '*Nodee,* swami,' he says, 'there is no call for that kind of language. Especially against these children.'

So it was a 'bad word' that he used, we realise. The only thing that salvages our mortification is that Ajji's face is not among the ones turned to us. Beside me, Anisa is pale. She draws breath as if to say something, and I clamp down on her hand, hard. 'Don't.' There are other murmurs around Gautham uncle.

'Control your boys,' someone else that we don't recognise says. 'We won't have this kind of talk about our girls.'

'Of course, of course,' the man in saffron says, to Gautham uncle. 'I did not realise that she was your daughter, *kshamisi*. You should take her inside with you, not allow her to wander around outside.'

Gautham uncle does not bother to correct him. 'Come with me,' he says to us, and we follow him down the hill. People disperse behind us, but I can feel their scrutiny as we pass by. Lakshmi smiles at us as we go down the hill, and motions for us to come over, but Gautham uncle walks on ahead to his parked scooter and we follow.

The joy of a few minutes ago is gone. This is the first time that I have been up the hill to the temple and not been inside to pray or stopped at Lakshmi's stall for my flowers. It feels like a punishment. Everything feels dirtied, as if that word the balding man used is a shower of muddy water that soaks through my clothes to skin. I have a sudden urge to go home and take a bath, scrub until his word washes off.

'The pig, the absolute pig,' Anisa mutters meanwhile, twisting the ends of her dupatta into furious little knots. 'Did you see the way he looked at us, as if we were dirty or something?'

Ajji meets us at the foot of the hill. Gautham uncle hands us over to her. He gets on his scooter, and says, 'Some fool of a boy fell against Anisa, and that man over there was shouting at these girls. I talked to him. What is the world coming to when our children can't go to the temple in peace?'

Ajji is less angry with us than I would have expected her to be. After she and Gautham uncle have enquired after each other's health, talked about her knees and his wife, he leaves.

'Tell me if that fellow says anything to you again,' he says to us as he leaves. 'Anisa, don't forget to tell your father about this.'

After he is gone, Ajji says, 'What is all this drama?' to us. It is good she didn't hear what he actually said, I tell myself. She would have been furious. Both at him for saying it, and us, for drawing that kind of attention.

'Show me the man,' she says, but can't quite see his face on the hill when we point. Amazingly, that is the end of the matter for her. I should be relieved, but I feel as if the punishment is only delayed, growing somewhere, as it usually does when it is not immediate.

We walk back along Sampige Road, Ajji talking to someone every few minutes without breaking stride. '*Oota aitha*?' Have you eaten? '*Chanaggiddira*?' Are you well? Greetings, not questions, designed more to mark encounters than to elicit information. But these interruptions ensure that she cannot have a real conversation with us, and I am thankful.

When we turn into our street, we see Gautham uncle and Anisa's father talking under a streetlight. Our news has preceded us. In a minute Girish uncle walks over, and we see all of them gathered under the pool of light, like actors on a distant stage. They talk for a minute or two longer, and then the sound of their laughter reaches us as we get closer. 'Useless fellows, all of them. This Devidas is a small-time goonda trying to get into politics. Even his name is new, it used to be Sathyaprakash,' Girish uncle says, evidently in a follow up to the joke he just told. 'Nothing to worry.'

Farid uncle smiles at us as we turn towards my gate. 'When are you coming home?' he asks Anisa, but before she can reply Ajji insists that she should stay for dinner.

'Let them eat here today,' she says, because Anisa and I have eaten together almost every night for several years. All that the adults can do is keep count, so the meals are roughly equal in distribution between her home and mine. Not that it matters, they always rush to insist, though, if the matter ever comes up.

It is reassuring, the sight of the three adults laughing, even after they presumably heard what happened. Anisa relaxes by my side. 'I wonder if that was the man who shouted at us,' she says, 'this goonda, Devidas.' We never call adults by their name without the obligatory uncle or aunty tacked on, and calling him by his name, and a goonda to boot, is sweet revenge. She laughs, all anger gone.

She steps forward ahead of me to enter our house and misses the last thing that Gautham uncle says. 'It's a good thing he thought she was my daughter. It's probably nothing of course, but it may be a good idea not to let her go to the temple again.' He says this hesitantly to Farid uncle, in the tone that adults use when they insist that they are not keeping count of dinners and favours.

I hang back to hear what Girish uncle has to say, pretending to fumble with my sandals. 'You're right. Nothing will happen, but he will use it to bring in all this Hindu-Muslim business. Don't tell Anisa anything, it might upset her. I'll tell Mira not to go.'

4

Ajji

Ajji had been in and out of consciousness all night. When awake, she had seen her frightened daughter-in-law at the foot of her bed. She had been impatient at the sight.

'Don't just sit there,' she wanted to say. 'Can't you find something better to do? A grown woman looking like a child that has seen a ghost.'

But before the thought was complete, she had slipped away. To a place hundreds of miles away, where the Sahyadri mountains sloped westward off the shoulder of the Deccan, down to the azure Arabian Sea and the blissful verdant miles of the Karavali coastline. Where stretches of sand were thrown up like a blessing between rugged mountain and surging sea, studded thick with coconut and palm. This was land that was ceded, unwilling, by the sea, when the sage Parashurama threw his axe into it, Ajji had been told as a child. But she could see now, at last, how each meander of the Karavali encroaching into the sea was a city, each slip of land in between, a town. One such town was her Malehalli, a place so small that mapmakers and travelogues ignored it, not pausing to draw breath in their gushing litany of larger places: Mangalore, Karwar, Belthangade and Udupi.

But this was the town at whose centre a statue of her husband stood, and beyond which the streets diverged, to police station and school, or the small college further out where her son Kishore first glimpsed his wife, Radhika. Beyond which still smaller unpaved paths led further out, past acres of arecanut covered hillside and small, tiled roofs, to the sandless stretch where rugged hillside met surging ferocity of cheated sea. It was such a place that glimpsed once should have been the gift of a lifetime, Ajji thought, and yet had to be forgotten, left behind, because there was no other choice. A longing seized Ajji for Malehalli, for respite, for the struggle to forget to end.

She awoke, to her hospital bed, to the machines that beeped alongside, and a longing that persisted and gained in strength.

Perhaps this *was* the end, she thought, surveying the room that was so alien from all that she knew. It had to be. Why else would she be here, with no memory of how she came to be so? Why else would Vimala sit by her bed and look so afraid?

This was the end of her life.

The thought acquired a certainty she could not deny. And improbably, she felt her heart lift, in relief, in joy. Ganesha would not deny her this one last wish. She did not have to consider the consequences of her words. She did not have to forget anymore.

'Vimala,' she called. 'Vimala.'

'Get some paper and a pen. Write down what I have to say for Mira. So she will know. When I die.'

She saw Vimala leave to find paper, and could not wait for her to return.

'Ganesha,' she began, almost as soon as Vimala's back was turned, as she did with the making of chaklis or stories, with a prayer to Him, 'keep me alive till I have said the things I have to say. Make my words tell the truth, no matter what I say.'

Her voice grew stronger with use, and there was Vimala back with loose-leaf paper, to hear the rest.

Mira, you insisted on knowing the beginning of every story. But why, Ajji, did they do that, you asked, or why did they not do this? All the time, as if I knew all the answers. As if I could always tell you how and why everything happened. Things happen, sometimes for a reason, and sometimes not. Things happen to people in stories and in lives because of things that happened much before, even before they existed. You think, 'No, my story began such and such day, the day I was born.'

How wrong you would be then, because, Mira, your story probably really began the day I walked into Malehalli, a new bride in July 1940, though you were not born until many years later, in November of 1975. Maybe it began even before that, in 1930, a full ten years before our marriage, when your grandfather ran away from school to listen to speeches on the radio, about the Salt Satyagraha. Because he listened to those troublemakers on stolen afternoons, he spent more time in jail than at home and died early, and that is part of your story.

Or maybe it began even before that, with the epidemic of typhoid that wiped out parts of whole families, your grandfather's and mine, in 1925, when I was two and lucky to be left alive, a girl, when more precious sons died. Or even further back, centuries before that, when they say our forefathers, the ancient Havyaka Brahmins, moved southwards over the Vindhya mountains, then trekked across the plateau of the Deccan, to Karnataka and Malehalli. People say they were directed there by a king who wanted atonement for a sin. But I cannot tell you those tales and the results of those events in the time that we have left. Lord Yama knots his noose and readies his buffalo to mount and you know as well as I do that he is never a patient man. So, forgive me, but I will hurry up and begin, in the middle, at the time that I came to Malehalli, a young bride of seventeen, just before the monsoons of 1940.

It was on a late summer day with an overcast sky and heavy clouds that I married your grandfather. We left my village for

Malehalli even before the guests had finished talking about the wedding feast, about the gingery tartness of the tamblis and the sweetness of the genasale. The genasale had been steamed in clove leaves for an hour, as was customary, and then, was eaten in a flash. That was my wedding for you. For months, my parents had planned the event, going from astrologer to cook and moneylender, only to go back and change everything twice over, because the groom wanted a Gandhian wedding and his parents, a traditional Havyaka one.

'Who is this Gandhi?' my father would ask, sometimes exasperated and sometimes in jest, 'that he demands that my daughter wear khadi, not silk, at her wedding?'

After all that fuss, and the drama, the day of the wedding dawned and we were married, almost as an afterthought. I only know that it was the khadi that won, because of the picture that we took, sitting stiffly in chairs on the veranda of my father's house after the ceremony. I remember leaving that house of my father and his father before him, in the company of a smiling stranger. My cousins whispered in my ear as we left the house, that he worshipped a living man, a mahatma, who was called Gandhi. This mahatma, who, they said, always won.

We left my village in a bullock cart that was festooned with flowers. We do not have those bullock carts anymore, even in villages far smaller than Malehalli, the covered carts with soft cushioned seats of silk and satin that rocked you with each step that the bullocks took, while their silk-lined canvas roofs and tiny curtained windows kept out the sun.

Your grandfather refused to be driven to his home with his new bride in a motorcar. That car was one that my father had on loan from a friend, who had 'borrowed' it from the district collector, who that friend worked for. You see, it appeared that this mahatma, apart from his views on silk and khadi, had rather strong views on 'borrowing', on motorcars, and on the white men who ruled us, such as that district collector. Or so I remember your grandfather explaining to me on our way up the winding, beautiful roads by the sea that would take us to your ancestral town, Malehalli.

Ah, the beauty of those sights, Mira, I do not have the time to describe to you in any way to do them justice. Leaves in every shade of green, even the ground so densely carpeted, interrupted only by mossy barks of the trees that reached the sky, and the sea always close at hand. How can I tell you what each sight was? Every corner you turned was a new amazement, like apsaras dressed for Indra's court, each to compete for his attention. But they were not enough to stop me from pouting all the way there, because I had never ridden in a motorcar before.

When he finally noticed my pout, your grandfather tried to cheer me up with stories of the places we passed on our way to Malehalli. In the motorcar we would have made the journey in a half hour. The bullock cart took three hours, and I do not think that I said a single word to him in all that time. It would not have been proper to do so, and I would have seemed too eager. We were almost at the foot of the hill where his house was before I even allowed myself a smile at his jokes. He laughed and said, 'So my new bride is not both deaf and dumb after all.'

The monsoons were late in coming the year of our marriage, despite the clouds that day. The earth was parched. Our little house, surrounded by groves of fruit trees, was on a sloping hillside by the sea. We lived there with his parents, as was custom.

But soon, very soon, the rains had come, and in torrents and gullies the water had rushed all around our small house, nourishing the piece of land with the bananas and coconut that would sustain us for the years that my husband went in and out of jail following his mahatma, even as it stole every bit of top soil that was not tethered down by root or plant.

I can see the little rings in the puddles outside when raindrops splashed into them, feel them splash up in a fine spray. My husband stood outside in the rain, calling me, and he was smiling. His bearing was so regal, even half-drenched in the first rain of the monsoon, that it reminded me of some king I had imagined from a childhood tale. I examined his face and his heart, the way I held up tomatoes and peered at them for bruising or softness, this way and that, at the weekly market. No matter what the angle or the light, no blemishes came to be seen, either in the face, or the heart inside. It was for such a short time, but I felt such gratitude for the good fortune of our match. So easy and so perfect, given to me like a gift.

Still, there was a lot I had to learn. My husband, your grandfather, your Ajja, did not care if there was too much salt or too little in the hagalkai gojju that he ate, or if there was any vegetable in the gojju, or even if there was any gojju at all. His attention was reserved for bigger things. The world was his family, he said. The burden of worrying about the rain and rice and money fell on me instead. Oh, I grumbled and I quarrelled, because there were mouths to feed, Mira—mine, his, and his parents'. And his mahatma was too far away for me to ask questions, so I asked your Ajja. But I could never be angry for too long, because your Ajja would have me laughing in an instant, forgetting whether it was hunger, fatigue or fear that made me so angry, or jealous.

Your Ajja cared greatly about many things, things he heard on the radio and read about in the newspapers, things I had no knowledge of, then. He would teach me during the evenings and into the night, by the light of a kerosene lantern, as darkness crept in around the edges of our veranda.

'You learn quickly,' he would say, but only very rarely, and before I had a chance to bask in his appreciation, we would be off on another lesson. History, geography, English, wherever his

fancy took him. But more important than all of that, for him, were the things his mahatma taught. Which were not just about Independence and freedom from the white men who ruled us.

'Embrace the Harijans,' he would say, unaware of how shameless he sounded, of how badly he flouted the laws of our ancestors. 'Embrace the Harijans.'

Embrace the people who cleaned the lavatories and lived at the edges of Malehalli, who no one in our family could look in the face without the need for purification? The untouchables, for whom his mahatma had coined the term Harijan—people of God. We fought. I could humour his whims and pretend to care about his newspaper, not notice his lack of steady employment, but this was different.

'The laws of caste are truths decided before our births, they are bigger than you and your mahatma,' I said to him. 'They go back all the way to Manu, the first man. Caste is the fruit of sins or virtues in previous births. Their sins make them Holeyas; our good deeds and the good deeds of our ancestors make us Brahmins. You betray your caste and us when you go to their houses. When you eat with them you bring their pollution here when you return. How can you disrespect your ancestors, and all they did, like this?'

'Think. Don't repeat the things your father says like a parrot,' he'd say and laugh at my anger and my stubborn tears. 'Think for yourself.' He'd say a lot of things that were new to me then, but things that you have grown up accepting as fact. That all men are equal, and how our treatment of those low caste people was the sin, not the pollution of our caste.

I remained stubborn, and he told me the only story that he ever told me in all our years together. It was the story of Kanakadasa, which I have never told you before.

'Meenakshi,' he said, 'this Krishna, who you worship every day, do you know what he thinks of your caste or theirs? Nothing.

It doesn't matter to him, if you are Brahmin or Harijan. Why, in Udupi Matt, the idol of Krishna faces the back. Do you know why? You believe these stories more than you believe your husband—you should know why. Didn't your father tell you about this?

No? I'll tell you. Kanakadasa was not a twice born Brahmin. But he prayed to Krishna, just like you. He went to Udupi Matt to pray. But the priests at the matt would not let him enter the temple because of his caste. So when Kanakadasa went to the back and tried to look in through a window, they say Krishna Himself turned around on His pedestal to see him. Someday, when you go to Udupi, you will see, the idol still faces the window at the back, Kanaka's window. Even your God is against this, Meenakshi, it is a crime that we commit.'

Your grandfather was not a good storyteller. Udupi is not a Havyaka Matt, only a Madhwa one. Who knows what their practices are like? Perhaps there was something else to the story, and nothing about the untouchables. This is what I thought when he told the story, and proceeded to ignore it altogether.

But I did go to the temple at Udupi by the sea, years later, without him, I saw the temple with Krishna turned to a tiny window in the back. His back was still turned stubbornly to the priests who bathed and adorned Him and sang His praises. After we had stood in lines that snaked around the temple to be able to peer through that tiny window to see His face, it was time for lunch. And outside at the line for lunch, the priests still asked for your gotra to assign you a place to sit, so no pollutions should happen. Brahmins here, everyone else over there.

I marvelled then at your grandfather and this arrogance that he shared with his mahatma, that they wanted to change the things that even God, the lord Krishna, could not.

But this was years in the future, and had no effect then on the fights we frequently had. He insisted on going to untouchables' homes, teaching their children and talking to them of his mahatma and our freedom from the white man. Of course, I refused to let him enter the house if he did not take a purificatory bath in the courtyard, after he had been visiting those that he called Harijans. He refused to bathe, and refused to enter the house. If he brought one of the boys that he had been teaching home with him, he would insist on being served food with him. Not bothered that he was sitting on the floor outside his house, like some uncaste. Otherwise, he would not eat. My mother-in-law finally told me to relent.

'He is a good boy, and you will drive him away if you do this. Let him come inside.' Somehow, as the days turned to weeks and months, I seemed to be giving in more and more, and one afternoon I found myself receiving people whose castes I did not know into my home, and feeding them as I would my brothers or cousins. My face burned with shame as I bent over their plates, dropping huli and tambli, following the rules of madi, as if it was proper and as if it mattered. If my parents were to see this, my mother would faint, my father would drag me back to his house in anger. But your Ajja smiled, as if all was well with his world.

Soon, he had me going to the women's centre during the day, where they were teaching people to use the charkha, to make khadi. Usha—the wife of one of your grandfather's friends, Mahalinga—took me under her wing. She was one of those tall women who seemed to do everything better than everyone and with less effort. She had her hair scraped back in a bun, and all she wore was khadi sarees and long-sleeved khadi blouses, and the way she wore them you would think they were the finest Mysore silk. She did not seem to worry about her family or her house, if she cooked the evening meal or swept her kitchen, as long as she spun that charkha, the mahatma's beloved spinning wheel, every day.

You have never seen a charkha other than in pictures, Mira, and you will never know the pain that it takes to draw the yarn from the cotton, in unbroken lines, especially when it is a pregnant woman that sits there trying, cross-legged, with fingers swollen in the heat. My back would cramp up in protest at my clumsiness and then there would be Usha, by my side, smiling, 'You can do this, Sister, you can. I struggled too, in the beginning.'

As I smiled to her face, I would think, 'If only the British memshahibs had to sit next to this woman every day and spin the charkha, they would convince their husbands to leave us quickly.' Yet I went every day and tried harder than I did the day before because I wanted your grandfather to look me in the face with all his attention, and appreciate me.

I was pregnant with our first child. My mother-in-law told me that this child would make him responsible and bring his attention to the family. Instead, he said, 'But look at Usha,' a hundred times a day, it seemed to me, whether it was about her calm disposition, or her spinning at the wheel, or her devotion to the ideals of satyagraha. My discontent swelled with my belly and unsaid words pushed against my tongue.

'It is such a scandal,' my mother-in-law said, when I refused again to go to my mother's house in the seventh month of my pregnancy. 'People will say I kept you back to work for me in your state.'

'Go,' your Ajja said, when I hoped that he would ask me to stay. 'The customs are old, but we do not want to hurt your parents. And you will get more rest there.'

Finally I could refuse no more and my parents came to fetch me in another silk and canvas covered bullock cart, with flowers and fruit in baskets. After the rituals of the shreemantha, the blessing of the first pregnancy, it was finally time to leave. The guests gathered and gossiped in front, waiting for lunch to be served. I went to the back room, to gather a few belongings and books to take for the months away. Usha followed me there and was talking to me about some book or the other that I should read, so my child would be born with the right temperament, as she called it. Then, your grandfather, your Ajja, walked in. He smiled at Usha before he saw me. He looked happy. That, oddly enough, was enough to send me into a jealous tantrum.

'Neither of you can wait to see me leave, it seems,' I said, the words innocuous but their meaning clear.

Usha froze. The laughter in your grandfather's eyes died and he said, quietly, 'Meenakshi, you should apologise.'

Usha laughed, a small forced laugh, and said, 'Brother, she is tired and anxious about the journey and the pregnancy. There is no harm done, no need to apologise.'

Your grandfather was angry with me. He said something about the sins of jealous, foolish girls destroying women's reputations and lives.

'You say this thoughtlessly,' I think he said, 'because you are angry with me, or someone else. But what you say so casually could hurt a good woman forever.'

For years after that, even though the accusation was merely that there was more affection between them than was seemly, and though it was baseless and unspoken, it would hang between us. Unspoken yet present, in the way Usha and my husband would never be alone in conversation, in the ever so slight emphasis she placed on 'brother', and in the slight hesitation that preceded the rare times he said 'Usha' again. So, even among these satyagrahis, who only worshipped the truth, this lie would find a home to live. I should have listened more closely and learnt my lesson then, but I did not. My jealousy would burrow down deeper to a place I did not know I had, surprising me when it finally revealed itself, years and years later.

But he was a kind man, your grandfather, much kinder than I deserved. He said, 'Maybe you will have a little girl soon and I can teach you both not to be so wilful, at the same time,' smiling again. He promised to visit me often at my parents' house. It was a promise broken soon, because weeks after I left, his mahatma would call on the British to 'Quit India', and be thrown into jail. Your grandfather would go on marches with his friends, where the satyagrahis would march on to face steel-tipped lathis, where they would not even lift a hand to shield their bodies. There would be pictures in the papers of broken bodies and blood on the streets, reports of shootings in faraway towns and villages, and all the while more satyagrahis would walk on in silence to take the place of those that had fallen. Somewhere in the beginning of those marches, after they had beaten your grandfather and he had his limbs broken in the name of his mahatma's ahimsa, his non-violence, he would go to jail.

I went into labour early at the news from Malehalli of the march. My womb contracted, stronger and stronger each time, and yet I would not cry, not a tear would slip from my eyes, or a sound my lips. I was not a peasant woman who would give birth like some animal, even if all I could think of was my husband. My mother held me in her arms, praying aloud, while my father paced the floor outside, clearly dreading a messenger from Malehalli with news of death.

Finally, the child that had grown in my womb with my discontent was born into the darkness of fear and doubt. When they held him up for me to see, he had my husband's face. Still, I could not smile. I knew they would not tell me if my husband had died, because they thought that women so close to childbirth were delicate and to be shielded, like children. So, I held my first-born as if he was the neighbour's, all of my mind engaged with the question of my husband's life. It would be days before my father would return with news of seeing my husband in the district jail, in Mangalore, a city I had never seen. I would only see him when I visited him there, months later, when it was permissible for a new mother and baby to travel that far. I would hold a baby boy in my arms, your uncle, Girish, and for the first time since his birth, we would all smile.

When I finally saw my husband, it was through the bars of the visitors' room at the jail. There was commotion and crying when families all around us examined and exclaimed, at injuries and bruises, and at cheeks and temples hollowed out by inedible food, brown and deep like coconuts grated close to their shells. I smiled at last, glad that the broken limb and thinning body still held my husband's life. He stretched his arm through the bars to touch his son's head and his face, to examine the tiny feet and hands that had to be unsheathed from blankets and towels, even in the heat of summer on the Konkan coast.

'You should not have travelled this far,' he said. 'He might fall sick.'

I smiled, saying nothing of the quarrels and the tears it had taken for me to come this far, or the impatience with which I had hurried my father through stops for meals, biting my nails at his slowness. I said nothing of the gratitude for his life that elevated the dirty public hall of our meeting or of the love that could now slowly flower from the tight, closed bud in my chest for this baby whose face was my husband's.

Then there was the namakarana, the naming of the newborn. Another ceremony, more guests and food. A celebration, even when hunger never went far from our home. We had waited for your Ajja to be released from prison, putting the ceremony off for later each time the headlines turned optimistic. Until finally everyone had tired of calling him 'the baby', and neighbours clucked their tongues at our tardiness in acknowledging the blessing of a firstborn son. Astrologers were consulted and an auspicious time was picked. The priest came to our house from the temple to whisper our son's name in his ear for the first time, 'Girish.'

And finally, your grandfather came home in 1945. Suddenly, he came, when I was hanging clothes out to dry on a hot day. Your uncle, Girish, was playing in the mud around my feet, putting his hand out to grab little droplets of water that dripped from the clothes that I wrung, twisting one arm over the other, before I hoisted them on the line. He had just turned three. I saw someone come up the path to our house on the hillside, and in the distance I could see the khadi cap that your grandfather sometimes wore, and his familiar long-legged step. I looked away, as if wringing my mother-in-law's newly washed saree required all my attention. I was convinced that there was no one walking up the path, that I was imagining the thing that I had waited every day to see.

Then my mother-in-law was running down the path to him, calling out his name, and shouting, 'Meenakshi, Meenakshi, bring Girish.'

My father-in-law picked up his mud- and water-splattered grandson and ran down the hill behind her, tripping on bumps and stones that his cataracts hid. The neighbours who lived by the path up the hill came out, to greet your Ajja and follow him up to our house. I watched this little procession, with my husband carrying Girish at its head, wend its way up to our house. All I could do was stand where I was, tears falling from my eyes, wrung by the years of waiting that had finally ended.

When he saw me, your grandfather said, 'Meenakshi, silly woman, dry your tears, or they will have to build a dam at the bottom of the hill.'

Everyone laughed, in happiness, not at his joke. He was home now, and anything that was said could be an excuse for laughter.

Your grandfather had a hero's welcome. There were guests in our house all day, bringing fruits and sweets. It seemed that all of Malehalli turned out to see him, to ask if he was well. An arecanut merchant in town offered him a job. He asked your grandfather to oversee the accounting in his store.

'Don't you have someone doing that already?' your grandfather asked, doubtful of charity that might be cloaked in the offer of work.

'I have relatives,' the man replied, 'but I need an honest man. A Gandhian.'

And so it went. And then there were more people, people I had never seen, people from neighbouring villages and towns who visited. A lot of the satyagrahis had already been released. Usha's husband, Mahalinga, had come home months before. A few were still in prison, and their relatives came to ask for news of this person or that.

Usha and Mahalinga were among the last to leave. Usha had helped me in the kitchen all day with making buttermilk and slicing fruit for the people who visited, helping wash plates that were sticky with sugar syrup from the serving of sweets that they brought. In the years that our husbands had spent in prison, we had become friends. She was softer, less rigidly idealistic than she had been in the years before. It might have happened the first time she had to sneak into a pawnshop with some gold jewellery or when she had to accept being in debt for the month's groceries, but there was softness to the hard-edged zeal that she carried so proudly before. We had found more common ground in our years of shared humiliations and worry than we had at the charkha. I was sorry to see them go and sorry for my thoughtless words only a few years but almost a lifetime ago.

Ajji paused. She realised that she had not been sorry then, even though she had just said so. She had been happy and exhausted, as much from the emotional upheaval as from standing in the kitchen all day. At the back of her mind, while she worked in the kitchen and turned around surreptitiously from time to time for a glimpse of her husband in the hall, there was a niggle of some unfinished business with Usha. She should have been sorry, Ajji thought, and wasn't that enough as she lay here dying, that she thought she should have been sorry? Just as she should have been more sorry for something much bigger, that was to come years later between their families. And so the lie and its justification spread, an anodyne through her veins, following the sedative that had been injected into her vein only moments before.

'Yes, it should be sufficient,' Ajji thought next, yielding to the sudden drowsiness that arrived, deceitful and merciful. 'That is how it should be.'

5
Mira

Appa and I are in Seattle. We walk to yet another gate, into another plane that will take us on the next leg of the journey. Our journey is a patchwork in creativity rustled up by one of Appa's travel agent friends. Our flights may cross-over and retrace paths where they connect, while my memories are, for now, relentless and unidirectional: I follow Anisa inside. The conversation under the street light has ended.

We sit down to dinner on the kitchen floor like we always have. Hands washed, legs folded and crossed, left arm safely stowed away, before plates of steaming rice and hagalkai gojju that my aunt serves us. She bends over at the waist and drops the gojju on our plates, careful not to let the serving spoon touch the rice, or the plate. Ajji sits to the side, her eyes following the trajectory of Vimala aunty's serving spoon. Her hands are busy. She has been rolling the cotton garlands for our tulsi plant and the next day's pooja. She doesn't look down at her hands to fashion them and yet they emerge perfectly formed, little white strings of bulbous globes and even waists, on to her lap.

In all the years that I eat in this kitchen, the rules of madi do not change, nor does Ajji's scrutiny for lapses. In the centre of complex webs of touching and not being touched that is partly what madi is, is Vimala aunty. She has cooked all the food and cannot be touched. Touching her would defile any food she makes after, necessitating another bath and a different, untouched saree before she can cook again. No one else can touch our plates, defiled not only by our touch, but the residue of saliva that might make its way back on our hands returning for the next morsel. Right hands may touch food, left hands, even washed ones, may not.

Ajji presides over every meal in her kitchen, and enforces madi like the natural order she believes it to be. In a minute, satisfied that all is well, she says, 'You girls are too old for stories these days. You would beg me to tell you something as you ate. Now, I suppose you are just too fashionable for this old woman's stories.' This is a recent hurt of Ajji's. Over the last few years, there have been highly popular television shows of her favourite epics, the Ramayana and Mahabharata. Families have gathered to perform aarthi before their television sets when actors portraying Rama or Krishna came on. Ajji, of course, has considered this not only foolishness, but unfair competition for the telling of tales she considers hers alone.

So this is a cue that Anisa recognises as well as I do.

'No, Ajji, of course not,' she says, smiling her dimpled smile. 'We want to hear your stories, like always. Why would you think that we didn't want to?'

'Yes, Ajji,' I echo dutifully. 'Please, please tell us a story. It has been such a long time.'

'Oh, all right then,' Ajji says, gathering up the jars of turmeric and vermilion with the cotton garlands she has just finished to move a little closer. 'There was a yakshagana at the temple today that you girls missed, about Rama and Lakshmana when they were young boys. So beautiful, so beautiful. The costumes, the expressions. It reminded me of when I was young like you, watching my father on stage in our village. You missed the performance. You should at least hear the story.'

Tipping the waists on the cotton garland with vermilion and turmeric, she continues, 'You may not know this, Anisa,' though we all know that she does, 'Rama was an incarnation of the great Lord Vishnu, the Preserver. He was born in Ayodhya many hundred years ago to King Dasharatha, and his wife, Queen Kousalya.'

It is an ordinary enough beginning, but I squirm beside Anisa. It has only been a few months since saffron-clad Hindu zealots climbed a centuries-old mosque in Ayodhya that they said was built on the site where the Lord Rama was born, and pulled it down. Less, since the ensuing riots where thousands, Hindu and Muslim, died. Anisa and I have negotiated this minefield of our conflicting histories many hundred times in the years we have known each other and emerged unscathed. Yet, today feels different. No one has ever said about us what Girish uncle did in that too-polite tone: Hindu-Muslim business.

Ajji continues, oblivious to my squirming. Anisa does not share my unease. Vimala aunty serves us ginger tambli, dropping a spoonful on the side of our plates. Ajji runs through the familiar story of Sage Vishwamitra coming to Ayodhya to ask for help from King Dasharatha. Demons have tormented the sage, interfered with his penances and polluted his sacred fire. He needs the warrior princes, Rama and Lakshmana, to defeat the asuras, so he can pray in his hermitage again.

'Anyway,' Ajji says, her mind evidently on the yakshagana, 'even the asuras looked so real today. I wonder where they got the costumes from.' And then, she says, 'Keep eating, do I have to remind you like I did when you were babies?'

I bend my head down to eat, barely tasting the ginger tambli, my favourite. The faraway glance I had of the yakshagana dances in my head, the clap like thunder, the dark costumed asura falling to the floor.

Ajji continues with her story. The princes vanquish the asuras, as I listen with half an ear. They are blessed by the sage, earn greater powers, and then for some unspecified reason, go on a journey with him, where Rama encounters his biggest devotees, Shabari and Ahalya.

Shabari breaks all the rules of etiquette and madi by offering food that has been tasted to Rama. Rama, though entitled to the purest of the pure, accepts her unclean offering because she only tasted the fruits to ensure that he gets the sweetest ones. It is a way to tell, Ajji says, that devotion makes even the most reprehensible thing pure. It was Shabari's innocent devotion that made Rama eat the thing no one would.

Then there is Ahalya. 'Rama showed the world he was a true God, when his big toe touched the stone in the hermitage, and she came to life,' Ajji says, of Ahalya. 'That is why we call Rama "Ahalyodhraka", when we sing his praises. He is the "Ahalya-redeemer".'

Ajji wraps up Rama's journeys as Vimala aunty carefully pours buttermilk over the last serving of rice. She promises to tell us the rest later. It is an assurance that is less necessary than it seems. We know the story, and also that Ajji enjoys telling us her versions as much or more than we like to listen.

When our plates have been carefully rinsed in the sink outside so they are safe to touch again for their washing, Anisa and I walk outside to the gate. We talk there awhile. Our neighbours turn in for the night in sequence, announcing their intentions by lights suddenly extinguished and windows that fall dark in the silence of the street. Ajji finally joins us at the gate, clucking her tongue at the lateness of the hour, and Anisa walks back to her home as we watch.

When Anisa arrives the next morning, it is with news that Adil has left early with Farid uncle. It is the first day of his internship. Also that Rehana aunty would like to make carrot halwa for tea in the evening, and is missing cashews. So we set off together, to buy them at the shop on Sampige Road. It takes us the good part of a morning to actually leave my house between one thing and the other, and we make it back to Anisa's home in the late morning. Rehana aunty puts us to work grating carrots when we arrive. She intends to teach us to cook this summer. And she decides today that halwa is as good a place to start as any. 'It *is* Adil's favourite, you know,' Anisa giggles to me as soon as Rehana aunty's back is turned, 'so maybe you should pay attention.'

I stick my tongue out at her.

We make our way back to my house after lunch. It is part of our routine. If I don't go back home for at least part of the day, Ajji will make her way up to Anisa's home looking slightly out of breath from climbing the stairs, to say, 'Mira, when were you planning to come home? I see you even less over summer than when you are at school.' Her long-suffering tone will strike guilt she swears she doesn't intend into all of us, Rehana aunty included. So it is an unspoken sort of agreement, and Rehana aunty hurries us through lunch to get us out the door before any of that can happen.

In the evening, Ajji leaves for the temple as always. Girish uncle tells us it might be better for us not to go with her. 'After all that drama yesterday,' he adds. For once, Ajji is in agreement. And so we rush back to Anisa's house as soon as Ajji leaves.

Adil is in the drawing room with Farid uncle, and Rehana aunty is setting up the dining table for dinner. Adil's face lights up when I walk in, and I pretend not to notice. We've missed tea, which was earlier in the evening. Farid uncle compliments us on the halwa, 'Better than anything Rehana has made in all the years that she's been cooking.' Both Adil and Rehana aunty laugh at this piece of hyperbole, and Rehana aunty tells us there is enough left for dessert, and some for me to take home later.

We sit down to eat after Rehana aunty has rolled out and cooked a few more rotis for the two of us. We talk about Adil's project, something with fluid dynamics. He is animated when he talks about it. The researcher he's working with won the Bhatnagar award the year before, and Adil is in awe. I should pay attention and be inspired, as no doubt Farid uncle intends for Anisa and me to be. Instead, I find myself noticing the fine brown hair on Adil's forearms and the way it catches the light as he gestures under the lamp that hangs over the dining table.

I am so conscious of everything I say and do, that I find myself unable to eat very much. Rehana aunty clucks her tongue at me, as usual, and makes up with an extra-large helping of halwa, which, unsurprisingly, tastes exactly like the one she always makes.

We sit down to a game of cards after dinner, and my pleasurable unease grows at the close proximity to Adil, the directness of his gaze. I look down at my cards and tell myself firmly that it is no different from the way he looks at Farid uncle or Anisa. 'Daydreams, child,' I say, as the Sisters in school would, 'are the devil's handiwork in an empty mind.'

Though it is late when I finally leave, I might have succeeded in emerging with my supposition unscathed. But when I get to the end of the street, I remember the halwa that Rehana aunty gave me that I have forgotten on the dining table. Ajji has unbent enough over the years that she will eat certain foods from Rehana aunty's kitchen, but she only eats it on the day that it is cooked. Eating leftovers the day after is not something that madi permits. So I walk back up the street and to Anisa's house to get the halwa, realising that most of our neighbours are asleep.

When I get to the door, it has been only a few minutes since I left. I push open the still unlocked door and come face to face with Adil. He stands frozen in the drawing room, shirtless. The lights are on and the room, empty. The fold out couch is open, and a T-shirt he probably intends to wear for the night is on it. But all I really notice is the expanse of chest and shoulder, and the look in his eyes, when I look up to meet them.

It is only a second before Rehana aunty bustles into the drawing room with pillow and sheets, and he has slipped the T-shirt on, and I have retrieved the small container of halwa for my family to taste. But it is enough. I walk back down the stairs and feel my stomach slowly unclench, even as my skin tingles in the cold night air. I have to stop at the gate before I can go in to Ajji. Shirtless boys or men are commonplace—labourers on the street, priests at the temple or urchins in the rain. My reaction to Adil is anything but. I have never felt this exhilaration, or this hunger. I walk up the path to the veranda and, in the approaching familiarity of my home, a sense of wrong-doing grows.

Ajji has waited up for me and lets me in with an admonition over the hour. Everyone else is asleep. I make my way to my bed, and there beside it is the picture I've held close for years, of my mother.

There have been murmurs that I have heard about my mother over the years. All the way from the memory of Girish uncle's reaction to her picture to more recent whispers that died away when I entered a room. Until today, I've known it without question, or having to ask, for the gossip it is. How could my mother, this woman utterly and impossibly beautiful to my eyes, be anything but blameless? But suddenly today those whispers are less easy to discount in the darkness of the night, and with the knowledge of how very easy it would be, to do wrong.

For the first time, her expression seems different from the motherly adoration I have always thought it to show. Perhaps it *was* a different kind of love that she felt when the light bulb flashed and froze her expression on to film. Something more akin to the moment of intimacy I have just come from. I turn it face down. But her expression stays with me, as does Adil's from the moment before Rehana aunty arrived.

Later, I lie awake listening to Ajji's rhythmic snores. When sleep finally arrives, it brings dreams that are sad. There are colourful yakshagana performers in the street before the temple, their majestic costumes shimmering in the sun, who bar me from entering the temple where Ganesha stands indifferent. I turn away from the temple. Adil and Anisa wait down the street. Suddenly, there is thunder and fog. Anisa and Adil laugh at me behind the wall of fog and I cannot reach them. I turn around to go home but everything has disappeared. Ajji, the home where I live, all vanished into nothingness by rain.

When Ajji wakes me up the next morning, I still feel the chill and the loss. I hug her, both arms wrapped tightly around her waist, and refuse to let go.

'Oh you silly-silly girl,' Ajji laughs, surprised and pleased. She does not even complain that she has to bathe again before her pooja. 'Still such a child,' I hear her say to my aunt. 'Anisa and her, they walk and talk like they know everything these days, but our Mira is such a child. So innocent.'

I return my mother's picture to its face up position in the morning light. By day, her saree is elegant as it has always been; her smile as open and without innuendo. Then I help Ajji with the tulsi pooja. We hang the garlands she made the previous night over the brick column that holds the holy plant in our courtyard. It stands sombre and tall, dark green and newly washed from the rain. Ajji lets me light the clay lamps that she will use for the pooja, and we set them, together, into the little recesses that the painted brick column bears, one for each side. We dab turmeric and vermilion and circle the holy plant. The damp floor is a persistent reminder of the rain that passed.

'Please,' I hear myself pray, 'let it just be a silly crush that I will grow out of. Please let everything go back to the way it was.'

There are many things in that prayer that I do not mention; their presence is clear even so many years later. Adil, my mother, my wakening urges that I am convinced no one who is respectable, shares. We are hemmed in by Ajji's tales of piety, the traditional neighbourhood we live in where wives do not touch their husbands in public, the quaintly chaste movies where passion and ardour are only suggested, where heroines will not kiss their leading men onscreen for several years more, and then to much hand-wringing and brouhaha in the media. That is the world of my impending adulthood. Within it, is that prayer, with all its urgency.

I see its futility.

6
Girish

The sky was barely tinged with pink to the east, a three-quarter moon translucent in the receding night, when Vinay brought Girish's car to the front of his mistress's building. Ajji had been taken to the hospital the night before, and Girish had stayed the night. Choreographed to perfection, the car arrived only seconds before Girish emerged from the foyer. He stepped into his car before the thin morning air could penetrate his cotton shirt and cool his skin still warm from the shower upstairs. Once inside, he turned invisible behind the tinted back windows of the grey Ambassador sedan. Only the chowkidar saw him leave, and he saluted the car as it exited the gate. Vinay rolled down his window to pass out a folded fifty rupee note, the usual payment for his continued silence.

It was a successful getaway. The government plates on his car did not catch the sun or the eye of a nosy neighbour when he left his mistress in the morning. Good thing people sleep late in this part of town, Girish thought, as Vinay sped down the street. If this were more traditional Malleshwaram, there would be the occasional gossipy housewife up even at this hour, splashing water on her doorstep in preparation for rangoli. Here, in fashionable Benson Town, large apartment complexes alternated with houses behind high walls and closed gates tended by somnolent watchmen, where the traditional chalk patterns at doorways would either be impractical, or passé. This is the life, he told himself, lingering on the presumed late mornings and their implication of indolent luxury. After years of swallowed insults and gains won one painstaking toehold after the next, the world behind those high walls was finally at hand. Or so he hoped. All that remained was the election.

Girish shifted in his seat, restive against the urgency of this thought. If his mentor, Surendra, won the election for their party, he would become deputy chief minister of the state and Girish would have his own ticket for the next bye-election. Or maybe Surendra would be generous, and there would be one instead for parliamentary elections, for the central government.

'MP,' he said aloud, 'Member of Parliament,' uncaring that Vinay would hear, testing the pleasant weight of the phrase on his tongue. He wound down his tinted glass window once in the safe anonymity of Nandi Durga Road, empty save for an occasional two-wheeler or auto rickshaw speeding in the relative freedom of the early hour. The promise of impending gratification turned everything more beautiful in the brightening golden morning. All he surveyed was his private fiefdom. Sidewalks flew by empty, stately homes glimpsed quickly between crowded branch and tree stood silent and supplicant to him as he sped past them. Even the scattered billboards seemed brighter, the happinesses they peddled gilded by the growing dawn, and by the joy of his expectation. Member of Parliament. MP. Or MLA?

Maybe if my mother dies I can sell that old house in Malleshwaram, he thought, tearing his mind away from those twin possibilities. He had visited the hospital last night and managed to leave without actually seeing her. Not that it was necessary, and not that he should feel guilty about that, he told himself firmly. An image of his wispy wife crossed his mind, from years ago when she stood at the gate with flowers in her hair. He dispelled it with an equal firmness. Perhaps *she* would have the decency to disappear; not many men would be as patient as he had been with her. But his mother would probably die. And the funeral would have to be arranged before he could sell the house. Right in the middle of the elections, of all the *soole-maga* times this could have happened. His brother would come from America and stand around like a guest, as if he had forgotten how things worked here. Everyone would expect things to happen all by themselves like magic, while they stood around and talked pretty. One happy morning, he told himself, if I could have just one happy morning without thinking about these people.

'Shivaji Nagar. Stop by Thimmappa's house,' he told Vinay. Better to take care of the issue before it became a distraction. He could already feel the inadequacy that came upon him when he thought of his brother. He had not worked this long or this hard to feel like this again.

Thimmappa could handle the shamianas at the house in Malleshwaram. And the chairs that would have to be rented; transport to the electric crematorium that needed to be arranged. Ajji would not have picked the electric crematorium, of course. She would want the burning wood pyre at Harishchandra Ghat and the melodrama of crying relatives. But things could finally start to happen the way he wanted, Girish thought with a sigh; better-so-many-years-too-late-than-never. Nevertheless, there niggled a faint superstition, that he was planning the funeral of someone who still lived, his mother no less, and this made his voice unnecessarily testy when he told Vinay, 'Slow down, are you trying to kill us?'

Vinay slowed obediently as they passed Cantonment railway station. It was a short drive beyond that, but the scenery changed quickly. They turned right past State Bank, and the streets grew slightly more crowded, busier by the kilometre. Homes became smaller and pushed up against each other, interrupted frequently by still shuttered or half open storefronts, and fronted by littered pavements. More vehicles claimed the street, careening buses filling with early morning commuters, cars and motorbikes, all racing to work ahead of the usual morning gridlock. Further still, narrowing streets heralded aging buildings stacked tall and even closer, noisy roadside tea stalls beside the occasional mutton shop open early for business. Girish ate meat without contemplation, relished it even, but the sight of the hanging carcasses annoyed him.

'Unclean fellows,' he told Vinay, reverting automatically to the comforting superiority of his twice born Brahmin status. 'Flaunting their filth.'

He scanned the walls alongside, nevertheless, to make sure that his party's logo was at least as prominent as the others. Now in Shivaji Nagar, a decidedly more Muslim and less affluent part of town, Vinay slowed to a near crawl as they tried to find Thimmappa's street in the warren of radiating lanes, some only big enough to let one vehicle pass.

The walls around them were covered with posters, crowded together and overlapping, some written over with graffiti, some torn or otherwise disfigured, others completely covered with another party's. The detritus of all of this activity, every torn scrap of poster, discarded pamphlet and pulled down flag, was piled on the street in untidy clumps, scattered or gathered by the whims of passing winds. A battlefield, like every other part of the city at the height of electioneering, only this seemed blatant, more brazen. Maybe because there was more green on the walls than Girish cared to see, more signs of the crescent and star. This had once been a safe bastion for his centrist party. All they had needed to do to win was field a Muslim candidate. But those days were long gone, into the clamour of Hindu jingoism that pulled down mosques and staged openly divisive saffron processions, and its echoes in equally hardline Muslim parties glad for the excuse and the attention. And so here they were, with a newer, openly Muslim party whose lurid green posters and emphatic crescent and star mocked, it seemed to him, his party's milquetoast secular-but-Muslim alternative.

'It's this one,' he called to Vinay, as they both spotted the distinctive banyan at the street corner, almost as wide as the street it bordered, towering over the little shrine that it shaded. Thimmappa's house lay just beyond, on a predominantly Hindu street that looked, except for the unobtrusive shrine, like every other street around it. An anachronism, Girish decided, a legacy of several generations for whom religion had been less label and more way of life.

Vinay carefully edged the car into an empty spot on the street, adjacent to a wall that held more than its fair share of green posters, with names emblazoned in Urdu along with the usual Kannada. All over Bangalore, Muslims now wore skull caps and burkhas, more Hindus wore saffron bands that conflated mainstream beliefs with marginal agendas, handed to them by right wing Hindu activists at their neighbourhood temples, even the small ones like this one. All of which left secular centrist parties like his isolated in the middle. He grew irritated at Thimmappa. Could he not have at least cleaned his compound walls? Such laziness, not to show even the appearance of supporting his own party. Allowing his walls to be overrun by these upstarts.

Girish, with Vinay close behind, entered the street where Thimmappa lived alongside his tenants in a sprawling house now rented out piecemeal. They approached his door, and sure enough, there was a young woman there, making rangoli patterns in white powder. Her saree was hitched up at the waist, exposing a widening sliver of left leg from just above knee to ankle. Girish could not help the glance that it drew, and when he looked up at her face, he was surprised by the scorn he saw there. She made no move to drop her saree on to the wet street, continuing to look him in the face instead, as if she expected him to look away or be ashamed. Impertinence, he decided, pure *kobbu*.

'Thimmappa *iddhana*?' he asked her, using the less respectful suffix, just to show her that he could. She flounced indoors without a reply. He heard her call out inside, the words indistinct. Seconds later, Thimmappa emerged, lungi-clad and hastily buttoning a shirt over his torn undershirt. He looked surprised to see Girish at his door. 'I would have come,' he said over and over, 'you should not have troubled yourself.'

They went inside, and there was no trace of the girl. Thimmappa's wife, a middle-aged, thick-waisted woman, came out from the kitchen with coffee when they sat down on the metal chairs Thimmappa unfolded in haste. Not a mistress then, Girish decided, must be a daughter, or from the lack of resemblance, a niece. A pity. But they had to get to the business at hand. Coffee and pleasantries completed, Girish beckoned to Vinay, who passed over the black bag he carried from the car.

'Three lakhs,' Girish told Thimmappa, as he passed over tightly bound packets of rupees. Five hundred-rupee notes so the packets would be slim, the preferred currency for this type of transaction. A smiling Gandhi, toothless, on each one. 'This is for the regular expenses.'

Thimmappa nodded, looking as if he had been expecting the payment. There were many uses for the money, as there was in every election—lorries to be rented to take people to vote, biryani and cheap toddy for after. Even legitimate expenses like loudspeakers and cars, everything had to be paid for. It could not all be 'white' money that they could declare to the election commission. Men like him knew that, as did Girish.

'Another thing,' Girish said, expansive in the transient afterglow of good coffee, and of dispensing his largess. 'There is another job to be done. My mother is in the hospital, the news is not good. It may be any day now.' He paused. 'We may have to arrange a funeral, at short notice.'

Thimmappa looked relieved. It was both unexpected and incongruous, and Girish wondered if he should have asked for accounting of the last payment, some of which may have gone into the thick gold chain his wife wore. It looked new.

'Of course, of course,' Thimmappa said, suddenly jovial, as if this was a wedding he had been asked to arrange. His wife glared at him from beside Girish, and he composed his features. 'We will take care of everything outside the house.' The ceremony inside the house was beyond his purview, as they both knew.

But Girish could see the calculation in his eyes. Goddess Mahalakshmi Herself had arrived in Girish's black bag early this Friday morning. Perhaps She would be even more beneficent if he asked, he seemed to be thinking. Unsurprisingly, when Thimmappa spoke, it was to say, 'Payment for the other matter, *saar*, before or after?'

Girish laughed, slapping his thigh, turning in his chair to face Thimmappa's wife. 'Amma, your husband is so smart, he jumps to the point. Doesn't he? Payment?' He turned to face Thimmappa again. 'My mother is not yet dead, and this is your concern?'

'*Kshamisi, kshamisi,*' Thimmappa said. 'It is early in the morning. I don't know what I was thinking. Your family is my family. I will spend for it out of my own pocket. Leave everything to me.'

Girish stood up. It was a minor victory. The whole thing would have cost a few thousand rupees, money he would not have missed. It was the principle to the thing, he decided. That and the girl's impertinence. They all thought so much of themselves; once in a while they had to be shown their place. He turned at the door. 'You can use some of the money I gave you today. I want to see the bills for everything.'

'Of course,' Thimmappa said, standing up as well. Girish knew he could arrange for bills, all he had to do was imagine the amounts. But he would at least make the bastard work a little.

'But there is no need, Girish-*avare*, I will take care of the expenses. Your family is my family. You just caught me at a dull time this morning. I did not have time to think about it.' Thimmappa walked Girish to the car, still talking. They were both in agreement that no more money would be forthcoming for the funeral, which was the only matter that needed deciding. The rest was politeness. When they reached the car, Vinay held the door open for Girish. 'Where next, *saar*?' he asked after Girish was seated, an ostentation that he, for one, knew his place and could be counted on to do his job.

'High Grounds,' Girish said, meaning, to work. At the Public Works Department, close to all the places that really mattered in the city, the legislature, the high court, five star hotels and a golf course closed to new members. But only after breakfast with Surendra, at the Legislatures Home, by his office. He had not been long in Thimmappa's house, but in that time the sun had taken over the sky, dispelling the mellow dawn. The streets were fuller with people leaving to work, or to whatever mischief youth and unemployment occasioned. Faraway loudspeakers on the first circling cars could be heard, and as if to taunt Girish, it was not his party's slogans that he heard override the sounds of the already bustling city.

'*Baddi maga*, rascal,' Girish cursed again, meaning Thimmappa. Lazy fellow. Ready to ask for money, as if he did all that he needed to without being asked. Soon it would be up to Girish to dispense favours, and he would remember this. That would teach Thimmappa, and the girl, for her insolence. He ran her over again in his mind like a rewound movie clip, lingering on the exposed leg. Not much she could do to stop him from doing that, was there? Did she think she was some maharani that he couldn't look at her leg?

He saw Vinay turn to look at a large billboard advertising a newly released Kannada movie at the next red light. It was the new Vivek Nayak movie, and he was drawn larger than life, his head and shoulders projecting above and outside the billboard. Some intrepid fool had managed to scale the billboard to garland him, as if he were some deity. Next to him was the thin, almost boyish heroine in jeans and a skimpy tee. As if there was anything to see in these skeletal women, Girish thought; she might as well have worn a saree. But Vinay's gaze lingered.

Girish tapped him on the shoulder. 'Have you seen it yet?'

Vinay shook his head. 'Not yet released, tonight is the first show.'

'Remind me,' Girish said. 'I will give you the evening off.'

The boy deserved at least that, he decided, movie-crazy as he was. But it was more than that, of course. Absent father, a mother who worked to support him and all the attendant humiliation of growing up like that. People like Vinay, like himself, were never really given anything, deserved or not. No, the world belonged to people who were born under a luckier star. Perhaps it was finally time somebody did something about it.

In the nine-and-a-half minutes that it took Vinay to drive from Thimmappa's house in Shivaji Nagar to Girish's destination near the imposing Vidhana Soudha, Girish had dismissed the girl and the episode with Thimmappa from his mind, and decided that Vinay was due for a raise. Even if the happy glow of dawn was gone, there was a busy day at hand. The bustle of electioneering grew farther and fainter behind them as they got closer to the legislature, Vidhana Soudha, and Raj Bhavan, the governor's residence. It was as if these were places far removed from, and not the result of the rough and tumble battles in places just like Shivaji Nagar all over the state. The grandeur, even if often experienced and unsurprising, brought back Girish's habitual anxiety. Perhaps the seat for the bye-election would be put off again, even if Surendra did become deputy chief minister. It might not be in Surendra's power to give or remain his intent when the election was won. There might be bigger players to appease; things that he could not know now or predict.

Girish was early to his breakfast meeting with Surendra at the Legislatures Home Canteen. The canteen was in the basement of the Legislatures Home, where out of town legislators were given rooms to board, for when the legislature was in session. Surendra had one of the rooms on the third floor. Girish was already at the table when Surendra arrived, without his usual entourage of personal assistant and two other hangers-on, whose functions lay somewhere between those of errand boy and bodyguard. Surendra, tall and fair-skinned, and dressed in his usual immaculate white strode across the room when he spotted Girish. This was unusual, because he thrived on the social opportunities that the canteen provided, and would often stop to talk to each person in the hall before he sat down to his meal. Today, he pulled his chair around so his back would face the room before he sat down, forcing Girish to move his own chair to face him. When he sat down, it was easy to see why. Surendra's eyes were bloodshot, and a sharp red streak, like a nail mark, ran from the corner of his cheek down his neck.

Surendra was tall and regal appearing, youthful for his age. A little over sixty, and a few years older than Girish, he was well tended, with few marks of the hard drinking and living of the preceding years. He allowed the edges of his decorously styled hair to remain grey while he dyed the rest, and Girish knew he patronised a certain brand of imported women's cream that delayed wrinkles. He continued to exercise near obsessively on a bull worker that he had acquired years before. The effect was to arrest his age at a fashionable maybe-less-than-middle, one that suggested both the wisdom of maturity and the vigour of youth. This was tactically necessary for politics, he often told Girish, who rather suspected Surendra's not inconsiderable vanity, and with it, a taste for younger women.

'Mallige,' Surendra said shortly, picking up the coffee that Girish had ordered for him.

Girish nodded, and successfully suppressed the smile a lesser man would have let show. So there had been a feisty one at the newest brothel in town. Girish had never been, but he had been the one to introduce Surendra to the madam.

Before Surendra could say any more, there was a hand on his shoulder. It was the MLA from Karwar, Vasant Gowda.

'Surendra-*avare*, *heggidira*?' he began, voice trailing into laugh when he saw Surendra's face. But Vasant needed a favour, so the laugh died quickly. 'My nephew, you met him last week, any news on the matter?' He needed a licence for a large commercial complex on disputed land and permissions were handled by Surendra's ministry.

'He will get it. You don't have to ask me this daily. Do you want me to go find him and give it to him on a silver plate?'

Surendra said and turned away quickly in dismissal. Perhaps the laughter had rankled.

Vasant walked away, ignoring Girish's '*Namskara*.'

Girish noted the slight, and made a mental note to increase the bribe his nephew would have to pay by a few thousand rupees. But the sting of it lingered, a reminder that perhaps he was only an itinerant in this rarefied world, a mere impostor.

'Tell that woman of yours,' Surendra said, when Vasant had moved out of earshot, 'we have to arrange dinner at your apartment today, for Sadhu Devidas.' He emphasised the 'sadhu', giving it an ironic edge. 'Every two-anna goonda can become a "sadhu" these days. Drives around in a foreign car, calls himself a sadhu.'

'Who, that Devidas, from the theatre fire?' Girish's surprise had gotten the better of him.

'Yes, yes,' Surendra said testily. 'Stop looking at everything just from your perspective. He beat you in your backyard, even when he was just that two-bit hoodlum. Do you know how many people listen to his radio address now? Or watch him on TV? How much money he gets from all those one rupee, five rupee donations? Crores, I tell you, crores.'

Girish considered it for a minute. It was true. He had watched the hoodlum turn holyman. He had known him when he was Satyaprakash, and worked for a local politician who was the leader of the opposition in the legislature. In the span of seven years and a miraculous transformation later, people now believed in the sadhu, Devidas. They did not realise, as Girish did, that the transformation owed more to political patronage and money than to divine intervention. No, people thought that God spoke to Devidas and showed him visions and revealed to him His intentions for the world. A whisper had started that Devidas was actually God, an incarnation, a rumour that Devidas swatted away less modestly each time, as if it was not his own apparatus that planted the stories and watched them grow.

Surendra tapped on the table, an impatient rat-a-tat that interrupted his momentary silence. 'What, still thinking about it?'

'No, no, I don't care about all that, it is in the past,' Girish said, realising that it was true. 'If we can get him, we will win. What we lose in Muslim votes will come in on the Hindu side. How did you arrange it?'

Surendra had been meeting Hindu religious leaders all over the state, to offset the new reality of the aggressive Muslim parties and the belligerent Hindu right that made noises vastly out of proportion to their still miniscule showing in the polls. Most of the religious lot had cast their lot with the Hindu nationalist parties, there was no surprise there. But there were a few who were apolitical, or undeclared, and Sadhu Devidas was one of them. The one with the largest following, the most money. He could be kingmaker before he became God, Girish thought, smiling both at his own wit and Surendra's foresight in courting him. But how had Surendra managed it?

Surendra only sipped his coffee, smiling at Girish.

'He agreed to come to dinner?' Girish asked again.

'Yes, but as if he is some Lord. Not as if he was some goonda who used to fall at my feet once.'

'Did he tell you what he wanted?' This was key of course, the price of Devidas's benediction.

'What is your job, if I must be the one to find that out?' Surendra said, snapping his fingers at a waiter. 'The usual.' Surendra turned back to him and said, 'He probably wants a few hundred acres of land somewhere for an ashram fitting his new status. Anyway, it does not matter. The harder he plays to get, the more the Fox has to rely on us. He can't negotiate or be seen in public with Devidas, because then all his friends would leave him for the next convent-educated bastard who can talk English. For now, it's all right.' The Fox was code between them for the current chief minister, whose chair Surendra was working up towards in steps.

Girish nodded.

The waiter brought Surendra's usual, which was benne masala dosa, with an extra-large scoop of butter that was melting over the sides in rivulets. 'What, you are not eating?' he asked Girish, his tone almost affectionate. 'Do I still have to take care of you like I did in Malehalli? Bring him the same thing.'

'No, I ate some uppitu already, before you came,' Girish protested, but Surendra would hear none of it.

'Eat with me.'

So, of course Girish did, because this was the man he had followed from one party to another. Secular, Communist, even a brief foray into a caste-based party notable only because it was a caste neither of them belonged to, before returning to the party where they had both begun. He had followed Surendra through every horse trade, to every stepping stone, from one faction to the next, doing what he asked of him. Each time his loyalty had been rewarded, and the rare moments of affection that Surendra showed him affirmed to him the special status that Surendra accorded him. 'This is my relative,' he would say to people sometimes, of Girish, in an inaccurate statement that elevated them both.

Surendra could be anyone to anybody—that was his gift. Girish was nobody in his own right, but his pedigree was impeccable. Surendra's connection to the freedom fighter Srinivas Murthy, Girish's father, caused people to look with less askance at a handsome, smooth-talking climber with no roots or antecedents. Things were different now, of course;

Surendra was his own man and did not need Srinivas Murthy's reflected glory. But he was still bound to Girish from their times together in Malehalli. Not for the first time, Girish thought back to those days with something like gratitude, fondness even. No one else had taken an interest in him then. And without these moments of Surendra's concern, there were only the injustices that were his lot. A wife who did not understand him, a family that did not value him or help, a father who left him nothing of profit but his name. There were Surendra's occasional and unexpected rages, of course, but they passed quickly, with no grudges held afterward. Who else had ever done more for him than Surendra?

'And how is the girl?' Surendra continued, winking broadly. 'Taking care of you? Or are you ready for a new edition?'

Girish laughed and continued to eat without speaking.

'Call her, call her,' Surendra said. 'Tell her to arrange dinner. And be careful, nothing can go wrong tonight.'

Breakfast done, Surendra stood up. He would go to his room upstairs to sleep off the excesses of the night, and Girish would make his way to his office, with a stop or two on the way. Soon, his cellphone, advance issue and not available yet to the general public, would begin to ring as the business of the day started.

He had to go home first, so he could pick up Vimala's clothes and have them sent to her at the hospital. Maybe I can throw all her clothes in a pile and send it all to the hospital, he thought, and it made him smile. His sense of well-being restored by a full stomach and Surendra's goodwill, he walked to his car with a light step.

Once he picked up the clothes, he would get the keys to the old ration shop on Sampige Road. Girish had made the owner a loan several years before, and facilitated the permits for a ration shop. But the fellow's wife had run off with a neighbour, and he had taken to drink. The debts piled, and he had finally come to Girish for help. Girish took on his debts in exchange for the shop. Prime real estate for a pittance, the way he saw it. Either the man was a fool, or he did not care. Maybe he believed the children's tales about ghosts and curses, Girish thought as he stepped into his car, remembering the stories Mira had breathlessly brought home when she first played on the street with the other children, of the previous owner who had died and returned nightly as a ghost. He looked like the kind of fool who would.

Vinay drove out of the Legislatures Home, and Girish saw the crowd on the street step aside for his car, parting before him like a portent of times to come. Soon, he told himself; soon. Perhaps the stars had begun to smile on him. Soon there would be motorcades and garlands, more money than he could dream of or count. It could all happen. He had Surendra's favour. It would.

He picked up his phone, and dialled Sitara's number.

7
Mira

Appa and I are on the flight to Frankfurt. We have been served our first airline meal of the day. Mine is vegetarian, his is not. We have talked about inane matters, except for a spirited discussion on who makes better bisi bele bath: Ajji or Vimala aunty. We fail to reach a consensus. Vimala aunty's has a touch more jaggery, which I like more than he does. It is only remarkable because we have never in all these years discussed even such peripheral details of my life in Bangalore.

~

In the week that follows my fervent prayer, I tell Anisa my first half-truth: my uncle does not want either of us to go to the temple.

Outside, cars strapped with loudspeakers begin to circle the streets. Multicoloured flyers litter the sidewalks. Pamphlets fly with denuded petals from the trees above them in the tails of late afternoon winds. Hindu devotional music blasts from the temple at four in the morning when all but a few of the very faithful curse at the noise and turn over in bed. In response, a distant mosque raises the volume on its speakers for the customary call to prayers at five. People turn over again, curse some more. Posters of Lord Rama appear on private compounds that homeowners rip off in exasperation, only to see them appear again. Gone is the beatific smile on Rama's face in those portraits. He looks resolute, martial even, ribbed and muscular, as if He has discovered a celestial gym. The rains still arrive most afternoons, frequent and welcome, but they leave less of a mellow afterglow behind. They seem innocuous, not radical or new as they should, these departures from the life we have known.

When the adults have forgotten the altercation at the temple, we finally go back one evening with Ajji. There are more saffron-clad outsiders, both in the temple and on the street below. They hand out pamphlets in the streets: Sadhu Devidas Coming to Town. Join Sanskrit Classes, Learn about Our Glorious Heritage. Hindu Values, the Need of the Hour. Lord Rama, the Epitome of Righteousness. Anisa takes care to walk a wide loop around them. Thankfully, the man who shouted at us is not with them. But we know his name—Sadhu Devidas; my uncle says he was a goonda only weeks or months before.

Ajji walks by them with disdain. 'There's nothing these fellows can teach me,' she snorts, and that seems to be most of our neighbours' reactions. Some of the most fervent TV serial-watchers of the years before seem glad, however, as if all this is an extension of the *Ramayana* they loved and watched every week. And in some ways, it is. Just as the television drama supplanted varying regional retellings of the story with a gentle and unifying authority that bemused people like Ajji, so too do these fervent saffron youth. *This* is being Hindu, they say, not all the other nonsense you've thought it was. The priests at the temple are happy enough, because there is finally some excitement at their door. More visitors mean more cash in the hundi, more collections when the aarthi plate comes around at the end of the pooja. Indeed, they puff up with importance as they come around with the aarthi, a new assertiveness in place of their former servility.

'Yakshagana performances, all old-fashioned things,' a young priest tells Ajji, oblivious of her appalled disbelief. 'We will bring sadhus for discourses so they can talk about our true Hindu values. Lots of people will come.' For once, Ajji is speechless.

No one remarks on Anisa's presence at the temple. Anisa has always come to the temple with me, because we have always gone everywhere together. The ones who know her have not minded before. They are often the housewives who have received us when we went Ganesha visiting together, when we were five or six. On Ganesha's birthday, all around, when except inside Anisa's home there would swirl the distinctive smells of ghee and jasmine, sandalwood and incense. Schools would close, loudspeakers would scream and these ladies would set before the newly fashioned clay images of Ganesha in their houses the sweets they laboured over since daybreak. We banded together, as children and urchins did, in mutually exclusive groups, to go Ganesha visiting. The first year, I had begged and badgered Rehana aunty, hopping on one foot outside their door, until she let Anisa come with us, against her misgivings and her better judgement. Vinay, who straddled that line between street child and better born, was the leader of our little group. He would ring the doorbell first and say 'Ganesha *nodbeku*', we need to see Ganesha, his shoulder thrust out, almost a challenge to the lady at the door. Daring her to point out that one of us was dressed not as well as the rest, and that another was a camouflaged non-believer. Not one did, of course. They opened their doors, because children are like God, and who could refuse Ganesha on His birthday? Anisa was arguably the most enthusiastic Ganesha-viewer, and asked often, dimpling prettily, when offered a laddoo, for '*Godambi irodhu*,' one with cashews. Because another of our goals, less stated, was to sample a hundred and eight different offerings for pot-bellied Ganesha that the smiling ladies made with their finest ghee, and handed to us, even as they saw through our fervent piety.

The others see us with Ajji and assume that we are sisters, or more likely, cousins. In truth, Anisa and Ajji are both fair-skinned and petite, and I am the tall, dark-skinned, perhaps-not-relative standing between them.

Anisa, however, seems less assured than she usually is, hesitating before stepping into line in front of the idol. Ajji motions her forward, 'Step up, step up, people behind you can't see.' The young priest, who is new, frowns at Anisa's name when Ajji mentions it for the archane, the blessing. 'What kind of Hindu name is that?' his frown seems to say, but there is a big crowd, and the frown disappears when he moves on to the next family.

On our way down from the temple, Lakshmi shouts at the outsiders to clear the space in front of her stall.

'Interfere with business, and I'll make you wish you were never born,' she threatens, sending a saffron-clad recruit scampering. I smile widely at her when I get my flowers. 'Look at you girls,' Lakshmi says. 'Such young women already. You haven't come by in so long.'

And yet, two days later, we hear that her son and the boys he plays cricket with have signed up to hand out flyers. It is easy money. Besides, there will always be time for cricket afterwards. We see them from the terrace late one evening, knocking on our neighbours' doors, calling out to each other on the street, 'This one is mine.'

Girish uncle gets the flyer from Vinay as we watch. We are too high up in Anisa's terrace to hear what is being said, but it is a short conversation. My uncle walks him to the gate, and we can hear him call out to the boys on the street, 'If you boys want better work, come to the party office.'

Meanwhile, I have been so successful at timing my visits to Anisa's home that Farid uncle complains, long and loud, that he never gets to see me these days.

'Where is my other daughter?' he demands, standing outside our gate one evening. 'Mira, have you become too grown up for us?' He has bought a jackfruit on his way back from work, and Adil stands a little behind him, balancing it on his palms. It is huge. 'We'll never be able to finish it all if Mira isn't there to help us,' Farid uncle tells Ajji, who is standing at the gate. Even the boys loitering in the street with flyers laugh.

That evening, I sit on the floor of Anisa's drawing room with her family, as Farid uncle sits in the centre, his oiled knife gutting and slicing the jackfruit. I get the first fruit as it emerges, orange-yellow, slippery and slick.

'For Mira,' he teases me, 'because she is such a rare visitor these days, needing a special invitation.'

Adil gets the next, then Anisa, then Rehana aunty, who then sets aside the next one for Farid uncle as he works. The pile grows higher, even after we can eat no more. Farid uncle continues to skin and gouge until the last piece is extracted, not stopping to taste the pile that grows by his side. 'Plenty for all the neighbours,' he tells me at the end. 'Later Anisa and you can go around and give it to everyone.'

I try not to look at Adil, but there are odd moments when our eyes meet. When I first bite into the luscious sweetness of the fruit, awkward and aware. When I laugh at one of Farid uncle's jokes. Each time that happens, a now familiar tug somewhere deep within appears, and I grow silent. Anisa talks into my silences, nudging me when no one is looking. Rehana aunty and Farid uncle seem to not notice anything untoward. Adil seems to be quite at ease, arguing with Farid uncle about the most efficient way to skin the jackfruit. It is impossible, in the end, not to let my guard down with Adil.

I can talk to him, I tell myself, and it will not be the end of the world. Maybe he does not even remember the way I looked at him before. Maybe it was all in my mind. Maybe I just need to spend more time with him, and the awkwardness will disappear. And so begins a slippery slope. We spend almost every evening at Anisa's home. Adil pays me oblique, understated compliments. I 'don't sound too bad' when we're mock-singing our *Kaboothar Jaa Jaa* song—maybe I should just sing something nice instead? My handwriting is beautiful; my manners are vastly better than Anisa's. He never alludes to anything more personal than that, but I notice the way he looks at me when he talks. Just as I notice the way his eyes settle on my face when he thinks I am not looking.

The next week I begin to find little scraps of poems in random places, in a magazine that I ask to borrow, under my bag or my plate at dinner, or at my elbow, once. They are not addressed to anyone in particular, but they are written in his hand. Luscious verses, profound and intimate, words in arrangements I have never seen. At the end of each he scrupulously includes the name of the poet, Pablo Neruda usually, or Ghalib sometimes. He is nothing if not honest.

'I can do physics, not poetry,' he says one day, 'strictly a logic and numbers kind of guy.' It is half statement, half apology and altogether endearing. My resolve to work towards normalcy flies out the window. How can I resist him, this boy who aspires to poetry, for me?

The air tingles with awareness when we are together, even at opposite ends of a room. Accidental touches still scorch my skin and yet they become more frequent. Glances grow in intimacy. I walk around in a delicious fog during the day, smiling indiscriminately at people in the street, misgivings stowed away deep inside where I cannot feel them. I even smile back at Vinay, who, for reasons I cannot fathom, has taken to sending strange little half smiles my way.

One evening, Anisa and I make our way to the local lending library as usual, a weekly expedition over summer. The library is a neighbourhood enterprise common for its time, started by a couple of housewives in a garage that one of them owns. It is smallish, but stacked with books from ceiling to floor. The books are obviously bought second hand or in bulk, but they can be rented cheaply by the day. Anisa and I usually leave with a few to read under the fan on hot summer afternoons when even talking is too much effort. But today, in place of one of the aunties who usually mans the check out desk is her nephew, newly arrived from out of town.

He raises his eyebrows at a Mills & Boon that I've picked for the first time and slipped between our more usual stack of Agatha Christies and Perry Masons. We've almost exhausted the stash of acceptable reading the library owns, and this is my first Adil-inspired foray into daring. He lingers, specifically, on its mildly racy cover. 'Why not the real stuff,' he asks, leering, 'you know, like Harold Robbins or James Hadley Chase? Or *Lady Chatterley's Lover*—I have a copy.'

'We'll tell your aunt,' Anisa says, bravado thinly papered over discomfort. 'And that's a banned book. You shouldn't be offering it to minors.'

He leers some more, and looks her up and down. 'You are the ones renting dirty romance novels, not me.'

'Not dirty!' I say, horrified. I haven't read a Mills & Boon before, but I've seen his aunt read one as she waited for people to finish making their selections. We back away with our stash, and decide Adil will have to be despatched to return the books when they come due.

Outside on our street, the absence of the cricket-playing boys is disconcerting. There has never been a time when we have not had to watch for the wayward ball at this time of the evening.

'We can walk in the middle of the street now,' I tell Anisa, more to distract myself from the leering clerk than anything else.

'Why are men such creeps?' she wonders aloud, undeceived.

'He was just being an idiot. Probably hasn't talked to a girl all week,' I say. 'Let's go to the City Central Library instead, one of these days.'

I spot Adil's motorbike first, even though his helmet completely covers his face. 'That is a long way off, but maybe the bus—' Anisa breaks off mid-sentence when the motorbike stops on the street by us.

'Would either of you ladies care for a ride?' Adil asks, revving the engine, and we can see the laughter in his eyes through the visor.

'No,' Anisa hisses at him, 'and you're being an idiot, Adil.'

'Oh, that's good,' Adil says. 'I only wanted to ask Mira, anyway.'

'No,' we say together, Anisa and I. Adil and I on a motorbike? That would be so improper. Even Adil and I in conversation on the street outside our homes, without Anisa, would be strange. Not improper, just strange. Everybody would notice. If Ajji didn't see it for herself, she would hear about it. Does he really think I would go?

'Okay, then,' he says, laughing aloud now. 'See you brave young things at home when I get back.'

'Why are you home so early anyway?' Anisa asks, frowning at him. She looks like a younger version of Rehana aunty when she does that, drawing herself up tall and taut so the top of her head comes up to my ear.

'My project ends this week,' Adil says, 'and I am going to meet my friends at Casa Piccola. Thought you'd like to come.'

'As if you'd take us. You've never wanted us around your friends before.'

'You'll never know now, will you, after you've both refused already?' Adil says, ignoring Anisa's irritation. He looks into my eyes, and says for me alone, 'But I'll be back early, around six. Maybe we could play cards or something?' He looks like a little boy when he says that, I think, as if a toy would make him really happy.

'Maybe.' I find myself smiling, even though Anisa is shaking her head at me.

'Don't encourage him,' Anisa says after he leaves. 'He's my uncle, but he's still, you know, a boy.' She emphasises the boy, and it comes out like a swear, like the mild ones we use on the sly: damn, and hell.

'I didn't really do anything,' I say, 'and you're still thinking about that guy at the library. You don't really think Adil's like that, do you?'

'Oh, you know what Sister Lalitha says.' She laughs. 'It doesn't matter; all boys are the same.

'And it doesn't matter,' she continues, in the Sister's Malayali accent, 'if the cotton falls on the fire, or the fire on the cotton. Remember, you are the cotton.'

We laugh together in the street. Vanitha aunty, one of our neigbours, hears us laughing as she pays for the bananas she has just bought from a street vendor. 'You girls are getting older,' she says, 'don't laugh so loudly in public. We know you, but other people will talk.'

We stop laughing, of course. 'It's a good thing you did not get on the motorbike with Adil. She would not have talked about anything else for a month,' Anisa says under her breath as we walk past her, duly chastised. We giggle decorously and softly all the way home.

There is a white Ambassador sedan with government plates outside our gate. Someone must be in to see Girish uncle. This is a rare occurrence, visitors from work for my uncle.

The gate screeches as usual when we push it open, and a handsome man dressed all in white looks up at us. We gape at him before we remember how impolite that is. He looks like an older movie star, but one that would probably still be paired with a teenaged heroine in a new movie. He sits, long legs cramped, in one of the wide wicker chairs in the veranda. Ajji stands at the door to his side, her face stone-like in displeasure. My uncle is nowhere to be seen.

I feel the man's eyes on me every step of the way up the short cobbled path to the veranda. I bend my head; turn my eyes to the floor. I can still feel his scrutiny. He laughs as I approach the veranda. 'Ah, this must be Mira! So many years, she was a baby when I saw her last. Well, well, the fruit does not fall far from the tree.'

Ajji cuts him off with a snort. 'Surendra, she is *my* granddaughter.'

He seems unfazed. 'Mira, come, come. Sit here.' He motions to the chair by his side.

I don't want to sit by this man, I want to go inside where he cannot look at me the way he's been doing. But before I can respond, Ajji says to me in a fierce whisper, 'Go inside. Now.' I have never seen Ajji so angry.

But the man smiles, and says, 'Come, come, don't be shy. I knew both your parents. Here, come sit down.'

It seems rude to refuse, and the idea of being rude to an adult is an outlandish one. Even if Ajji is the one asking us to be rude.

So we sit down, ignoring Ajji's sharply indrawn breath.

I have my back to Ajji, which is just as well. I can sense the anger that seeps from her in the way she breathes behind me, a suppressed fury that is out of all proportion to my disobedience.

He asks us about school, the way adults usually do. He

asks us if we have seen the latest Hindi movie. He does not mention my parents again, and I surprise myself by asking, 'How do you know my parents?'

He laughs. 'I knew them from Malehalli,' he says. 'I knew them both from before you were born. And your mother—beautiful woman, just beautiful.'

Ajji explodes when he says this. She steps forward and drags me up roughly by the arm. 'Go inside when I tell you to, shameless girl!'

She thrusts me into the house and shuts the door.

We stand as close to the door as we can to hear what is being said on the veranda.

Ajji's voice is soft, a furious whisper as if she realises just where we are. 'Have you no shame? Coming here today, sitting in my house, talking like this?'

'I am here to see your son,' Surendra says, making no effort to lower his voice, so it carries into the street, 'he works for me. If you remember, he was an intermediate-failed good-for-nothing before that.'

'I have told you this before—do not come to the house. Even you should have more shame than that. And to actually talk about my daughter-in-law? You have the insolence to do that?'

'You must forget, the whole world talks about your daughter-in-law,' he sneers, in a way that is completely at odds with the way he spoke to us.

Anisa turns to look at me, white-faced.

'My son gave me his word that you would not come to this house, Surendra,' Ajji says, still quiet, still furious. 'It was the only way I would live under his roof after Mahalinga died.'

'Ah, the great Srinivas Murthy's wife speaks of words and promises! Don't forget, before all that, that your whole household feeds on scraps from my table.'

'I live on my husband's pension,' Ajji says, and I can hear a break in her voice. It scares me. This is Ajji; I have never heard her cry or be afraid.

'Of course, of course, and you remember whose recommendation you needed before it was sanctioned?' Surendra laughs. 'You must not forget such things, Amma, even if you believe some old fool like Mahalinga and his silly stories.'

We hear a scrape of a chair, he is standing up. 'Ah, the boys are here. Tell Girish I came,' he says, 'and it is so touching to see the love you have for your granddaughter and your daughter-in-law's memory. We both remember a time when that was not the case, don't we?' More laughter. 'Girish will be upset you did not offer me coffee, but we are almost family, no? No need for formalities.'

We hear him walk down the garden path, calling loudly to Vinay and his friends. 'So, you are the boys who are so eager to work, eh?' His loud voice continues for a while, the words fading as they walk away from the gate together.

We step back from the door so Ajji does not find us eavesdropping. My eyes catch Vimala aunty's as we do so. She has been standing a little behind us, listening as well. She turns away from me when I see her, heading back into the kitchen. A minute later, we hear the retreating roar of the car as it speeds away and leaves our street, but Ajji still has not come in.

When I am brave enough to go outside to see where she is, I see her walking far away in the street in the direction of the temple. She seems older, more bent in the distance. How fanciful to think that, I tell myself. Ajji is as she has always been. Unflappable.

Anisa, behind me, says, 'Who was that?'

I shake my head.

'Poor Ajji,' Anisa says. 'I should be nicer to her.'

I head back into the kitchen. 'Vimala aunty,' I say, 'who is this man? What was all that about?'

My aunt looks up at me, and for a while she says nothing.

'Your Ajji would not like me to tell you,' she says, finally, when I am beginning to think that she has pretended not to hear me. Her eyes are tired. I notice her creased sari, the absent-minded knot of her hair, the streaks of rice flour that run willy-nilly across her chest. She is always dressed like this. As if her world is the kitchen. Not a world that includes visitors, or guests, a walk to the temple or even to the street to buy on an impulse from the man who pushes a street cart laden with bananas. It is true. She would do nothing that displeases Ajji. I am almost back in the hall, when I hear her speak again.

'But I have to tell you this, Mira. If you ever come home and find him here or see him somewhere when you are alone, turn around and run. Don't tell Ajji or your uncle that I told you this. But remember this, run away as fast as you can. Even if it seems rude or people notice. Run.'

The conversation, such as it is, ends on that unsettling note. Anisa and I wait in the hall while Vimala aunty resumes working in silence.

I pace the hall with Anisa, and that is when I remember that I have heard the name Mahalinga before. It brings to mind a train journey and cold curd rice to eat, a hall with grieving relatives and a white-swaddled corpse in the centre. And a tall woman, khadi-clad, with greying hair drawn tight into a bun. She is folded quietly into Ajji's arms, in a grief almost regal in its restraint. I wonder if I imagined it, as Anisa suggests when I tell her this. But that woman, I think. I could not have imagined her.

And there is more. It was in this very hall that it happened, one night when I was very young. I cannot place it in time. I woke up to loud voices. Ajji's mainly, interspersed with Girish uncle's, in this very hall that I was pacing.

'I do not need permission, anyone's *permission*,' Ajji had said, flinging her saris into an open suitcase. 'I did not live to be this old to ask *permission to do anything*! My granddaughter and I *will go* to Mahalinga's funeral. We owe him a debt *that I, at least*, want to repay and know that *I* cannot.'

'Amma, he was not quite right in the head. People will talk if you go. It is not like he is our relative or even of our caste. It is not proper. Appa would not approve if he was here.' Girish uncle, pleading.

'I know what my husband would have wanted better than some young fool who barely knew him,' Ajji said, voice scorn-sharpened, finding more things to throw into the open suitcase. 'Surendra cannot show his face here either. I forbid it. If he comes, I will go back to Malehalli. And not come back.'

'Surendra is our benefactor, our saviour. It is because of him that I have this job. Be reasonable.'

'Vimala,' Ajji said, ignoring Girish uncle completely, 'we are taking the train in the morning, even if I have to walk to the railway station. My husband may have died, but he has not left me here to be a burden on your family, *or a servant*, to listen to all your whims and fancies. I know *better than anyone* here what he would want.' A minute after she had used up a final weapon, her widowhood and her dependence on the whims of her children, she'd said, in a sudden change of tone, closing the suitcase and locking it, 'Pack some curd rice for Mira in the morning, to eat on the train journey. She'll get sick if she eats the food they sell there.'

I tell Anisa, who looks mildly disbelieving. She never remembers the things that happened to us when we were young the way I do. She doesn't remember that her sweater in kindergarten was red, and had buttons shaped like white elephants, or even that it was her mother who had a five star for us that first day after school. I wonder sometimes if her memories of those days are her own, or merely things I've told her about years after they happened.

'Are you sure, Mira?' she asks again. 'It's not something you think happened because of what we overheard?'

But I am sure. And it doesn't tell us much of anything that we don't already know, or hold out a promise that it concerns anything we care about.

Anisa watches me pace for a while. She finally chooses a book at random from the pile we brought, and it turns out to be the Mills & Boon I picked. She rolls her eyes at me, but begins to read anyway. I sit by the window. It seems selfish to leave without seeing Ajji. I can see the hands on the clock creep up closer and closer to six. Even though it is a white-sareed, bent woman that I am looking for, it is passing motorbikes that catch my eye.

Girish uncle arrives before Ajji does. 'Somebody was here looking for you,' I say, careful not to mention the eavesdropped conversation. 'I think his name was Surendra.'

He is startled. 'Was Ajji here?'

'She went to the temple after he left. Who is he? Ajji didn't like him.'

'He is my boss,' Girish uncle says. 'Ajji doesn't like him, of course. There are a lot of people that your Ajji doesn't like.'

He paces up and down the hall for a while. He tries to call someone on the phone, whoever it is evidently does not answer. My aunt continues to make dinner in the kitchen.

'Why don't you go to Anisa's house?' he says. 'Ajji probably will not come home until the evening pooja is over.'

I know Girish uncle says this because he does not want us to hear the fight that is coming when Ajji returns from the temple. Ordinarily, nothing would make me want to leave.

Nothing that is, except the distant roar of the motorbike that I hear making its way into Anisa's building.

8
Ajji

The celebrations should have lasted weeks after Nehru's speech on the radio, which we heard crowded around the big transistor radio in the hall. When I awoke the next morning, your Ajja was pacing the ground outside the house, still unable to contain his happiness.

'This air you breathe, Meenakshi,' he said, 'it belongs to us. To us, you understand? Wake the children. This is not the time for sleep.' He rushed them through their prayers and breakfast, smiling all the while as if his face would tear open like an overripe cotton pod. 'This is the best coffee you have ever made, Meenakshi, and the thatte-idlis are feathery, like clouds.' Even his breathing seemed better, and he was less winded when he picked up your father, Kishore, a plump one-year-old, so fat that he could not walk yet. 'Kishore, Girish, this is your ground, your land, do you see?' Pointing outside. 'Yours and no one else's.'

'It was theirs yesterday, and will be theirs tomorrow, as long as we pay the loan off,' I said finally, tiring of the need to celebrate. I did not add that the only ground that would ever belong to them was held for them by my sweat and toil, not his mahatma's grandiose ideas. Those only took away husbands and their livelihoods. 'Freedom did not mean that we were free of our debts, or even the interest on them with the moneylender. But your Ajja knew what I was thinking, and instead of our usual

fight, he laughed and said, 'When you both grow up, maybe you can teach your mother to see more than her petty concerns.' And he spent the day in irrational joy, seeing everything anew.

'Kishore, Kishore, my son, of all of us, you are the only one who will know life only as a free man!'

'Girish, never forget this day, that so many have suffered and sacrificed for,' he said, 'but this is the time to look at our future, at the future of our free country. We may be poor, but we are not slaves anymore. Hold your head upright, straighten your shoulders and stand like a man.'

He quoted Nehru's speech to anyone who would listen, about waking up at the midnight hour, and trysts with destiny, shouting it from our yard into the street and homes below. On and on, until he grew tired and started coughing, pink-tinged patches of phlegm that I only saw when I washed his handkerchief the next morning.

But that afternoon, while I curled up in my discontent, and missed important contents of dirty handkerchiefs, his joy was being slowly poisoned. What should have been a long celebration turned into a bloodbath that we heard about on the radio, many weeks after it had begun. Hindus and Muslims killing each other and far worse, women assaulted and children killed all along the new border with Pakistan. People whispered about gunny bags tied shut arriving on trains on either side, that when opened revealed nothing other than sliced off women's breasts. Things we could not have even imagined. Tales we only partly believed, sure that no human being could do this to another.

Malehalli had no Muslims, and I could not imagine that, even if we did, my neighbours or I would rush out to kill them and loot their homes, much less the other things.

'The people who live there,' I said to your grandfather, 'they must be animals.'

Your grandfather said nothing.

As I went along with the washing, I thought about it.

'It is the kind of food they eat up there,' my mother-in-law, your great grandmother, said. 'All that meat and wheat, it heats the blood.'

My father-in-law, peering into the distance through his cataract, said, shortly, 'A man has to do what he has to do to protect his family, no matter what he eats. What would we do in the madness?'

That was when your grandfather left the house, walking all the way down to town without telling anyone. He left without saying goodbye, even though it would take him at least an hour to climb back up to the house, with multiple stops along the way.

I thought about it more as I soaped my saree on the washing stone. There was the arecanut merchant who came to visit us when your grandfather was released from prison, he had a big shop. People were envious. If he were Muslim, would they attack him? And who would? Maybe Rachiah, the man with the curving mustache who worked for him would, I thought. He was big and muscular from lifting arecanut sacks all day, and the stories in town were that he drank illicit toddy on the sly. Perhaps he would be capable of something like that.

But then there was the mild-mannered Krishnappa, who killed someone last year over a gambling debt. No one knew he gambled until the day they dragged him off, handcuffed, to jail. Who knew, really, what anyone was capable of?

What if our ancestors, the ancient Havyakas, had gone north instead of south? What if that king who wanted atonement for his sin had dreamt of the river Yamuna instead of Kaveri? I imagined our home and the small grove of trees that I fought to keep, in another place, surrounded by Muslims. Hardy, hot-blooded people toughened by beef and wheat, at our door, brandishing blood-stained knives, while we cowered within, our rice-and-vegetable-thinned blood ready for the spilling. I shivered as I lifted the sari and brought it down hard on the washing stone.

'Rama,' I thought, 'so infinite are Your mercies, that you protect us from that day of their migration to this.' And all around me people called out to their children to come indoors, and waited for their menfolk to return, crowded around transistor radios, even though we were a thousand miles from the violence.

It was then that I saw the pink phlegm-stained handkerchief. As I thanked Rama for His mercies, perhaps He smiled the enigmatic smile they give Him in the pictures we worship. Perhaps as He smiled, He revealed the shadow encroaching steadily on my husband's life, even as I shivered unnecessarily over distant things. The handkerchief lay there nestled in my dirty saree, its bold specks of blood showing. I picked it up, and in an instant all else fled from my mind. I could explain away the tiredness and the difficult breathing to the food in prison and the punishments his body took. Not coughed-up blood. I left the washing unattended to sit on the steps and wait.

Your Ajja arrived with Mahalinga, Usha's husband. I watched their slow ascent, and the multiple stops to catch his breath. Your Ajja had been to the Congress office, to see if he could help. There was a group of people going north, another following the mahatma to the east, to Calcutta and the border with Bangladesh. Another group was going to a village on the way to Mangalore that had Muslims, to do the things that satyagrahis do in the face of evil. This, to my understanding, was standing up and being beaten or killed, in the hope that those doing the beating and killing would be shamed into stopping. Or fasting, like their mahatma did frequently and to much attention. Not the most practical way to handle the rage and lusts of heated blood. But, I learned later, your Ajja had coughed and had to sit down, and they would not allow him to join.

'Just a cold, Meenakshi,' your Ajja said, the satyagrahi who worshipped the truth, when I mentioned the blood in the

handkerchief, too impatient to wait for Mahalinga to leave. 'The blood, just a little, came from coughing so much.'

Mahalinga left quickly after, refusing buttermilk or coffee.

I watched your grandfather closely the days after, and the coughing seemed to improve. My concerns were lulled by his words, and it did not occur to me to doubt this man who only and always spoke the truth.

Your Ajja's mahatma went on a fast in Calcutta. Like parents rushing to placate a petulant child, people threw their weapons away. The riots stopped, at least in Bengal. Your Ajja began to spend most of the day by the radio, in his easy chair, listening, silent. When he spoke, it was to the children, and he spent hours teaching them this or that, the way he would teach me when we were first married.

Sometimes he said, 'Meenakshi, you work so hard.' Or, things I had never heard him say before, 'How are we going to pay off our debt?'

He took a job with the arecanut merchant, to oversee the books. To calculate again what the man's relatives had written and counted, to calibrate their suspect honesty. He would go down to town twice a week, and sometimes a boy from the shop would come, bringing books on his bicycle for your grandfather to work on at home.

In time, the riots ended and people who had left town returned. The news turned positive again, for a while. Your grandfather began to sleep sitting up in his easy chair, listening to the radio at night. A few weeks into this, inexplicably, the boy from the shop began to bring the books home every day. Your grandfather worked on them at home, and did not leave the house, except to go visit the Congress office about once a month. Kishore began to walk, finally, his chubby legs strong enough to support his weight at last. Girish joined the government school in town and brought home slates with perfectly fashioned Kannada letters in white chalk. We were a family like any other.

It was so fleeting, like collected rainwater on the sloping hillside that was our front yard. Your Ajja became sick when the monsoons were on their last legs. The months dragged on and the dampness in the air reduced, but his coughing increased. As he slept in the easy chair, I would sometimes wake to see pink froth at his lips. He hungered for air, as if he sank under water. No kashayas of ginger or tulsi could bring him relief. Then the doctor arrived, the one from the town that your Ajja had gone to see in secret every month when he said he went to the Congress office. He came up the hill in his car and strode into our house with Mahalinga behind him, sheep-like, carrying his black bag.

*'I told you this would happen, Srinivas-*avare,*' he chided, stern, as he listened to your Ajja's chest with his shiny black stethoscope. 'Have you been taking your medicines?'*

That was how I finally heard the truth, of your Ajja's fever as a child that he shivered through, the joint pains for which they took him to the government hospital in Mangalore. Rheumatic fever, it was called. I looked it up years later, Mira, when I returned to reading and books, when I had to help you with your homework, to see how it was spelled, the disease that took my happiness. That day, however, it fell on our ears almost a Kannada word: Rumatic jwara*. The fever left, they said, but it marked the valves in his heart and narrowed them. As he got older and his heart grew bigger, the openings became more narrow. Narrow openings that were stingy with his blood, making it wait and collect in his lungs. Until he could only sit like an old man in his easy chair by the radio and drown in his own pink spit.*

Mahalinga had taken him to the doctor when he spat up blood at the Congress office that afternoon when everyone else left town. He had taken him there despite their mahatma's distrust of such medicine.

'I told him, sister,' Mahalinga said to me, still sheepish, when the truth came out, 'think of your wife and your young children.

Now is not the time for ideals.' Your grandfather had reluctantly taken his medications as if they were treason, and hidden his illness from me.

Now the doctor made daily trips with his injections and tonics, his assurances to me more strident by the day.

'You can give me my fees when he is better,' he would say, as if it could happen, that we would walk down the hill to his office with his fees, your Ajja and I. We prayed to every deity, my mother-in-law and I, the big Gods and the minor ones, all the way from Vishnu to His dwarapalas. For a while, he seemed to get no worse. I began to hope, as the year drew to an end, and a new year beckoned.

A few weeks after that, a month into the New Year in 1948, your Ajja sat by the radio one morning, and I sat at the grinding stone outside. There was an announcement that broke through the concert that your grandfather was listening to, that I missed. In faraway Delhi, some madman shot your Ajja's mahatma on his way to prayers. Muniya, the Holeya boy your grandfather had taught in his healthier days over my misgivings, came running up to our house with the news only minutes later.

That was how I heard the news your Ajja had heard moments before. He sat unmoving in his chair, the tears running down his face. That was the last day he spoke. Even to this day, I wonder what his last words to me were. Had he asked for water at breakfast that morning? Or had he asked me to fetch a shawl when the cold air rushed in behind Girish as he left for school? I had thought nothing of them and nothing of the silence that day, because I thought that after his sorrow faded, he would speak again.

But your Ajja died before his sorrow left, as if it were a blessed release from his hunger for air, sitting up in his chair by the radio that night.

He died that day. I was twenty-five years old.

I saw him die, as I sat by his chair. There was nothing to be done. Mahalinga slept outside in the veranda, as he had done for some days. My mother-in-law woke him so he could go down on his bicycle to get the doctor. I saw your grandfather's face and knew that it would be pointless: your Ajja was dead and he looked more at peace than he ever had in life. More relaxed than he looked the day we were married, less careworn than when he unwrapped Girish's foot from the blankets in jail, less anxious than when they put Kishore still warm from my body into his arms. It was a peace that mocked my tears, my children and our life together.

Being robbed was what it was, Mira. Robbed in my prime by Rama, your Ajja and his mahatma. Yes, mostly his mahatma. Forgive my indulgence in telling you this, the robbery that took from me all that I ever wanted for myself.

I tore at my hair and beat my chest. My husband was gone. I was alone in the world. But underneath that sorrow, already I could feel the anger begin. The women from the neighbourhood dragged me away from his body so they could prepare him for the cremation. As we sat that morning around the cooling shell that had housed my husband, far away in Delhi important people made speeches. The nation wept, and we wept by ourselves, alone. The nation mourned and we mourned alone. Our sorrow for your grandfather was too large for a corner to accommodate sorrow for old men past their prime, shot by madmen over ideas that had nothing to do with us. Religion, country—what did they matter to me or my children? There were no sandalwood pyres for your grandfather, no speeches on the radio, only two young boys without a father and a wife who knew that her husband preferred death to a world that killed his mahatma.

I watched the flames that Girish lit, and felt his newly shorn scalp rough under my palms. When the time came to perform the rituals of widowhood, everyone, my in-laws, my parents, neighbours said I didn't have to shave my head or wear white. These are newer times, they said, and you are so young. We don't have to keep up with the old ways. Your husband would not have wanted it, they said, this is everything that he fought against. Even the older widows who sometimes seem eager to perform the rituals would not come forward.

But I broke my bangles myself. I wiped the kumkum away with my own hands. I cried and hit my head on the wall until they called a barber. I would not stop rending my clothes until they brought me a white saree. If the mahatma could throw tantrums all his life and get people to do the things he wanted, I could too. Finally, the one they brought was made of khadi, of my husband's weaving.

Not one thing did I ask for myself, but my husband. Not jewels, not silk sarees, not trips to the cinema with strings of jasmine in my hair. But he, your mahatma, stole him from me in life, and in death. All I was left with was two young boys to raise and no way to die. Because if I did, they would have no one at all.

Soon our piece of land with the coconuts was gone, as were your Ajja's parents. The meager existence we scraped by was based almost entirely on my work making pickles or chaklis for the village ladies. I taught the boys to work hard, to study, so they could get ahead in life, not run around on the streets with things that did not concern them. Girish was always the more excitable of the two, getting into scrapes with the village boys when they talked about his growling stomach in the mid-morning, or his bare feet. Our poverty bothered him, while Kishore ignored it, just as he ignored everything else outside of his books. He carried his hunger and his wants lightly. Girish would scheme and cajole me for sweets or delicacies, only content when he had a small bit more than his younger brother. Kishore never thought to check how much his brother got. If I saved some to give Kishore later in secret, the first person he shared it with was Girish. He looked up to his brother then, just as he does now. Girish was always the older brother who fought the bullies if they bothered Kishore, the older man that my younger son turned to for advice. Yet, he was as different from his older brother as it was possible to be, the way it is sometimes with brothers.

'Look at Kishore, why can't you be more like him,' I would say to Girish, after yet another complaint from some lady in the village. We depended on the goodwill of those ladies and I wanted him to curb his tongue and his fists for at least that reason.

'It reflects badly on your father,' I'd say, and it was true.

They now had a statue of your grandfather in the main roundabout, and every time a new person came to Malehalli, they would be taken to the statue or the foot of our house on the hill. 'Srinivas Murthy,' native Malehalli folk would say to the visitors, 'he was so honest, a true Gandhian, not like today's politicians. Look at his wife, and his children, they live in such poverty to this day.' Or, with slightly less truth, 'And look at his wife, she only wears white because she honours his memory.'

'It would be better if they gave us an anna,' Girish would say at those times, 'or even two paise, every time they go by the statue or our house like they do when they go to the museum. It's of no use to us, all this empty respect.'

Perhaps this was how I felt too, because I never rebuked him when he said that. Perhaps somewhere I was happy that this boy was nothing like his father, that he would not squander his life in foolishness. Kishore was another story. I worried about him and how he would survive this world, with his bookishness and innocence.

I prayed in my puja room every day, to Rama smiling His beatific smile, to Krishna standing by His herd of cows, coy Radha by His side, to ascetic Shiva grey from the ashes He rubbed on His body, mother Ganga flowing fountain-like from the matted hair on His head. I prayed to them all, and not one of them set me right. They smiled at me from behind their frames, as I sat before them in my self-pity and my smouldering anger at your Ajja that never left me.

But as is the way with our Gods, They show you soon what they mean, even if They are trapped by the smiles we give them, and the glass frames we imprison Them by. Perhaps that was why They sent two people into our lives, to show me what I still had to lose and the sorrows that I still had to bear. One was Surendra, when he was a young politician and had not yet belonged to as many political parties as there are in Karnataka. In those days, he was a youngster, a Congressman in his Gandhi cap like any other.

When Surendra walked into our house for the very first time, smiling and saying, 'Namaskara, namaskara,' Girish had failed his intermediate exam for the second time. He was dissatisfied and idle. There were more fights that I heard about, rumours of card-playing and meat-eating on the sly. I was at a loss. I could not say that his father would not have approved of such behaviour, because he would have laughed to my face. I tried to tell him that this was unbecoming of his Havyaka lineage and the respect that our family always had. In the end, I would have to resort to tears for Girish's contrition to appear. It would take all the guilt I could invoke to make him sit down by my side and promise to give up his bad habits.

One morning in September, Surendra made his way up the hill in the mid-afternoon. He stood in our front yard, and when he left we would all remark upon how polite and handsome he was. Perhaps that was why we never noticed that he introduced himself by just his given name, without any reference to where he came from, his lineage or his caste.

Not that any of it seemed necessary. Surendra stooped to touch my feet, called me Amma, and talked about how much he admired Srinivas Murthy. 'I asked all around the village, Amma,' he said, 'until they pointed me to your house.'

'Such a shame it is on us,' he went on to say after he was seated and had been offered coffee, 'that you, who have given so much for this country, have gained so little in return. In Delhi, ministries are handed down from father to daughter like kingdoms. And here, in Malehalli, all we do is watch others take the things that belong to us.'

He was, we learnt, making a pilgrimage of sorts to the home of a man he considered his mentor, though they had never met. I should have recognised then that this was not a man like Srinivas Murthy. Because your grandfather, for as long as he lived, was happy to let other people take the things that belonged to him. And yet, I was charmed.

Maybe Girish needs a male influence, I thought; maybe this young man will be like an older brother to him.

'This is my older son, Girish,' I said to Surendra that day, not knowing all that this would bring upon us. 'He is a good boy, but struggling a bit with his studies.'

'Ah, Srinivas Murthy's oldest son,' Surendra said, almost triumphant, 'I am glad to be of help.'

Was it only later that I saw this remark for what it was? Maybe I did not suspect then that the only reason he favoured Girish was so that he could point to him as his protégé and claim for himself the mantle of a freedom fighter's son. Or perhaps I saw it and chose to ignore it, because Surendra's connections might bring Girish a government job and opportunities that a failed intermediate exam could not provide.

'Girish,' Surendra said, 'you must ask me for anything you need.'

Surendra was a frequent visitor to our house after that. Girish followed him around the village and to the party office. Despite his stated fondness for Girish, Surendra managed him with a firm hand, I was pleased to note.

'How many hours did you study today?' he would ask in the veranda, as I listened approvingly from the kitchen. When I came out, I would see that he had brought along something small for Girish, a magazine or a sweet, a pair of binoculars once. It was a new experience for Girish, the attention and the small gifts that he did not have to share with anyone, even Kishore. There were also jobs or errands for Girish to run, so he had a sense of responsibility. And if he failed at any of them, Surendra's temper was hard to watch. Yet, through all this, I sensed that my son stood a little taller for Surendra's interest, and slowly but surely there seemed to be more order, more discipline in his life.

And Surendra helped us in other ways. There was a new scheme to pay a pension to widows and families of freedom fighters. Your grandfather would have cringed at this charity, this attempt to pay for what he considered his duty. But we were poor and hungry. It was a small amount, but no less welcome for being so. To get it, however, there were forms and affidavits to be filled. Ashamed as I am to say this, also bribes to be paid, to a clerk or peon, even in Malehalli, where everybody could see the statue of Srinivas Murthy in the town centre.

Surendra raged when he heard this, his handsome young face distorted in anger. He took Girish to see the MLA from our district, and then as rapidly and surely as afternoon rain that follows a clouded morning, the pension arrived.

So by providence and by design, Girish and our family were being bound up with Surendra, with his hunger and his ambition. Had I known how far this would take us, and the price that mounted to be paid, I might have gladly picked deprivation, even starvation, instead.

9

Mira

Our journey continues. Appa and I have walked through two airports in America, and one in Europe. We are on our final flight to Bangalore. Appa has worked through a book of crossword puzzles. Now he watches movies in the tiny screen embedded in the backrest before him and complains on and off about his cramped seat. We doze to the drone of the airplane engine and wake to crying infants. We acquire the patina of disorientation that comes with a journey across continent and time zone.

~

The gulmohar trees are in full bloom, their spreading branches a burning bright orange. Adil has finally finished his project. 'Nothing to do now, but loll around and bother the girls,' he says, pulling Anisa's long, plaited hair. A year ago, he would have reached over and pulled mine at the same time, but now, of course, that is impossible.

'Childish, childish,' Anisa clucks her tongue at him. 'Such a big body with such a tiny brain. What a tragedy.'

'Anisa, you poor thing, to talk about yourself like that. I never knew you felt you were a cretin,' he laughs, ankles crossed on the coffee table, head tipped back on the sofa.

'Look at Mira,' Rehana aunty says. 'I think she's the only

reasonable one here. Do you two have to spend all your time arguing? I get a headache when you do this all morning.'

'Yes, Mira,' Adil says, 'since you are so reasonable, how do you put up with Anisa?'

Before I can come up with a safe response, Anisa says, 'She just thinks about how much easier it is than to put up with you.'

'Mira, Mira,' Adil turns to me, hands crossed theatrically over his chest. 'I am the easiest person in the world to put up with, please just give me a chance. One chance is all I ask.'

'No, thanks,' I say, praying the rush of blood into my cheeks doesn't show. 'I really prefer Anisa's company.'

'Try your luck somewhere else, Adil,' Rehana aunty laughs. 'Those two have never given each other up, for anything or anybody.'

The banter goes back and forth until Rehana aunty decides to put us all to work. Adil is dispatched to buy mutton. Anisa and I are to slice onions and grind up spices. Rehana aunty has decided to make biryani, and decided also that it is time we learnt how. 'When I was your age, I could make biryani all by myself,' she says to both of us.

Adil arrives when we are giggling through our onion tears. I lift a hand to wipe them, and the stick-on bindi that I am wearing slides off my forehead on to my arm.

'Wow, Mira, without that bindi, you could be a nice Muslim girl.' Adil's voice is serious. When I turn around, he looks like someone who has come up to a wall and stopped short.

Rehana aunty is turned to the stove and has her back to us. She says, 'Careful, Adil. She's a nice girl, true, but the rest could make her Ajji very upset.'

For a moment, there is a frozen tableau in her kitchen when she says that, and even Anisa is at a loss for words. The next, Rehana aunty asks for the onions, and the effect passes. This is all still my overactive imagination, I tell myself; Rehana aunty only means that Ajji would be upset if someone called her granddaughter Muslim. There are no deeper messages in Rehana aunty's words, and no hidden warnings.

Later, when Rehana aunty goes to cook the rice separately from the mutton for me, as she usually does, I stop her. 'Don't bother, aunty, I'll just eat the rice from the mutton biryani. As long as I don't eat the mutton, it is still vegetarian.'

'Mira, are you sure?' she says. 'Your Ajji might not let you come here again.'

'Oh, aunty, remember when I first came she said I could only eat whole fruit? She will be fine. This is not such a big deal.'

'It tastes better, Ammi,' Anisa says. 'Let her eat it just for today if that's what she wants.'

When Adil watches me at lunch, there is no pretence of the sidelong glance. Rehana aunty has been called away by a phone call. He sits opposite me at the table, and his eyes rarely leave my face. It is a shared recklessness. He should not look me in the face as he does, gaze skimming every exposed dip and rise. I should lower my gaze to avoid their wanton exploration. Instead, I lift the mutton-flavoured rice to my mouth, where it sits on my tongue, tantalising and forbidden. I savour its richness, and the concentrated attention of his gaze slips past my forehead to my eyes, slides on the bridge of my nose to find my lips. It might have been a lifetime, though it is probably only a minute. Anisa kicks him under the table when she hears Rehana aunty get off the phone.

'Exactly how long do you plan to hang around here, now that your project is finished?' Anisa asks Adil, even as Rehana aunty clucks her tongue at her rudeness.

'Don't answer that Adil,' Rehana aunty says. 'Anisa, that

was very rude. Adil is older than you *and* he is your uncle. Where are your manners?'

'Don't worry,' Adil says, 'I know she can't bear to see me go.' He forces a laugh, as if this is the continuation of the morning's banter. 'But I'll probably have to go in a week.'

'A week?' Rehana aunty says. 'What is the hurry? You haven't been home at all with your project, and now you want to leave so soon?'

A week. Only seven days, I tell myself as the flavours of the biryani saturate my tongue. Then everything will be back to how it was.

Downstairs, there are cars with loudspeakers making their rounds. 'Tonight, seven o'clock, Sadhu Devidas. Come one, come all.' Disembodied loud voices that say the same thing in English and Kannada travel up and down our street and then the next, where we can still hear them.

'Why are they so loud?' Rehana aunty asks, more than once. 'And how long are they going to keep this up?'

If she is uncomfortable with their openly Hindu agenda, she does not mention it. Anisa has taken to looking outside the window each time a car circles past, but she does not say anything about it either. We talk only about all the unnecessary noise. I feel their unease in my bones, and know that none of my other neighbours would recognise it. Though they also talk about the cars, it is in tones that suggest only a mild annoyance.

We help Rehana aunty clean up after lunch. Adil leaves, saying only that he needs to meet a friend. Anisa offers to go up to bring down the washing hung there to dry. She is silent as we make our way up the three flights of stairs.

Anisa ignores the washing, even as I unclasp clothespins to take a towel off, then a shirt. Adil's. For a quick second I hold the shirt up to my cheek, allowing it to sink into the soft fabric. Anisa snatches the shirt from me in a quick, furious jerk.

'Leave it,' she says. 'Mira, have you gone completely mad?'

I do not pretend to misunderstand.

'I haven't done anything, Anisa. Nothing wrong has happened.'

She sighs. In all the years that Anisa and I have known each other, we have never fought. Never with each other. We have had schoolyard tiffs with other girls, arguments with her parents and with Ajji. But it has always been understood: she and I are on the same side.

'You are barely sixteen, Adil is nineteen, not quite twenty yet. Even if you were Muslim or Adil Hindu, this will not work. Not now. You are both being very silly. This third-rate filmi business, staring and sighing. It has to stop. Both of you could get into trouble. Do you hear me?'

I bend my head.

'There is so much going on,' she says, 'and all this chatter about your mother to add to it. I don't understand how people can talk like that about her. It would be like saying that about Ammi. I would be so upset, and yet here you are, swooning over Adil as if he's the most important thing in the world.'

I cannot tell Anisa that the picture of my mother still alternates between face up and face down on my bedside table. Or describe the way that Adil makes me feel, which somehow also makes me think that there may be something to the stories about her. To say it out loud, even to myself, sounds hollow and illogical, if not disloyal. So I say nothing.

When I look up, Anisa is crying. 'I'm fighting with you,' she says, 'and things don't seem the same anymore. Not on the street, not in our house with Adil here. Everything feels different.'

I take the shirt and the towel back from her. I want to say

I'm sorry, but those are words we've never had to say to each other—sorry, please, thank you. To say it now would be to acknowledge that our friendship, too, has changed. I hug her tight instead, the same way I hugged Ajji the morning of the tulsi pooja. She stops crying, and we manage to laugh.

'Such drama,' we tell each other, 'mountains out of molehills,' 'tempests in teacups,' until we run out of clichés to describe our disagreement. 'We could all be in a Hindi movie.' We smile determinedly through more tears as we pull clothes off the line to take downstairs to fold.

'We'll spend next week at your house,' Anisa says, with a new firmness, as we turn towards the stairs. I see the spreading gulmohar tree on the street below us, completely covered in orange blossoms, and not a hint of green leaf. All of which will probably be gone in a week.

'Of course,' I say, 'that would be best.'

We can hear the loudspeakers in the stairwell; the cars have circled back to our street.

'Maybe we could go to the central library,' I say, more to distract Anisa from them than anything else.

'Yeah, maybe we should,' Anisa says, 'though it is probably already closing time today. Maybe tomorrow?'

We dump all the clothes on the sofa where Adil sat such a short time ago, and fold them in silence. I am careful to avoid Adil's clothes. Rehana aunty walks into the hall and is surprised to see us folding clothes without being asked, and probably by the absence of our usual giggling.

'Hmm, you two must be really bored today.' She helps us fold the last of the clothes. 'Why don't you go down and take a small walk until your father gets home? Or maybe you could rent a video cassette for the movie you keep singing songs from—what was it, *Kaboothar, Jaa, Jaa*? Maybe we can see it tonight.'

'It's *Maine Pyar Kiya,* Ammi,' Anisa says shortly. 'That's the name of the movie. And I don't want to see it. I think it's very silly. Stupid teenage love story.'

'Okay, Anisa,' Rehana aunty says, 'don't rent it then. I was just making a suggestion. There's no need to be angry with me. Why don't you girls go down and do something else instead of being bad-tempered?'

We make our way downstairs and cross the street to my house. Just before we push open the gate, Anisa says, 'Ajji is probably going to make suggestions too—like going to the temple.'

We look at each other, step back into the street. The cars and loudspeakers are gone for now. We walk aimlessly back and forth, not really talking to each other, busy with our own thoughts. Mine linger on the biryani, Anisa's displeasure, and the hints of impropriety that swirl around my mother. Anisa is right. This is what I would have said, if Anisa were the one acting like me. This is not how well brought-up girls behave; girls from good families and better schools. Girls who plan to have careers and upstanding futures.

If Ajji or my aunt knew how I acted, how could I face them? How could I have been so silly? And yet. Adil. Why is it that at one glance everything that I know to be right vanishes?

As if to answer, Anisa nudges me. But it is to point something else out. We have walked all the way up to the front of the theatre, now showing a Malayalam movie with large billboards up front. For those who cannot read Malayalam, there is a helpful translation of the title. It says, in English, 'Her Nights'. In the forefront is an ample-chested woman in a traditional Malayali mundu-veshti, eyes averted, face turned to the side. There isn't the extra layer of cloth across her chest, as there would have been had she been wearing a saree. The effect of the partially turned face, the slightly undressed nature of the image, though she is, in fact, fully clothed, is somewhat dirty. Much like the boards outside upstanding textile stores, which choose for some reason to only advertise bras. Pictures of women, sometimes pretty, and sometimes faceless, all wearing bras out in the open in their windows. Perfectly legitimate on the surface, yet the women who are ostensibly targeted by the advertisement usually avert their eyes, pretending not to notice them. It is as if there is something to the picture that excludes us, shames us even. On the bottom right of the billboard, as if to drive home the message, is a large red A—adults only. We look away, scandalised, and hope no one saw us looking. We cross the street with hurried steps, glad to turn our back on the shameless picture. That is what Ajji, or Rehana aunty would say, had they been with us: 'Shameless, shameless.'

It is then that we see them. The small crowd of saffron-clad men and boys standing across the street from the theatre. Shouting. We recognise a few of the boys—there is Vinay and his cricket-playing band of friends. The clerk from the lending library is there too, and some older people we've seen at the temple before. We see them cross the street and make their way over to the theatre gate, shouting all the time. The watchman at the gate shouts back in return, and then the ticket seller from the box office joins him. More people emerge from the theatre. I recognise the owner. He looks as if he has been surprised in the middle of a nap with his tousled hair and crumpled trousers. Between shouted sentences, he spits splotches of bright red betel juice into the ditch alongside.

The theatre owner is a friend of Girish uncle's, or perhaps an acquaintance. I have seen them greet each other in the street. We have had fruit baskets from him—which Ajji ordered me not to touch—delivered to our house at Diwali, doubtless in return for some favour my uncle's officialdom allowed him to bestow. He is a brawny man, substantial and wide, with a thick gold chain around his neck, large rings on several fingers, and a gold chain knotted bracelet-like over one wrist for good measure. He pushes the leader of the saffron pack, the man we know as Devidas, with one hand, almost contemptuously.

Everyone is shouting all at once. It is hard to understand what the argument is about, the gist of the conversation being, essentially, on both sides:

'Who do you think you are?'

'I know the chief minister. Don't mess with me.'

'And I know the prime minister, but do you think he knows me? Don't bluff with me. As if the chief minister is your bum-chum. You think you can fool me?'

Many variations of the same, all shouted, with some pushing, and threatened injury. In the melee, Vinay and his friends break away and clamber up the compound wall to reach the largest billboard. They jump up and down on the narrow compound wall, trying to tear parts of it down. As it happens, they can only reach the corner with the large A, and it comes off, piecemeal, in their hands, along with a small sliver of the woman in the mundu-veshti.

'*Kattegala*,' the owner shouts at them, *Donkeys*. 'I'll tell your mother.' The last he shouts at Vinay, who stands on the compound, holding a fragment of the hoarding like a flag.

'Do you even have a mother?' Vinay shouts back, and then we understand, the group is protesting the vulgarity of the billboard. The theatre workers clamber up the wall to dislodge Vinay's friends. Passersby stop and gather around, yelling all kinds of opposing instructions.

'I am calling the police,' the owner finally screams.

We walk past them as fast as we can, ignored by both sides. We can hear the confusion behind us even further down the streets. The language gets more colourful, the voices louder. Somebody starts throwing stones, but is quickly subdued by the crowd. That seems to be the signal for the crowd to break up. Either that, or the threat of police, shouted by the theatre owner, over and over at the top of his voice. By the time we reach our street corner and look back, the crowd seems to be dispersing, the saffron people still yelling threats at the owner, along with insults in Kannada that we imagine are more colourful than the ones of a few minutes ago, because we don't understand them.

Anisa and I finally look at each other and say, 'Crazy people,' at the same time, and then suddenly it all seems so funny. 'Can you imagine, that sleazy guy from the library was there, protesting the picture?' Anisa says. 'What do you bet he's going to be there tonight, watching the first show?' It seems like such a relief to laugh together at last, and we push open the gate to walk up the path to my house.

We pass my uncle in the veranda and don't stop to tell him about the altercation. It would involve mentioning the billboard and the fact that the woman's chest was semi-exposed even if fully clothed, so we don't. Ajji and my aunt hear us from the kitchen and ask if we want to eat something. Ajji asks us, predictably, if we want to go to the temple with her. 'We've already walked a lot today, Ajji,' I say, and we settle down in front of the television. Anisa flips channels until we are watching another top-ten Bollywood countdown. I take this to mean that our disagreement is behind us.

Barely ten minutes later, there is a commotion at our gate. We run to the windows to look out, and see the theatre owner there, followed by some of the theatre workers. They are talking loudly with each other, and bang on the gate before they push it open. My uncle rushes to meet them, as they are mid-way up the path to the veranda.

'*Banni, banni,* Bairappa-*navare*,' he says to the owner. 'Please come.'

The owner does not really seem impressed by his welcome. It is not often that Girish uncle actually rushes to greet someone. He must be rich, I surmise, because he certainly is not famous.

'Girish-*avare*,' he says, 'this is too much. You really must do something about these goondas.'

'What goondas? What happened?'

'Your niece was watching, didn't she tell you?' We hear him ask, and brace ourselves for a scolding that can't be far behind.

'No, you know how children are,' my uncle says. 'What happened?'

'That goonda Sathyaprakash, or what does he call himself now, Swami Devidas? He sent some people over yesterday, asking for a donation for his talk. The same people who used to collect his *mamool* from the market before, maybe. I refused. And today, he came back to make mischief outside my theatre. Trying to tear down pictures, turning away decent people.'

'But how can they do mischief? You have all the permits,' Girish uncle asks, and we can hear the screech of the wicker chairs as they both sit.

'Some nonsense about vulgarity. As if it is their father's property—all this nonsense about decency and family. As if I don't know the kind of fellow he is.' We can hear him hawk up spit, but the sound of the splotch does not happen.

'Oh, yes.' My uncle's voice. 'I saw the picture this morning when I went to the office. I wondered if it was wise, you know, in this environment, when they are trying to stir up trouble. Maybe some other movie would have been a good choice ... There are plenty of good Kannada movies, I'm sure.'

'Good choice? Good choice? Who pays twenty rupees a ticket to come and watch movies nowadays that I can afford to take every fool's opinion?' Bairappa says, voice louder than before. 'Especially when the same movie is available on the street on a cassette for a rupee a day? And every house has a VCR—tell me, *swami*, how is a man to do business?' His tone suggests that he thinks my uncle is being a fool.

There is a moment's silence, and then Bairappa continues, '*Nodee*, *saar*, it is only business. We show people what they want. If they don't want to watch it, they don't have to buy tickets and sneak into the theatre after dark. I pay good money, to the government, and everyone else.' A pause. We register the pointed reference to a Diwali fruit basket, or something more. The hangers-on mutter and shift their feet, but we don't hear anything intelligible.

'Girish-*avare*,' he says, again, when uncle is silent, 'take care of this. Speak to whoever you have to, but I will not be blackmailed by this two-anna goonda. I am a bigger goonda than him.'

'Bairappanavare, don't worry,' Girish uncle says. 'You have been a loyal friend. Nothing will happen. I will speak to the minister. We'll see what charges we can bring. It is a sensitive issue, you see. If the papers get hold of this, they will make him a hero, you see. All the women will support him.'

'It is not a blue movie we are showing,' Bairappa says, exasperated. 'It is an Adults-only movie approved by the Censor Board. Just like any English movie on Brigade Road—a little bit of skin, some talk. There is no need to get so angry over this. If I had given him the money yesterday, nothing would have happened. But there is a limit. We can't give money to every fool who asks. I am Bairappa Gowda, not some two-anna vegetable seller on the street to pay *mamool* to some two-anna goonda.'

'I know this, and you know this, but you know how these journalists are, they will write anything to sell papers. They will put pictures of that woman in the paper, say you are peddling smut. It will make Devidas look like a hero. Please, be patient. We will deal with him the best way we can.'

Girish uncle offers Bairappa coffee, but he is too angry to stay. We hear him refuse and stand up to leave. His underlings have been silent for all the conversation, and now we hear them, muttering their goodbyes to my uncle as they leave behind him. '*Barthini, saar*', '*Barthini, swami*'.

Anisa and I turn up the volume on the television, hoping to stave off questions, from Girish uncle or Ajji. But when my uncle enters the hall, it is to only say, 'Stay away from the movie theatre for a few days, and the temple. I don't want to see you girls anywhere on that side. Walk the other way, to Margosa Road, if you have to go out.'

After Anisa and I have watched television for about two hours, we eat dinner in my house while Ajji tells us the story of How Rama Wed Sita. My uncle's warning begins to fade into the space where all the other thousand things that adults tell us every day crowd each other and clamour for attention, losing daily battles with one another. Ajji's story is much more interesting that night than anything we had seen or heard that day, just by the richness of its detail. She speaks of the first glance that Rama and Sita exchanged, where they recognised each other as the Lord of the world, and His eternal consort.

That glance, she says, poets would write about for centuries. The swayamvara, where Sita could choose her husband from all the assembled kings and princes of the land. Except, there was a contest. She would wed the prince who could string a mighty bow. ('But that means that Sita did not really have a choice, did she, Ajji?' 'Anisa, as usual you are missing the point of the story.') The thrill that passed through the gathered assembly when Lord Rama easily lifted, strung and broke the mighty bow that no other king could move.

Then, there was the wedding. Ajji embroiders freely as she goes along here, and we hear details of feasts and clothes, all more fantastic than when we heard the story last. 'Everyone expected the Pattabhisheka next,' Ajji says, of that auspicious event when Rama would be crowned king. 'But something else happened before that, something sad and unexpected. But it is getting late. We'll continue the story tomorrow.' She stands up, as we do, all secure in the knowledge of what comes next. Kaikeyi's tantrums, Rama's exile and Sita's abduction, and Ajji's embellishments that make each iteration more compelling than the last.

Despite that hopeful, commonplace wish to continue a story past its feeble cliff-hanger, we will not hear the rest of the story. Anisa and I will not sit together for dinner again. Anisa will never bother Ajji with her inopportune questions in the middle of a story, causing Ajji to frown and bite back a hasty retort. We will not ever skip down the path from our veranda to the gate like we do that night, my uncle and I standing at the gate to make sure that Anisa enters the door of her building.

10
Vimala

Vimala saw Ajji pause. Her breaths were shallow and fast. The machines beeped. It was not just physical, of course. It was the story. The stalling, the self-indulgence of history were all over. Here were the unpleasant parts, and Ajji would have to start talking about them.

She took Ajji's hand in hers and told her to rest. 'I will tell Mira the next part, Amma.'

It was the first time that Vimala had told Ajji to do anything, and she was surprised at the small pleasure the action brought.

Vimala had arrived in Malehalli for the first time, head bent so low she only saw the winding path up the hill and the doorstep in any detail. Or the way sunlight slanted into the courtyard at her feet, where she stood quietly with Girish as they waited for the auspicious time to enter. Minutes later, they crossed the threshold together, right leg first, and her joy was as quietly exuberant as the brief cascade of rice and jaggery to the floor as she entered. It was the moment that she remembered with such clarity all these years later, when she became Ajji's daughter-in-law and Girish's new bride, arriving into her new home.

Vimala had been an afterthought in the house she was born into. Her parents had her in their later years, and died when she was young. Her brother, with a growing family of his own, had been the one to assume her care, along with land and house. He was not unkind, but she had understood that her place there was temporary, until she could be married off into a family of her own. She had passed the years of only partially meant slights and exclusions by dreaming up a life that would be hers when she left. It had been the waiting and dreaming, those years that had gone before, that buoyed the joy of her arrival.

Girish and Vimala stood in the hall with all the visiting relatives gathered around. Girish was only a little older than she was, and she remembered his slight frame and his sidelong glances at her with some surprise. There was wonder in his eyes, as if he had imagined a future wife who was less attractive, the hint of the furtive eagerness of a child with a treasure to unwrap.

Her brother-in-law Kishore was shy those days, and usually had his head in a book. She only saw him clearly days after the wedding, when all the guests were gone. He had smiled at her as she served the brothers their breakfast. The brothers, even Girish, had been too shy at that point to include her in their customary banter. It was Kishore who had glanced her way frequently, however, to see whether she was amused or offended. This unexpected concern for her feelings felt like a welcome, finer than any she expected.

Their household stretched itself to include her, and the routine of the days before her arrival re-established itself. Girish was studying again, for the intermediate exam he had failed three times. It was now the same exam that Kishore was to take.

Girish, while studying, was always at a spot where he was within range of demands for coffee or Vimala's attention. From time to time, he found her in the kitchen or at the washing stone with some imagined need—a book to be found or a shirt to be ironed, excuses for a few stolen moments before she would run back to the abandoned clothes or cooking. He also had a job, at the local party office, running errands for the new politician in town, Surendra. Their marriage was Ajji's final attempt to seal his distance from the wayward crowd of boys in town to responsibility, to life. For those brief months that Vimala glided through her new home with the air of a woman loved, it seemed that Ajji had succeeded.

In the evenings, while Ajji went to the temple, Vimala and Girish walked down past the town centre and the arecanut fields beyond, to the rocky coast and the tiny beach, talking about the futures that Girish imagined for them, each more grandiose than the next. Those visions were gifts he laid at her feet, in equal parts hope, swagger, need and vulnerability.

Then the results arrived. Kishore had passed the intermediate exam. Not State First, as Vimala finally realised everyone had expected, but well enough to merit a picture in the newspaper and the pride of a rank student. Ajji promptly hid the newspaper among her sarees, from whence it emerged a dozen times a day when she thought herself alone. The smudged and faded newsprint around Kishore's picture became, to Vimala, a testament to Ajji's wondering fingers.

Meanwhile Girish had failed, again.

Kishore had continued to smile at her shyly every morning, eat what he was served without complaint, and move through their home as if he were a polite and temporary guest. Vimala could not resent him if she tried.

Girish told her it did not matter. There are many roads to success, he said, on their evening stroll together, and only one of those involved exams. She would see. He would be more successful than anyone Malehalli had ever known.

In the weeks that followed, Ajji seemed to agree. She stopped nagging Girish in what appeared to be a grudging acceptance of his work at the local party office: a career now instead of a step-stone. It was only Vimala who knew about the newspaper between the sarees and perhaps only she who wondered if Ajji had given up on one son because of the other.

Kishore would go to college, of course. There should have been worries about money, Girish's nominal employment with Surendra had not changed their gnaw of debt and want. But, as Girish said later that night as he settled down beside her on the straw mat in the back room, things always came easy to Kishore. For the first time in the months that she had known her husband, there was bitterness in his tone. She held him close, trying to stanch his hurt with her skin even as she pretended not to notice it.

True to Girish's estimation, shortly after Kishore's picture was in the newspaper, a promise of a scholarship arrived unasked. It was from a local arecanut merchant, now aging, for whom her father-in-law had once done some book-keeping. There may have been others from societies and philanthropic clubs—Kishore's picture in the newspaper and news of his impoverished status had indeed generated much interest. Ultimately, however, it was the arecanut merchant's gift that he took, impelled perhaps by a tenuous connection to a father he remembered with difficulty. When the old man stopped by their house one evening, Vimala saw how unselfconsciously Kishore had stooped to touch his feet, as if that would bring him the blessing of his father by some extension or alchemy. Perhaps the old man understood. There was wetness in his eye as he surveyed Kishore's bent back, a tremor to his voice when he spoke.

'Your father was a great man,' he said, as Kishore straightened up, 'and we all owe him such a debt. You will do well. You will do very well.' His own children, he said, were lesser men in comparison, one a wastrel and a drunk, the other his wife's slave. Not a man like Srinivas Murthy in his own family, not even a shadow. 'You will be your father's son,' he said, peering into Kishore's face, ignoring both Girish by his side and Kishore's embarrassment at the oversight. 'You have my blessings always.'

It was soon the first day of college. Even before dawn, Vimala had woken, as Ajji had, to the clatter that Kishore made as he picked his way around the still dark house, gathering clothes, toothpaste, soap and books.

'It is only five o'clock,' Ajji said, sounding simultaneously annoyed and proud. 'You look ready to leave. At least let me make some coffee, a small breakfast.'

Vimala nudged Girish awake.

'It is not that far,' Girish grumbled, but Kishore had been adamant.

So Ajji and Vimala had rushed through their cooking. Vimala had done all she could in the previous months to make herself indispensable to Ajji. There was not a need she could not anticipate, not a task she could not learn or perfect to Ajji's taste. It was the job she had a lifetime of training for, and the aspiration. And that morning, in the joy of Kishore's first day at college, Ajji had been unexpectedly magnanimous.

'Would you like to go along with them?' she'd asked, as they stood together in the kitchen, having managed a reasonable meal in half the time it usually took them.

'Yes, you should come,' Kishore had said, addressing her directly for the first time.

At that, Girish had looked a little less reluctant to leave.

When Vimala arrived with them at the college, it was still early in the morning.

The college was brick and mortar evidence of socialist self-reliance, a towering red and white temple of modern India. It was built on the coast, rising taller than any building in town and set back from the sheer rock face and the sea below it by a manicured garden. A winding paved road extended to it from the main street, ending in rock stairs cut into the sloping hillside at its base. Stairs led up to the entrance of the college, flanked by white pillars and topped by a stone arch, above which was set, like a final arbiter, a giant clock. Three floors of smaller arched doorways and shaded open corridors stretched on either side of clock and door, each looking out over the roaring water that assaulted the building's foundations under the acres of well-mannered English garden. Indeed, it looked as if the British might have built it had they been around at the time it was designed. Vimala was awed by it. It was only years after that day that it occurred to her what a fawning emulation it was.

Despite the early hour of their arrival, there were families already gathered, and more climbing the steps behind them. For many, it was a day that they would tell their grandchildren about, the day their farmer-cobbler-merchant family changed, with a college-educated son or less likely, daughter, a first in the family. A dream that entire families came to share, of education, advancement, a better life. Girish was there as older brothers should when the father is absent, walking up the stone stairs with Kishore, Vimala trailing only a few steps behind.

Girish kicked a stone as he watched the college come up in front of them. He swallowed, turned his eyes away from the edifice and patted Kishore's shoulder.

'Do well,' he said, biting back other, bitter words Vimala knew he would save for their pillow that night, 'but don't forget, outside all these books and this talk, there is a real world. That is the world we live in, and it matters more than all this.' He gestured expansively, including building, garden and sea, as if there was a nebulous entity around them that he could define with that gesture, one that signified superfluity, a does-not-matter-in-life-ness. As if he truly was the older and wiser brother, one that a failed exam could not unmake.

Vimala followed the arc of Girish's arm, knowing herself powerless in that moment to stem his hurt. Kishore turned as well. Girish's arm swung to encompass the land and sky around them, and in following it, their eyes fell on Radhika, who stood by the white banisters with the climbing roses, a nun in full habit on either side. Girish turned around to see what they were looking at, and noticed her the minute after.

Vimala saw both brothers stare, even the older married one. It was not because she was beautiful, they might have told themselves, before the next thought arrived in surprise, but she was. She was dark. Her skin glowed, but it was with a burnished amber that recalled smooth mahogany tree trunks or dark honey, not the prized paler complexions of their mother, or Vimala, or any number of female relatives that they probably recalled and discarded in comparison. It was an unexpected paradox for them, Vimala decided, this darkness and beauty, and the reason for their attention.

Radhika was tall; the habited nuns beside her stood three or four inches shorter. She wore a saree in a plain pale yellow that day, the sleeves of her contrasting white blouse decorously long, almost to her wrists. It might have been from prudery that the nuns insisted on, but for the wide boat neck and the cut of the blouse, which recalled an actress in a movie they had seen that summer. She wore her hair pulled back into a bun, but one set high on the head, which in an inch-and-a-half of placement had reclaimed elegance from severity.

Vimala studied her a little longer, this woman who had briefly stolen her husband's attention. And she saw other men look at the slender wrists emerging from the severe blouse sleeves, the impossibly thin waist under the swell of bosom, generous to say the least, in a seventeen- or eighteen-year-old. She saw how they turned away, perhaps in guilt masquerading as disapproval, as she suspected Girish did. But Radhika also had a way of looking everyone in the eye that, despite the demure attire, suggested boldness, a knowledge beyond fashion, beyond her years, that caused Vimala's own eyes to fall away in embarrassment.

As it was, the nuns seemed to be giving her a last-minute homily as they stood on the stairs. Work hard, do the orphanage proud, they said, uncaring that their voices descended the stairs to straining ears other than hers, while mothers were telling their own daughters to watch their reputations and not laugh out loud, hard work be damned.

But Vimala also saw that of all the glances that fell away that day from Radhika, there was one that did not, and that it belonged to Kishore Murthy. Radhika had smiled at him almost immediately. As if it were the most natural thing in the world. It was this, and the nuns, that made Vimala realise at once, and with complete certainty, that this poor girl had no mother to school her in the social graces. She probably never did.

An hour or so later, after the formalities were completed, Girish and Vimala returned together, down the steps where Girish had made his speech. They were almost at the foot of the hill when they heard Kishore call out, and he came running down the stairs to them.

'Anna,' he said, the childish appellation oddly reassuring to them both, 'I did not say goodbye.' Kishore said this awkwardly, because of course it was not goodbye that he meant, but thank you, or I need your blessings, your good wishes, or some other affirmation of his older brother's love.

Girish pulled his brother into an embrace.

They stood at the hill, patting each other on the back, until Kishore had to leave.

'He has everything, but he needs this, like a child,' Girish said to Vimala after he left, and she noticed his voice held a strange mixture of relief and scorn. 'He has never asked me if I needed help, ever. Must be nice to be the younger son.'

Vimala shushed him as one might a child. She took his hand in hers, for once in her life uncaring of who would see or hear of such an indiscretion in public.

Girish was surprised. But even as he freed his hand gently from hers and reclaimed his bravado, a swashbuckling hero ashamed of his momentary weakness, she saw for a moment the unspoken gratitude, perhaps even tenderness, in his gaze.

'Don't worry,' he said to her. 'Surendra will get me a better job. You'll see. Kishore may have his books, but I have real knowledge, and friends who can help.'

Over the months that followed, a new household routine established itself. Girish, freed from his need to study, began to spend more time at the party office. Surendra became his brother, friend and boss. Vimala felt the space around her expand, as if the break from Girish's incessant need was a respite that she had not realised she wanted. Both Girish and Kishore were gone all day, though Girish was always the last one to come home. His friends returned, as did the occasional alcohol and card-playing. The evening walks and promises came less frequently, even if they did not change in the strength of their ardour or conviction.

Meanwhile, Kishore had a routine that seldom wavered. He came home directly from college, drank the coffee his mother made in anticipation of his arrival, and then settled down to study. It was a short and intense bout of attention. After that, he relaxed, and could be found walking down the hill, talking to the neighbours or their children. Over a few weeks, perhaps because he noticed the anxious air Vimala had as she waited by the door for Girish, or the way she hurried indoors at the first sight of Girish at the foot of the hill, he took to keeping her company on the veranda instead.

It was from their conversations on the veranda that Vimala realised that Kishore and Radhika had become friends almost right after they met. The story of their friendship was embedded in the anecdotes her brother-in-law told her, the details hidden in plain sight. There was much that Radhika and Kishore shared that did not need telling. Of poverty, hers abject, his, a shade better. The lack of a parent, though one was better than none. Both scholarship students and ambitious, even if one was quieter than the other. Despite the obvious obstacles, such as a gender divided classroom which placed girls on the right, boys on the left, she realised that they had settled into their seats across the aisle from each other, and into a friendship that seemed easier than it should have.

Kishore had never been inside a church until the day he walked after class to Radhika's orphanage, class notes in hand, when she had not come to college for a day. It struck him suddenly that Radhika was Christian, a fact he considered and forgot the implications of soon after. He learnt that she could sew, that she made her own clothes on another such day, and smiled when she grumbled about the Sisters' criticisms of her creations. Or her admission one day that she frequently thought about becoming a bride of Jesus, like the Sisters who had loved her all her life. It would be a good life, she assured him, even as the thought of a nun with eyes like hers filled him with amusement, one that Vimala shared with him on the veranda later that evening.

There were other details that Kishore did not share with Vimala until much later. Kishore and Radhika took their Bachelor of Science exams in the summer of 1969, and as they walked out from the exam hall, it seemed likely to both that their easy friendship would end as they went their separate ways. They lingered in the garden outside, saying the things that their classmates said to each other, stay in touch, write often, when without warning Radhika turned to Kishore and told him what she knew of her parents—her mother was a young girl who gave her up at birth.

'She's probably married now, and has a family of her own somewhere,' she told him. 'No one else knows that I know.' Her tone was matter of fact, as if it was not the devastating secret that it was. Kishore did not make the mistake of pitying her. He took the gift of her confiding in him, in awe of the trust it showed, and wished he had a dark secret of his own to reveal.

As it turned out, they need not have said their goodbyes. Radhika and Kishore remained behind at college. They had both been accepted to the Master of Science program, Radhika in physics, and Kishore in chemistry.

Most of their classmates moved away. The women married off to distant grooms, and the men, to cities where jobs could be found for their new diplomas. The world they lived in had other distractions, such as the war with Pakistan that made patriotism paramount. For those that did get jobs in bigger cities, there was also a modicum of drama, with the black-painted windows and air raid sirens, if nothing else, since no bombs were dropped in south India. When they travelled out of Malehalli, Radhika's frank gaze became less of a novelty since so many women in these big cities had similar ways.

In the absence of their classmates, Kishore and Radhika spent more of their time together, cocooned in the college which had grown to grudgingly acknowledge their unusual friendship. Kishore often remembered that he was somehow behind in the give and take of their relationship, since there was no dark secret that coloured his own ordinary life that he could proffer in return. So, instead, he told her every thought and desire he had, every childhood story, every familial fable until she knew him as well as he knew himself, or better.

Then there was the day when Radhika found him in the garden, as he waited for her under a spreading gulmohar that had littered her path with petals.

'I am a princess,' she had said, laughing as she approached.

'Look,' she said, pointing, 'did you see this? All these flowers to cushion my steps. It almost makes up for the torture of the class I just finished.'

Kishore found himself incapable of laughter for the first time in his life, or some clever repartee that she clearly expected. He was conscious of two things in that moment. One, there was a completely new emotion that he could not explain away with any number of platonic protestations, and two, if there was a universe comprised only of beautiful things, it could still be no match for the golden sheen of sunlight on her mahogany skin. It filled him with want, furious and voracious.

He left her in the garden with some halting excuse—he had forgotten a book, a pen. He hurried away from her as she stood there, needing to examine this sudden and new longing that came upon him, a despairing knowledge that she existed quite outside of and separate from him. It came as a surprise, this love that impelled a dissolution of skin and independent personhood. He felt impatient with himself, surely this could not be, after all the protestations of friendship he had made. She would think him a cad. His friends would call him, rightly, a hypocrite. Yet, it was an emotion that brooked no question, or compunction. He stood at the edge of the cliff and watched the sea rage. And he accepted that there could be no other way, no escape from the joys and struggles he could see ahead.

So, finally, here then was a secret that was his to give in return. He braced himself for all that might follow his declaration—disappointment, scorn, the loss of a friendship. But to not tell her was worse, a betrayal. He rehearsed his speech, careful to allow for her possible embarrassment or surprise, room for some graceful exit she could make.

He returned to her. She was sitting under the gulmohar, a wayward petal in her hair.

'I've realised something,' he began, 'and I am not sure how to tell you this.'

He looked up to meet her eyes, and the speech flew out of his mind faster than he could retrieve the words.

'I cannot bear to be away from you,' he said instead. 'Everything is lesser when you are not with me. As if something is missing. It's as if the only thing that makes the world worth living in has disappeared.'

She smiled, and the joy of the world declared itself to him.

'You are everything to me, Kishore,' she said, 'you have always been.'

It should have felt impulsive. But it did not, even to Kishore, who had only just realised what she had perhaps known for a long time. Maybe they should have waited, examined their feelings or the possible outcomes of their plans to spend their lives together. Neither felt it would change anything. So all that remained, they thought with the heady inevitability of young love, was to tell Kishore's family and the Sisters at the orphanage.

Radhika went in to see the Mother Superior, the forbidding woman who had watched her grow up and never so much as patted her head in passing, to say, 'Mother, I am in love with a boy in my class at college. I want to marry him.' She met the Mother's gaze as she did everyone else's. There was no hint of shyness, or shame.

As the conversation proceeded, it was obvious to the Mother that this wedding was going to be more difficult than either Kishore or Radhika had surmised.

Kishore could trace his lineage, ancestor upon ancestor, all the way to the first Brahmin who walked over the Vindhyas to the Deccan and Malehalli. Radhika was not Brahmin, and worse, as the Hindu scriptures had it, of Sinful Birth. So, even if Christian and casteless, she was still lower to them than the lowest of castes. None of their vaunted similarities would work against this insurmountable barrier.

'Let us pray over this, child,' she said, taking the girl's hand in hers, drawing her to the altar where the Saviour looked down upon them from His cross. 'Show this innocent child mercy, Lord Jesus, keep her safe in Your infinite love that is greater than all earthly riches. Allow her to find happiness in Your will. Amen.'

It was a prayer that was particularly apt, for more reasons than either supplicant could know at the time.

Kishore told Vimala first, that very evening, when Ajji had gone to the temple for the evening prayer. That was when the stories came together for Vimala, and she saw this thing that was improbable yet true, the love her brother-in-law had for the bold and dark-skinned girl she remembered. Despite herself, she was charmed. It was a romance that she may have seen only in a movie before.

'Talk to your brother,' she told Kishore, secure in the knowledge she had then that her husband could right the wrongs of the world. 'He will help with talking to Amma.'

Vimala heard the result of her advice from Girish the next night, when he whispered to her in the darkness of their room. She heard of how Kishore had found Girish in the party office at day's end. And as Girish told Vimala that night, when he saw that his brother looked so ill at ease, he knew immediately. His brother had found trouble for the first time in his life. His mother would soon know that her younger son was not perfect, though he managed to fool her all these years.

After the whole sorry tale was aired, Girish told her, they had walked on in silence all the way up the hill to their home where both Vimala and their mother waited at the door, anxious over how late the men were.

'I knew it had to be your fault, Girish,' his mother had said over Kishore's protestations. 'Kishore always comes on time or lets us know if he is going to be late. Don't spoil your brother with your ways.'

11

Mira

It is easy to walk up to Anisa's house the next morning, though I know she would have preferred for me to wait at mine. Easy to pretend that I do not want to catch a glimpse of Adil, who will be gone this week. When I ring the doorbell, it is a mirror image of the day that Adil arrived. I still have my hand on the switch when the door opens; Adil is on the other side.

'Mira,' is all he says.

'Anisa is taking a bath,' Rehana aunty says, in the middle of cleaning up the breakfast things, walking in and out of the kitchen. 'She said you were going to the City Central Library today. You have a long walk. Did you eat a good breakfast? Can I give you some toast, or a glass of milk while you wait?'

'No, aunty,' I say, moving automatically to help.

'Leave it, Mira,' Rehana aunty says, 'just sit down, you don't have to touch the dirty plates.'

But she has some mangoes to pickle, that she needs to dry in the sun. 'Why don't you take these upstairs instead?' she asks, gesturing to the platters of cut mango on her kitchen counter. It is more to get me out of her way than anything else, I suspect.

It is the most natural thing in the world for me to take one plate upstairs and for Adil to offer to help with the other. So we end up on the rooftop, platters behind us on the floor in the sun, the gulmohar a flaming canopy beneath us as we lean on the short wall, looking down into the street. The street is empty, or as close to empty as it gets in Bangalore. The odd pedestrian walking to work in the not-quite-early morning in summer, when the schools are closed, and people with real jobs have long since left for work.

I look into the street, thinking, we should be going down, Rehana aunty will wonder where we are. Adil peers into the street alongside me as well, and for a moment we stand, as if we are searching the street below us for a way to end the silence.

Finally, it is Adil who speaks. 'I'm leaving on Friday,' he says, 'don't know if I told you.'

'I know,' I say, inane and safe, as I always am with Adil.

'I will miss you, Mira,' he says, heading unheeding into dangerous territory. 'Look at me, for a second.'

I half-turn; look at him out of the corner of my eyes.

'No, properly,' he says, stepping back from the wall, so I am forced to turn all the way to look at him, my back to the short terrace wall.

The clotheslines behind Adil are laden with the washing of twenty households, shirts and towels of every stripe, a saree in every hue. They flutter gently in the breeze all across the terrace, all the way to the door, screening us from anyone who might walk up into the terrace that morning. We could be the only two people in the world, surrounded by veils of every colour.

'I will think of you every day,' he says, as I lift my eyes to his.

The terrace floor that is warming in the sun and will scorch my feet in a few minutes, the clothes that flutter in the breeze, the pressure of the wall on my back, all disappear. It is as if I have seen him for the first time again. Is this what Sita felt? Even as I think the thought, I know it for the blasphemy it is.

'Wait for me,' he says, and my glance slips down past his eyes to his mouth, and then to that perfect cleft of his chin.

I lean forward. My tongue darts out, and before I can be surprised by my own daring, finds that dip in his face. I see the surprise in his eyes in the instant before his mouth comes down on mine.

I feel the pressure of his lips on mine and the world disappears until I feel the scratch of stubble on my cheek. I don't know if it is that scratch which jolts me out of my dreamlike state, or the sudden loudness of catcalls and whistles behind us. We spring apart, and I can see Adil looking across the street. I turn my head even as Adil tries to stop me, hands cupping my face, attempting to shield my identity from the crowd of boys stringing up a banner from the top of a building on the next street. It is useless. I see them, and they have seen my face. Vinay stands silent in the middle of a crowd of jeering, catcalling boys, a look of complete and utter betrayal on his face.

I run to the door. Adil follows close behind, saying things like, 'It's okay, Mira, there is nothing to be ashamed about. It's fine really.' Fine, really? Does he not realise what just happened?

In the stairwell, he turns me around to face him, speaking urgently, 'Mira, listen to me. This is important. I love you. I will come back for you. In a year, I'll have a real job.'

I look at him, but the catcalls are fresh in my mind. And why did Vinay look like that, as if I had done something terrible to him? How could I have been so stupid anyway? And, I love you? Really?

'You're crazy, Adil. In a year I'll be eighteen. Eighteen, and barely out of high school.'

'Did you hear me?' he asks, and suddenly I think about how our voices echo in the stairwell.

Adil lowers his voice to a whisper, but it is no less urgent when he says, 'I love you. And I will wait until you are ready.' It sounds like a vow, a promise he holds dear.

It suddenly seems too much to take in. None of this was supposed to happen. It was only supposed to be a pleasant fantasy, a private crush that only existed in my mind.

'Okay, I'll think about it,' I say, and he seems not to hear the doubt, or the anxiety in my voice. He whoops, softly, looking so much like a little boy who has been given his best gift.

Despite myself, I smile.

'What if I'm not ready until I'm thirty?' I ask, my heart lifting in his joy, the doubts of a minute ago pushed away.

'I said I'd wait,' he says. 'But I will be back soon, just in case.'

I cannot help my laugh that echoes in the stairwell, or the way my doubts melt against his certainty. This must be what it feels like to be in love. And who else would make me feel this way, but the boy I was meant to be with? What happened was not Adil's fault, it was mine. Things could have been worse. It was only the neighbourhood boys who saw us, not adults, not Ajji. None of them will hear about it, in all likelihood.

Adil steps forward. 'If I'm going to be waiting years for you ...' and he bends down to kiss me again. I lift my face to his. It is the briefest of kisses, and it has to be the most glorious of kisses, even if I have nothing to compare it against.

Then somewhere below us is the sound of a door closing. We step back. And it is not a minute too soon. I can hear Anisa's voice from by her door, 'Are you two coming down?'

We go down the stairs to Anisa's floor, and she meets us outside the door. My eyes slide away from Anisa's. 'We should probably leave,' she says, to Adil. He offers to come along, she refuses.

Anisa and I walk down the stairs to the street. 'Adil says he'll wait for me,' I tell her, not needing to add any details.

She looks at me in surprise. 'You mean, wait, as in wait for you to—'

'Until I'm ready.'

Anisa smiles wide, dimples appearing on her face as they haven't in a long time.

'So he found his backbone after all,' she says. 'Good for him.'

'You mean you don't mind?' It is a surprise, after the session we had on the terrace, the tears and the awkwardness of the days since.

'I was worried, Mira, worried that he was just, you know, playing around, and that you'd be hurt. I know you—you would have been crushed. You know, like Sister Lalitha says, cotton and fire, and who knows, maybe you'd have ended up an unwed mother ...' She says the last cheekily, as if there is no chance in the world that I would end up that way.

I remember the way my tongue left my mouth of its own volition, and the catcalls. How could I be so very stupid, I think, and decide that I can't tell Anisa that part after all.

'Maybe we should have let him come with us,' I say, hopefully, as Anisa laughs. 'What, so you two lovebirds can be together and I look for books all by myself? Not a chance.'

We are almost at the road to the theatre when we see the group gathered there, shouting slogans. It is a happy mish-mash of people who want the whole world to speak Kannada, people who don't like obscene pictures and some of the boys who used to play cricket. It is a dharna, and that is when we remember that we are supposed to take Margosa Road. I don't want to face these boys after what happened earlier, even though it is only their friends who saw me with Adil. We turn around before any of them spots us.

But this will make our walk even longer. The sun is already high in the cloudless sky today, and starting to warm up pavement and tar. We walk back all the way to Margosa Road.

'So' Anisa asks, 'will you marry him?'

'It looks like it, doesn't it? There isn't much point to it otherwise.' I laugh. And then, as it occurs to me, 'Good god, I'll be your aunt.'

'Only if Adil gets mature enough to act like my uncle. You're safe.' She laughs, and it seems to me that our happiness fills the street.

A half hour's trudge later, after we have constructed a multi-layered fable of Adil's and my future together, complete with children, one of whom will have Anisa's dimples and be her favorite niece, we are at the City Central Library.

The librarian at the front desk is an older man in glasses. He smiles and waves us through. We wander around, and are spoilt for choice. There are so many books, and so many authors we have never heard of. We discover row upon row of Agatha Christie and P.D. James. It is a bigger and better version of our school library that we have missed all summer. Anisa looks like a child in a sweet shop. A week ago, I might have been the same.

But now. Adil. I am a girl who has been kissed. I wander off to the window. I wonder if it shows, if people can tell. Maybe my lips are redder, swollen. I check in the glass. It is silly, of course. My mother, I think, all of a sudden. Maybe if she were here, I could ask her what she thought of Adil. Not that I could tell her of course, about the kiss or the rest of it. But I could slip Adil in sideways, in another conversation. Ask her if she thought Adil was a bore, or a show off, just to have her disagree. I imagine her laughing at my questions. I see her smile in the photograph by my bed. I can see right through you, Mira, she seems to say. Of course she would love him. Who wouldn't?

'Can you help, Mira? We can't possibly take all of these home,' Anisa says presently. I attempt to read the descriptions at the back, but they do not hold my attention.

She finally decides by herself, and we head out with two of the most promising ones.

'We can always come back,' I tell her, when she hesitates by the door, looking longingly at the books we've had to leave behind.

The scorching sun gets higher in the sky as we step outside the library. There is a lull in the late morning crowd, with few other people on the street. It is the kind of day when storefronts are partially blocked off with sheets that hang down from their awnings to keep out the sun. A couple of middle-aged women in cotton sarees, baskets weighed down with their purchases, pass us. We envy the umbrellas they carry. Sampige Road stretches long and difficult before us.

'I'm thirsty,' Anisa admits, after we have walked past the third tender coconut seller, four cross streets from the library. Rasna in frosted glasses, condensation beading on the sides, taunts us from a billboard on the other side of the street. Even the overcrowded buses seem appealing, as they careen to a stop near us. We have forgotten to bring money, so there is not much we can do about our thirst, or the long way home.

'Should we go back the way we came?' I wonder aloud, hoping, of course, that we don't.

Anisa does not reply, and we continue in silence on Sampige Road, passing cross streets that would take us to Margosa Road. The books feel heavier as we walk, and talking seems more effort than it is worth.

'Let's just take the back way, behind the theatre,' Anisa says, when we are almost at our side street. So we walk on past the cross street to the theatre, and on to the narrow alley that will take us back to our street, looping past the tonga stand. We are still within the letter of Girish uncle's directive, because we are not going to cross the front of the theatre.

12
Ajji

Ajji had stayed silent while Vimala spoke, weaving the tale of her brother-in-law and his wife as it were a movie she had seen and not a patchwork of other people's remembrances. Ajji ignored it as she had ignored the murmuring responses of a small crowd of listeners to her own story before. When she spoke again, her voice was surprisingly strong, cutting across Vimala's, as if Vimala had never spoken, without an acknowledgement of the things they had just heard.

There were two people who destroyed my happiness, such as it was. The second person is one I have never spoken of, Mira, though you asked me a hundred times a day about her, before you learnt not to. Your mother.

Your father was an innocent, for all his intelligence. I had always known it, and had watched over him to make sure that no one took advantage of him, as boys or playmates do. I relaxed when he went to college, and that was my mistake. They tell me he saw your mother the first day he went to college, and she lost no time in making eyes at him. The other boys, they knew her for what she was, but your father, the innocent, was completely taken in. Five years after the day, when they graduated, and both had jobs to work at the college, I still did not know that they planned to marry, so deep was her deceit. Or so I thought at the time, when I heard about this from Gowramma, our neighbour down the hill whose son had joined the college.

I was so proud of your father. He was a model son. I felt I knew him best of all in the world. When I looked into his eyes, I saw the soul I had carried nine months in my womb and nurtured with my toil, mine alone. He was my son, not even his father's. Incapable of secrets, not with me. Gowramma's son had no scholarship, no picture in the papers. He was an ordinary boy who was lucky to be able to go to college, not the prince my son was. Perhaps this coloured my conversations with her, perhaps I seemed too proud. Maybe that was why she walked up to our house one morning looking as if she had won a lottery, her smiles visible to me all the way down the path before she came to the door.

She sat down on the stone bench outside the door, while I continued cleaning rice, picking out the tiny stones that ration store-bought rice had in abundance. Vimala left to pour her some buttermilk. Then this shameless woman leaned in to tell me, as I am sure she planned to all along, 'I hear there is a wedding planned for your son, Meenakshamma. So far gone, and you never told me?'

I said all the usual things; I laughed, saying how could that be, he is still studying or some such thing. We had not even talked to the matchmakers, or sent for girls' horoscopes.

'You mean you don't know,' she said, openly smiling now, eyes dancing in her mirth. 'My son told me. The word is that he plans to marry some girl from the Christian orphanage. Dark like charcoal too, he said. Who knows what uncaste had her and threw her at their door?'

I drew myself up. 'You are mistaken, Gowramma,' I said. 'Your son is still a child, and for all his studying is easily confused. That cannot be my Kishore. You must tell your son that it is a sin to spread such stories.'

'Yes, Meenakshamma, that's what I told him myself. Yours is such a good family, it would be a shame. Better that he found

some honest Holeya girl. At least her parents would be married. But he insists that it is true. And that girl Renuka, from two streets away, she told her mother the same thing.'

Vimala came out with the buttermilk, and I saw the guilt in her eyes. Girish must have told her, I realised. Had he heard the gossip too and been misled? My Kishore was incapable of such betrayal, not only to deny me a chance to find his bride, but to find someone so unsuitable. Girish, maybe. Kishore, never.

'We will have to see what the truth is,' I told Gowramma, still confident, but her smile irritated me. I couldn't wait to be rid of her, but she ignored all of my hints to leave, enjoying her buttermilk to the last.

I waited at the door for Kishore that evening, remembering his late arrivals, the way he had avoided my glances of late. I had thought nothing of it then. But it still could not be true, I insisted to myself in the arriving dusk. There had to be some other explanation. He would set me straight. He probably pitied the wretch and helped her with something, innocent of the gossip it would generate.

I waited until he removed his shoes, and washed his hands and feet for his evening prayers. As soon as they were done, I asked him, 'Kishore, are there girls from the Christian orphanage in your college?' An innocuous enough question, but guilt showed itself in his eyes.

'Amma, I have wanted to tell you this for a long time,' he said, as if this was a relief for him, to have this conversation.

He lies like his father used to, I told myself, lying to himself first so he is convinced what he speaks is the truth. You probably wonder why I blame your Ajja for everything, Mira, but some of what I say is true, and some a habit, from the bitterness his death left me with. While I waited, the story spewed forth from your father's lips, as if he did not know it for the abomination it was. He loved her. She was a goddess. He was unworthy of her, so perfect was she. I am not sure if those were his words, but that is the impression I gathered, from the sentimental trash he spoke. Why could it not have been Gowramma's half-wit son, I found myself raging, why did it have to be this fool of my son that she set her sights on?

'I know this is difficult for you, Amma,' he said, 'but once you meet her you will see. She will be the daughter to you that you always wanted.'

Indeed.

He brought her to the house the very next day. There was no one to ask permission from, not a horoscope to see, not an auspicious time to be found. The way he brought her was the way cattle are brought into the yard, with no consideration for tradition, no fear of the stars, not a care for right and wrong the way it has been for thousands of years.

I did not go to receive them at the door. Vimala fetched me from the kitchen as they waited in the hall. She was sitting on a chair next to him when I entered, and their heads were bent to each other, excluding the world. When they saw me, though, both jumped up and rushed to touch my feet. When she straightened up, I saw her. It was worse than I thought.

Like charcoal, Gowramma had said, but she was fairer than that, more like coffee made when there is too little milk in the house. She had regular, perfectly symmetric features, as if a master painter had put them there, so regular that she might have been a picture instead of a real breathing person. These were the features that in your face I would grow to marvel over and love, but I saw them first in hers. I almost gasped when I saw them. I shook myself. Hmpf, I thought at that time, so this is how she caught him.

I questioned her tactfully. That was my right, of course. How long had she been at the orphanage? Since birth, she said. Did they treat her well? Yes, they were the only family she had known.

And so on. She could not cook. Her only womanly skill seemed to be to sew. I did not ask her about her parents, what was the point? She had the manner of a man, too, and an arrogant one at that. The way she looked at me, it was the gaze of an equal, not some wretch without family or gotra, who had cheated her way into my son's life. She held her head high and her shoulders squared as if she carried the burden of the world on her head, as if it all depended on her. And she was tall. It was when she was turned away from me that I saw it. This was exactly how Usha used to be. Usha looked nothing like her, of course, but her manner was identical to Usha's when I had first met her. If it was possible to, I liked her even less than I did before.

I realised many years later, Mira, that it would not have mattered if she were fair and the daughter of my cousin or some other cherished relative—I would have still disliked her. If only because I could not bear the thought of having my son stolen from me. I did not realise it then. I saw the way Kishore followed her every gesture and word, the way they anticipated each other's sentences and thoughts. When she was in the room, Kishore could not look elsewhere. Your Ajja had never looked at me like that, not on the day we were married, not the day I bore him one son or the next, not the day before he died. The bitterness in my heart swelled and threatened to drown me, but there was nothing I could say.

'You know this, Amma,' he had said, unmoved by all of my arguments, my entreaties and threats. 'There is nothing wrong with marrying her. If Appa were here, he would have approved of it.'

In the end, I surprised everyone, Gowramma, my sons, even myself, when I gave in, worn down by his insistence, the way I once had been by his father's.

They were married in the way he had brought her to the house for the first time. Without a priest, no astrologer and certainly no mother in attendance, because I had stayed away from the register office where they became man and wife. What priest would marry them anyway? Perhaps they went to the church after that for a blessing, but at least he spared my sensibilities and did not speak of it to me.

They held a little celebration in the yard before our house the evening of their wedding. Their friends arrived from all over, bringing flowers, gifts and stories of their cities and lives. Some had spent the afternoon hanging rented lights on the trees that sparkled and blinked. Somebody else brought food, Maddur vade and Mysore pak, bottles of Coca Cola, which you could still buy in India then. I sat inside but I could see them through the windows, laughing, enjoying the evening as if it belonged to all of them. One of the gifts that your parents got that day was a camera, that two or three friends had gotten together to buy. They had used it to take pictures of the ceremony, such as it was, and now they took pictures of the bride and groom, and themselves.

Kishore finally came in to coax me outside for a picture. I went at last, standing next to your father, who looked tall and distinguished in his suit, and beside him your mother in a sequin-splashed blue saree that she wore for the celebration. Apparently it was a saree that your father had bought for her with his first salary. As soon as that picture was taken, your father laughed and grabbed the camera.

'This one is for me,' he said, and took a picture of your mother, while she smiled at him, an amalgam of joy and intimacy in her eyes. For that one moment I felt my animosity slip away, so obvious was her love for him.

Surendra arrived just as I was turning away from your mother. I had not invited anyone, preferring to ignore the wedding altogether. The only people there were your parents' friends. Perhaps Girish had invited him, I thought. Indeed, at the gate, Surendra was asking loudly for Girish. People made way for the loud stranger, and soon he was upon your parents. Saying loudly, 'So this is the beauty you have been hiding, Kishore,' as he handed your mother the most extravagant arrangement of flowers that I had ever seen.

Somebody stepped up to take their picture, of your parents and Surendra, perhaps it was Girish. Surendra stood next to your mother. The next few moments I have thought about many times these past years. While Girish fumbled with the camera, and your parents held their smiles and poses, Surendra moved closer and closer to your mother. She edged away from him as he did that, and I could not tell if she was even conscious of it. Her smile stayed in place.

The picture was taken and Surendra said, 'How about another one, just with the bride and her brothers-in-law?' He pulled Girish closer, handing the camera to Kishore.

It was an odd request, and one he perhaps would not have made if this were a proper reception with elders and family. On the surface there was nothing wrong with it, except that I could tell that your mother was uncomfortable. As she should have been, to be in a picture with two strangers on her wedding day and without her husband. If she were my daughter, I would have spoken up, or if she had once looked at my face for direction, I would have put the pup in his place. As it happened, she did not. She looked at Kishore, who accepted the camera with a good-natured laugh.

*'Of course, Surendra-*avare*, you are like a brother to me, so both of you are Radhika's brothers-in-law.'*

She did not object, for all her arrogant ways. She continued to smile through her unease at the way Surendra's shoulder was pushing ever so slightly into hers, his body edging closer with each second that Kishore took to focus the camera. She was quick to escape as soon as the picture was taken. By that time though, in my mind, the damage was done. The softening that I had felt towards her was gone, and the situation with the picture set the final unsavoury ending to the whole episode of their wedding. This is how the world sees Srinivas Murthy's daughter-in-law, I thought to myself, with such disrespect, and it could be no one's fault but hers that it was allowed to happen. I went back into the house, and ignored the sounds of the celebration that went on into the night.

Was it any surprise then, that the relationship that got off to such an inauspicious start became steadily worse in the passing days? When I came in a new bride to the house your mother did, it was after years of patient tutelage by my own mother. She had instructed me on prayers and rituals, on every aspect of life that my mother-in-law could expect to see. My mother lived in fear that my mother-in-law would fault my upbringing—what greater insult could there be? Yet, your mother traipsed into my house with none of those lessons, and still expected to be treated better than I was from the minute she set foot inside.

In the early days, we tried not to fight. I cloaked my insults with concern, though she probably saw right through them, and Kishore, fool that I knew he was, did not.

'You do not have to trouble yourself with cooking, you already work so hard at the college,' I said, to keep her out of the kitchen. 'I respect your beliefs, you do not have to follow our ways,' to keep her out of the pooja room. 'Don't you want to go to church?' Every Sunday, so I would be rid of her for another few hours.

Vimala evidently took pity on her, because I would occasionally surprise her teaching your mother simple things behind my back, like knotting flowers into garlands, doing rangoli, or the recipes for your father's favourite dishes. For a while, your mother was content with that, and to live in my house like a guest. She may not have realised it, having never lived in another home, that perhaps the life I allowed her was no different from the one at her orphanage. There wasn't another way, I told myself, feeling the same shame and tightness in my chest that I had felt when your Ajja forced me to serve lunch to his low caste friends in our home. When I closed my eyes every night I found myself letting out a breath that I did not know I had been holding all day.

'How long will you torture me?' I found myself praying to my Gods, thinking guiltily that a marriage that did not happen before Them was not a real one, anyway. Perhaps the marriage that was nothing more than a scrap of paper could fly away like one, or be misplaced or forgotten. Or, as I thought in secret, in the deepest reaches of the night, and in my most guilty moments, maybe she would just disappear and Kishore could have a real marriage. A marriage that his birth entitled him to, to a girl who was everything I wanted for him.

The Gods must have smiled when they heard me. Isn't it a wonder how capriciously They approve our requests? Sometimes it is one in a year, or one in a decade, and always for years after the boon is granted, it is the one you wish you never had asked.

The days turned into weeks and months. Preoccupied as I was with this unsuitable marriage, I tried to find other ways to engage my mind. I could no longer walk to the neighbours or down the street, the false expressions of sympathy, like Gowramma's, were too much to bear. So I took to reading the newspapers again, the way I had done so many years ago with your Ajja.

In the years that I had been busy raising my boys, the mantle of power had passed from Nehru, the man I knew to be the mahatma's favourite, to his daughter. All that Malehalli ever saw of Nehru was when he came to inaugurate the college that he had built here years before, and what a production that was. All the children were given the day off from school, and lined up along the sides of the road for hours before his motor car arrived, so they could wave the roses they had been handed. His love for children was legendary they said, he was called something in

Hindi that escapes me now, but meant 'Uncle', like 'Chikkappa', something like that. He loved roses. He always kept a fresh one in his button hole, they said. I saw him standing up in the motor car, waving to us all, and he looked like a prince. No wonder the mahatma picked him, I remember thinking. He looks like he could be our king. In any case, while I had not been paying attention, he had died, as had his successor whose name also escapes me now. Then the responsibility for the country passed to Nehru's daughter. She was our prime minister. The newspapers were full of her.

When Surendra had first come to help me get the freedom fighter's pension, he'd said, 'In Delhi, ministerships are passed from fathers to daughters,' and it was undoubtedly her that he'd meant, saying it as if it were an outrage or something. But the way I saw it, that was the natural order of things. If I had a daughter, I would give her the gold chain my mother gave me at my wedding. Only idealistic fools like my husband, or maybe Kishore, would do otherwise. Really, that was what you would expect. Unless you were foolish, of course.

But the newspapers were full of anger over something that she had done. There were rumours of rigged elections, and someone called Jayaprakash Narayan was agitating against her. He was a Gandhian, the papers reported, and he was conducting satyagrahas, just like the mahatma once had. Exactly what we need again, I remember thinking, for more boys to quit school and college and ruin their own lives and that of their families.

My own sons were safe. Girish could not fast to save his life, and Kishore had never been interested in politics. For a while I was entertained though, by all the action and the passion that people were writing with. Over the next few months there was more happening in the world outside that was interesting, if only to distract me from the strife in our house. Then came the Emergency.

A court had found Indira Gandhi guilty of something small, using official government machinery for electioneering. That and the constant sniping in the papers made the country ungovernable, she said, and it was done. The democracy of her father's days was gone with one stroke of the President's pen. That first day everything was calm, as was the day after and the day after that. People wrote about those days afterwards, after the Emergency was lifted. But during that time, all was quiet, in the streets and towns. In truth, we may have noticed nothing different except that the newspaper arrived with entire segments coloured in black: unpredictable mysterious shapes that were censored columns of print. The newspapers that had so harangued Indira Gandhi before were now silenced behind them. They threaten our country's integrity, Girish was quick to tell us, the newspapers aid seditious elements who would do us harm. That was the reason those columns were hidden.

But all of this drama was quietly upstaged when your mother came to me a few months after the marriage. It was the morning that the world around us changed, when Indira Gandhi took the country and its laws so easily into her hands. I looked up from the newspaper I was reading, expecting some ingratiating question or request. Instead, she announced, quietly, that she was pregnant.

13
Mira

The street is quiet. The tonga stand looms empty in the distance, the stalls vacant but for feeding pails and grime. The distant houses on either side have shuttered their windows against the sun, and only faint cooking smells escape. The air is still. We miss the trees of Sampige Road and their generous shade. We turn the bend past the tonga stand, to the stretch of road that hugs the back wall of the theatre. We are surprised by the silent crowd gathered there.

About twenty people are huddled together, and almost immediately I recognise Vinay. The others in the crowd are his friends from the cricket-playing days, along with his new-found companions, a lot of them in saffron. The balding man who was in the fight with Bairappa before is not with them, nor the men who threw stones at the hoarding. The boys are gathered around the edge of the back wall, where a short compound wall meets the edge of the theatre.

Anisa and I look at each other. The winding deserted street behind us, or the short walk onward past them? Anisa turns back, half turning towards the tonga stand. Her expression is the same as the one that she has when the cars circle our street with loudspeakers.

I hold her arm before she can turn all the way back. I gesture towards the watchman at the end of the road, dozing on someone's moped. Safe to go on. She shrugs, and we walk forward.

A few steps later, we see one of the boys emerge from the window high on the theatre's back wall. He flashes a thumbs-up sign. Then the boys gathered below help him clamber down, talking in muted voices. We are almost abreast of the crowd when the clerk from the local library looks in our direction, and sees us.

'*Nodoo, alli*,' he chortles, suddenly loud, pointing at us. 'Your girlfriend has come looking for you, Vinay.'

All of the faces turn towards us, but Vinay looks away immediately.

'Not my girlfriend,' he says shortly. I remember the strange half smiles and the glances over summer. So that was what it was all about. If the circumstances were different, Anisa and I might have laughed. Vinay, with his Kannada, and his beedis? We have nothing in common. The easy and unquestioning snobbery of this thought is the first of many regrets to come, and the smallest.

Anisa and I both bend our heads down, pretending we haven't heard. We try to walk faster without appearing to hurry. They might get in a joke or two before we reach the watchman. We'll be gone before they can think of more. A brief memory of the morning's episode on the terrace crosses my mind. The betrayal on Vinay's face, the embarrassment when I looked up to see all of them hooting and jeering. I bend my head lower.

Suddenly, all of them are turned around, facing us, almost in a line against the theatre wall.

'How come, Vinay?' someone I don't recognise asks. 'You've always defended her before.'

'Yeah, she's sooo innocent,' someone else mimics.

'He knows what's what, now.' One of the boys laughs, and I guess that he was with Vinay on the terrace this morning. I want to tell Anisa, warn her really, but the boys are too close and will hear everything. I try to gesture to her with my eyes, but she does not understand.

The boys have been moving in front of us, forcing us to walk more and more to the left as we try to walk by without a confrontation. I take a tiny step back, hoping that Anisa will follow. Maybe we can run to Sampige Road.

But a boy in saffron moves behind us, as if to block our path, saying, 'Oh, yes, such great devotees, who come to the temple daily.'

Somebody else says, 'Yeah, even Muslims. I wonder if they know to take a bath before?'

Anisa shivers beside me at this, and freezes in place.

It is too late to run back now. The boys are in a line in front and curving around behind us. And the first of them starts to walk around. As if they are going to circle us. They are laughing. The watchman is still asleep a few yards away. I wonder why he has not woken up. We walk backwards and to the right, steps smaller and faster now as we look for some way out without a direct confrontation.

'So fashionable, wonder if they even speak Kannada? So high and mighty.'

Then from somewhere behind us, 'Dirty Muslims, beef-eaters.'

'Run, Anisa,' I mutter under my breath, pushing her as unobtrusively as I can towards the side. A circle has already formed in the last few seconds, but there is a gap to our right behind us, where the back gate to the theatre stands open.

She hesitates for an infinitesimal second. 'Run,' I say, more urgently than before as I push her sideways. There is no doubt in my mind that Anisa is in danger. It feels as if the whole Hindu chest-thumping of the last few weeks has crystallised around us.

She makes it through the gap in the circle, and I follow. But the circle seals off behind her as the boy in saffron steps almost triumphantly in place. She does not notice until she is almost at the theatre. The ring of boys is loose around me, but each time I take a step to cross them, they step closer together, sealing off gaps. Almost as if it is a game we might all have played when we were younger.

Anisa stands at the theatre, finally seeing that I have not made it through. She says, 'Vinay, let her go! Vinay! You know us. Tell them.' Her voice is shaking, but she stands there, drawing herself up tall against the fear.

Vinay looks at her, and spits. The other boys laugh.

'Get out,' someone says.

I try to read Vinay's face, to find a way to remind him that we used to be friends. But his expression is closed, opaque. We might be strangers.

'Run, Anisa,' I say, exasperated and afraid. Does she not realise I am Hindu, they will just let me go? It is her that they want, and she is lucky she got through. 'Don't waste time.'

Anisa turns around and tries a door that leads inside the theatre. It opens, and she enters.

No one breaks off to follow her, or even turns around to look at her. They continue to circle me slowly.

I am Hindu; I don't have to worry, I repeat over and over in my mind, counting the seconds.

'So happy to be with us,' one of Vinay's cricket-playing friends says, and they all snigger.

'Let me pass,' I say to the boy nearest me.

'So proud, as if I am your servant,' he says.

'I'll scream. People will come running ...'

'Oh, like that Muslim boyfriend of yours? Let him come.'

I see, suddenly. This is not about Anisa, but Adil.

'You know what's worse than Muslim?' one of them asks. 'Sluts that open themselves to Muslim dogs.'

I look up at the boys, and they are leering. I feel truly afraid for the first time.

'If you are so anxious for a kiss, why couldn't you ask one of us?' the clerk from the lending library says, and when I look at him he makes the loud kissing noises he made before.

'Sir, Watchman-*avare*—' my voice is suddenly thin, even to my ears. I try again, louder, but he does not stir.

There is more laughter around me. The boys are circling around, and now Vinay is up in front of me. He does not look me in the face but spits, again, as he steps past. This cannot be happening, I think, but it is.

'I thought you were so good,' he says, 'and you are like this. Just like your mother.'

'Like mother, like daughter.' This is another of the boys that Vinay plays cricket with. I don't know his name.

'My mother is dead,' I say, more afraid. 'Don't talk about her.'

'Oh, she gives us orders, now.' The clerk from the library.

'Like mother, like daughter.' I turn around to follow the voice. Vinay, again.

'Slut.' He looks me in the face as he says this. 'Kissing that dirty Muslim. In the street, in front of everyone. No shame. Just like your mother, slut.'

I start at the contempt in his face, but he continues to talk.

'And I defended you all the time. You and your friend, walking around in those short skirts and your tight sleeveless clothes. Parading yourselves, standing on the balcony when you know we are on the street below. Begging for attention. I thought you were so innocent, even when all of them said you must be like your mother. And you do this. Shameless. Both of you deserve everything you get.'

The circle has gotten tighter. I bump into an arm behind me when I step back from Vinay and his anger. They will get in so much trouble when someone comes, I tell myself, trying to quiet my fear. How are they so loud, so unafraid? And why does the watchman not wake up?

Suddenly, to my left, there is a loud sound, like an auto backfiring, only louder. It is from inside the theatre.

The sound obviously means something to the boys. They seem surer now, more aggressive. Another arm reaches out from the back somewhere and pulls at my duppatta. I clutch at it, but it is gone, leaving a burn in my clenched fist.

'Vinay, please,' I say, finally, all pride gone. 'Ask them to let me go. Anisa will be back with my uncle. You will get in trouble.'

'My uncle,' he mimics. 'No one is coming back. Not *her* and not your *boyfriend*.'

I push at the boy nearest me, who looks about my height. If he stumbles, I can run past him. It may not work, but I am desperate. He doesn't. He grabs my arm instead. The clerk from the library grabs my other arm. I shake my arms free even as I feel a rip in my kameez in the back, the neckline pulled back with the force of that rip, so hard and fast that it cuts into my throat.

There is a second, louder noise like a boom, followed by short, loud sounds.

The next minute I see flames licking their way out from inside the theatre. The walls may be paper, the ease with which they melt.

'Anisa,' I scream, 'where are you?'

Someone shoves me to the ground and I do not see who it is. They are yelling obscenities in Kannada, and they all, even Vinay, look half crazed.

'Vinay,' I plead, 'we went to see Ganeshas together.'

He grabs a handful of my kameez in response and another strip comes away, which he holds up the way he did the part of the hoarding the day before. The contempt on his face silences me. 'Isn't this what you wanted, slut?'

We all hear the scream from somewhere within the theatre.

I try to get up, but get pushed down to the street again. When I start to scream, a hand covers my mouth. It smothers my nostrils, and for a minute everything disappears from my mind, except that I need to get a breath. I twist my head from side to side, kicking, clawing, struggling for air.

Then there is just blackness.

When I wake, Lakshmi has thrown her saree over me. She is standing over me, screaming, saree-less, in her blouse and petticoat.

'Look at me, you bastards,' she shouts, 'look to your heart's content.'

The boys are running away.

She screams obscenities, flinging stones at their retreating backs. The books Anisa and I carried only a few minutes before are strewn on the street at her feet.

The theatre is a raw, untamed blaze. The watchman lies unmoving on the moped.

14

Mira

Lakshmi has her arms around me, and does not let me go into the burning theatre. She drags me home, kicking and fighting. Ajji runs out of the house when she sees us outside in the street, and between the two of them they drag and carry me indoors.

Lakshmi tells them that Anisa might be inside the theatre.

'I told you not to go there,' Girish uncle shouts, picking up the phone. 'Now what have you girls done?'

While he calls for fire engines and police, Vimala aunty sweeps me up, Lakshmi's saree and all, madi forgotten. 'Not again,' she says, not explaining herself, merely looking as if someone has died.

Ajji comes back with a saree for Lakshmi, saying, 'Here, cover yourself,' distaste in her voice.

Lakshmi tells them the details, how she was looking for her son, Vinay, and came upon the group of them behind the theatre, ripping off my clothes while the theatre blazed in the background.

'*Devar punya, saar*,' she says, hastily tying the borrowed saree before my uncle's carefully averted eyes. 'If I hadn't been there, who knows what would have happened?'

'They didn't do anything to her, Amma,' she says to Ajji, and pausing delicately, 'she still has some of her clothes under my saree. She may just be scared and bruised, nothing worse happened.' And then her tone turns wheedling; now fully clothed, she grabs Girish uncle's feet without warning, '*Dodd manasu maadi, saar*,' she begs for Vinay to be spared.

Bad company, no father, the excuses tumble from her lips, with her tears. 'They were talking about her mother, when I came up to them. God knows where they heard. That she had taken a lover, when she was already a wife and mother. It shocked even me when I heard it, and I hear so many stories. You know how boys at that age are. You cannot blame them fully, can you *saar*?' She looks around at all of us. 'Your family has so much to lose, *saar*. Save my son and I will hold my tongue till the day I die.'

'Listen to me,' Girish uncle says, steely-eyed in a way I have never noticed before, 'I will make sure Vinay stays out of trouble—but only if you shut your mouth. Do you hear me?'

'Whatever you say, *swami*, you are like God to me,' Lakshmi says, relieved, bending down to touch his feet again. But my uncle is ready for her this time, moving away as he says, 'No drama, Lakshmamma, listen carefully. Your son is mixed up in big people's affairs, starting a career in murder. He could be hanged, or be in jail for life, do you understand?'

Lakshmi nods, tears starting again. 'You will protect him, *saar*, I have saved your family honour. If you don't help us, who will? Not even Ganesha.'

'Spare me the acting, Lakshmamma. We don't have time. I told him not to work for Devidas. He is not as innocent as you say.'

'You know this already? That Devidas was behind this?' Vimala aunty says, but she only voices what we are all thinking.

'Stay out of this,' Girish uncle says, contempt in his voice. 'Men have to go out and do business in the world. Sometimes these things have to be allowed to happen. I told Bairappa to be patient. But he had to go above me and talk to the chief minister.'

There is a silence when he says that, just before we hear the sirens, far away on Sampige Road, getting closer and louder by the minute. The fire engines are coming.

'Lakshmamma,' Girish uncle says to her, finally, 'no one can know that you were there, or my niece. No one. If you open your mouth, I will throw Vinay out on the street and allow the dogs to feed.'

I try to run to the door, to run out on the street. To ask if someone had seen Anisa. She may have gone back, I think, with help. She is probably looking for me behind the theatre right now. That scream I heard was someone else, or maybe I had imagined it. Rehana aunty, Farid uncle, I have to tell them. But Ajji grabs me before I can get to the door. She puts me in the bedroom, and locks the door. I beat on it, kick it, scream.

'Enough,' Ajji says to me from the other side of the door. 'You have done enough for today.'

Girish uncle paces outside, on the veranda, in the hall. Ajji leaves to look for Anisa and Rehana aunty.

I bang my head on the wall, pound the floor, shout. We have to find Anisa, I say, over and over, for minutes or hours, or something in between, while the cars and sirens scream up and down the street.

Somewhere in the clamour, a doctor arrives at our house. My aunt holds me down while they give me something in my vein.

'Small dose,' the doctor murmurs, 'just enough to calm her, not enough to make her lose consciousness.'

'I have to find Anisa,' I say, 'I have to find Anisa.' But I have no energy to kick the door or scream, or beat on the walls with my head and my hands anymore.

There are more cars and jeeps on the street than any of us have ever seen. Journalists, TV crews. Police cars. Even government vehicles.

We hear the news inside the house as it happens outside. The fire engines douse the burning theatre. Bairappa and the clerk were the only ones inside, somebody says. There was a dharna in front of the theatre, that morning. No one had been allowed in for the morning show. An electrical fault, somebody says; good thing it happened the day of the dharna, so more people did not die.

Then more details emerge—people heard something like an explosion. A gas cylinder, they say. Leaking gas that no one knew was there, and then perhaps an electrical fault. A tragedy, an accident, waiting to happen. An unidentified body, also in the theatre, that might be a girl.

I have no energy to get up and go to Rehana aunty when she arrives, only a few minutes later, even though the door is now unlocked, and half open.

'Have you seen Mira or Anisa? There are vehicles all over the street, and I haven't seen them come back from the library.'

They all look at each other. Ajji says, 'Rehana, I came to your house earlier. Where were you? Lakshmi just brought Mira back. They are looking for Anisa. Here, sit down.' Ajji and Vimala aunty rush to hold Rehana aunty, who crumples, as if her whole body just turned to rubber.

'Can't find Anisa?' she says. And then, 'Is Mira okay? Does she know where Anisa is?'

'Wait, sister,' Girish uncle says. 'I have called Farid bhai at his office. He is coming home now. We can talk about everything after he comes.'

'Mira, Mira,' Rehana aunty comes running into the bedroom. She has seen me through the half-open door. 'What happened to you, why are you wrapped in this old saree?' She parts the folds, and sees the shredded salwar kameez hanging in tatters.

'Where is Anisa?' she asks, voice shaking.

All I can say is, 'I have to find Anisa; I have to find Anisa.'

'Where did you leave Anisa?' she shakes me. 'Where did you leave my daughter?'

She runs back to the hall. 'Have you called the police? I need to go there. Why are you all here, inside the house? We need to go search for her.' She is almost out of the door before Ajji restrains her and brings her in.

'Of course I called the police, sister,' Girish uncle tells her. 'Let us wait for news. It is not safe for you to go out.'

Rehana aunty tries to go out again, pulling her arms out of Ajji's grasp. Ajji puts her arms around Rehana aunty, half embrace, half stranglehold. In all these years, Ajji and Rehana aunty have never touched each other. Rehana aunty stops short, looking at Ajji's face and her arms, which are now holding her firmly at the shoulder. 'Why were you crying?' she asks, her tone puzzled, angry, even.

'Anisa is hurt. They took her to the hospital,' Girish uncle finally says, while Ajji starts to cry, silently. 'When Farid bhai is home, we can all go see her. It will only be a few minutes.' Ajji helps Rehana aunty into a chair. Vimala aunty takes her hand, and Ajji sits down beside her.

There is the muffled sound of a scooter at our gate. Farid uncle has arrived. Girish uncle meets him outside. I do not hear their conversation. Nor does Rehana aunty, who is still in the hall with Ajji and Vimala aunty.

Rehana aunty is crying, and she does not ask any more questions. Perhaps this is an adult code they all understand, but she seems to know that things are worse than they seem.

Farid uncle helps Rehana aunty stand up, walk to the door. His face is frozen into the expression he probably had when he saw Girish uncle at the gate—a half smile in greeting. Only the eyes are different, twin pools of shock, and something else that I do not recognise. He does not look in my direction. Rehana aunty looks at me over her shoulder before she leaves, but she does not say anything.

I will my body to move. I want to go out, follow Farid uncle and Rehana aunty, to see Anisa. Maybe Anisa is in the hospital, wounded but alive. But it is either the drug they gave me, or the look on Rehana aunty's face. I am unable to move. Her last words to me stay in the air after her.

'My daughter,' she'd said. 'Where did you leave my daughter?'

15

Anisa

Anisa enters the door at the back of the theatre and is in the auditorium with its giant screen and dirty carpet. She recognises it, despite the darkness, from its smell of stale cigarette smoke and sickly sweet jasmine wilting in women's hair. The door snaps shut behind her and disappears. But the smell's familiarity lulls her anxiety, reminding her as it does of much anticipated childhood outings, greasy too-crisp samosas and Ammi's fierce, almost comical, disdain for public bathrooms. Her eyes adjust to the darkness, and she knows she is at the front of the room between the screen, alight and sending pools of green and orange light to her feet, and the first row of theatre seats.

Mira should have been able to make it through the circle of boys. Why was she just *standing* there? They are just *boys* and they are in for so much trouble when Abbu finds out. Or Girish uncle. It will only take her a few minutes to get to someone. Perhaps there is an adult that she knows here, watching the movie.

But the seats are empty, as are the aisles. Of course, the dharna, she remembers, no one was allowed to enter today. Maybe the protestors are still in front of the theatre. All she has to do is get to the front. Above the closest aisle is the column of light from the projector in the back, like a beacon.

She wonders if the owner is playing the movie despite the empty seats, in a show of defiance.

She hurries up the aisle past the empty seats, calling out in English and in Kannada, just in case. Her voice echoes around the room and she realises suddenly that the theatre is silent. The movie is playing with no sound track. She turns around for a moment and sees the woman from the billboard, dressed exactly as she was in the picture outside. But she is beautiful. Her face fills the screen, luminescent and smooth. Her eyes are wide and kohl-lined; the eyelashes impossibly thick. She blinks and Anisa follows the line of her nose to the generous glistening red lips. On the next shot, the camera cuts in close, sliding past her neck. Her cleavage fills the screen. Anisa turns away, her momentary captivation broken, snorting, thinking, *Oh Mira, you should see this*, running faster up the aisle. There *must* be *someone* in the theatre, if only the man who runs the projector.

A few seconds later, she is almost at the end of the aisle when Bairappa enters from the side. He is a flash of white shirt in the darkness. She might not have recognised him had she not been expecting him, and for the glint of gold at his neck and wrist.

'Help us,' she says, breathless and too loud.

'What is all this shouting? And how did you get in?' he says. 'Stupid children. First the boy and now you. Can't watch for free just because you can sneak in.'

'No, it is Mira, do you remember, Girish uncle's niece? She's caught in the back, the boys—the boys are creating trouble. Can you talk to them?'

There is a loud sound, off to the side, and she feels the ground rock a little under her with the vibration.

Bairappa turns away from her. 'Now what?' he says.

'Get out,' he calls over his shoulder to Anisa as he walks away.

She turns to her left. She knows there is a door at the far

corner which leads into the lobby. She has reached it when there is a second sound. She feels the wave of compressed air that hits her as she turns around, knocking her past the open door into the lobby. She sees the wall on the far right of the auditorium that she was just in, collapsing, flames springing up like jinn.

Was that where Bairappa went? She hesitates.

But Mira, she thinks. I have to get out and find somebody, or a phone, to call.

She stands up and sees the lobby is still intact. There is no fire here yet, only searing warmth, hotter than outside, and smoke. Was it an earthquake, she wonders, and how is there fire?

She turns towards the door, finds herself hobbling. Her ankle hurts; she is still winded from the fall. She should be outside soon, but the smoke slows her, clouding, disorienting. It is only a few steps, and she will make it even if she can no longer be sure of where the door is. She is scared. She tells herself she is not.

Mira, she thinks, Abbu and Ammi, as the smoke fills her nostrils and her lungs.

She sees them all together in this lobby on their last visit here all those years ago. They are standing at the concessions stand, waiting for their samosas and Torino. All dressed up, even though it was only a short walk from home. Mira, fidgeting and wide-eyed, next to her; Ammi watching the vendor to make sure he uses clean plates. Abbu turning to them, eyes twinkling as usual, saying, 'Who wants ice cream?'

She can feel the sweet and cold of ice cream in her mouth and the fizz of orange soda. Her Abbu loves her. She is his noor, his diamond. He holds his arms out to her to pick her up and toss her in the air. She knows she is too old for this and too heavy for Abbu. But the wind lifts her up as he tosses her. She sees him smile at her from below, steadfast and indulgent, and she feels herself lift away and above, higher and farther.

16

Mira

When they take Rehana aunty to the mortuary to identify Anisa, I hear she tears her hair out in clumps that she tosses on the floor. That she collapses on the dirty floor without a sound passing her lips. That she screams abuses at the police who stand outside the door. That she says over and over to Farid uncle, it is your fault, I told you we should have been stricter with her. We should never have come here to live. That she says not one word when they draw the white cloth back to show her what is left of her daughter. That she stands like a statue while her husband's tears flow unchecked. That she turns around and walks out, saying, no, that is not Anisa, I don't know who that is.

The neighbourhood ladies all stream in through our door, each bearing a different morsel of gossip, where each contradictory detail contained within is a triumph of discovery. They crane their necks and walk inside to the kitchen hoping to catch a glimpse of me. It is useless, of course. The door to the room remains shut to their gaze, and I weave in and out of a drugged sleep behind it, seeing the Rehana aunty I know and love doing all the things they say that she did. I can hear the stories Ajji and my aunt tell the women who visit, heading off scandal with lies.

'Mira was home when this happened. We don't know how Anisa ended up behind the theatre. Mira is upset of course, they have been friends all their life. But she does not know anything about this.'

Ajji begs me to eat, again, or drink some water. 'We'll have to take you to the hospital,' she says, the tears gathering in her wrinkles, spilling over one by one. Why does she cry for me, I wonder, when it is Anisa who is gone? I turn my eyes to the ceiling, hoping that she will leave. 'It has been a day and a half since you drank anything, even a sip of water,' Ajji tells me.

How does it matter anyway? I do not care. Anisa is dead and I am alive. It is impossible, and wrong. This is a nightmare that I will wake from to find her at the door, impatient to start the day. I will endure this nightmare, I think, and wait to eat and smile, wait to live and breathe until Anisa arrives.

Anisa does not arrive, of course. But we have other visitors late in the evening after the tumult has died down a bit, and I lie in my bed.

It is Surendra, dressed all in white, and there are two other men with him. They look like subordinates of some kind, or assistants. Girish uncle has been waiting for them at the gate, and they walk up the garden path together to the veranda as I watch. I unlatch the window, and their low-voiced conversation reaches me easily.

'I could not talk over the phone,' Surendra says, sitting heavily in the wicker chair in the veranda. Girish uncle continues to stand, as do Surendra's companions. The two of them stand back with their arms folded, scanning the garden path behind Surendra as if there may be someone there, crouching to hear. Perhaps they are bodyguards. 'The Opposition leader came to see me today.'

After a beat, Surendra continues, 'We cannot proceed against Devidas. Blackmail—some sordid business with the fellow's wife. Devidas has pictures and recordings.'

Girish uncle is surprised. 'I did not know. That changes everything.'

Surendra snaps his fingers. 'Yes, and that is how your brilliant plan to let the theatre burn and send Devidas to prison fails, Girish. I told you it would not be that simple.'

Girish uncle mumbles, shifts his weight from one foot to another like an errant schoolboy. I cannot make out the words.

'I know I agreed with you,' Surendra says, impatiently. 'Bairappa should not have gone above your head, or mine, to talk to the chief minister.'

Girish uncle says, 'Who could have predicted that Devidas had this hold on him?' There is a faintly accusatory tone to Girish uncle's voice, a murmuring hint that it was Surendra's fault that they did not know this before.

'Yes, but that is not the point now, is it?' Surendra says, exhaling heavily. 'Think a little—if word gets out that Devidas was able to do this in your backyard, to someone who has been by our side all these years, and get away with it, how does it make us look? How does it make *me* look?'

They wait in silence for a while, the bodyguards behind Surendra swatting away mosquitoes in the growing darkness.

'You have to find a way to clean up this mess,' Surendra says finally. 'And it is your mess. Don't make excuses. Find a way to make this right.'

He gets up and he turns away from Girish uncle. He takes a step down the garden path, and the underlings turn likewise to follow. It is at that moment that Ajji arrives at the gate, back from the evening pooja.

She stops mid-stride when she recognises Surendra. It is too dark to see their faces, but they are two figures in white that stand out in the darkness, facing each other on the garden path outside my window.

Surendra stops, and says almost meditatively to her, 'What is this I hear about your niece?'

I cannot make out Ajji's expression.

'It is only people with no shame,' Ajji says, 'who go where they are not welcome.' She seems calmer than when she spoke with him last. 'I don't know what you heard, and I don't care.'

Surendra laughs, loud and coarse in the darkness.

'You don't care that the great Srinivas Murthy's granddaughter was kissing some filthy man on the street? Is it because his daughter-in-law did all that and more, with how many more men, who knows?'

'Shut your mouth,' Ajji says, her voice shaking in anger. 'Your tongue will rot with the lies you tell.'

'You are the one telling lies,' Surendra says, even as Ajji tries to step past him. 'But even you see the truth now, don't you? They say it all shows up in the blood. Only seventeen and already so eager.'

Ajji rushes past him to the door and outside my sight.

She comes in and shakes me by the shoulder. 'What did you do?'

So, she did believe him, after all. So much for her protestations that Surendra was a liar. 'It was Adil, not some filthy man.'

She takes a step back, paler than when she walked in. I look outside the window, and Surendra is already at his car, with one of his lackeys holding the door open for him.

Girish uncle is at the gate.

Vimala aunty comes into the room.

There is a look that passes between Ajji and Vimala aunty that I cannot decipher.

Vimala aunty says, 'You should tell Kishore.'

Then I hear Ajji in the hall, making one of her rare international calls to Appa. I hear her side of the conversation, and her pauses.

It's Mira. There's been an accident. It was a fire. She's okay, but Anisa died. Yes. No, she's better now. Yes, it was an accident. She was in the wrong place at the wrong time. Yes, I think it is better if you do that.

'Your father is coming,' Ajji tells me, only a few minutes later, but she looks as if she has fought a battle and has lost. She rummages through the Godrej cupboard with the locker for valuables to find my passport. That is how I understand that I am to leave with Appa.

Later, sleep arrives after a glass of milk that Ajji forces upon me. Before the chemical aftertaste of whatever it was laced with disappears from my tongue, I hear her say, apologetic, 'It is for the best, Mira.'

When I hear the blaring songs from the temple at daybreak, it is another day. It brings the realisation that there is no Anisa at the door, and that there never will be. And it is my fault, in ways I cannot escape. I kissed Adil while they watched. I walked down to them, shameless where I should have been ashamed. Anisa's half turn, her instinct to go back as soon as she saw them, is as clear as my foolhardy conviction that dragged her with me to them.

I look at the picture by my bed. A woman in a blue sequined saree smiles into the camera, her eyes at once joyful and knowing. Her glance so confident and so intimate in its timber it must be directed at someone who loves her and is loved in return. A private moment between photographer and subject. How could I have mistaken that glance as being meant for me? What was the story that Lakshmi told, that she had taken a lover when she was already a wife and my mother? It seems suspect, and yet the truth of her is obvious in Ajji's silence, which is as wily as her stories are. My mother, I think, and the rush of love that usually accompanies that thought is absent.

I hear the waking sounds around me. Ajji stands up, next to me. She has slept nearby, between the door and me, sitting up, back to the wall.

'Are you awake, Mira?' she asks unnecessarily, to my wide-open eyes.

Above Ajji's head there is a blaze of pink sky in the window. I do not answer.

Ajji knew. She has always known. She could have told me. Why didn't she? It had to be because the story was too shameful, because my mother was the woman that Surendra said she was.

Ajji looks at me, eyes patient, waiting for me to speak. 'Do you feel a little better today?'

I close my eyes. The skirts that Anisa and I wore as part of our school uniforms appear shorter in retrospect, the folded down socks vulgar instead of fashionable. Vinay defended us until I kissed Adil. Had I not kissed Adil, perhaps he would have continued to defend us. Maybe he would have helped us escape.

There are kitchen noises next, and then sounds on the street. The milkman, a newspaper thudding on the floor outside. My aunt at my side with a glass of warm Horlicks.

'Let me give it to her, it needs to cool,' Ajji says, reaching for the glass from my aunt. But the doorbell rings again, too late for the milkman, too early for visitors. Ajji shuts the bedroom door carefully behind her as she steps out into the hall. There are voices, Girish uncle's and Farid uncle's, in the hall.

'Sorry to bother,' Farid uncle says, and his voice carries soft and clear into my room in the silence outside. 'But I could not think of anyone else to ask.'

'Of course, of course,' Girish uncle says, 'we are like family, please do not hesitate. Is there some more paperwork they need before the funeral? I spoke to the medical director at GH yesterday. He promised me they would release everything today.'

'No, Girish-*avare*. It is not that. The funeral will go ahead.' Farid uncle hesitates. 'I am sure it is all a mistake. And it will be cleared up soon enough. But,' he hesitates.

'But what?' Ajji asks.

'They arrested Adil this morning, just before daybreak,' Farid uncle says.

'Arrested Adil?' I can't be sure who said that. Maybe it was my own voice. Arrest Adil?

'The inspector who came said it was precautionary. There was no warrant,' Farid uncle says.

'But your brother-in-law is a college student, not a goonda,' Ajji says. 'What is the meaning of this? Precautionary for what?'

'They said it was for the funeral. I don't know. That is why I came,' Farid uncle says. 'Rehana has not been herself since we came back from the mortuary. And when they took him this morning, I thought she would go mad. She does not have anything left, you see, that she can lose.'

Through the closed door, I can see him, my Farid uncle, who I called Abbu sometimes and in secret. The father that Anisa shared with me like she shared everything else she had. The gentle man whose voice I hear breaking, and I see him as if he stood before me instead of outside beyond a closed door. I see the tears in his eyes, the sorrow that cannot be borne. I know I have destroyed Anisa, and broken her parents. Now, Adil?

I want to rush out in to the hall, warn Farid uncle about the help he is seeking. Your trust is misplaced, I want to shout. But I am too weak or drugged to move.

Girish uncle clears his throat. 'Let me find out,' I hear him say, and imagine the pat on Farid uncle's shoulder that must accompany those words. I hear the back and forth of the dial on the phone in the hall. Hall chairs scrape the floor as they are drawn back, sat on. A newspaper rustles.

There is a long conversation, mostly with just a phrase or two on Girish uncle's end. Monosyllabic words or short phrases, like yes, yes-yes, and I agree, I see. And no, I don't think that is true, no, of course not, you are right, yes, of course, thank you, interrupted only by occasional newspaper rustles. Perhaps it is Farid uncle who is fidgeting.

When Girish uncle gets off the phone, Farid uncle says, 'Did you see this?' instead of waiting for him to speak, and the newspaper rustles again, changing hands.

A pause, and 'Let me see it,' Ajji says.

'What is the meaning of this, Girish-*avare*? What is this about "a girl of a certain community"?'

'You know, Farid bhai, they don't say Hindu or Muslim in the papers, because it can create communal tensions, riots. That's why they say "certain community" so people don't read the paper and you know, create more trouble.'

'I know as well as you why they say that,' Farid uncle says, a thread of anger in his voice. 'But what does that have to do with what happened? Such nonsense, communal riots in Bangalore, when has that ever happened? This is not some godforsaken town in Bihar or somewhere like that. And they quote the commissioner of police for this, about communal issues? This was the same man who told me it was all an accident two days ago—you were there.'

'Yes, Farid bhai, I was just getting to that—I spoke with him just now, please be patient. Sit down, sit down. Don't be hasty.'

'I'm listening, Girish-*avare,* tell me, what did he say today?'

'They found a kerosene bomb in the theatre, Farid bhai. And there is CBI involvement, so they cannot keep it quiet either. It is a mess.'

'So they found a bomb in the theatre. You called him to see why they arrested Adil. Why did he tell you about the bomb? What does that have to do with arresting Adil?'

'All these things take time, Farid bhai, please be patient. Your brother-in-law was working on a science project.'

'Which had nothing to do with making kerosene bombs.'

'But they found your daughter's body in the theatre, and the theatre owner is a Hindu ...'

'Girish-*avare*, you can't be seriously suggesting that Adil and Anisa had something to do with this?'

'I know they didn't, Farid bhai, but like I said, it does not matter what I think. They work through their theories. The commissioner told me that if it were up to him, he would just forget about the bomb, but now with the CBI, they have to investigate.'

'They can investigate, but they need to find out who did it, not arrest some innocent because he belongs to "*some community*". What kind of stupidity is this?' Farid uncle is loud.

'Farid bhai, you need to be calm; remember, I am on your side. Don't be angry with me.'

'But Girish-*avare*, you are acting as if what he said is reasonable. I did not even hear you protest on the phone.'

'We need to free your brother-in-law, Farid bhai. We cannot do that by making speeches about what is right. Even if he did not do it, you have to agree it looks bad for him.'

There is a moment of utter silence in the hall.

Then Girish uncle continues, 'The commissioner thinks there is a way out—the real culprits cannot be arrested, there is too much political pressure.'

'What, what does he think?' Farid uncle's tone is measured, angrier than it has been when he was shouting. When he says, next, 'And what suggestions does he have for us?' it is as if he knows the answer that is coming.

'He can arrange for the report to be altered slightly, so it will seem like it was a gas cylinder bursting, and that Anisa was found outside the theatre. But, you know—'

'But, what, Girish-*avare*, please don't stop now.'

'It will cost money, you know, to pay off all the involved people. It is high profile, CBI involvement; the work has to be pukka. He thinks there are about five people who have control over the report.' I listen for the shame that needs to be there, because he has just passed on a request for a bribe. There is none.

'He doesn't need the money right away,' Girish uncle says. 'As long as you agree to pay, he knows you are a man of your word. They will release him in time for the funeral.'

Anisa has died, Adil is arrested, and now Farid uncle needs to pay money to get him released before the funeral. That is what my uncle has just told him.

'How much, did he say?' Farid uncle's voice is diamond edged, when it arrives to cut into my flesh behind the closed door.

I stumble to my feet. I have been lying down for so long I sway as I get up, and have to grab the bedpost so I don't fall.

'Girish!' Ajji's voice cuts through the air whip-like, and suddenly I know I have never heard Ajji ever address her son directly before. Not in happiness, not in anger. She has never spoken his name even though they live under the same roof. And I have never noticed this before. How could that have been?

I have taken two steps towards the door, holding on to the bedpost, when Girish uncle continues as if Ajji never spoke, 'Two lakhs.'

'Have you no shame?' Ajji asks, in the silence that follows his words. 'You stand under your father's picture, and you ask for a bribe?'

No one responds. The words melt away into the silence.

I hear a chair scraping back, a thud as the newspaper lands on the floor. I take a few more steps. I let go of the bedpost.

Through the waves of dizziness, I see the door. It is only four, maybe five steps away.

'*Barthini,* Amma,' Farid uncle says, to Ajji, the traditional 'I will return' that is customary to say at leaving. 'Don't blame your son; he is just doing us a favour, giving us a message. It is our bad luck.'

'Tell the *commissioner*,' he stresses the word in a way that makes his disbelief clear, 'that the money will take time to arrange. I will have to get a loan until I can sell something.' I hope that he is turned away from Girish uncle when he says this, contemptuous, tossing the words over his shoulder the way men throw coins in the sand for urchins to scramble and find outside the temple. But the gentle voice that I know is wounded, as if this unmasking of a man he considered his friend injures him, not Girish uncle.

I am almost at the door. One more step and I can run into the hall, to Farid uncle. I open the door just as Farid uncle is putting on his slippers in the veranda outside. 'Farid uncle,' I say, at the door, but my voice is a thread. Even Ajji, standing in the hall, does not hear it. I try again, and Farid uncle looks up at me from the veranda, as he straightens up. He will hold his arms out, I think, and I can run to them.

'Mira,' he says, looking straight at me, but so formally that he might be addressing a stranger. He looks at the empty space next to me for a moment, and it is as if a weight of sorrow descends on him again.

In the space of that moment, I remember that Farid uncle always asked after Anisa first when he came home, before he had greeted Rehana aunty at the door. I remember Rehana aunty's mock exasperation, and her frequent joke that he would follow Anisa to her married home, against all convention, self-respect even.

I cannot face the emptiness in his eyes.

I hear Rehana aunty's words instead in my mind, now more accusatory than when she said them, 'Where did you leave my daughter?'

Even though Farid uncle says nothing, this is what I expect him to say. These are the words I hear him think.

A moment later, he turns around and walks out.

I watch his straight-backed, square-shouldered walk to the gate, and I cannot cry.

Ajji holds me close. 'He cannot bear to talk to you now,' she says, 'but don't think that he blames you. It is not your fault.'

But I know the truth.

I drink the cold Horlicks that my aunt has forgotten on the floor of the room.

I do not ask to go to the funeral. The Mira that Anisa knew might have gone. Instead, they all go, even Girish uncle, locking the door carefully behind them.

'Rehana aunty asked for you,' Ajji says, when they return, 'she told me you were the only daughter she had left.' I wonder if she is lying and conclude that she is.

'Adil was released, but he had bruises,' Vimala aunty tells me, as if I should care.

I see those bruises later that afternoon, after the funeral, when Adil arrives. I hear him at the door and Ajji comes in from the kitchen to stand beside me. Vimala aunty invites him inside over Girish uncle's objections. When she brings him to where I sit propped up in bed, there is a small map of blue and black over his right eye and a bandage on his right eyebrow. There are scratches on his neck and cheek. He has aged years in the day and a half that it has been.

He stands at the door and seems relieved, then surprised, to see me looking so well.

'Why didn't you come to the funeral?' he asks, and I

wonder if that is anger that I hear somewhere deep, all the way down. But there is only concern in his eyes.

I cannot tell him why. Do the culpable walk among the grieving at funerals? 'I am sorry,' I say, and the words come out strange and formal.

He takes a step back in disbelief. 'You're sorry? As if it is some party that you missed?'

He takes a breath and tries again. 'You're probably in shock. I know how close Anisa and you were.'

I feel myself start to cry inside, but there are no tears that come to my eyes.

Girish uncle comes up behind Adil. 'All right, you've seen her, now leave.'

'Adil,' Ajji says, 'Mira is leaving soon. Her father is taking her to America. It is for the best.'

Adil looks only at me.

'I'll wait for you, Mira,' he'd said, before his niece died, and he was arrested and beaten up. A girl that I used to know had kissed him, once. It was a promise meant for her. Not for the girl who might find herself incapable of restraint despite a husband and marriage. I think of the fables that Anisa and I constructed, and the niece she hoped would have her dimples. I think of Surendra saying, only seventeen and already so eager. Waves of revulsion come up my throat, for that eagerness, and for the grasping, grabbing hands of the day before. I almost retch, before I remember to breathe the way Ajji taught me to on long bus journeys, when I was younger and motion sick. It does not pass.

Adil waits. I see his disbelief that grows at my silence, the anger. 'Mira,' he says, 'what the hell is going on?'

No one answers him. He is only nineteen, I think, when he kicks over a table, and Girish uncle comes running in, threatening to call the police. Adil pushes him aside, even as

Ajji tells Girish uncle he will do no such thing, and Vimala aunty attempts some soothing inanity in the melee that ensues. There is some shouting and breaking in the hall after that, and then I see Ajji and Vimala aunty walk Adil to the gate, one on either side. Adil looks up at me when he passes by my window. I turn away, but not before I have seen the anger in his eyes.

At the gate, Ajji goes so far as to pat him on the back. The assurances she murmurs are too soft for me to hear.

I go back to looking at the picture by my side. A woman in blue smiles falsely into the camera, her eyes mocking, and knowing. So many lies, she seems to say, and what fools you are to believe them.

Appa arrives early the next morning. I see Ajji turn Adil away at the gate twice, as Vimala aunty packs. Perhaps Farid uncle or Rehana aunty attempted a visit, and were similarly diverted. It would be Ajji's way, to head off confrontation with politeness. After all these years, she has decided to let me go with Appa, and she will not allow for failure or a change in her plan. I am glad not to face any of them again. I am also angry. With Ajji, and the way she always gets what she wants. My anger at her grows with each passing hour, perhaps because it is an easier companion than guilt.

When I leave with Appa, later, there is a crowd of neighbours gathered in the street and on their doorsteps, ostensibly to say goodbye. Perhaps they stand there to watch for the way I look, days after I kissed a boy on the street and my best friend died for it. Perhaps this will fuel a few sessions of afternoon gossip to much conjecture and moralising, with expressions of sympathy for all the families involved. I cannot summon up the energy to care.

This is where my memory ends. I see myself step out into the street for that very last time. I pull down my sleeves, wishing they were longer, even though they already reach my wrists. My neck, my hands and face, all feel exposed. My eyes are turned to the ground. I do not look up to see the colour of the sky or the streets of my childhood for one last time. I do not scan the faces gathered for the ones I love. There are no hugs of farewell, no good wishes or goodbyes.

17
Girish

The table was set. Girish had spent the day in preparation for the dinner, and Sitara was straightening the flowers one final time when Sadhu Devidas arrived, saffron-clad novice in tow. Girish rushed to receive them at the door. His 'Namaskara, namaskara, please come in,' was almost obsequious in its deference. Devidas acknowledged the welcome with a graceful incline of the head, and Girish was relieved to see no hint of irony.

Devidas was soon ensconced in the comfortable sofa. The novice monk stood just a little behind him, having refused a seat, and together they were an exclamation in bright burnt orange in the pastel drawing room. Girish had barely settled in on the sofa opposite when he saw Sitara's maid, Chellamma, come out of the kitchen. She went straight up to Sadhu Devidas, to stoop down and touch his feet in a marked departure from the thinly veiled insolence that usually marked her interactions with Sitara and her guests.

Of course, Girish realised, Chellamma was a devotee.

Sadhu Devidas's speeches were telecast at a little past five in the morning, and had been for the last five or more years. A few weeks ago, while Surendra was trying to court Devidas, Girish had finally watched one in Sitara's living room, risking leaving after daylight. He had cursed and wondered: was

Devidas so bad that he could not get a later, better spot? Now he realised the genius of the timing, which was perfect for Chellamma and the rest of her kind. They probably woke at four every day, bathed, cleaned and said their prayers before they headed out to work. So this was how Girish had been able to leave comfortably that morning before Chellamma arrived, and Devidas had the piddling two-rupee and five-rupee donations that grew into crores.

In the minute that he saw Chellamma stoop to touch his feet and straighten up as if she had taken a dip in the holy Ganga, Girish finally understood. For the half hour that he had watched that morning, the camera stayed on Devidas's face. His elastic features were in turns beatific, pained, angry or puzzled. His expressions were made so much more arresting by the monochrome saffron that he wore and stillness of the screen behind him. His voice had the cadences of peaks, valleys and meandering soothing rivers that recalled old teachers, forgotten childhood friends or a mother's lullaby, mesmerising Girish, even though he was studying him as a scientist would a specimen under his microscope. It was this ingredient that made the brand, Girish realised, a long-held puzzle now explained. Lots of people had political mentors and the money to gather the gullible into their fold. You could turn a street corner and trip upon a sadhu.

But this was how Devidas alone had followers that grew in numbers every day, who were gathered a little closer daily into the ever-expanding luminous circle of his influence. It was the day labourers, construction workers, maids and drivers. As they waited at bus stops and grumbled about their lives, or the capriciousness of people they worked for, or even about the noise from the mosques calling the faithful to prayer, Devidas's name probably came up. And his fame and his reach spread, insidiously from one to another, like the most contagious of viruses. As Chellamma straightened up, Girish's eyes met Sitara's. Chellamma would have to be given the night off, he telegraphed, and Sitara understood.

The doorbell rang again, and this time it was a more frequent visitor at the door. Surendra had arrived. Their intimate dinner party was complete.

Surendra walked into the room, apologising effusively for being the last one in. The angry streak on his neck had faded some, and the lower part completely obscured by his stiff, high-necked collar. His white Nehru cap was slightly askew, almost rakish in its angle. He walked in past Girish, palms pressed against each other, saying, 'Namaskara, namaskara. Sorry, so sorry to be late.' He was smiling widely, and the combined effect of his looks and good humour was striking. Even Devidas stood up to receive him. He nodded and smiled beatifically at Surendra, who offered up a paean of praises. 'Swami-ji,' he said, as if he thought of Devidas as a holy man, and himself a devotee, 'it is such an honour to have your darshan, like having God Himself come down to our humble abode. You are like Krishna, who comes to assure the victory of the Pandavas. With you on our side, the righteous will win this election.'

'Surendra-*avare*,' Devidas began, and Girish, who had not heard him speak yet this evening, had a sudden vision of a warm gulab jamun that his mother had made for him as a child, a golden-brown honeyed sphere of perfection that he could now suddenly feel on his tongue. He was surprised. Girish had spoken to Devidas many years before, when he was still a small-time hustler in the street and went by his given name, Satyaprakash. His voice was rougher those days, and he lacked the rounded vowels and the baritone he now possessed. He wasn't sure if he ought to be amused or impressed. He turned around and spotted Sitara returning from the kitchen after dispatching Chellamma. She had heard Devidas speak as well, and she looked entranced.

'Surendra-*avare*, you give us too much importance,' Devidas continued, 'with all this talk of support and elections. We just ask the questions for the common man. We do this for God, for Rama rajya, not to be governors or ministers. We don't think it is necessary to support anyone. God will support, God will dispose.' He smiled again, and Girish saw Sitara open her mouth. It was as if she wanted to ask a question that would make the sadhu turn around and address her instead. But Surendra started speaking again, and he saw her close her mouth in disappointment.

'Swamiji, you are very humble, of course. But the truth of the matter is that you are the people's voice. It does not matter if it is you who speak, or they, it is one voice.' Surendra was sitting at the very edge of his seat, grinding into it, and leaning over, as if he could not stress this enough, his fingers pushing forward in emphasis. 'And everybody, all the way to the chief minister, they all acknowledge it. You are a true leader. All that he asks, the CM, is that he has one meeting, no press or anything, just a casual meeting, him and you, like this, at any of your trusted devotee's houses. And then we can discuss the importance of your support with the CM. He will be most grateful.'

'But your CM,' Devidas said, regret dripping off his dulcet tones, 'your chief minister does not show enough respect for the Hindu way or for us. Especially with the way he ignores the true devotees of our Kannada *Mathe*. He seems to think it is more important to keep certain people happy.' And at the mention of those people, the sadhu's voice dipped lower and became more regretful. 'These Hindu-haters, these so-called-journalists and mullahs, who will destroy our dharma, our way of life. Stooges that the British have left behind,

Macaulay-*makkalu*. They have no respect for dharma, the way things should be done. And your CM, every time he stands up with all those people who cheer when our enemies win cricket matches against us, he stands against us. And now he wants our help? Because there is an election coming?'

Surendra seemed to be formulating a response when Sitara cleared her throat and asked, 'Swamiji, would you like some tea?'

Surendra turned to Sitara in irritation. They all saw for just a minute the good humour slip, and clear fury in his eyes. Even as Sitara took a step back in surprise, the novice priest stepped forward. 'Guru-*devru* does not eat or drink anything that is cooked or served by women.'

'Unless, of course, it is cooked with devotion. In rare occasions, exceptions may be made,' Devidas interjected, turning his smile towards Sitara. 'Even Lord Rama ate fruit from Shabari's hands.'

'Yes, yes. Sitara is a great devotee of yours, she wakes up every morning to hear your discourses,' Girish rushed in, telegraphing a do-not-speak to Sitara.

But Devidas still shook his head, regretfully, making preparations to stand up. Evidently, his message was delivered, and Sitara had given him the perfect cue for an exit. Surendra's eyes narrowed on Sitara, and there was a brief flash of fury or menace that flitted again across his face. This time she did not notice.

Girish tried again. 'Perhaps this young sadhu here can serve you, all this food that she has made with such devotion, with her own hands.' Some of that was true, because the food had been cooked by Chellamma, earlier in the day.

'Maybe some other time,' Sadhu Devidas said, standing up.

Everyone stood. Surendra turned jolly again, smiling and scraping. 'Of course, of course, you know best. We are your servants, your devotees, of course.'

Devidas and the novice monk made their way to the door. Almost as an afterthought, at the door, Sadhu Devidas turned around and said to Surendra, 'Your CM is lucky to have people like you. Though he seems to have some foolish ideas about everything else. Perhaps we can meet again, at this young sister's house,' he beamed at Sitara, 'and we can talk about how our humble services may be of use to you, if not your CM.'

And then they were gone. As soon as the door closed behind them, Girish said, 'He's just playing with us. He'll sign on eventually. He just wants more.'

'Yes, of course, the great Girish Murthy knows best, son of the great freedom fighter, Srinivas Murthy. A great man from such a good family.' Surendra laughed, and it sounded almost genuine. 'Only none of the men in your family can control their women, can they? So full of ideas.' He laughed louder. 'We might have been able to get him in the bag today, and I would have had the deputy CM post next month. But no, your maharani had to offer him tea. She just had to insert herself between us.'

'I'm sorry, Surendra-*avare*,' Sitara began, missing the warning glance that Girish threw in her direction.

Surendra would not look at her. But he swung a wild arm in her direction that connected with her face and snapped her head back, sending her sprawling to the floor on her back. Even when the breath left her mouth—*whoosh*—as she fell, head just missing the edge of her teak coffee table, the sound of her fall only partly muffled by her chiffon saree, he gave no indication that he had even heard her.

'I can discipline her,' Girish said to Surendra. Without turning to Sitara, much less offering a hand up, he said, 'Just go inside, now, without a word. Not a word.'

Idiot of a woman, he should have asked her to leave with Chellamma.

She got up and ran to her bedroom.

Girish pulled out his cell phone and called Vinay. They would need someone to serve them dinner, and he would need to salvage Surendra's good humour. He cursed in his head. If the bitch had just kept her mouth shut, it would have all been fine.

When Vinay arrived, he began pouring out glasses of Black Label and ladling mutton biryani onto plates, while Girish and Surendra sat at the carefully set table with the flowers in the centre. Surendra chewed loudly on his chicken 65, fine spittle intermittently escaping his lips. His fingers groped the biryani on his plate, discarding rice for meat that he gathered piece upon piece. Girish, a fastidious eater in comparison, sat by him in silence. He looked up only to signal Vinay to refill Surendra's glass.

'Tell me, Vinay,' Surendra said suddenly, with a loud laugh. 'Did you know your girlfriend is coming back?'

Vinay paused, mid pour.

'Yes, yes, your childhood sweetheart,' Surendra again, between chews.

'What is her name, now,' Surendra paused dramatically, chewing still. 'Mira?' And then he laughed again, loudly and alone.

'Tell me, tell me,' he said, 'did you know or not?'

'No, he did not know,' Girish said. 'Vinay, go down, we can serve ourselves.'

'Oh, don't tell him to go now,' Surendra said. 'We are just starting to talk, man to man.'

'Surendra-*avare*, I am very sorry about what happened today,' Girish said, as a panic built in his chest. Surendra could not be taking this tack, it was not reasonable punishment. 'You are upset. It is late, better to let him go down.'

Surendra continued to eat as if Girish had not spoken. Vinay paused, awaiting the verdict: stay, or leave?

'She looked just like her mother, you know, when she left.' Surendra said. 'But she was only a girl then, she must be a woman now.' He smacked his lips around the mutton. 'Her mother... now, she was a beautiful woman, so beautiful.'

'Surendra-*avare, tappaithu, dodd-manasu maadi.* Let us not go into the old stories now, you may say something you regret.' As he spoke, Girish realised to his dismay that his desperation was showing. His voice sounded high and thin even to his own ears.

After a minute's pause, Surendra laughed again. 'Okay, send the boy home.'

Vinay rushed to the door. Girish did not blame him, he would have run too. When drivers heard things they were not meant to hear, there were not many options. Jail for a robbery no one committed, if they were lucky. Turning up in a ditch somewhere, cold and rat-nibbled, if they were not.

The door closed behind Vinay.

Surendra licked his fingers. 'You know, Girish, you were nothing. A good-for-nothing wastrel, who would still be roaming the streets of Malehalli, playing cards and drinking cheap liquor.'

'*Tappaithu*,' Girish said, weary. He knew the drill as well as Vinay did. He would apologise, no matter how many times it took.

But Surendra was not finished. 'No prospects, no job, intermediate failed. Now people recognise you on the street. All this money you get under the table every time you approve a project, that's what you live on. You, your mother, that good-for-nothing wife of yours, and now this piece on the side.'

At the mention of Sitara, his voice rose again, 'And you forget, all this that you have, I gave you! Me, Surendra. I lifted you from the gutters and brought you here. And now you raise your voice to me over some bitch in heat?'

'Sorry, sorry, I spoke out of concern, not in anger. I would never raise my voice to you,' Girish said, and then, again, '*Tappaithu. Dodd manasu maadi.*'

'Call the bitch out,' Surendra shouted. 'Call her out right now.'

Girish went to the bedroom door. She probably had the door locked, if she had a grain of sense.

'Sitara, come out.'

He heard her move a chair up against the door, trying to be as quiet as she could.

He knocked again.

Surendra walked over himself to bang on the door.

'Come out, come out.'

Girish said to Surendra, 'She takes sleeping pills, she must be asleep already. The neighbours will wake up.'

'Hunh,' Surendra snorted, 'sleeping pills, asleep—trying to tell me tales, now?' But his hands came down softer on the door. The election was only weeks away. Girish knew his constant and only fear. Who knew which good-for-nothing journalist lived close by?

He used the momentary change in Surendra's mood to say, 'They have new girls at Mallige, I'll call them now.'

'Beat her, when you see her. She can't sleep forever.' Surendra stepped away from the door. 'You have to have a strong hand, or they will sit on your head. Weak, weak, that's why she takes advantage of you. Ask my driver to bring the car.'

After Surendra left, Girish exhaled as if it was a breath he had held for hours. The drawing room with its silly pastel colours annoyed him as it never had before. Women, he thought, each is more trouble than the other. But he had mollified Surendra. Tomorrow he would remember that Girish was his trusted confidante, the one who always set things right. All would be well. The evening was still young, and his.

Girish called Vinay to bring his car around. Then it suddenly occurred to him—he had not given Vinay the night off as he'd promised. And the boy had not reminded him, either. Maybe he would have to ask Sitara to arrange a meeting with Vivek Nayak for Vinay. He could do that. Even Vivek Nayak with his garlanded billboards and the teenage heroines would have to agree, because he was Girish Murthy. He waited for the updraft of joy at that idea, but it did not arrive. The unpleasantness with Surendra lingered, and Girish knew he would not escape it even as he rushed downstairs and away from the pastel drawing room.

18

Mira

How did I get to be different from the girl who left? The answer lies somewhere in the years after Celia gathers me into her arms when I arrive in San Francisco, in a jangle of bangles and blur of long, tie-dyed skirt.

'There, there,' she says. 'You are home with us now, and everything will be fine.'

Instead, I have night time terrors of melting walls and raining ash. Days pass in fugue.

Appa and Celia are professors in a small university town. Their home is alive with laughter and students that drop in unannounced. It is as different from the squat house in Bangalore as it is possible to be. Ajji and Appa think this is for the best. Easier to forget, I hear them say to each other on the phone. I float unmoored; nothing is forgotten.

When the school year begins, I go to the neighbourhood school. The transition is easier than expected in some ways. The lessons and work are a welcome relief from my thoughts and the phantom limb pain of Anisa that persists. But there are memories of grasping hands and tearing cloth that come upon me in the most unexpected instances. I'm uncomfortable with being touched, and shrink from scrutiny or even eye contact. People murmur behind my back, and it is mostly kind. Is it a language problem, they wonder, or perhaps something cultural? Maybe she's just shy. The high schoolers around me seem as real as actors in an American movie once watched on Brigade Road, and their lives and interests flow around me unacknowledged. After a few weeks, no one gives me a second glance.

Celia insists on therapy. We go to one counsellor after another, all expensive, and highly recommended. We speak the same language to each other, but it is as if we mean completely different things. The kiss, the mob, Adil. The Hands. Anisa. The Fire. There are words I can use to describe all that happened, but all feel inadequate, small and quaint. How can I explain Ajji, and the guilt that is more real and earned than the 'survivor's guilt' that they murmur, soothing and deceiving, into my ears? There are stories I have grown up with, an entire culture coded into right and wrong, virtue and sin. A life lived in Malleshwaram with its narrow streets and open-hearted neighbours. In their bright, hermetically clean offices so distant from it all, it feels exhausting even to begin to describe. In the end, I find myself unable to speak very much, about anything at all. I nod at everything I am told, and walk away unchanged. I am not what they would call a good patient.

After a while, I refuse to go. In the meantime, letters arrive from Bangalore, sometimes in Rehana aunty's graceful hand, sometimes in Farid's uncle's square lettering, and reduce me to a quivering mess before I open them. Celia takes to hiding them unopened. None arrive in the hand that once wrote me poems.

Celia talks to friends from India, finds ashrams and talks given by visiting monks. Perhaps something more culturally appropriate, I hear her tell Appa. But after the first leaves me shaking in the car at the parade of saffron visible just beyond, she understands it will not work. These people are old and respected, she tells me, finally and fully defeated. I have no doubt that they are. Perhaps they bear no kinship or commonality with the thugs who appropriated their colour. I still cannot leave the car. It is after we've returned from that drive of a hundred miles each way, that I have the disastrous conversation with Appa about my mother. It leaves me convinced that there is something unsavoury there, that I am lucky not to know. I hide her picture away in a drawer rarely opened.

Then Celia finds Soldier. He arrives like a little tornado, and asks me no questions. Perhaps it is in remembering to walk and feed him, that I slowly find purpose. I do not have to be worthy, or virtuous. All I have to do is know that it is time to find the bowl, or stand at the door with the leash. In time, he makes me smile. I begin to volunteer at the local shelter for abused women and a senior citizen's home. Simple tasks, I ask of them, just ones that someone needs to show up consistently for. Not too much interaction with the residents. But despite my best efforts to live in penance or punishment, life slowly finds me again.

I am in college when I begin to make friends. There are people I meet at classes or the places I volunteer at. I begin to see that people will smile and probe no further than my name, which they will call pretty, or interesting. It means clear like glass in Spanish, one of them tells me. So I know then that I am as ironically named as Soldier, and it makes me want to smile. At the shelter, I talk sometimes to women whose stories I sense are darker and more terrible. We never exchange experiences. But it allows me, in some strange and paradoxical way, to revisit the past in my own mind, in ways I couldn't before. It allows a possibility that perhaps my demons are human-sized, and within the realm of things that are conceivable, even if they are not ordinary.

There are milestones. There is a girl whose dimples remind me of Anisa, and I am able to look her in the eye. I begin to work after school, and begin to pay my own way, at least in part. I learn to drive. With that delayed American rite of passage comes more independence and responsibility. Soon, I graduate from the university where Celia and my father teach. I am admitted into a post-graduate course there, and find an apartment to share only two streets away from the home that he and Celia own. And then, a job at a laboratory one of my professors runs. It is a life circumscribed by a hesitation to move too far out. I have travelled halfway across the world, but this feels just about far enough.

I accumulate potted plants and watch them grow with the devotion Ajji had for tulsi in our courtyard. Soldier waits impatiently for me to get home every day, and as we walk together in the evenings, children ask, daily and reliably, to pet him. I begin to go out with friends. I am a dependable and sympathetic ear, and an even better designated driver. My days become peopled, cheerful even. Though none of my friends could ever be Anisa, my sister more than friend, I see her sometimes in their laughter. In a curve of cheek suddenly glimpsed, or a child's eyes that come alive in sudden mischief. I can think about her with only love, and heart-stopping regret.

Celia's sister and nieces visit off and on. On one of those occasions, I see Celia's wistfulness when she remarks on her niece's shade of eyeshadow, which matches exactly the tint of her lipstick—both are things that I have never worn. I find myself wandering into a hair salon one afternoon, intending to get my hair cut. I emerge in a cloud of curls that seems to lift my shoulders and my spirits. I tell myself I look nothing like my mother, and that I do not care what her story might have been. But there are days and evenings when I am alone, that I do wonder.

After years of silence, I begin to talk to Ajji on the phone. Our conversations are never about the things that happened. I am still angry with Ajji, though I cannot explain why that must be so. She pretends not to notice, quizzing me about the things I eat and the friends I make. It is as if she believes I am still somehow under her care. She tells me details of her fasts and prayers. We do not talk about her loneliness, or other people I have left behind. I do not ask Celia for the unopened letters, or even if any new ones have arrived.

More years pass. Ajji drops hints about marriage, and goes so far as to suggest I meet the suitable sons of her friends or acquaintances with some regularity. It makes me angrier with her than might be warranted. Weeks later, I meet a tall and courtly man with burnished chocolate skin. His laugh is gentle as soft rain. Perhaps it's Ajji, or just the passage of healing time. I lift my eyes to his obvious admiration, and think, yes, lunch, why not? Then the phone call arrives.

And here. The end of the gruelling journey is upon us. Bangalore's lights glimmer in the distance; its roads are jewel-edged ribbons of tar. Appa wakes up at the pilot's announcement of descent, and together we watch it come up to meet us, this place we once and still call home.

19

Ajji

I had hoped for a grandchild for years. Vimala, the daughter in law I had brought home under the right stars and after all the right prayers, remained stubbornly barren, despite the fasts that we both kept every ekadashi and every chaturthi. Yet, instead of joy, it was distaste, I have to admit, that began to grow in my belly.

Yes, the idea of you who I love beyond everything now, left me with the bitterness of neem flowers in my mouth that day. It must have shown in my face. Her own face fell, and I realised that she had told no one else yet. I tried to make amends, but she had already turned away. When I saw her later that day, she affected a haughtiness that I had not seen before. It was then that our fights began in earnest, and in the open.

She began to challenge my authority, subtly at first, then openly. She insisted on going into the kitchen. She had learnt the ways of madi from Vimala, and I could not object on those grounds, because she followed the rules to the letter. The only way I could object was to call her unclean even if she were bathed and attired according to the rules. But that would have made Kishore angry. It would have made him passionately angry to have his goddess, and now the mother of his child, so insulted. He would have turned away from me forever. Perhaps that was what she wanted. So, I faulted her cutting of the vegetables, the seasoning of the huli she had helped make, or the way she washed the dishes. Insignificant things, but small persistent complaints that allowed her notice of my displeasure. There was nothing that she could cook that I would eat, finding some excuse or the other to not touch what she had made.

It made the menfolk restive, both Kishore and Girish, as men often are when they are caught in women's fights, threatened by waters whose depths they cannot plumb. Girish tried to distance himself by coming home later than usual. It was clear to me that he now spent almost all of his time with Surendra, but there seemed to be less card-playing and alcohol, so I counted it an improvement. Vimala, for her part, traitor that she turned out to be in those days, supported your mother. I wondered at Vimala—she was the older daughter-in-law, the one who should have been pregnant first. Had I been in her situation, I would have experienced at least a little resentment. But Vimala became almost maternal in her concern for Radhika. Both of them thought that I was not aware that she whispered solace to your mother in corners, but I was. It made me angrier, and more petty.

I ignored her growing abdomen as the weeks fattened into months, never enquiring once the way I had with even the neighbours' daughters, if there was any special craving she had or a wish that we could fulfil. It was as if I could wish it away, if I avoided every reference to it in passing conversation. Eventually, even Kishore could not pretend to not notice my displeasure. Instead of coming up to me to ask me what the matter was, as he should have done, he took to staying late at the college. They would both come home late at night and disappear into the bedroom after a rushed dinner. If Kishore had come up to me, maybe I would have shouted at him, said my hurtful words, and gotten it behind me. Maybe we would have all gone back to being some semblance of a normal family.

Instead, he avoided me, and it made me angrier, that she sought to take my son away from me like this. She probably complains to him about me, I thought, telling him half-truths and exaggerations. In my better moments, I hoped that she had a place to rest in the college if she had to come home this late in the evening, with her advancing pregnancy. But I have to admit those moments were few and far between, as angry and confused as I was with the way events had gotten the better of me.

Gowramma came to visit again. I thought that perhaps she sensed the opportunity for more gossip in the strife in our household. But the joke was on her. Her halfwit son (I blamed him still for being the one that brought this affair to light) had gone and joined the students' union. His closest friend, a first-year named Sudhir, was one of the student leaders. They were both students of my daughter-in-law, she said. It stumped me for a minute, Vimala had students?

'Oh, her,' I said, realisation dawning about who else would be considered my daughter-in-law. 'The students' union. At the college. It is pretty harmless, you worry too much.' My mind was already on other things. The evening paper that Girish had brought home had a lurid headline.

'It is this boy, Sudhir,' she persevered. 'My Gopal would not be involved in this by himself. It is all because of this boy.'

'Yes,' I agreed, since I could not seem to be rid of her. 'You think you know your children, and then they go to college and do all the things you never think that they could.'

She was too distracted to notice that I gave her an opening to inquire into my troubles with your mother. It was almost as if she had forgotten the glee with which she had announced her advent into our lives. It must be easier to ignore if it is not your son who brings home the unsuitable girl, I thought, turning over the page of the newspaper. Why didn't she leave if she did not even want to gossip?

Gowramma was waiting for your parents to come home, as it turned out. She jumped up as soon as she saw them at the door. She unknotted a small bundle from the end of her saree as they approached. 'Kadle burfi,' she said, handing the package to your mother. 'My daughter asked for these all through her pregnancy.'

The way your parents reacted, those sticky, sweet peanut squares might have been gold. Your mother would have cried, I think, had she not been aware that I was looking. Still, she bowed and bobbed, thank you, thank you. Even Kishore had a tear in his eye. I stamped hard on the guilt that I began to feel; had I been so harsh that even this small gesture of kindness appeared so magnified?

But Gowramma had an agenda too, that your parents in their overwhelming gratitude did not realise. She wanted your mother to talk to Sudhir, her son's friend, who appeared to be a firebrand in the students' union.

'I would have gone to his parents,' she said, 'but they are not in Malehalli, he is from out of town. Could you take him aside after class next week, and tell him to at least not encourage the other students to neglect their studies?'

When she left, your mother had assured her that she would speak to Sudhir. I grudgingly made your mother some milk with saffron that night, the way my mother-in-law had before Girish's birth. 'So your child will be fair,' I said without thinking, just the way my mother-in-law had, and she looked as if I had slapped her. Of course she left the milk undrunk, and I went to bed cursing myself for having unbent to this arrogant woman. She was dark, we all knew that. So I was not supposed to say the obvious to her face? So the maharani would not be insulted?

I will not bore you with the details, Mira, of all our sniping and disagreements. Suffice to say that by the time she left for the hospital in labour in a taxi that your father hired at great expense, we were no longer on talking terms. I spent more time in resentment about the way he threw his money around as if she were some queen, than I did contemplating the joy that would soon arrive in the world.

Your mother arrived home from the hospital with you in her arms. I had not gone to see her at the hospital, though they kept her there five days. She had bled after you were born, they told me. As if bleeding is something so extraordinary in a woman, I snorted when I heard; I am sure I will see them both in good time. She stood at the door with you in her arms and Kishore by her side, her face a mixture of joy, tiredness and yes, apprehension. Vimala swung the plate with red water three times around you all to ward off the evil eye, before your mother stepped across the threshold with her right foot first. I tried to remember if we had welcomed her thus after the wedding. We had not. I had not wanted to, and Vimala had been too timid at the time to go against my wishes. But now Vimala circumvented my approval by not asking me about it beforehand, and pretending that I would have approved if she had asked. I found another reason to blame your mother, and it was for Vimala's new and growing disobedience.

I expected your mother to come to me where I was sitting, in front of the pooja room, stoop to touch my feet, and show me your face. I was, after all, an older woman, the eldest in the house, and her husband's mother, no less. Had I been in her place, that is what I would have done. She stood undecided in the centre of the hall in front of me, for a minute. Then, as if she saw something in my face, and had come to a decision, she turned and walked to the bedroom as if I had no right to expect her respects. Kishore had been just a little behind her, as she crossed the threshold, and he stood in the centre of the hall in her wake, looking, for once, completely surprised by his wife. I watched the struggle on his face, go to his wife or his mother? I would have been amused, had I not been so insulted.

Girish came to Kishore's rescue as he stood there in the hall, saying, 'We should go to the shop in town, it is too hot for the baby without a fan in the house.'

Vimala disappeared into the kitchen. For the next hour, until my sons returned, your mother and I stayed in our territories in our own silent war. Kishore brought you to me when he came home, a pathetic attempt to cover for his wife. I had not heard raised voices, or an argument over her conduct. What his silence condoned, I would not make right, I decided, turning my face away without a word, ignoring the silent bundle in his arms. I never did see your face that day. It would be weeks later, and in a completely changed world, when I first set eyes on you.

Your mother was on her maternity leave, of course, and could not leave the house. She spent all her time in the bedroom. Vimala spoilt her so far as to take her meals in there, and to do her washing, as if she were her maid. 'She has no mother, Amma,' Vimala said to me once, gentling her tone so I would not take offence. 'We are all she has.'

I would hear your mother cooing to you, or singing or talking to you, as if you were already an adult and could understand every word she said. They were remarkable one-sided conversations, and she would seek your opinion on everything, from your father's choice of shirt, to whether the rains would come that year. If we had a guest, and they heard this through the thin walls, they would be charmed into laughter, so fantastical were the responses she imagined from you. I steeled my will, and ground my curiosity into the dust. I would not lower myself, and go to her to see the baby. It was my right to expect her to bring my granddaughter to me.

In the evenings, with the novelty of a new baby in the house, Kishore and Girish would both come home early, and the four adults would coo over you, and take turns holding you. They would exclaim over imagined smiles and preferences that you had before they had any reasonable chance of being true. 'This is the most intelligent baby I have ever seen,' Girish would say, after he thought that you looked towards your uncle or aunt if their names were mentioned. 'There cannot be another baby that does this at three months.'

After many years, Girish's resentment at his younger brother's success seemed to be fading, and I heard genuine joy in his voice as he exclaimed over you. They all laughed in the hall over some antic or expression, and I felt utterly alone. I meant to exclude and shame your mother for her disrespect, but I slowly began to see that it was I who was being excluded, from my sons and my home.

During the day, if you were awake, I would hear her talking. The only silence was when you slept. So even though I did not see you, I was aware of your wakings, and your sleep, even your struggles with being nursed. Every time you cried, and the two inexperienced women, your mother and your aunt Vimala, struggled to calm you, I noticed as well. What foolishness, I thought to myself, for her to be so proud when she needed help. Was it such a humiliation for her to come to me?

One evening, when you were about three months old, your father arrived early from work, suppressed excitement in every step. I could see him climbing up the hill from my vantage point at the door, and I knew from the way he bounded up the hill. When he got to the door, his expression confirmed my initial impression. He said nothing to me, however, disappearing into his room to his wife. Such are the rewards of motherhood, Mira.

When I heard the news after she had been told, it was that he had been awarded a four-month scholarship to go to a university in America, a country whose name I had heard only once or twice in my life thus far. It was an honour beyond our imaginings. Even Girish looked genuinely happy for his brother.

I could hear your parents talking that night. I am not ashamed to say it. The walls of the house were thin, and I could not have avoided it if I tried.

'How can I leave you?' he said, over and over, my son. As if he had ever truly considered not going. I knew him better than he knew himself. Nothing would have stopped him. He says this so many times, as if he were leaving her behind to an army of ogres, I thought to myself, or maybe it is just me that he considers equal to the band of ogres. She convinced him to go that night, and by morning all was decided.

I wondered if it would be difficult to get his papers with the Emergency. It turned out to be the opposite. The government clerks who used to come to work at ten, and then take hourly breaks, came early to work, and Kishore had all the documents he needed the day he asked for them, without the need of a bribe. After all the strikes and dharnas, and a huge strike where all the trains ground to a halt the year before, things were quieter and smoother. Girish once even gloated that the trains ran on time. Maybe it takes a woman to make this country right, I thought to myself then; this Emergency works better than her father's democracy.

Kishore left Malehalli by train with Girish, who would see him off at the airport in Madras. It struck me then, how little had changed between the brothers despite all the upheavals in our home. Even though their jobs were different as could be, and Kishore more educated than his elder brother, he still deferred to him as he did when they were both in school. Even though my younger son was a grown man with a child of his own, he accepted that his elder brother would go with him to look out for him, ease his way as he was able. And before he left, just after he touched my feet and took my blessings, Kishore stopped by Vimala, saying, 'Take care of Radhika,' and then he was gone.

20

Vimala

Radhika, Vimala thought, was the whirlwind they were all caught up in. Radhika and Ajji had orbited separate paths under the same roof, and the rest of them had been drawn to Radhika, helpless against her youth and charisma. There was so much, she realised now, that Ajji had not known.

Vimala had watched Radhika come into the house that first time with Kishore as Ajji had, and stayed to celebrate with the happy couple at the reception long after Ajji left. It was Vimala who had consoled Radhika when Ajji left the reception in a huff. They were both young women, and newly wed. Both in love with their young husbands. There had been the drama of Radhika and Kishore's courtship and marriage that had captured Vimala's heart, of course. But more, Radhika had arrived unschooled in Ajji's ways, needing surreptitious instruction and covert support. Vimala had found it irresistible. No one had looked up to her before.

Even before the wedding, Radhika had sewed for Vimala, on occasion, blouses in the latest fashion. Now she daily tweaked the pleating and drape of Vimala's sarees. She stepped back to admire, and then adjust. Vimala could not recall a single instance in her old life, or the new one, where she had been the centre of such attention. So they huddled in corners and talked recipes with genuine pleasure, sometimes sharing naughty jokes in whispers so no one would overhear. They discovered the old Wren & Martin that their father-in-law had used to teach Ajji before their husbands were born. They read his notes in the side-lines. They were little markers of progress. *M now able to write a letter excusing herself for sickness, read one, and another: need to test parts of speech tomorrow.* They tried and failed to imagine Ajji as a young and happy student, one who would take rather than give instruction. They giggled. It all felt like the give and take of sisters.

A few short months into the marriage, Radhika suspected that she was pregnant. She told Vimala, right after she told Kishore. It was the first bittersweet moment that Vimala had in their months-long interaction, and one she recalled in sharp clarity all these years hence. Radhika's announcement, even so doubtful and diffident, had made Vimala wish suddenly and concretely for one of her own. That was Vimala's secret, that unspoken wish. That they could grow big with child together, like sisters should. She dreamt open-eyed that they would tell their mother-in-law together, give birth alongside one another, and that their children would grow up together—playmates and siblings more than cousins. It was the weight of that daydream that impelled Vimala to lean in towards Radhika, and whisper, 'Wait until you're sure to tell her. Give it just a bit more time.'

Vimala, for reasons she did not explore, failed to whisper the development into Girish's ears as they lay in bed that night. Girish was preoccupied besides, with troubles of his own. The strikes and demonstrations against the prime minister had multiplied. People railed against corruption. Farmers, student leaders, union workers—no one seemed immune. It seemed as if everything had changed in the months after the train workers went on strike. The trains stopped as did all commerce and industry for the time. Finally, the strike broke and thousands were jailed in the aftermath.

But instead of resolution, it seemed to have set off incessant carping about the woman in charge. Here they were, months after, and the papers were still full of it. They all seemed out for her blood, and that of the party that Girish and his mentor Surendra were part of. It wasn't the cacophony in the papers or the physical unrest around them that bothered Girish as much as the realisation that they may have picked the losing side.

Weeks passed. Girish tossed and grumbled. Radhika was now well over the three-month mark. Vimala had watched the rhythms of her own body with such attention for the time, and now had to concede that at least one part of her dream would be postponed. And so it was that Radhika went up to tell Ajji about her pregnancy right around the time the unrest around them boiled over, and Indira Gandhi suspended their democracy with a 2 a.m. stroke of the president's pen.

Girish came home that evening, quietly exultant. All of the Oppostition had been jailed, in Bangalore no less, where they had come together the day before to demand the prime minister's resignation in a rally. He had waved the newspaper in Vimala's face. 'See, all that shouting they did? This had to happen. Fools.' It was the last newspaper he would wave so triumphantly. Because after that, for Girish, happy news became a matter of course. This would also be the last newspaper that arrived unscathed. From this day on, newspapers would arrive with empty white pages of dissent, or black bars of censored text around news that was considered safe, and sanctioned by those that knew better. For twenty-one months.

That evening, Vimala told him about Radhika's pregnancy as well, finally, just before the evening meal. She expected some bitterness. Perhaps some shadow of the days when his and Kishore's exam results arrived. But Girish was expansive in his happiness instead, patting his brother on the back and asking why no one had thought to make a sweet to mark the occasion. Kishore looked abashed and proud, all at once. Ajji sulked just a bit at the bonhomie, and Radhika's smile grew more luminous regardless. Perhaps it was the depth of change that Radhika's news wrought in their household, or the beginnings of unacknowledged disappointment that did it. Vimala let go of her pride that night, and asked Girish if they could walk together in the village in the evenings as they once did. And for once Girish agreed, as if he were king of the world and agreeing to her request was just another demonstration of his magnanimity.

It was on those walks that Vimala discovered the things that Ajji did not yet know. There were the walks that took them past the town centre, where a statue of her father-in-law stood, and Girish's party office. Where she saw the first billboards appear that were all white and bordered in brown: Work More, Talk Less. Or Rumourmongers are Enemies of the Nation. Exhortations against gossip, when it seemed that all of Malehalli talked in whispers and huddled at street corners. When the rumours reached Vimala in circuitous ways, they were of a government run amok. That there were sterilisations of people in droves. Even young and unmarried men swept up into quotas for vasectomies. Reports of shooting at slums and settlements, so the areas could be cleared. Fawning judges, who wrote judgements calling their prime minister a Mother, a Goddess. There was no right to protest, no right to life even, outside of her merciful gaze. All were stories so fantastic, and from so far away, that she dismissed them as unworthy of serious consideration.

But what she did see was that in that town centre and under those giant billboards where people had shouted and raised flags before, there was now silence. In that already quiet space, people fell silent when they passed. Middle-aged men who would have ignored them before stopped to enquire about Girish's health and hers, with a solicitousness that was almost obsequious. There was the sense of a changed and wary world that had just begun to look upon her husband with respect. The pride of it made her spine just a bit straighter when it happened. It was also clear that if Girish had risen in the world, there were multitudes that had fallen. The offices of the godless communist party were as deserted as those of their saffron adversaries. The people who had rallied behind a Gandhian in protest, now nowhere to be found. 'All in jail,' Girish had scoffed, 'or hiding like rats somewhere.'

One evening, they walked a path rarely trodden. It was down the narrow, unpaved furrow between arecanut groves to where the sea surged up daily into a thousand rainbows. It was here that Girish had once laid his aspirations at her feet. The memory of that evening had made Girish and Vimala smile and murmur to each other as they walked down the path that seemed deserted as always. Except that it was not. And instead of a couple newly-wed or in illicit courtship that they might have surprised, it was a small band of young men, deep in low-voiced conversation. They looked no less guilty, however, at the interruption.

Vimala recognised their neighbour's son, Gopal. They had made a joke about him only minutes before, about how Ajji still bore him a grudge for what she saw as his role in Kishore's marriage. She did not recognise the other boys. Evidently Girish did. He stepped up in front of a taller and fair-skinned boy by Gopal's side.

'And what are you college boys doing here so far from the campus?' Girish asked, and though his tone was pleasant, the greeting she'd intended a second before died on Vimala's lips.

'Nothing,' the boy said, looking down at Girish who stood a head less tall, and the other boys drew breath at his tone. There was no sir, or even Anna, to soften the terseness of his reply, and he stood loose-limbed and arms akimbo, as if this were none of Girish's business.

Gopal stepped up. 'Just taking a walk, Anna, to break the exam tension.'

Girish ignored him. 'We heard about your speech,' he said to the boy he first addressed. 'All those fancy words, but even men like me can understand.'

Gopal paled. Everyone stood frozen for a moment. The boy said nothing.

Then the boys murmured apologies under their breath, stepping around them to leave. Except for the boy Girish had challenged. Vimala noticed Gopal tug on his arm, then half-drag him as the rest of them left. It might have only taken a minute. But the lightness of Girish's mood was gone. They made their way down to the rock, and he fumed in some private anger. 'Bloody naxalite,' he muttered to Vimala, and her puzzled look. 'Did you see how insolent he was?'

It set her back, that word. Naxalite. The papers were full of the naxalite threat. Of the bombs they intended to make, the lives they could take. The need to report, if one suspected a neighbour or friend had those sympathies. But surely not these boys? Not Gopal, the shy boy she had first met weeks into her marriage when he had come asking to borrow sugar for his mother?

'Didn't you see the way he acted?' Girish asked, as if that was not proof enough. And there was more. The taller boy, Gopal's friend, was Sudhir. He came from outside Malehalli, from Kerala. Everyone knew they were all communist sympathisers in those parts. He had made a speech in the college quadrangle the previous evening. There was a play staged, a satirical take on politics, the week before, that he had written and organised. The prime minister had been lampooned, though she was never mentioned by name. 'He never says it clearly, so we can take care of him,' Girish fumed, 'but everyone understands what he says. Bloody naxalite.'

'Maybe they're just college boys,' Vimala said. 'I've heard they make jokes about everything.'

'You don't understand, do you?' Girish had said, turning almost fond in the opportunity to explain. 'That is where the real danger lies. You underestimate the youth, and you lose every time. Look at us,' he paused. 'The youth Congress, I mean. We are the country's hope. We are the people in charge. Even our chief minister, now only in name. He answers to us.'

They had made it all the way down to the shore, and they paused a minute at the rocky edge. Sea spray rose up all around them in welcome. Rainbows danced. The altercation receded. They stretched their arms out into the shimmer of rainbows and fine mist and laughed like children. Girish turned happy again. 'Tell Gowramma to check on her son, and the company he keeps,' he told Vimala when they had made their way back to the house, where Ajji waited with dinner.

That evening, Radhika looked drawn and tired. Vimala felt a pang at the way her cheeks had hollowed instead of filled out. Her belly was well and truly showing now. Just for a moment, Vimala felt guilt. Was it the fear of Ajji's displeasure or her own disappointment that had caused her to draw away from Radhika these past weeks? She gave Radhika's arm a squeeze as she passed, carrying the tambli Ajji had made into the hall to serve. Tomorrow, Vimala promised herself, she would make a tamarind chutney that she knew Radhika would enjoy. And in the short space of that time and the moment of that regret, she forgot all about Gopal, that strange boy Sudhir and their antics at the college, and the need to warn Gopal's mother.

She was not surprised, however, when Gowramma made her way to the house the week after with kadle burfi for Radhika. But it did give her a pang of remorse for the things she had failed to do: warn Gowramma, and make the tamarind chutney for Radhika as she had intended.

Months crept by. Newspapers grew more soothing, while people turned to the radio and uncensored news from outside the country, which were anything but. Radhika began to spend more time at the college, working late to escape Ajji's moods. But Vimala and Radhika finally sat together outside in the veranda one evening, cleaning rice while the menfolk were gone on errands, and Ajji to the temple.

Radhika told her that she talked to the boys—Gopal, Sudhir even. On many occasions. But there had been another play that they staged the night before, in the hostel foreground and after dark. One of the students had complained, and there had been trouble. The principal had called them in. But at least the authorities had not been called in, for now anyway.

'They are just boys,' Vimala said to Radhika, as she had to Girish.

And Radhika had disagreed, as Girish had, her eyes flashing in the dusk. 'Yes, but they are also talking about important things.'

'I feel bad to tell them to hold back,' Radhika had gone on to confess in the half-light. 'It is not as if they are doing anything wrong. Even in Bangalore, right under the noses of the government, there are people staging street plays, asking questions.'

'But that's dangerous, Radhika,' Vimala was surprised into saying. The long walks with Girish guided her view of the world. The government was right, wasn't that what everyone said? If you didn't say that, well, that was just asking for trouble. Especially in these times.

'Yes, you are right, Akka,' Radhika had said, reaching over for Vimala's hand. 'Kishore says that too. He wants them to stop the politics on campus. He's worried about Gopal, and he thinks they will listen to me. Gowramma asks me every time she sees me, as if her son is my responsibility now. I just want to make sure they are not mixed up in something worse, like all this naxalite business. But giving a speech here and there, or a play even, they are not such bad things. Are they?'

Only speech-giving and acting, Vimala had wondered. As if it were truly such a small thing. She remembered how angry Girish had been when they came upon that little group. It was something she had not thought of for so long, but suddenly it filled her with anxiety. For the foolish boys, and for Radhika, who for all her education seemed unable to see what Vimala so clearly could. Where was there room for confusion, or doubt? You had to be safe. That was the most important thing. But she could not find the words for that ill-stated anxiety, and so she turned away from Radhika to the small pile of rice in front of them.

It soon got too dark for them to pretend to be able to see the stones in the rice, and they made their way indoors before the rest of the family arrived. The week after, Radhika had left for the hospital in a taxi that had made its way carefully and slowly up the narrow road to their house and departed in similar fashion.

Vimala braved Ajji's displeasure to go to the hospital with Girish. Kishore looked up with relief at their arrival. They walked together to where mother and baby lay. As soon as they entered, Radhika had carefully taken her baby out of the cradle alongside. And she set her, as carefully, into Vimala's arms, with a generosity that was as immense as it was unassuming. 'Here, Mira,' Radhika said, 'here she is at last—your other mother, your Doddamma.'

Vimala had never forgotten the realisation she first had when Radhika had smiled at her brother-in-law on the college steps. This wasn't a woman for social niceties, or the occasional white lie. Radhika meant it, as much as anything she ever said. The baby yawned and stretched ever so slightly in her arms. Vimala's heart swelled in a way that banished daydream and disappointment. She forgot her barren womb and the way the townspeople gossiped. She looked up at Radhika through her tears, quite wordless in the joy of a newborn in her arms.

Girish held the baby next and was noticeably charmed. 'What you named her, already?' he teased Radhika, who smiled as she lay spent on the hospital bed. 'What will we do at the namakarna then? You'd better keep it quiet for now.'

Was there a time when she had been happier in her life? Vimala could not remember. Those were the months after Radhika came home, where the baby had united the four adults into a shared devotion. There could not have been a time when they were more hopeful or had laughed quite as much at or with each other. And in the midst of those happy days, Vimala remembered the event that had given her pause. One that she had thought back to so many times after everything changed.

Weeks after they had come home with Mira, Gopal and Sudhir arrived one mid-morning, on a weekday. It was ostensibly to see the baby. Neither Girish nor Kishore could be expected to be home. Ajji was not home either. Vimala had wondered if they waited at Gopal's house until they saw her leave. It was an uncharitable thought, but Vimala could not help but notice the furtive air they had, and the way they spared no more than a glance at the baby they had come to see, who Vimala held in her arms. No, it seemed that all of their attention was for Radhika alone.

They stood stiffly in the hall until Radhika arrived from

within. They continued to stand, even though she asked them to sit. But Vimala noticed the way their shoulders relaxed when she entered, and the way their eyes lit up at her smile.

Vimala handed the baby to Radhika as she usually did when visitors arrived, and went in to the kitchen to make some coffee for them. But she could hear the conversation that ensued. There were the usual pleasantries. Radhika telling them it was so nice to see them after so long. News of common friends and professors.

'How are the studies coming along?' Radhika asked, and that is when Vimala heard the boy, Sudhir, speak.

'How long are you going to pretend that everything is normal?' he asked, and Vimala noticed that his voice was deep and rich, even in its now evident irritation.

She half-turned from the milk heating on the stove to watch.

Sudhir had taken a step towards Radhika where she sat, and now he towered over her in the centre of the hall. 'Have you stopped paying attention just because you have a baby?'

Radhika straightened up in her chair and held Mira out ever so slightly so her face was turned to Sudhir. 'Yes, Sudhir, I've haven't heard much news since Mira arrived. But I did hear about the drama at the hostel. My brother-in-law told me. It was lucky they did not call the police.'

'Lucky?' Sudhir scoffed. 'Have you forgotten what you used to say? About speaking truth to power?'

Radhika sighed. 'I think that was a mistake, Sudhir. It was long ago, and I did not think that it would all get this serious. I've told you so many times since—think of your parents. Just stay quiet until things settle down. You don't have to be the only one to save the world.'

'It was not a mistake,' Sudhir said, and then suddenly Vimala saw him drop to his knees in front of Radhika. 'You know it is not right. And you can help. Talk to the other professors. You are an old student, and so is your husband. You can bring everyone together, and we can all stand up as one.'

Vimala saw Radhika shrink in her chair and lean away. Then she was pushing her chair back and standing up. 'Sudhir, what is this childishness?' she said.

But he continued to kneel in front of her, head bowed, and Vimala wondered if he were crying. Gopal stepped up, put his hands on Sudhir's shoulders and attempted to lift him up.

It was all so odd, and Vimala stood in the kitchen, coffee cups in hand. Should she go into the hall or should she stay?

Radhika bent towards Sudhir and said, 'Sudhir, what is all this? Come, come, sit on the chair. Let us talk.'

As she cajoled the two into chairs, Vimala went in, careful to be noisy and cheerful. 'And here is some coffee for our guests.'

Radhika's eyes met hers in gratitude.

'Both of you should listen to me,' Radhika said, when they were both settled into chairs, coffee cups in hand, and in the orchestrated pretence that all was as it should be. 'If my daughter were sitting here in front of me, I would say the same thing. Stop. It scares me where this is heading. I hear rumours of students being picked up from their hostels and tortured in jail. Maybe it is just a rumour. It probably is. But what if it isn't? How will I show my face to your mother, Gopal?'

Vimala saw Gopal's eyes drop away from Radhika's, but that Sudhir's burned still when he looked at her. Was it fervour for the cause, or a different kind of hunger? The alternative arrived out of nowhere, and Vimala was ashamed at the thought. This was her sister by marriage, a married woman and a mother to boot. The boy was her student. Why did that thought arrive so insidiously, and out of the blue?

Coffee done, the boys stood up to leave.

'Promise me,' Radhika said, as she walked them to the door, 'that you will stay quiet, until I get back to college after my leave, at least.'

Vimala could not remember for months and years after, hard as she tried, if they did promise Radhika they would stop, or be quiet. Radhika was quiet herself for long after they left, and when she referred to them again to Vimala, it was to say, 'I worry about them. Especially Sudhir. And somehow it all feels like my fault.'

Later that evening, Kishore arrived with his news of a scholarship to study in America for four months. That bit of news, so hopeful and happy and such an honour, drove all else aside.

Then Kishore left. And everything changed, of course.

21
Ajji

Only four months, we all told ourselves, missing him before he reached the railway station, he would be back before we even noticed, as if the lie would help ease his absence. He had never been away from home, and I had felt him drawing away from me over the months. It made this physical separation seem like a final seal to losing him. I shook myself at this inauspicious thought, said a prayer for his long life, and focussed on the moment when he would be back, climbing up our hill with a suitcase full of toys for his baby, and maybe, forgiveness for me in his heart.

Before any of that could happen, however, trouble arrived again, in the form of Gowramma. She arrived the week after Kishore and Girish left, with an older couple in tow that I did not recognise. The gentleman was silver-haired and had a pencil-thin moustache, and the woman was plump, in a polyester saree too young for her age. Not from our parts, it was easy to tell. They came in to see your mother, and it was soon obvious that this was not a social call, a new baby visit. The woman had been crying. Her eyes had that dryness that one sees the day after funerals. Her son, whose name was Sudhir, was missing.

'I know your son,' I heard your mother say, going up to comfort his mother. 'I am sure everything is fine, did you check with his friends?'

They had, Gopal included, who had told them a strange story of sounds in the hostel after midnight, a police jeep and sounds of a scuffle in the hallway. No one had seen anything, but in the morning Sudhir was gone.

'There are no men in the house,' I said. 'Otherwise we would have helped, of course.'

Your mother glared at me, and offered to go with them to the police station. I should have held my tongue that day, and things may have been different. The more I said, the more I seemed to convince your mother of the truth of the opposite. Even Vimala tried reasoning with them; Girish would be back in a day, she said, and he would help them. They were all adamant, for different reasons, and your mother handed you off to Vimala that day before going with them to the police station.

By the time she arrived in the late evening, an hour or so after she had left, I had worked myself up into a rage that was greater for all its impotence. I had no idea how anyone could do this, go against an obvious stated directive by their mother-in-law. I would have died rather than show such disrespect. And to think that she was, after all, some half caste bastard thrown on the side of the street. Did she think that seducing my son would get her equal footing with me? The son I prized, she had schemed and planned to turn him against me. Living in my house like some queen, even keeping my first grandchild away from me. And now this insult as well? She had not even entered the house before I started screaming at her. Once I started, there was no holding back. I raged, I called her names, threw pots and pans on the floor, every dormant prejudice and every imagined slight making its way to my tongue. Nothing would make me stop, not even the whimpering that I heard coming from Vimala's arms.

She came up to me and looked me in the eye. I had not seen such contempt in anyone's eyes until then.

'You are welcome to your house, and your madi, and your son, if you can keep him,' she told me. 'I am leaving. I am not your slave. I am not some cow you bought at the market. I did

not ask your son to marry me, and I had no need to beg him. I have put up with your insults enough. I am a human being, which is more than you are.'

And that was that. She packed her bags and walked out, baby in one hand, bag in the other. This is what comes of not having a mother, I told myself, as she walked out, not knowing how to behave. Thinking that everything you do is right, that no one can correct you. I watched her all the way down the hill, expecting her to turn around at the last minute and come back up. Vimala had run after her, begging her to return, stay at home until Girish came back and could make arrangements for another house.

She walked on, without even stopping for Vimala, who had done so much for her. She was crying, Vimala told me later, and probably did not want us to see that. In any case, I supposed after she disappeared from sight, she would probably go stay in the orphanage and drag our family's name through the mud, until Kishore arrived and grovelled at her feet. Four months, I told myself, she would be back after she extracted all that she wanted from my son.

I had two weeks to ignore the growing bleakness in my heart, and despair over my rage before Vimala arrived one day with you in her arms. A day after that, your mother's corpse arrived at our door in a white mortuary van.

Vimala had made frequent trips to the orphanage, to watch you while your mother went to the college or on other errands. On that last day, your mother told her that she was going to the police station to check on the FIR that she had filed over Sudhir's disappearance. When she had called earlier from the college, the inspector had said it was misplaced and that she needed to file it again. When she did not come back hours after she had gone, Vimala came home with you, not trusting the orphanage enough to leave you there.

We called Girish, frantic, from the neighbour's phone. I sat before the Gods in the pooja room, remembering the things I wished in guilt. For the first time, I held you in my arms and looked at your face. The centre of my world had already changed when I did that, though I did not know it. My hands were busy with you. You refused the bottle, and cried until I squeezed a cloth with sugar water in your mouth, rocking you with all the experience and the love that I could summon. What are we going to tell Kishore, Vimala and I asked each other, a hundred times, before Girish came home.

'She never made it to the police station,' he told us. 'They are still looking for her. Somebody saw her talking by the cliffs with Sudhir, the boy who had run away, they said. He looked like he was consoling her or,' he looked suddenly embarrassed to say this before me, 'as if they were embracing.'

The next morning, the van arrived from the mortuary. Sudhir had disappeared again. No one else had seen him after that brief sighting with your mother. The police were seeking him as a person of interest in her murder.

Kishore arrived three days later, after her burial in the churchyard. He was inconsolable. It is my fault, he said, over and over again; I should not have gone. I wanted to go, that is why this happened. My life is over, he said, I have no life without her.

Girish spent every waking minute with him, attempting to turn his brother's mind from his sorrow. Kishore, irrationally, would not talk to me. He remembered how I had treated his wife while she was alive, and seemed to think that coming to me was a betrayal of her. His own mother, who bore him and raised him; and this was what he thought.

A day or two later is when Kishore asked Girish, asked us, 'How could this happen?'

'Maybe there were things you did not know,' Girish told him, delicately. 'They say she was seen talking to Sudhir. He had

told his friends that he was obsessed with her. Maybe she resisted him.'

'Of course, she would have,' Kishore retorted, incensed at the suggestion his brother was making.

Girish did not tell him what they were saying on the street, that she had been angry, she had left the house in anger, and had gone to Sudhir for consolation, and ended up dead. What more could one expect anyway from a girl like her? One paramour had not worked out, so she had taken another. And he had killed her over some disagreement. Perhaps it was because she had had another man's daughter.

Soon there were other people at our house, other stories. People that talked about seeing her in conversation with Sudhir after class well before all of this happened, while Kishore was working elsewhere in the college. These were the people who came by to offer condolences, though their intentions may have been to pick up tidbits of gossip. Perhaps they talked in street corners and on the steps up to our house, but the stories grew more detailed and embroidered. She always did have a soft corner for him, they said; it was obvious the way she looked at him, the way they used to talk after class.

Even Gowramma forgot that she had been the one to ask your mother to talk to Sudhir first, to convince him to stay out of politics. Her son, Gopal, came in with her, white-faced and silent. He nodded his head when Kishore asked him if it were true, that Sudhir spoke about his wife constantly. He did not even look up, and left as soon as he could, looking the very picture of guilt, as if he had shared those fantasies people said his friend Sudhir had.

Their friendship started well before the wedding, people said, she did not even stop to consider that Sudhir was so much younger than her. Shameless, really, that she would be seen talking with him in plain view of everyone, in the college quadrangle. It is what happens when you let people without good families, or any family, into polite society.

Kishore remained unconvinced. No one could tell him that she had run to Sudhir for consolation without it resulting in a brawl, much less their insinuations about their relationship. Finally Surendra arrived, and with Girish, sat him down.

'This must be painful for you,' Surendra said. 'We understand. You loved her, and you cannot believe that she is gone.'

*'But none of this makes sense Surendra-*avare*,' Kishore said, voice between anger and tears. 'You came to our wedding, you know her. You have to help me. We have to find out what happened.'*

'All in good time,' Surendra said. 'Your brother and I have been talking to the inspector in charge of the case, Dwarkish. He is a smart young man. He will get to the bottom of it. You don't worry. Leave this in our hands.'

'Yes, Kishore,' Girish added, 'leave this to us. We will not let this Sudhir go unpunished. Sooner or later he will have to show his face. If not here, then somewhere. You have my word that when that happens, you will be the first to know. We will find out from him why he did what he did.'

Surendra patted him on the arm, while Kishore finally broke down and wept, as if he were still the toddler that used to cling to my saree.

'I don't believe all this nonsense that people say either about an affair with Sudhir—maybe it was all a one-sided thing on Sudhir's part. I mean, there is no smoke without fire, but I agree with you, she would not have encouraged him,' Girish spoke soothingly well into the night, well after Surendra left, promising to follow up with Dwarkish.

Kishore stayed a few more days, making daily trips to the police station. He would not talk to anyone in the village because the whispers that had already taken hold were not the ones he believed or cared to hear. One night, three days later, Surendra came again, asking to see Kishore urgently.

Dwarkish was annoyed by Kishore's frequent visits, he said. 'During the Emergency, they have all kinds of powers, these policemen. Stay safe—it might be better to go back to America and finish your assignment. What is lost is lost—you need to be safe, at least for the sake of your daughter.'

Kishore went back to America at our insistence, mine and Girish's. The four-month assignment turned into something much longer. He was ambitious, and with her gone, had no desire to come back.

Later that month, we had news that Surendra had managed a job for Girish in Bangalore, in the Public Works Department. Surendra came by to tell us himself.

'It is a wonderful job, Amma,' he said to me, smiling like a film star. 'No less than your son deserves. It will bring him a good salary, and an opportunity to earn even more if he is smart.'

A month before, and I would have refused to leave this town where your Ajja's ashes had touched the ground, where my happiest times, as brief as they had been, were spent. I could not even remember clearly a time when I had not lived in that tiny house on the slanting hillside. And yet, the life that I had lived in Malehalli felt tainted. All your Ajja's doings and mine were obscured by the stigma around your mother's. The stories about your mother flew around town, growing heads by the day. There were whispers in the street when I went down to the market, and eyes turned away from mine at the temple.

I thought back to the day I had fought with your mother, when she walked out of our home. People said that I had put her out as soon as my son's back was turned, and perhaps that was the truth, though I did not think it so at the time. The faint shame that I felt at my own conduct was better borne as anger towards your mother, and I let it grow. It was all her fault. If she had not set out to seduce my son, I would not have a son who was a widower so young, so far from home. There would be no need to walk with anything but pride into the village or the street. As poor as we had been before, we had at least had our honour. Now this she-demon had taken even that from us.

While I tended the anger I had, fed it with the slights and innuendo the village women sent my way, you grew in my arms, more precious and beautiful by the day. Even in those early months, it was easy to see that it was her features that you had. But what I had distrusted in her, I grew to love in you. In the blindness that comes to the very beguiled, I almost went so far as to imagine that your skin was only a shade darker than mine, your eyes were almost my own mother's, and your nose from certain angles almost appeared Kishore's.

Good riddance, I remember thinking, even when I had the rare pang of guilt at a remembered night-time prayer for your mother's disappearance; at least she left my granddaughter to me. So it was easy then, to pack my belongings with Girish and Vimala and leave with them on the train to Bangalore. The witch had destroyed my life, my all. To move somewhere else where my granddaughter could grow up without the indecent whispers that followed her now—that was the only reasonable option we had.

As we left Malehalli on the train, I saw the church tower just outside town, its giant bells visible over the top of the rushing trees. Without the constant reinforcement of our neighbours' gossip and in the receding spire of her childhood home, the first doubts about your mother's death arrived. How was it possible that she had managed an illicit affair with someone when she had been home with you all day and night, and when we had heard her speak to you of your father with such love?

Vimala, sitting opposite me in the train saw the church as well, and her eyes met mine an instant after. The doubt I saw in her eyes, an echo of my own, gave me the strength to squash the question she did not ask.

'She must have done what they said she did,' I said to Vimala, convincing myself more than I did her. 'Why else would she be so eager to leave our house? It was not as if I was more than mildly annoyed with her. She wanted to leave, and she took any excuse she could.'

Vimala, my good daughter-in-law, the one who was trained in the rules of polite behaviour, said nothing. I saw her bite back her words and her doubts in obedience.

The months after we came to Bangalore were happy ones. Girish had a loan appear almost magically within a few weeks of arriving, and he was able to buy the house in Malleshwaram, just steps from the Ganesha temple I visited every day, head held high as before. We planted tulsi in the empty pedestal the previous owners had left, and she took root and grew to my delight in the same way you did.

Vimala tried to be the wife your uncle now needed, with his office job and friends in high places. There was not a step too big or too difficult for her to take to leave her small-town ways behind, so patiently did she watch and learn. She took such delight in dressing up every day like our neighbours did, waiting by the gate in the evening to receive her husband from his day at work. She even enrolled in English lessons, at the school that advertised itself in posters and pamphlets all over our neighbourhood, The London English School of Speech. I saw that she imitated your mother's style of hair some days, the pleats of her saree on others. I knew then that Vimala's doubts had never truly gone, and I knew also that mine remained as well. But I tried to believe. Your mother had to be at fault. Why would so many people lie? What other reasonable explanation was there to explain her death?

I had almost succeeded in believing, when Mahalinga arrived one day, many months after we had settled into our new home, half-crazed but with a story to tell.

22

Girish

When Girish got into the car that Vinay brought around, he realised that he had hours to spare before his brother and Mira were to arrive. And to think he had nothing to do, on a perfect balmy Bangalore night. Almost instantly, Lakhotia Jewellers came to mind. He had wanted to see the store ever since he met Lakhotia at the hospital, both to get a measure of the man, and to see the kind of enterprise that created 'black' money in such magnitude that it required the philanthropic cleansing of a hospital. Not that there was much charity that went on there, he thought, almost snorting audibly. He could probably count the number of patients who received free treatment by the number of times Lakhotia's wife had appeared in the Sunday supplement of the *Deccan Herald*.

He also had a vague idea of a trinket for Sitara as means for rapprochement. Surendra would recover his good humour at Mallige, but women expected their pound of flesh. Even if it was all her fault, she would come up with enough drama and make it seem as if the fault was somehow his. He had never bought anyone jewellery before, and perhaps it was time he did. Just to see how it would feel.

The money had come in this morning, in cash, in return for approval of a housing development in the Green Belt. Fifty lakhs after Surendra's cut, for a stroke of his pen that moved the border several hectares. For such a small piece of land that did not even belong to anyone.

He climbed up to the glass doors and was saluted by a watchman dressed in ceremonial attire that included shield, sword, turban and moustache. He almost laughed, before he stepped across the threshold and was swallowed up by an exuberance of gilt and gold. It was a maharaja's palace recreated, or an artist's imagining of one, with attendants in period costumes, lights disguised as lanterns and not a cash register in sight. He stood undecided for a minute before a girl appeared at his side, asking, in convent-accented English, what he would like to see. I could buy her something small, he told himself, and there would still be so much money left over.

An hour later, Girish emerged, a peacock pendant in hand, that cost more than he had planned to spend, its clustered diamonds and sapphires duller and less impressive in the passing street lights outside his car window than in the store. He laughed aloud, shutting the box. He should have it appraised tomorrow, he thought, appreciative suddenly of Lakhotia's cunning. They would be diamonds, he was sure, but maybe a lower grade than he was told. It would still be worth it, to be royalty for the hour, to feel the allure of metal and stone, and to succumb. It almost did not matter what you bought. Maybe he could take Kishore there, he thought, so he could buy something for that new wife of his. Show him what India had become these days.

It was slow going on M.G. Road, despite the late hour, because of the traffic and the jaywalking crowds. He rolled down his window, and the warm air rushed in, with the blaring music from passing cars, and the laughter of young people, easy and joyful for no good reason. 'Always Diwali here,' Vinay muttered, after they narrowly missed a weaving scooter that strayed into his path.

'Go slow, there's no hurry,' Girish said, leaning back, relishing the festive air that rushed in and embraced him, as if it were indeed Diwali. As everyday was, if you were young, and had money to spend. Vinay yelled an obscenity at an auto rickshaw that passed too close, and Girish met his eyes in the rear-view mirror. Vinay looked anxious. It was not the traffic, Girish decided; perhaps it was what Surendra said, or perhaps it was Mira coming back.

'I forgot about the movie tonight,' he said, clearing his throat.

'It's okay, saar,' Vinay said, turning around in surprise. 'I don't have to see the first show. I can go tomorrow, or maybe the second show, if we finish early tonight.' He looked grateful, Girish noticed, that he had remembered. Or perhaps he was just grateful that Girish did not hold him responsible for the fiasco with Surendra.

Soon they were off M.G. Road, and the crowds and the music disappeared. HAL Road was quiet and fast. They passed the Military Hospital, and the airport came up before them as usual, familiar and small.

'Stay in the car at the airport,' Girish said. 'We'll find a porter to help with the luggage. No need for you to get out at all. And wear your hat.'

At the airport, while Vinay bought tickets for entry, and dug out his little used chauffeur's uniform, Girish berated himself. Mira knew Vinay was responsible for the incident at the theatre, and for the Muslim boy's arrest. If she knew, it would be fair to suppose that Kishore did as well. He should have given the boy the week off. Oh well, he'd just have to come up with a good story before it became an issue, why someone like Vinay was in his employ.

Vinay left to park the car, and Girish walked to the arrivals zone where people were already lined up.

Having bought his additional and overpriced ticket to the arrival lounge inside the airport, Girish walked in. He found a seat by a bucket of ferns, which afforded him an illusion of privacy. His phone rang constantly. It was the usual hubbub before elections, a thousand decisions to be made. People who needed fawning over and those that fawned over him. The game is what I enjoy the most, he told himself, of the intricate decisions that he made every minute, the calculations that always ended in victory for his side, no matter the odds. But even that thought brought a kind of restlessness instead of satisfaction. He straightened up in the chair and shifted his weight, as if that would rearrange his sense of the thing. It did not. The phone rang again, and for once he ignored it.

Maybe the restlessness was from his brother's arrival, fraught with all the things that had happened between them, and the things that might have. Perhaps it was from Surendra's anger, which returned him, as always, to the boy he once was. Girish usually scorned this way of thinking, reserved in his mind for lazy housewives. Why do we have to live in the past or inside ourselves, he would say often to Vinay, when the world is so vast, and the future so bright? But tonight, in the momentary lull in the business of his day and in the rare moment of solitude he was allowed, a single moment of the past and his brother intruded. Girish recognised it to be a result of Surendra's taunt about his sister-in-law, one that was usually reserved for the most egregious of offences.

It was of the day when his brother had come to find him at Vimala's behest, at the party office in Malehalli all those years before.

'Kishore,' Girish had said, slapping his younger brother on his back, pretending to not notice his discomfiture, 'this is such a surprise. Come, come, did you lose your way?'

Kishore said, 'I have something to tell you. You have to talk to Amma for me.'

They were soon at the stand selling sugar cane juice outside the party office. The story tumbled out. There was a girl, Kishore said. Girish probably did not remember, but he had seen her once, a long time ago, on the first day of college. The girl with the nuns. He wanted to marry her. She had agreed, but Amma had to be convinced.

'Do you *have* to marry her?' Girish had asked first, as an image of Radhika on that first day in college came easily to him, the bosom and waist undiminished, years after the day. Just how far had his brother gotten, the lucky dog?

'I love her, I can marry no one else,' Kishore said, clearly talking about something else.

'I mean, Kishore,' Girish lowered his voice, looking his brother directly in the eye, 'did you do anything? Not that I blame you of course—but is she pregnant or something?'

'No, of course not.' Kishore blushed, for himself, and for Radhika. 'She is not that sort of a girl.'

Enjoy her if she lets you, and walk away, Girish had thought, wondering if he dared speak his mind to his brother. Penniless girls from orphanages cannot hope for much more, anyway. It might have been something he would have said to a friend, but his brother, idealistic fool that he was, would be upset. Not that sort of a girl, indeed. Not when he remembered the way she looked, still, years after.

But his brother had inexplicably grown even more embarrassed, to say, 'There is another thing that Amma will take badly.'

Kishore had spoken fast, as if to get the words out as quickly as he could. 'She does not know her parents. The rumours are that she is an illegitimate daughter that her mother gave up.'

'I'll talk to Amma,' Girish said. It would be his brother's battle, not his. He did not see even a faint glimmer of possibility for this marriage. Maybe it would take a fight with his mother for his brother to see that. And he, Girish, would come out looking good for once.

They started to walk away from the stall, and on a sudden pang of conscience, Girish turned to Kishore and said, 'You do not have to tell Amma any rumours unless you know them for a fact. No sense in making this harder than it is.'

The brothers walked along the main road in Malehalli, and their steps took them, as usual, past the large statue of Srinivas Murthy in the roundabout. They had walked by the statue all their lives, and Girish had long outgrown the novelty of seeing their father's statue in the town centre. But Kishore's steps slowed as they approached.

'Appa would have approved,' he'd said, looking up at the statue's face, now chipped in places, rather forlorn-looking in the busy circle.

'It does not matter what he would have done,' Girish said. 'And you never know. People change as they get older. It is different when it comes to their children. You might go clean latrines for the untouchables, but it is another matter to bring their filth into the house.'

They stood for a minute in silence, and Girish saw that he had offended Kishore, whose jaw was set, and hands clenched around the railing at the base of the statue.

'I didn't mean that,' he said, though of course he had, 'and if you are this sensitive, life is going to be hard for you. Those are the facts about your caste and hers. Christian or not, everyone knows it is the low caste people that convert, and people will say worse, to your face and behind your back.'

Kishore turned to his brother. 'Anna, I know you have always wanted the best for me, and that is why you say these things. People will say things, whether they are true or not. And I love her no matter what her caste is, just as much as I love you and Amma.'

Girish had looked at him then, and saw the tears in his eyes.

Poor deluded fool, he had thought then as he often did later; he imagines the best of every situation, and believes it as if imagining something makes it true. He could pass all the exams in the world, and he would not know an ounce about anything. Why would he even think that Girish wanted the best of everything for *him*? What kind of fool wanted something better for someone else?

Girish looked up at the monitor on the wall opposite to check if the arrival time had changed. It had not; his brother would be here soon. He returned to the rumination of a minute before. Kishore and all his harping on what their father would have wanted. As if their father was not a wastrel who died without providing for his children. And that marriage. It would have been better if that marriage had never happened, Girish thought, and not for the first time. It was not his fault that it was allowed to happen. And there was no reason to blame him for any of the things that happened after that, either. The girl was dead, after all, and his brother, remarried. All that remained was a gnawing worry that came rarely and only in his brother's presence. A suggestion that no matter how much his younger brother looked up to him, he would always be the older and yet lesser man.

He stood up. Even if he were, look where he was now, and how far he had come. He was the man who did the things that needed to be done. He was the only one who could.

23
Mira

People shoulder and brush past to waiting relatives in their eagerness. I feel Appa steer me between them as I stand lost for a minute, and then up in front of us is Girish uncle. Greyer and plumper than I saw him last, but smiling at me the way he always did, before everything.

'Mira,' he says. 'You are taller than me now.' And I am. I smile, though the tears and anger are fresh. It is what well brought-up girls do, smile when they are required to.

Girish uncle takes a step back at my smile. I see a strange recognition cross his face. It is momentary and swiftly replaced. He turns to Appa and the brothers embrace.

My uncle pats me awkwardly on my arm when he turns around to face me again, as if I am too old now or too different suddenly for a better welcome. He pulls a package out from his shirt instead, saying, 'Here, Mira, I bought this for you.' I take it even as I have the strange and distinct feeling that he did not. It is a peacock pendant, ornate and ostentatious, something an older woman might wear. It flashes and flares in the light, heavy and strange on my palm.

'How is Amma?' Appa asks.

'Still in the ICU,' Girish says. 'I talked to the doctor this morning, and he said she was critical, but stable. Whatever that means, you can never tell with these people. Either they are trying to bleed us with ICU charges, or she is really sick. Vimala has been with her.'

We walk out of the arrivals area to the pavement and cross the street to the island between the lanes into and out of the parking lot.

'Not really a loading area,' my uncle says, shrugging, 'but you don't have much luggage.' We can slip into the car here, and circumvent the line of cars waiting ahead of ours to get to the loading zone, he means. 'This is Bangalore, not your rule-obsessed America,' he says and smiles.

The billboards outside seem bigger, the cars crawling along the lanes in front of and behind, smaller than I remember. Everything is the same as it was in my memories, and yet different, in all the small, forgotten details that make the world before me more solid, more real. The air that refuses to be shy, the stray paper that flutters in the breeze, the litter that borders the street, the hum of a million people breathing in the night, the cars, the traffic, the honking, the relatives, the sense that nothing has changed at all under all that has.

'That's the car,' Girish uncle points, to the Ambassador fourth in line and making its way towards us. 'We'll be home in Malleshwaram soon.'

He says this as if it is a social visit, and he is a generous host. As if we are a family happy to be reunited at his home.

'Ajji, I need to see Ajji tonight,' I say, my insistence part concern and part rebellion. Girish uncle hesitates, it is past visiting time. We are probably tired after our journey. We could go early in the morning, he points out. It is not as if anything will happen overnight, so suddenly.

'I need to see Ajji,' I say in the face of his reasonable tone, feeling as if I am a little girl again, and need the Five Star I cannot have.

My uncle gives in, as if he indulges me. 'I will call someone,' he says, 'I know the owner of the hospital.'

Girish uncle gets in beside the driver in his white peaked cap, Appa and I in the back. I happen to see the driver's eyes in the mirror the second after.

It is Vinay.

Vinay, my uncle's driver? This is who my uncle trusts with the comings and goings of his life, the secrets that even his family is not allowed to know? Anisa and I matter so little that he would do this? Even so, I am not surprised.

So, this was the bargain my uncle struck. Vinay's loyalty and Lakshmi's silence for a bribe that Farid uncle paid. And Adil's bruises after the funeral. Was that the price he paid for his temerity in kissing Girish Murthy's niece? It is almost a stroke of genius, one that I did not appreciate as fully before.

I place the peacock pendant carefully on the seat between me and Appa. It will look as if it was dropped by accident, I decide, and turn towards the deserted streets again. I look out of the window, to streets so changed from when I saw them last. Blackness like ink covers them, interrupted only by quiet pools of light under the intermittent streetlights. Storefronts are shuttered, the windows of towering buildings opaque and shut.

Then I see Vinay looking at me through the rear-view mirror, furtive and bold at once.

It occurs to me in a way it hasn't before, that it was Girish uncle all along. It was he who failed to stop the bomb at the theatre, he who shielded Devidas from discovery, and he who attempted to place the blame on Adil. It is he who profits from the mishaps, and the grief. His immorality is far greater than that of a kiss on the street, even at its most lascivious. It is only gossip-mongers who think that sexual indiscretion trumps every other sin. And now, I no longer buy in.

I turn back to the window. It feels different, though nothing is changed. I feel the child's conceit fall away, that it all happens for me, or is of my doing. So many layers and so many agendas, the silent trees seem to say as we speed past; the world moves around us even if we do nothing. Are you so different from us?

'So who was finally found guilty?' I ask, suddenly reckless, turning to my uncle in the front seat. 'For the theatre fire?'

Vinay's gaze drops away in the rear-view mirror.

My uncle, without losing his composure, says, 'Oh, that was the thing—no one was ever found. Nothing came of the investigation.' He pauses, and in the same reasonable tone, continues, 'You know, this hospital you'll see, it is new. Nothing like it in Bangalore.'

We turn the corner on to M.G. Road, and even its brightly lit footpaths and parking spaces are desolate, for once empty of the life I have always associated them with. We speed by in its emptiness, even as I look for and find the familiar stores among the newer ones—Natesan's Antiquarts small and tucked away, the photography store at the corner, EGK, whose shut doors still feel like a mute welcome. The statue of a long-forgotten English queen comes up as before, at the entrance to Cubbon Park that we circle, passing the planetarium on the road to High Grounds. I recognise the side road to my school. Large, with grey stone-walled buildings arranged in a circle, around its very own roundabout that cars circle through as they drop children off in the morning. Behind the grey buildings, a series of steps leads downward to a playground, and a whitewashed chapel surrounded by eucalyptus trees.

This is the place where I saw Anisa for the very first time.

She was next to me in the line to go into the classroom. I recognised her as a familiar face from the school bus stop at Malleshwaram, on Sampige Road, that morning.

I tugged at my collar, wondering if it was too tight, because there was a tightness in my throat that made me want to cry.

Ajji stood in the distance beyond the locked gates, easy to tell as the splash of white among younger, brightly dressed mothers.

'My Abbu says I am his diamond,' Anisa said to my silence. 'Here, I have dimples, look.'

She chattered on that morning, despite the 'No talking, girls' that the nuns intoned periodically as they herded us into class. Her desk was next to mine. Her Ammi would have chocolate, a Five Star, for her, if she did not cry in class all morning, she told me in a sibilant whisper. She picked at the varnish on the old wooden desk, and around the hinges that allowed the top to lift. When she played with the clasp on the front, making a small tap-tap noise that only the two of us could hear, I almost giggled. We were marched off to recess, and we played together in the sand. My throat finally unclogged itself.

We made 'potatoes'. She showed me the hole she worried in her socks that she pulled tight over her skin to show me the milky beige peeking through.

'See, the brown round potato in my socks?' She helped me make mine. After we destroyed two perfectly good pairs of socks, we were friends.

'Yours is a real potato,' she pronounced, of the darker brown that bulged through my socks.

When we left that morning, Ajji and her Ammi were both at the gate, unlocked and crowded with children and mothers. Anisa shared her Five Star with me. First, she broke off a big piece for herself and gave me the smaller piece. Then she frowned, considering her larger half. A moment later, she broke off a piece of the larger part to hand to me.

'It's equal now,' she said.

My Ajji and her Ammi both smiled.

The next day, we were at her house in the afternoon. She partitioned off her Ammi's lap into two equal halves with her ribbon as Ammi sat cross-legged on the floor. One half hers, one mine, so we could put our heads down for the afternoon siesta, a practice that both our households shared. She wanted one side first, then the next, all the while looking to see if I'd object or fight.

When Rehana aunty objected to this ploy of putting off naptime, down we went. Into a warm cushion of knee and lower thigh under maroon georgette saree, to which clung a faint smell of mingled clove and garlic from the morning's cooking. When we woke up, we were on straw mats under the fan, sharing a pillow instead of a lap. Farid uncle was home. That evening, under Ajji's strict injunction of 'only whole fruit and milk,' Anisa and I snacked on sugary Bournvita and apples as Farid uncle—Abbu—looked at our homework.

He admired our perfect letters, and was amazed that we knew our numbers.

'Both of you know so much already,' he said, straight-faced. 'I don't think I was as young when I learnt all this.'

'Abbu, how old were you? How old?' Anisa clamoured as she jumped up and down, it must have been a game they played before.

'I don't know,' he said, 'maybe I was ten? Or twelve, maybe? Definitely much older. Both of you are very smart. Soon you will be teaching me things.'

Farid uncle's smile grew wider to include me, and the twinkle in his eyes grew more pronounced.

I hold on to that smile and that memory as my uncle waves to the salaam-ing watchman at Lakhotia Hospital. As he offers to take our luggage to Malleshwaram and we leave him to walk up the marble lobby to the receptionist.

'Mr Lakhotia conveys his regrets,' the receptionist says, 'he cannot be here to receive you in person. It is only because of the lateness of the hour. Of course you can see your mother; you should consider the hospital your own.'

It is a favour for Girish uncle that eases our way. I realise and resent this anew even as I show a gratitude that is small and grudging.

At a little past two in the morning, we are finally allowed into the ICU, where a nurse who tells us her name is Annapurna, leads us in to see Ajji.

There is a small crowd by Ajji's bed. The shock of it hits me. Something must have happened. Are they trying to revive her, or are they pulling up the covers over her face because they failed? Why else would there be a crowd around her bed at this late hour of night?

But when we get closer, I hear her voice and know my fears to be premature.

Ajji is telling a story. It is so unexpected, especially in the aftermath of my fear, that I laugh, and the sound jars in the silence of the ICU. Several of the people around her bed turn to me and frown. It is only when I see Vimala aunty so intent on writing that she does not notice us, that I begin to suspect.

It is the spectacle of Ajji's final story that we are seeing. It is one that she is telling with all her strength and resolve, to an audience that listens with attention even though it is the middle of the night. Just for a minute, before I realise what the story is, my heart swells with love for this steadfast woman who lives life on her own terms in every situation. No one else would tell stories in the ICU, and in the middle of the night.

But then I hear a name, Mahalinga.

'Mahalinga,' Ajji is saying, 'arrived to see me in Bangalore. I had spoken with him before, in the days that your Ajja had been a frequent guest of the British queen. Our relationship had receded in the years after your Ajja's death. They were struggling themselves, initially. In the years after Mahalinga found a job as constable, I had not wanted to be at the receiving end of pity or charity from Usha, so I avoided them both.

'But when he visited me in Bangalore, I received him out of courtesy for that old relationship. Even though I had no desire to see anyone from Malehalli, or to have the stories of your mother that were ever-multiplying pests all over town follow us here to Bangalore.

'Mahalinga looked unkempt in a way I had never seen with him before. His clothes were dirtier than might be expected, even with the journey. He did not seem to care. "I have to tell you this, sister, maybe it will ease my way to hell," he said, "though I am already there."

'After he had gone on in this vein for some time, it seemed to me that he was just working up his courage or his resolve to tell me something. I nudged him along as tactfully as I could, expecting some tale of hardship and maybe a request for money as a loan, or a job for one of his children. All those years, I remember thinking, and he finds us now when Girish is finally successful.'

Ajji's voice falters, and I step up automatically. Someone restrains me with an arm on my shoulder. I turn to see a stranger who is listening to the story. 'Wait, don't interrupt her,' the older woman says, 'She may not have that much time left for what she has to say.'

24

Mahalinga

It was afternoon. The fan whirred overhead as Mahalinga sat at the constable's table on the veranda just outside the police station.

Radhika Murthy had come back to the police station as directed, a week after her first visit. Now, she sat at the table across from the sub-inspector. She had waited awhile in the outer veranda while the sub-inspector had attended to important business, looking at her watch every few seconds. She had imagined aloud her baby's waking cry and the fuss over the bottle, worries she had shared freely with Mahalinga, asking him every so often, 'Is the sub-inspector ready to see me yet?'

When she was finally summoned in, he could see that impatience the wait had engendered in the way she spoke to his boss.

'What is happening with the FIR?' she asked, before she was even fully seated on the chair opposite him.

'You said you would file it when I was here last week with Sudhir's father. Now you're telling me the FIR was misplaced? How can an FIR be misplaced?' She spoke angry and fast, as if saying things faster would help her make up for the time spent outside. She was leaning forward in her seat, one palm face down on the table, shoulders hunched, looking right into the sub-inspector's face. Mahalinga watched her from his desk down the hall. She is so young, he thought.

The sub-inspector cleared his throat. 'These things happen, Madam.' He pronounced it 'Mey-dum', almost a Kannada word, not the way she'd say it, but the way one of the many boys she taught at the college every day would say it.

'But, how, Inspector? Don't you have rules about this sort of thing?' She seemed to think that this was her classroom and that he was a student who was tardy with his homework, the way she tapped on his desk with her palm, insistent. Mahalinga drew in a breath. Young, and foolish.

'Meydum,' he said, 'these times, they are not usual times. Tell me, Meydum, why do you trouble yourself over this? Your husband is away, you have a baby at home. Are you not satisfied with leaving her to go to work every day, that you must take on ...' he flicked a pen with his index finger and thumb, the way he would a dead fly that happened to land on his desk, 'this?'

She frowned.

Rajanna, the younger constable, arrived with tea in short glass tumblers.

'Please have, Meydum,' the sub-inspector said.

'Inspector,' she began, frowning again, 'I did not come here to drink tea. Please tell me if you will find the FIR, or file another one. It has already been a week.' Rajanna looked at her, eyebrows raised, the tray with the tea still held out, hand outstretched. She waved him away, impatient.

'All in good time, Meydum, all in good time.' The sub-inspector slurped his hot tea. 'There are a lot of issues with this case. You are not a child, surely you understand.'

She waited for him to continue, clearly not understanding.

'The Malehalli party leader, you know him, no, Shri Surendra—he came to your wedding, also, last month or last year? Ahh, you remember him, good, good. He is interested in this case, also, you see, and I am waiting to see what he says about the FIR. He told me last week that this boy, you know, this Sudhir, was in all this college union politics and was mixing with dangerous types, you know, comm-yoo-nist elements.'

Mahalinga was surprised. This was more polite than he had ever seen the sub-inspector be to anyone, since he had been transferred here to Malehalli at the start of the Emergency almost a year ago.

'But that's what you picked him up for, Inspector, and you sent him back to the hostel after questioning. He disappeared after that, so you still have to file the FIR for that, even if he was in the union, no? Why wait for party leaders?'

He continued as if she had not spoken. 'Surendra-*avaru*, you know, he has the line all the way up to the top, to Delhi. When he speaks, Meydum, sensible people, even big-big college professors like you, listen.' He looked up at her directly for the first time, so even she would not mistake the threat that lay not too far below the surface.

'*Inspectore, nodee,*' she said, lapsing into Kannada, 'he is a young boy, an only child—his fate may not matter much to Delhi, but his parents have no one else and somebody should help them.' Then, she made to draw her chair back, 'Thank you for listening to me, Inspector. I should be going. Please consider our request to investigate.'

Mahalinga exhaled, thinking the interview was at an end and had passed without incident.

But it was not to be.

'What is this, Meydum, you are leaving now? Surendra-*ru* may be on his way here. You should present your request directly to him. Myself, you know, I am only a government servant, like you. But he is a big man, very big. If you really care about this boy, you should talk to him.'

She hesitated, but to Mahalinga's relief she pushed her chair back anyway and stood up. 'I really have to go.' She had almost turned away from the desk before a black Ambassador sedan with government plates pulled up at the entrance to the police station. In swept Surendra, his loud voice and hearty greeting to Mahalinga in the veranda announcing his arrival before he actually stepped into the station. She was standing a few steps away from the desk when he approached her.

'Namaskara, namaskara,' he said, in a familiar way, 'what a surprise to see you here, of all places. It is like finding a rose in a bed of thorns, no, Rajanna? Your sub-inspector must be finding his work today very pleasant, no?'

'Meydum is here to discuss a case, Surendra-*avare*,' Sub-inspector Dwarkish said, as if they had not discussed this before, and as if Surendra had arrived by chance and not because Rajanna had called him.

Mahalinga stepped out from behind his own desk, and said, '*Thayee,* can I call a rickshaw for you? You were anxious to get back to your baby.'

'Mahalinga, you old man, what is the hurry? Let me talk to the lady and find out what she wants. She can go home comfortably in my car afterwards.'

'No, thank you,' she said, 'a rickshaw is fine. I can find one at the street corner. I am here to request help finding a student, Sudhir, who has been missing for two weeks. He is an only son and his parents are very worried. They were here to file an FIR last week, but the inspector tells me that he is waiting to hear from you. Please help them. They have no one else. They will be very grateful to you.' It was a request made formally, and she was standing up straighter and leaning away from Surendra who was standing directly opposite, leaning in, close to her, as she said it.

'And what about you, will you be grateful too?' He laughed, as if he had said something funny. Rajanna and Dwarkish laughed as well.

'Yes, thank you, and I should be leaving,' she said trying to step around him and walk towards the door, seeming to understand too late the lifeline that Mahalinga had thrown her.

Still, this was the middle of the day and these were government officers, not thugs in some back alley, she seemed to be telling herself, even when Surendra stuck his hand out in her way and said, 'But what is the hurry, Mrs Murthy, you were perfectly content to sit here and drink tea with Dwarkish here, and yet you run when you see me?

'It is so unfortunate when husbands leave young women like you at home and go away, really. I understand, you get bored and then it is like they teach at the convent school you probably went to, Mrs Murthy. An idle mind is a devil's workshop. You get involved in all this dirt over some boy's disappearance, in men's business. I know, I know, he was good-looking and your sympathy was probably stirred, husband being away and all.' He leered.

She dropped all pretence of this being a normal conversation at that, and said, 'I'm leaving, please let me pass. Mahalinga-*avare*, I would like the rickshaw, can you take me to the stand?'

When Surendra refused to budge, she tried to move his outstretched hand that was blocking her passage. That was the opening he seemed to have been waiting for, grabbing her by the arm, even as Mahalinga said, '*Saar, saar, bitbide*, let her go. Her father-in-law was the freedom fighter Srinivas Murthy, her brother-in-law is in your party. She is a young mother, a *thayee, saar*.'

'You can leave, you can leave, Radhika, all in good time,'

he said. 'Mahalinga, go on, go find a rickshaw. Her brother-in-law won't lose too much sleep, don't worry.'

Mahalinga remained frozen two steps away from his desk on the outer veranda, while she was asking him for help, struggling to free her arm, then the other one, then her waist, as the three men, Surendra, Dwarakish and Rajanna, carried her into the back room, laughing.

Scratching, kicking, clawing, screaming, and cursing.

Begging.

Weeping.

When they had all disappeared into the back room, Mahalinga overcame his shock. He ran to the sub-inspector's desk. He knew he was gambling his life, and Usha's, and his family's future as he picked up the telephone on it to call his old friend's son, Girish Murthy, at the party office. When the clerk at the other end brought Girish to the phone, he said, 'Mahalinga-*avare*, you were my father's friend, so I'll give you some advice. Don't meddle in big people's affairs. You have to think about your family. My brother will come back and marry again, maybe someone more suitable this time.' There was a lack of surprise in Girish's tone, a practical matter-of-fact-ness that brooked no argument.

Meanwhile, the laughter continued, interspersed with the sounds of ripping, tearing, beating. It seemed to Mahalinga that he had died and gone to hell, where he entered the pit of snakes that his grandmother had told him about, and they stretched and coiled and squeezed the breath out of him and insinuated themselves into his every orifice and sank their poisoned fangs into his flesh, and transformed his decency and his honour to this contemptible speck of less than a man, less than nothing that he was and was to become.

25
Mahalinga

Mahalinga sat beside the driver in the beige police jeep that pulled into the government hospital compound the morning after. People were lined up and their exhaled breaths were puffs of smoke in the frigid morning, all turning in the direction of the jeep.

Mahalinga got out with Rajanna when the jeep stopped. Together, they hoisted a long bundle between them from the back of the jeep. There might have been a suggestion of a movement from within the bundle covered with a torn bed sheet, it was hard to say. As they moved closer to the door and the line of people that snaked out from it, whispered conversations stilled. Eyes were averted, feet moved aside for them to step through.

Sub-inspector Dwarkish got out from the back of the jeep and walked leisurely behind them.

'*Jaga maadi, jaga*,' he called, unnecessarily, as he passed the line, his boots scrunching loudly on the gravel outside the hospital. Everyone stepped aside a little bit more.

'Accident case, Doctor *idhaara*?' Rajanna asked the clerk inside.

Mahalinga and Rajanna walked through, and placed the bundle, still wrapped, on a gurney in the back. They waited for the duty doctor to arrive. She was still at her home, and a ward boy had been dispatched to bring her. No one was allowed close, yet Mahalinga heard the staff whisper. It was a woman. They had seen her foot move. Rajanna stood by the gurney, swinging his lathi absentmindedly, like a toy. Mahalinga stood by him, sweating in the cold, eyes unwavering from a dust speck on the floor.

When the duty doctor arrived, he saw that she was a young woman. 'What is the meaning of this, Inspector?' she asked of Dwarkish, who was sitting on her desk, sipping coffee noisily from a thick glass tumbler. 'My staff has to be able to treat the patient, give first-aid.'

She couldn't have been much older than Radhika. She had the same kind of unthinking pride, Mahalinga thought, as if she was entitled to her loud-voiced opinions. The ward boy had probably knocked on the door as she was making breakfast for her husband. She had come right away. It probably wasn't often that emergencies came to her tiny hospital, where she probably spent most of her day on colds and cuts, aches and pains. The odd delivery by forceps or an appendicitis he guessed, maybe an emergency C section that arrived too late and could not be punted to the larger hospital in neighbouring Belmanur. But this, her eyes said, this was all so irregular.

'Yes, Doctor, yes-yes,' Dwarkish replied, putting his tumbler down carefully on her desk. 'This is an accident case, it is all for proper procedures, you see. We want only the doctor to see the patient. All these nurses, peons, everybody touching the body, destroying evidence, not good, you see. And then they will all tell stories, as if they saw it happen. In one week, the story will have ten heads, like Ravana,' he laughed shortly.

'Body?' she said. 'They tell me the poor woman is still alive?'

'You have to see for yourself, Doctor,' Dwarkish said. 'To us it is all the same, procedures and reports, you know.' He stood up. 'Let me take you there.'

After the doctor was led out of her office, Mahalinga and Rajanna moved the bundle to one of her treatment rooms. The doctor went in alone. She came out a short while later, face aflame.

'I need help,' she said to Dwarkish, 'this woman is alive, but just barely. I need my nurses, and after first-aid, we have to send her to the district hospital. She needs blood, maybe an operation. More than I can give.'

'Yes, Doctor,' Dwarkish smiled, as if he had expected her to say just that. 'But this is an accident case, special procedures are necessary.'

'Inspector, I have worked in Bangalore with all kinds of accident cases. As long as the forms are filled out, there is no restriction on who treats the patient or how they are treated.' She was angry now. 'She will die, if we stand here arguing.'

Dwarkish stood up, and with the lathi, lightly stroked her breasts, as if it were an introduction, a handshake. 'Of course, she will,' he said, and smiled. It might have been the smile that did it, coming as it did on the heels of his egregious presumption. She took a step back, angry at first, and then realisation arrived. He did this to her in plain sight of her nurses, orderlies, patients, and, as his underlings stood by. It was a warning as much as it was calculated humiliation. In that second, Mahalinga saw the confidence leave her eyes, and in its place an understanding, a fear that was unreasoning and immediate in its surprise.

'Give her first-aid,' Dwarkish said, magnanimous now, 'but there will be no transfers.'

They worked for an hour in the treatment room. The policemen did not interfere with the feverish pace of activity they mounted, sipping coffee, reading the newspaper with its customary black patches. In the end, there was too much blood loss and not enough time.

She pronounced the death an hour and ten minutes later.

When she went back to the office, Dwarkish was waiting. She stood at the door, unwilling to step inside. He smiled as he stood up.

'Don't trouble yourself too much about the paperwork,' he said, extremely polite. 'I have filled it out for you. Just sign, here and here.'

There was nothing for her to do but sign.

26

Mira

Ajji's voice flares across the dark room. Vimala aunty continues to write, but the listening women have all left. They had recoiled, retreated when Radhika Murthy was carried into the back room. It was as if they had reached a threshold they were loath to cross, and they hurried away, blaming neglected tasks. Appa and I wait in silence. My legs ache as I stand, but I do not step forward into the light around Ajji's bed, or ask to be noticed.

'I did not want to believe Mahalinga,' Ajji continues. 'I would have given anything not to believe him. I told myself that I did not, when I shouted at him that day, in my courtyard in front of the tulsi.

'You tell such lies,' I told him. 'It is a disgrace. It could not have been my son on the phone.'

But I knew somewhere deep within that Mahalinga was less likely to lie than Girish, that he was more of a man in Srinivas Murthy's mould than was my son.

I sent Mahalinga away with a promise to think about his fantastic tale.

'If only because you knew my husband in the old days. Anyone else,' I told him, my tone as magnanimous as I could make it, 'I would tell them their tongues would rot and fall to the ground if such were the lies they told.'

It was shameful, the way I treated the man who was with us in my husband's last hours. But a mother's instinct to protect her child would allow me to do no less.

Mahalinga left before Girish arrived that evening. A coward, I tried to tell myself, he does not want to face the man he accuses. He must lie.

Yet, we watched Girish closer that night, as he sat down to his evening meal. There was a new watch around his wrist, the newly acquired air he had of a man with means. I remembered the troubles with the things he did on the sly in the years before, the easy excuses that slipped as if oiled from between his teeth, delivered so easily they seemed to even lack the effort of thought. Vimala watched him closer than I did, I could see.

Later, that night, we prepared for bed. The kitchen things were put away and cleared for the next morning. Vimala came out to the hall with a mat and a pillow that she proceeded to unfurl on the floor beside my bed.

'I think I will sleep here from now on,' she said, as if it were the most commonplace thing in the world that she should lie outside in the hall on a mat like a widow while her husband lived and breathed and slept within.

That was all she said on the subject.

Your uncle said nothing that night. He did not mention it the next morning.

'Shall we go to the cinema this evening?' I heard him ask, however. Presents arrived in the evening, flower strings, a splashy saree with gold thread at its hem. Fruits arrived from K.R. Market the day after that, so fresh they might have just been picked off the tree. Tickets for the cinema, sweets that smelled of ghee even before you opened the packages they came in.

Vimala's mat remained stubbornly by mine.

The week after that he raged and called her names. Making a spectacle of himself that no decent family should see, uncaring that his mother heard, shameless in his tantrums for her to return to his bed.

Our house was a battlefield for months while Vimala remained steadfast. The presents he brought remained untouched. There were things she would do and things she would not. She would wash his clothes, cook his meals, sweep the floors and serve him his evening meal as she did before. She would not wear his sarees or his flowers. She would not dress up and stand at the gate to welcome him from a day at the office. She would only sleep in the hall by his mother like a widow while he still lived. She did not say a word.

I clung to the thread of my belief, tried to talk Vimala out of her resolve. What kind of family have we become, I asked her, and why are you so stubborn? Perhaps Mahalinga lied. What proof is there that he told the truth?

'You are so young,' I told her a hundred times, 'this sacrifice is bigger than you realise now. You will regret it in the future. Men cannot be punished in this way. He will find someone else.'

Then one morning, a few months after Mahalinga left, came news of his death. He had walked into the path of an oncoming lorry. His madness had increased.

'He wanted to die,' Girish said, 'he had been ranting for months.'

Vimala's eyes met mine that morning, and I discovered that I could no longer look her in the face.

I spent the day thinking while Girish was at work, gathering the things that I knew, weighing them against the stories that I heard, measuring and calibrating each for the truth. You played in the mud outside. You lifted yourself off the floor and walked, laughing with each step you took, never far from the picture of your mother that I had done my best to ignore. I looked at the picture again that morning, and saw your mother perhaps for the very first time as a woman. She was not just the daughter-in-law that I did not choose. Beautiful, it was true. But the stars that shimmered in her eyes were her love for my son. To that, I eventually decided that afternoon, there could be no argument.

By the time evening arrived, my mind was made up. If it was true, what Mahalinga said, and I now acknowledged to myself that it could be, we owed him a debt, you and I. Ours was not a family that forgot favours or debts. We would go to the funeral.

When we returned from the temple that evening, I heard from Vimala that Surendra had visited.

'It felt festive, when I went out to serve them coffee,' she told me.

We understood together that something they had wished for had come to pass. Was it only a harmless wish, such as the petitions I sent to the Gods while everyone slept, or something more concrete, such as a whisper to a man who drove a lorry? I was suddenly afraid to let my thoughts run their course.

I threw down my ultimatum with Girish that night—if Surendra ever came to the house again, I would go to Malehalli and never come back. You and I went to Mahalinga's funeral over his objections the next morning. It was a poor return for the loyalty he showed, but it was all we could do. I held Usha in my arms as she sobbed, and I knew what it was that I had to do.

After the funeral, I walked with you to the Christian church at the edge of Malehalli, a place that I never thought I would set foot into. One of the sisters there showed me your mother's grave. It had a block of granite at its head, a cross engraved above an inscription, Beloved Wife and Mother.

Kishore's work. When had he done this? Why had he not spoken of it to me? Most of the other graves were unmarked, or had simple wooden crosses, but with fresh flowers that I doubt your mother's grave saw.

We sat there awhile. I held you up to the headstone. 'Your daughter,' I said.

Then, I went to meet the Mother Superior at the orphanage. She was Radhika's mother as much as I was Kishore's, I thought. The respect that I did not accord Radhika in life, I would at least accord her in death.

Mother was happy to see you. 'The spitting image of Radhika when she came here,' she told me.

My daughter-in-law was once a child just like the one I held in my arms and loved, I thought in surprise. I had never considered this before.

'Mother,' I said to her, only because she was owed this as any mother was, 'I have something to tell you. I am not sure if it is true, but I suspect it is.'

We went together to the government hospital, to see the doctor there.

The lady doctor had not spoken of the events at her hospital to her husband when she went home in the evening. She had carried her secret better than Mahalinga and had hated herself less. But in the months that followed, she told us, it became easier to think of the morning, and examine the shame that she carried from it. She told herself that if someone ever asked her, she would tell the truth. When we arrived, and she saw the picture of your mother, we did not even have to ask.

She told us she saw us from the window. A white sareed widow and a nun, who looked as if they might be in an unlikely union of shared loss, and she had already guessed. While you played with the pens on her office desk, distracted by one that could write in four colours, she told us her story.

She recounted it briefly, without frills or fancy. It might have been a patient report that she was presenting to a superior at rounds, and unemotional as it was, it confirmed Mahalinga's account, every word he spoke about that cool morning where he had stood by her desk bathed in sweat.

'I don't know much more,' she told us at the end, 'but the police brought her in, and they wanted her dead. The body showed signs of extreme violence.' Perhaps she thought I was Radhika's mother, and did not need to hear the details that I could nevertheless imagine, the broken bones, the tearing and injury, the jagged edges of her insides pouring blood that they could not replenish.

We blessed her together, Mother Superior and I. We thanked her for all that she did for Radhika.

On the way back, Mother Superior spoke of forgiveness, but her voice spoke of her struggle rather than her faith. We walked to our old home instead of the church in unspoken agreement. It seemed as if she needed some time before she could face her responsibilities and her God. For me, there was only shame. If I never showed my face to the world again, I would be happy, I remember thinking, as we sat among the trees outside in silence. Your mother descended the hill a hundred times, suitcase in one hand, child in the other, as I watched. I would give everything I had to take that minute back.

There was nothing left to give, of course. Before, we had been poor, but we had our honour. The honour was gone with her death. But the shame of this truth went deeper than dishonour, deeper even than that. I had my granddaughter, but to give her up would be to give up my life, my hope, everything. I could not give you up, even to atone.

As I looked around the trees and the yard, my thoughts turned to your grandfather. This is the sum of it all, I thought.

This is what I have made of your family after you left. Don't think you are not to blame, I told him. He is your son too. You left me the sons but nothing to bring them up with, nothing to prevent this from happening. If you had been alive, none of this would have happened. And you have left me with nothing to even make a gesture of apology to your daughter-in-law for the wrongs that we have done to her.

It was then that I saw it.

There was the house. The little house that had been in our family for more generations than I could count, its floors and walls hallowed by a thousand prayers, its pristine purity maintained by centuries of discipline, of madi. There was that.

I went up to Mother Superior, interrupting her prayer as she knelt between the trees, asking, perhaps, for peace or the strength for forgiveness.

'Take this house,' I told her. 'I want you to have it, for the orphanage. There is only one condition. You have to name it after my daughter-in-law. My voice broke down finally when I spoke her name in apology for the very first time, Radhika Murthy.'

27
Mira

Ajji's voice stills. I feel the tears that I do not understand run down my face.

I step forward into the pool of light around Ajji's bed. My aunt looks up in the pause she is allowed in her writing, and sees me. She drops paper and pen, and holds her arms out to me. 'Mira, you are here.'

Ajji opens her eyes at my name. She cannot see me yet from her bed.

'Mira, Mira,' she says, struggling to lift herself off the pillows.

Despite everything, anger, regret, the things she has told that I still cannot comprehend, the sight of her weakness disarms me. I am at her side before I can think, holding her, saying, 'Ajji, Ajji, rest, I am here. It is all right.'

She looks me in the face for a minute, her eyes filling slowly with the tears she has probably not allowed herself through her story. I allow her to hug me.

'Radhika,' she says, and it is clear to me that her mind has wandered, as she weeps and caresses my face, 'Radhika, forgive me.'

'Amma,' Vimala aunty says gently, smoothing back her hair, crying herself. 'It is Mira. Mira is here, and look, here is Kishore.'

'Yes, Mira,' Ajji says, still caressing my face, 'my child. You came. You came.'

Appa comes up by Ajji's bed.

'Amma,' Appa says, reaching and taking Ajji's hand, 'it is not your fault. What happened to Radhika is not your fault.'

Appa looks as if he has aged in the few minutes since we arrived by Ajji's bed. But he looks more resolute, as if he says this to himself as much as he does to Ajji.

Morning advances and more people arrive while Ajji's hand is still tightly clasped in mine. There are those that come to relieve the ones that worked all night, and those that arrive just to hear the next part of the story, having tossed in their beds wondering about the parts that they missed. There are huddles outside Ajji's room, the tale flying without restraint now, whispered mouth to ear, called to friends and relatives over surreptitious phone calls, carried home and out by the ones that have stayed up all night to hear. It had started out as such a simple story, they whisper to each other behind opened cupboards or lifted up charts, until it became so different. When she reached the part in the police station, I hear one of them whisper, I could not bear to listen anymore.

'Could this be like a dying declaration?' one of the nurse's aides wonders, 'like that Vivek Nayak movie, where the villain's assistant confessed all before he died? They used the tape to arrest the villain.'

'Don't be silly,' a nurse mutters to her, 'it is not like that. This is not some movie. It was so many years ago, they will say the case has expired or something. And do you know who this Surendra is?'

'You had better hope he doesn't hear you,' another adds. 'I am surprised that she told them this story now, as if it could bring them anything other than more sorrow. She must have been delirious.'

The nurse's aide moves away to discuss the issue with the infectious disease specialist, evidently not impressed by their admonishing.

'You will not believe this, Amma,' she begins, telling her Ajji's story while the consultant forgets her waiting patients and forgets to check her watch that would have reminded her of the bleeding minutes from her day.

In the middle of all this, Ajji dies. She has been silent all morning. When the ICU bustles with visiting consultants and the tea boy hovers around them outside, alarms blare. Her breathing has slowed to nothing; the heart rate has fallen to a line. They rush in with the defibrillator and their vials of medicines, only for us to stop them.

'She deserves to go in peace,' Appa says. 'Let her be.'

We gather around her bed, the tears of the night spent. She looks at peace. No longer drawn in by secrets or the burdens she alone bears. Her lips may even be curved into a smile, as if she sees a sight of joy or welcome. Vimala aunty straightens her sheets.

'She must have smiled like this when she was a newlywed,' my aunt says, and it does not seem as incongruous as it should. Appa and I hold Ajji's hands on either side, saying our goodbyes to this woman we still love. If there are resentments or angers remaining, I cannot find them.

Dr Shenoy arrives soon after, as does Lakhotia. 'What, no one called Girish Murthy?' Lakhotia says. Ignoring the junior doctor's excuses, he makes the call himself. 'Girish-*avare*, I am so sorry to inform you—but we did everything we could.'

But it is soon apparent to Shenoy, even Lakhotia, that something is amiss. There is the air of shared secrecy in their domain, far too much talk that dies within their earshot, too many visitors that look as if they have no reason to be here.

'You need to run a tighter ship, Dr Shenoy, this is not some government hospital,' I hear Lakhotia mutter to Shenoy as they leave together. At the door, I see them pass a bearded young man who enters in a kurta and Kholapuri sandals.

He stops by Ajji's bed.

'Are you Kishore Murthy?' he asks hand extended, as Appa hesitates.

He's a reporter, he tells us, and he heard the tale from his aunt, whose daughter, his cousin, is a nurse in the hospital.

'I am sorry to intrude on your grief,' he says, though it is polite and untrue. 'I heard about the incident that happened during the Emergency, and wonder if I could speak with you.'

Appa looks me in the face for the first time since our world changed.

'Mira,' he says, 'it is your decision.'

I think of the woman in my childhood picture. Elegant, with eyes so full of love and life. She is not one I can imagine being violated, or petrified for years the way she has been. 'Beloved wife and mother', carved into a tombstone that no one visits, the words never spoken aloud in the same sentence as her name. All memories buried with her, forgotten into stone. There is no real choice about what must be done.

I step forward.

'I am Mira Murthy,' I say. 'What would you like to know?'

28

Mira

We walk down to the gleaming marble and wood lobby downstairs, now more peopled in the day. There are plush leather sofas scattered around the edges, and we find the one that is farthest from the receptionist's desk. Vimala aunty has walked down with us at my request, and it is she who does most of the talking to the reporter. Her account mirrors that of Ajji's and retains its horror, even on repetition. There is the hum of different conversations all around us, families engaged in their own anxieties, some with the loud, joyful laughter of those that arrive to welcome new babies. No one notices us. Barely an hour later, the interview is over. The reporter has all that he needs, and he thanks us.

'I'll have my colleagues check on the story in Malehalli,' he says. 'We will proceed carefully, given the names involved. I'll contact you again if I have questions.'

When he leaves, Vimala aunty reaches over to hold my hand. We have a sense of a fundamental difference in the world, that the secret that has left us has acquired a trajectory and life of its own. It has been only thirty hours since I left America with Appa, but it feels as if a lifetime has passed. There is no time to sit and tarry. There are formalities to be completed, a few short hours that we can sit by Ajji's side for the last and final time.

'You could go home for an hour or two,' my aunt tells me as we walk across to the elevator, 'take a bath, or eat something. There are auto rickshaws outside. Here, I have the keys to the house. I can come when they bring Ajji.'

But I don't want to leave her. So we walk to the receptionist instead, intending to find out if there is a hotel within walking distance or facilities that the hospital provides for relatives that Appa and I can use. The day has not exhausted its surprises for me, because as we walk up to the receptionist, there ahead of us is an older couple.

'Is there a Mrs Meenakshi Murthy admitted here?' the man asks, and we see the receptionist hesitate, her pencil hovering over a name on the computer screen in front of her.

He holds himself ramrod straight, the creases on his trousers and shirt sleeves as knife-edged as I remember them, and beside him is a woman who is harder to recognise because this is the first time I have ever seen her in a burkha. I know them before Vimala aunty recognises them, before they turn around at my voice and I see their faces—Farid uncle and Rehana aunty.

It is Rehana aunty's face that I search first. The strange mixture of sadness, anger, guilt and joy it holds, and the next minute I cannot see at all for the tears that come heavy and fast, that can no longer be held back. Not that it matters, because I feel myself being enveloped in two arms first and then another pair over the first, and the tears that are no longer just mine fall in earnest.

'Mira,' they say, over and over again.

'We heard Ajji was sick,' Rehana aunty says momentarily, drying her eyes and drawing back, careful not to let me go, while Farid uncle pats me on the head, smoothing back my hair to see my face better.

'Yes,' Vimala aunty says. 'She passed away this morning.'

Farid uncle says, 'I'm sorry we could not get here earlier. I would have liked to see her one last time. She was always a friend to us.' Unlike some others, I think, but he does not say.

'We will take you upstairs to see her,' Vimala aunty offers, and we are already turning away when the receptionist interrupts. 'I know you are VIP guests,' she says, hesitantly, 'but could you wait another half an hour? Usually we don't allow visitors into the ICU—but in half an hour at least the consultant rounds will be over.'

'Of course,' Farid uncle says, and I look at him for the first time in the face. He still has the hint of laughter in his eyes that he always had, and for that I am grateful. His moustache is salt and pepper now, and while he still has the straight-backed stance of his youth, there is something older about him now, an acknowledgement of time and defeat.

He smiles at me, and there is no shadow of anger in his eyes. 'Mira,' he says, 'were you planning to stay in America forever?'

'Yes,' Rehana aunty scolds, though her voice is gentle. 'Do you know how many letters I have written to you since, Mira? Did you even read them?'

I have no excuses to offer, no words that can be an acceptable response.

Vimala aunty murmurs beside me, 'She came last night, hasn't even eaten since.' And suddenly they are all united in a single purpose, to see that I am fed. Vimala aunty returns upstairs and I walk outside with Farid uncle and Rehana aunty. They saw a restaurant on their way in, they tell me, one right across the street.

Outside on the pavement, I realise that I am holding Rehana aunty's hand. It reminds me of when Anisa and I were younger and we went with her to the market, hanging on to her hands, one on either side. I know she remembers it too, when she says, her voice brighter for the effort, 'There, that's the one we saw,' as if there is no absence between us, no person we love and miss.

'I am not hungry,' I say again, and it is true. But we walk across the street anyway, to the little restaurant in the basement that has a newish sign that says, Starlight Café. It is an incongruous name, because the restaurant is clearly a relic of the old Bangalore, one more likely to bear a family name or that of a favourite deity. The blackboard on the street with the specials written in pink chalk in Kannada and English—Khara Bath, Masala Dose, Uddina Vade—is enough to declare it.

We make our way between the Formica-topped tables and chairs packed into rows, to find a place to sit. At mid-morning, almost every table is full, with, at a glance, white-collar government employees, auto drivers and college students playing truant. Over the buzz of their conversations, busy waiters bang trays and glasses of water about, and loudly recite the day's specials at breakneck speed. It could have been any generic eatery in the Bangalore of my childhood, one Anisa and I would have disdained as uncool. But every detail feels new with my absence, and reassuring in its familiarity.

Before Rehana aunty and I can unknot our aching fingers, a waiter materialises at our table. Sweeping his dishrag on the table top, straightening the macramé vase with the plastic flowers that sits on top, he addresses Farid uncle, 'So *saar*, *en kodli*?'

Farid uncle and Rehana aunty are not hungry either, but they will eat because they want me to. Farid uncle orders the Maddur vade for himself and khara bath for Rehana aunty. For me, a benne masala dose, the biggest item on the menu. 'And three coffees,' he tells the waiter, 'at the end.'

'You should eat,' Rehana aunty says, the way she used to at her dining table before. 'You are so thin. You need to keep your strength up, for the funeral.' Her face veil is thrown back, and I see the new lines around her eyes, the smattering of grey at her temples. The Rehana aunty I knew before would have reached for hair dye when the grey first appeared, but the one before me hides herself in a burkha. It is a conundrum, and I cannot find a way to ask her about it.

Farid uncle notices, though, and he says, smiling, 'Yes, she wears this costume now, to confuse me in my old age.'

'It's not a costume,' Rehana aunty retorts, as if this is a disagreement they have had for a long time. 'I wear a burkha because it is what I should have always done.'

Farid uncle says, resignedly, 'Rehana has discovered religion in a new way, and she thinks all of us need to benefit from it.'

'I should never have listened to him,' Rehana aunty says, 'I should have never left our ways. It was his mistake, and he still refuses to accept it. He always lectures me, Mira.'

They are interrupted in their squabble by the waiter who arrives with our orders.

'Eat,' Rehana aunty says again, and for a while we do just that in silence.

'Sometimes, we all have to pay for the mistakes of a few,' she says again, even as Farid uncle turns around to look at her in warning. 'Everything happens for a reason,' she continues, 'even when we can't see it with our eyes or understand it. Even if we cannot see why, sometimes He has to punish us. It is all Allah's will.'

'Rehana, you should ask Mira what she's been doing instead of telling her your half-baked theories.' There is an audible note of warning now in Farid uncle's voice.

'She would have been twenty-four,' Rehana aunty says, as if she has not heard him. 'She would have graduated, been married. Maybe I would have nagged her for a grandchild.'

She stops punishing herself with an effort, and says, 'As you would have been, Mira. Not living alone in some far-off place, as if you had no home or family. How could we have let it happen?'

She seems unable to stop now that she has started, and she seems not to know or care who hears her. The words come fast, as if she has thought or said this a hundred times before.

'He said all the time that Anisa was young, that she should do what she wanted. All this nonsense about religion not being important. Going to the temple, visiting Ganeshas, such blasphemy. As if she was some Hindu girl. It is a new world, he'd tell me. Don't think like your grandmother. And what happened, finally? It is all his fault, for not allowing me to bring up Anisa right. And he still refuses to accept his mistake.'

I am saved a response by the waiter who arrives with the coffee, which is just as well, because there is nothing I can say. We drink our coffees in silence in the wake of Rehana aunty's outburst, while she dabs at her eyes and straightens her shoulders.

Farid uncle sighs. 'She would have gone crazy, despite everything I tried. If not for Adil, she really would have gone mad. Now she just wears her burkha and tells me how wrong I was.'

'Yes, Adil,' Rehana aunty says. 'He lives in Bangalore now. We see him every day.'

Adil. A name I have not seen or heard in seven years. A man now, I think, not the boy who once promised me he would wait.

'How is he?' I ask, careful to keep my voice light.

They are happy to talk about him. Rehana aunty's smile appears again, Farid uncle relaxes by her side. He is an engineer, works hard, is successful, and was almost married three years ago. Saira, Rehana aunty says. That was the girl he almost married. She does not describe her, but the elegance of the name supplies my imagination with punishing detail. I can almost see her, petite and jean clad, shaking hair left long and silky, her fine-boned and fair-skinned hands with fuchsia nails bright against the white of Adil's shirt. I shake my head to dispel this image. It is not my concern.

It was to be an arranged marriage, Rehana aunty says as we get up from our table. She stresses the 'arranged', as if it is an adequate excuse.

'You did not read my letters, did you?' she scolds as we walk outside the restaurant, voice small and fierce the way Anisa's used to be. 'You would have known all this without us having to tell you. How could you be like this all these years?'

Behind us, Farid uncle says, 'Can you wait a day or two before you start nagging her?'

But in their scolding and bickering, their affection is clear. Despite Rehana aunty's regrets that have more to do with me than Farid uncle, there is the hope that they have forgiven me, if only in part. Rehana aunty puts her arm around me as we cross the street. 'It feels as if our Anisa is with us again.'

29

Girish

The gulmohar trees were ablaze in the sunlight again, their orange petals lighting up branch and tree, and settling in silent flames along the street. Relatives and neighbours, back from the hurried ceremony at the electric crematorium, were arrayed in diminutive groups along the garden path, in the rented chairs Thimmappa had brought in hours before. Sunlight puddled between their shadows, golden yet chill, it seemed to Girish, strange brightness without warmth that seeped through to his bones as he walked between them and silence descended abruptly into their whispered conversations. It was as if he carried the contagion, and everywhere he went, it spread and held, dense and cold.

Girish's phone remained an ever-increasing weight in his pocket, silent as if the work of a lifetime had never been. The programme had aired on a cable network the night before, as they brought Ajji home from the hospital. He had seen snatches of it in the lobby as they walked out behind her body, on a slab of ice in a black box. All it took was a glance, really. There was a lurid red ticker that ran at the bottom of the screen, lest anyone missed the breathless commentary from a popular network reporter. Breaking news: Powerful Politician Implicated in Rape and Murder During Emergency. Victim's Relative Involved in Cover-Up. Details Emerging. Don't miss the special at 9 p.m.

He had imagined something like this in the early years following Radhika's death, when they moved to Bangalore and carefully arranged their stories. But he had been lulled by time and success. Those fears had faded. He had held the world in his hand, spinning the globe between his fingertips, granting favours and climbing ladders. He had worried only about Surendra's goodwill. He had forgotten.

The previous evening, before the silence descended, he had paced up and down the garden path in whispered phone calls while the women in the family had washed and dressed Ajji's body inside. The chief minister had issued a statement in the early hours of the evening, calling the whole business an Opposition conspiracy, a framing of a respected statesman. Party spokesmen relayed his message to several stations. Then, Surendra had gone on television shortly after, to a rival news network, saying the story was a pre-election fabrication by the Opposition.

'This is an effort to sully my name,' he had thundered, and summoned tears when invoking the suffering of a dear friend's family. 'This is a time of bereavement for them,' he said, 'a death of a mother, no less. These vultures,' he said with every appearance of honesty, 'they have no sense of decency. They have used her delirious imaginings to blacken the family's reputation.'

It was masterful. It might have worked, especially in the old days with a single Doordarshan channel and its state-funded jobs. Instead, Surendra faced a younger man whose hunger for a scoop overrode any respect or decency that was invoked. It had not gone well.

'Is it not true that the government doctor who wrote the original report on the death is willing to recant,' he had asked, 'that she corroborates this story?'

In the moment that the camera captured the fear that

lanced across Surendra's face, the damage was done. It would be hours before someone actually tracked down the former government medical officer where she now lived in Mangalore, close to the obstetric clinic of moderate local repute that she owned.

'I remember the case,' she said, somewhat befuddled by the waiting cameras as she emerged from a late-night delivery. 'It weighed on me all these years. I am not proud of my part in what happened, but I was afraid for my life.'

But by that time, it scarcely mattered what she said. Surendra's expression when he was asked the question had made its rounds over every station in the country, as damning a confession as signed and delivered.

It was shortly after the interview that the silence had descended and grown. Girish stayed outside in the deepening darkness while the rest of the family gathered around his mother's body for the customary vigil before the cremation. He saw the flickering lamps through the hall window, the bowed heads around her body. Mira and Vimala sat silently, their arms around one another. Kishore's head was bent, his expression hidden. Rehana, Farid and Adil arrived later in the evening to find spaces around Ajji's body, adding their bent heads to those of her family.

Girish remained outside. It will all blow over, he told himself, again and again. We have been through bigger upsets. The chief minister needs us, needs Devidas. It will not work without Surendra. Thimmappa arrived with the shamiana and the chairs, and was careful to cloak his derision with an exaggerated show of respect. It only made Girish angrier, of course. He cursed Thimmappa audibly as soon as his back was turned, as if this mess were all of his making. When I get out of this, he told himself, I will make sure that he never gets a job again.

When Lakshmi arrived and walked up the garden path to find a spot by Vimala at Ajji's head, she did not see him. Girish watched her from the shadows, mistaking her oversight for an intended slight. Her son, he told himself, he will go to jail. Where was that dog? No loyalty, after all that I have done for him. The air grew chill around him, the streetlights acquired halos in the fog and still there was no ring on his phone. Not even Surendra called. He walked down the street, and all the televisions that he spied through open windows were tuned to the same story. It had all the elements of a hit movie—intrigue, sex, violence and power, with the irresistible possibility that it was also true. It was as if no one could look away. Mongrels, these journalists, he told himself, look at their glee.

He could not go into his own house to turn on the television, standing as it did a few feet from his mother's body. He called Vinay on his cell phone. Bring the car around, he said, I need to go to Benson Town. Minutes later, they were on their way, through Sampige Road still crowded in the early night, Miller Road with the still-open pubs and coffee shops, yuppie crowds milling between them, to Cantonment and Nandi Durga Road. Those houses have televisions, Girish thought, of the stately mansions and the world he coveted, and the same story is on them as it is in Malleshwaram. It was sudden, the realisation, and it settled like a chill into a corner of his brain. No matter, he told himself, I only need to talk to Surendra, and Devidas. And for once, I will walk into that apartment like an owner, not like a thief in the night. A mistress would not make much news now. He almost smiled.

Vinay had to park behind a large tempo at the entrance of the building. Someone was moving. Girish made his way to the apartment by the stairs; the lift had been commissioned by the movers. Sorry for the inconvenience, the sign above the lift said. He arrived on the third floor out of breath. I could have taken these stairs two at a time, he thought, of the day he went up the college steps in Malehalli with his brother, and with that thought came a glimpse of Radhika's face when he first saw her, standing by the roses with the nuns. It was another surprise, the clarity of that image, the way he remembered the swell of her cheek, the parting of her lips in a smile.

The door to the flat was open. He walked inside to realise that it was Sitara who was moving. The flat had been stripped, and everything that was in it neatly packaged, waiting in the hall to be taken to the tempo downstairs. The bitch. To do this at the first sign of trouble. I should have whipped her last night, like Surendra suggested. She was nowhere in sight. Chellamma was in the drawing room, obviously in charge of the move. For want of anything better to do, Girish glared at her. They all ignored him, Chellamma, the khaki-uniformed movers.

'What the hell are you doing?' Girish shouted finally, and made to stop the mover closest him, a slight boy in his teens. The boy sidestepped him, almost apologetic, moving swiftly to the door. Chellamma stepped up. 'She has gone, and she's taking her things.' The insolence, Girish thought, that she looks at me and talks to me like an equal. Sweeper woman from the gutters.

'Where has she gone?' To think that he had to ask her to find out.

'None of your business,' Chellamma said, obviously relishing her role in the excitement. 'You cannot find her.'

'I will find her,' Girish shouted, all his anger building up, at this woman who dared insolence with him, the movers, who to a man ignored him as they worked around him, and the bitch that dared leave him.

'Oh, and then what will you do? The same thing you did to your sister-in-law?' Chellamma hawked up and spit at his feet, on the expensive marble floor that he owned. He reached over to grab her neck; the insolent bitch, he would teach her to talk.

Suddenly, he felt a dozen hands on him, and felt himself being pulled back.

'Do you realise who you are dealing with?' he shouted as he was lifted up and moved back like another packaged piece of furniture in the hall.

'I'm sorry, sir.' It was the slight boy who spoke. 'But we have instructions. If there is a disturbance, we are to call the police.'

'Call the police,' Girish screamed. 'I am being robbed. I need the police. You don't know who I am. I will send you all to jail.'

Suddenly, there were faces in the hallway outside the door. All of Sitara's neighbours were out, drawn by the noise of the scuffle. Not one of them moved forward to help him up when he was deposited on the floor of the hallway.

He stood up, still shouting.

'Sir, I have to ask you to leave.' It was Mr. Bhandari from the flat opposite.

Before Girish could turn around and say, and who do you think you are, Bhandari continued, 'I am the president of the resident's association, and we have a complaint against you, that you cheated Miss Sitara. She gave us a document that shows that she is the real owner of the flat, and that false documents were notarised in your name. It is a police case. Please leave.'

Girish stopped shouting. The bitch, she thought she was so clever. He would show her, he was Girish Murthy. He knew people. Then it struck him anew—Surendra was gone. His phone had been silent all morning. He knew no one. A sudden tiredness descended on his limbs, as if somehow his energy had deflated with his pride.

'Laugh now, but I will show you who laughs last,' he said to Bhandari. 'And you will wish you were never born.' It sounded hollow and trite even to his ears, as if he was playing a villain in one of Sitara's movies. It is because I haven't eaten for hours, he thought, this tiredness. Tomorrow will be better.

No one stopped him when he took the lift downstairs. Vinay waited in the foyer.

Girish straightened his dishevelled clothing, smoothed down his hair.

'Legislatures Home,' he said to Vinay, who held open the door. There is an odd look on the boy's face, Girish thought, he looks guilty. 'What's the matter?' he asked, wondering what else was in store.

'There will be newspaper people there,' Vinay said, hesitantly, and Girish realised that while it was undoubtedly true, it was also the first time the boy had offered an opinion. At least he didn't turn tail and run, like everyone else.

In a momentary softening, he asked, 'And why do you look so worried?'

'It is not true, is it, *saar*, about—about Mira's mother?'

So that was it. He did feel guilty, probably about the incident with Mira. Fool, he thought, silly sentimental fool. Just like my brother. He sank back into his seat, seeing his brother at Vinay's age. Trusting, looking up at Girish as if nothing he spoke could be anything other than the truth.

I am just tired, Girish thought; it is not pain that I feel. I am not some sentimental fool. The weariness grew in his bones regardless, and he summoned up a final vicious impulse. 'No it was all true, she was a slut who slept with anything that moved. My brother was lucky to be rid of her.' He sank back into his seat, avoiding Vinay's eyes in the rear-view mirror. 'You have eaten my salt, you remember that. No matter what anyone says.'

Vinay drove past Girish's office at the PWD building. The building looked desolate, empty and dark windowed. Yet, there was a television crew camped in the front.

'They will be waiting at Legislatures Home, too,' Vinay said again.

Finally it was decided. They would wait it out somewhere. It was already midnight. In a couple of hours, the vultures would go home, especially with no success.

Vinay went in to book a room at a hotel nearby, and Girish went up a little later. Vinay left to buy food, and Girish turned on the television. He was prepared for unending rehashes of the evening's news and experts shouting at each other over their respective viewpoints. Was it murder, or is this an Opposition conspiracy? Everybody would get their turn to shout.

So it was a surprise, when minutes after he turned on the television, there was more breaking news. The chief minister had come out of his house to address the television cameras parked outside.

'I support our home minister Shri Surendra, and believe with all my heart that he will be cleared of these accusations,' he began, and yet Girish knew that something was amiss. The first tendril of chill misgiving wound itself around his weariness, and the chief minister continued, 'But I feel that as long as the matter is open to question, he should step down from his post to allow the authorities to investigate. I have talked with Shri Surendra, and he has proved that he is a man of integrity by agreeing to resign. We both feel that this is the best way to defeat certain elements in our society who seek to distract us from important issues that the common man faces, by sowing doubts and discord.' He proceeded to list his party's campaign pledges, but Girish did not stop to listen. He dialled Surendra's number, jabbing at his phone in fury, as if that would impel Surendra's phone to ring louder and force him to pick up. On his fifth try, someone did pick up. It was one of the bodyguards.

'Don't be a fool, Murthy,' he said, 'Surendra is gone. There is going to be a CBI case tomorrow. You should leave too.'

'Gone? Gone where?' Girish asked, feeling stupid, as the chill slid along his body and settled on his skin in goose bumps.

'Wherever his Swiss bank account will take him,' the oaf laughed, as if it was funny. 'All the deals have been made. He was given a false passport. Everybody got a few crores. It is all settled. Maybe you can go hide in that small town you came from, what was it, Malehalli? Famous place nowadays.'

Girish disconnected the phone. It was a strange feeling, the warm metal against his icy skin, and he dropped it quickly into his pocket. It cannot be, he thought. Surendra would not leave without telling me, after all that I have done for him. He will call. Maybe there is a second passport in a different name. But that idea was strange too, like a fairy tale ending written for children.

He walked out of the hotel room, down the stairs and into the street. It might only take him a couple of hours to walk to Malleshwaram. He would make it back in time for the funeral. Kishore would be lost without him, and as the older son Girish would have to light the pyre.

He could have called Vinay and asked him to bring the car around, but that seemed to be too much of an effort. It seemed easier to walk in the cooling night, walking along the sidewalk like a ghost in his white clothes.

Vinay found him a short way off and bundled him into the car. He wanted to tell Vinay that he would rather walk, but he did not. It seemed easier not say anything.

The hearse arrived just before dawn. More relatives were

gathered on the veranda, and more neighbours lined up all along the garden path, spilling outside the gate. There were no television vans. Kishore and a couple of the neighbours had talked to waiting journalists and asked for privacy, Vinay told him.

They went to the electric crematorium; the priest was there for the ceremony. When he asked for the son to step up, Kishore brushed past him to the priest. Nobody turned to him, or looked in Girish's face. This was how his mother had treated him when she lived, ignoring him as if he did not live under the same roof that she did, and had not once come from her body. As if he did not exist.

The sun climbed higher into the sky when they left the crematorium. Once home, as if by accident, he caught Mira's eye. She is a child, he thought, almost my own. I have hoisted her on my shoulders more than once. But the face she turned to him was her mother's, and he saw the same sultry eyes that seemed to mock him once, before he had known her. Before she was his brother's wife. It was a dark, knowing glance, he thought; her mother's look. Perhaps that was the thing that made him give her up to Surendra as he did. But had she ever looked at him like that? Or did he now imagine it in retrospect, to make what he did easier to bear? Mira turned away before he could reclaim her face from her mother's.

But it did give him strength, that look. It was a reminder of the times before. He felt young again, and his brother even younger.

'Kishore,' he called to his younger brother, suddenly hopeful, 'don't believe all this nonsense that you hear.'

Kishore turned around to face him, his back to the veranda.

'Kishore,' he said again, when his brother said nothing. The silence around them grew with the chill in Girish's bones, and everyone stopped to listen.

It was the face of a middle-aged man that Kishore had, not that of his younger brother. Not the boy who willingly gave up his share of the sweets that their mother gave them, not the face of the young man who believed his brother's tale of his wife's death.

He had the expression of a man who had his unquestioning faith betrayed. Girish supposed that he would scream, hurl curses and excoriate him for his loss. He expected it—it was what he would have done. And after, perhaps there would be forgiveness. They could return to some semblance of their old relationship once the words were hurled and the hurts mitigated. It was so long ago, and he had married again, after all.

But Kishore only said, 'Go away,' after the silence had stretched and deepened between them, and Girish knew that there would be no mitigation. Go away. It felt like banishment.

He turned around obediently, walking to the gate, feeling as if his feet did not touch the ground and that the air and the sun passed through him instead of around. Vinay hung back and did not follow him this time. All that he could do was walk along the street, carrying his burden of icy contagion, spreading silence as he passed.

He wondered if the phone had grown colder too, lying so close to his body. He pushed his hand into his pocket, and encountered another piece of metal instead. A key ring. He still had the keys to the old ration shop. Minutes later, he could tell that it still worked.

He went inside. The room was dirty. The furniture gone, probably removed by creditors. But there was a convenient hook on the ceiling, and a rope in the corner among the scattered gunny bags of ration issue grain and sugar. There it was at last, a place that was his, alone. If he was the man he was yesterday, he might have turned around and walked out, to humiliation or imprisonment, or the things he saw in his brother's eyes. But he felt hollowed out, as if the bits of himself that he had sold over the years had vanished along with Surendra, leaving a shell, a ghost.

He had heard the stories, of a man who hanged himself here and came back as a ghost that wandered the night, but surely they had that backwards. A ghost who wandered the streets would come, is what they meant to say, and find his solace here in a final rest.

He picked up the rope, and began his patient knots.

30

Mira

Adil. I recognise him almost before I see his face, from the small shock in the pit of my stomach that is stronger than in my memory. His face is fuller. The passing years have added fat to the bony contours and softened the edges around his eyebrows and along his cheekbones. His hairline inches higher above the familiar broad eyebrows. His forehead is a tad more generous. A small scar over his right eyebrow is new, a lasting reminder of the bruises he had when I saw him before. His eyes are different as well, or maybe it is just his gaze, more guarded, distant. A beard hides his cleft chin. For shame, why did he do that? He steps into the light in front of me as I sit at the vigil beside Ajji's body. For a minute his eyes find mine, and he inclines his head in greeting. It is a formal acknowledgement, and not one he would have needed to make before.

They all come to share in our grief, every neighbour that Ajji has known and stopped to greet in the street, including the ones who moved away years ago. Even Lakshmi, though my uncle is missing for most of the night and the early morning, and Vinay, presumably, is with him. When we finally leave for the crematorium, the house and street are full with the people who care about Ajji's absence. It is a comfort. We stay together, Rehana aunty, Vimala aunty and I. When we return, everyone disperses. I do not see Adil again, though Farid uncle and Rehana aunty are the last to leave.

It is the next day before I realise all that has happened, so quickly while we still mourned Ajji. So rapid is the unravelling of Surendra's reign. The stories I braced myself for, the accusations of immorality that I expected are absent in the suddenness of its demise. Surendra and my uncle disappear quickly, like demons in dreams. In only two days, there are more reporters, more questions, opinion pieces and editorials than we can read. The story has been useful to Surendra's enemies. There are whispers that the chief minister is happier to be rid of him, and that he is responsible for the prominence that Ajji's story has received. Yet, it cannot be this easy.

They bring us news of Girish uncle's suicide when we are in the garden, cleaning up after the neighbours. Thimmappa has taken down the shamiana and hauled the rented chairs away, but there is mud on the garden path brought in by scores of shoes that needs sweeping. The floors inside still wait for their ritual washing. My aunt and I had started outside earlier. It was a relief to work after the vigil, the visitors and the commiserations they brought, and the dead sleep of profound fatigue. Vimala aunty and I are together in the silent morning. Appa has left to pay for the chairs and the shamiana.

'Girish-*avaru* was planning to pay after, but I haven't seen him since the funeral,' Thimmappa had said earlier still that morning, avoiding Appa's eyes. 'I can take the money and settle the account for you, *saar*. Or you could come and see to it yourself.'

Vinay is the one to tell us. He rattles the gate for our attention.

'They found his body in the old ration shop,' Vinay says. 'It looks like he hanged himself.'

Vimala aunty says nothing. Vinay repeats himself, 'Girish-*avaru*, they found him in the old ration shop. You should come, do something. Otherwise the police will take the body to the morgue.'

My aunt sighs. 'Perhaps it is just as well that we haven't washed the house yet.'

She drops her broom and walks back indoors, ignoring Vinay. I can see the pain in her eyes as she turns away that she refuses to acknowledge.

I stand on the path alone, facing Vinay. He looks me in the eye, as if he is not the same person that tore my clothes, and said, isn't this what you wanted, slut? I say nothing, wondering at this man who once was a child that went to see Ganeshas.

'Mira,' Vinay says again, 'he was your uncle. You should claim the body, do your duty. I will help you. It will be like before, when we were children.'

We played on the street together when we were children. Hide and seek when the boys joined in, hopscotch when it was just the girls. We chattered away in Kannada together with the neighbourhood kids, Anisa, Vinay and I. One of them started a chant once, 'Mira, Mira s*annakki,* peppermint *thinakki,* rail *gaadi hatthakki, gandan karkondu odakki.*' It was a silly ditty about a girl named Mira who ate peppermints and ran away with her husband on a train. It made me cry and Vinay got into a fight over this. The scuffle ended in a torn shirt and a complaint to Lakshmi, which ended play time on the street with us for Vinay. He still chased me on the street for old times' sake after that, when his mother gave me her strand of flowers on the hill. But he was careful never to catch me, or yell '*Gubacchi*' when he spied me on the street still far from the temple, calling me the name for the brown and white sparrows he thought I resembled, the way he did before.

We went Ganesha-visiting the year after, and the year after that, until I was eight and Ajji forbade me to go anymore. 'Too childish,' she said by way of explanation. Our friends had fallen off slowly over the years. It would be just us and Vinay. So when he came around the morning of Ganesha *habba*, I met him at this gate where he stands, to tell him that Ajji had forbidden me to go. His face fell, and then he shrugged and said, 'It's okay. Too boring, *ilva*?' It was careful accented English that he spoke then and still does, and if one of our other friends were here, they would no doubt chortle and call it Butler English. Vinay's shoulder stuck out then as it does now, daring me to do the same.

Vinay continues as if nothing has happened since. 'Don't get carried away by everything you hear. It is all lies on television.' His face changes, when I still say nothing. 'Unless all you care about is that—that dirty Muslim.' He spits the words out as if he can think of no bigger insult for Adil.

And the chasm that separates the boy I used to know from the man in front of me reveals itself in that ugly phrase, which takes me back to a narrow alley behind a theatre that is soon to burn. I cannot bear to look at him anymore. But he is the last of the human-sized monsters I must set to rest. 'There is no friendship,' I say, and I feel the bitter taste of the words in my mouth as they leave, knowing that they will haunt him for long after I have forgotten them. 'No forgiveness. Not for the life you took. Not for the ones you destroyed. The boy Anisa went to see Ganeshas with is dead.' Anisa's name, spoken aloud, gives my words the weight of some ancient curse, one I do not intend.

I turn away to follow my aunt. When I look towards the gate again, he is gone.

Vimala aunty has been listening. When I join her indoors, she tells me, gently, 'Vinay always saw himself as the hero of one of these Kannada movies, and you as the heroine, Mira. One where the poor boy always gets the princess in the end. I am not sure that you ever realised it. Maybe things would have turned out differently if he saw some hope for himself, some way for a better life that he could work towards. Instead he ended up with your uncle—'

Perhaps one day I will learn to forgive, but for now my aunt's words only seem the inadequate excuse that they are.

When Appa arrives, I see the momentary shock in his eyes at the mention of his brother's death. But he does not leave to go to him. Together, we dust the house and sweep it. We wash the floors and the walls, the curtains and the bedclothes. The day advances. There is nothing left to clean.

I sense, however, that there is sorrow that Vimala aunty and Appa feel, that I do not. They bring up old anecdotes of the life the two of them shared with my mother and Girish uncle in Malehalli. It is as if they mourn, even if they do not admit it, even to themselves.

There is a cremation for Girish uncle that very day, we hear. But it is not one that we attend. Vinay and Lakshmi are the only ones at his final journey. They stop at the gate on their way back in the evening. Vinay is subdued, but he seems determined to say what he came to.

'We may not have money,' he says to Vimala aunty, careful to avoid looking at me, 'but we at least have our loyalty, our gratitude. What is wrong with you people?'

Gratitude, I wonder, at Vinay. For being pulled out of school and into servitude? He thinks that my uncle merited all that. Just how bleak of a future had this boy seen for himself that Girish uncle had represented a hand up, a way out?

'You are young, Mira-amma,' Lakshmi says to me, 'and your elders should teach you better. You cannot give up on your own blood, no matter what they do.'

It is Vimala aunty who answers her. 'This funeral, it happened a long time ago for us, Lakshmamma. It was only his body that was left.' It is true. I search my heart, and it is only an emptiness that I find, not sorrow. There is no tug of love, of belonging or blood. An absent space where there should have been my uncle, my father's older brother. Perhaps it is as my aunt says.

We sit down on the veranda as night approaches. We have left the lights off, and it is a small oasis of half lit darkness. The street outside is busy with pedestrians and two-wheelers, the street lamps bright as if this is an evening like any other. The fatigue of the last few days, the lack of sleep, the emotional upheavals and the day's hard labour has worn us down. We tell each other that we should get up, go indoors to sleep. But we sit instead on the old wicker chairs in silence, minds too tired to think.

'I should call the travel agent,' Appa says eventually. 'Not much to do anymore. We should be getting back.' He pauses, and asks my aunt, 'Vimala, would you like to come with us?'

She shakes her head. 'I always hoped I would go to Malehalli, though I did not think that it would actually happen,' she says. 'Maybe I can go now. Maybe the orphanage will find me something to do. It will be a relief to get out of this house.' She gestures to the squat home around us. I follow her arm to see the garden with tulsi in her pedestal, the garden path that Anisa and I ran down so often, and behind it, the tired walls that have witnessed so much. I cannot find the relief in my heart that she speaks of to leave this, this home that housed my happiness.

She continues, speaking more to herself than to us, 'Every minute that I lived here, I did because of Amma. As careful with my madi as I was with boundaries with—' She does not speak my uncle's name, but we all know what she means. 'It will be such a relief to get away, to go back. It doesn't matter what people think anymore. I don't have to care.'

Appa sighs. I see the relief Vimala aunty speaks of in his shadowed profile, and it irritates me, especially with the way they have allowed themselves to talk of Girish uncle all day.

'What about you, Appa?' I ask him, voice harsher than I intend. 'Did everything work out the way you expected? And now you can go back to the way things have been for you?'

'What do you mean, Mira?' he asks, though I suspect that he knows.

'All those years, did you not even ask Ajji for the truth? Did you believe them? Is that why there have never been pictures of her in your house? Is that why you left me here with Ajji?'

'I knew her,' Appa says, and his tone is mild. He turns to face me and the street lamps light up his face just for a moment before it disappears into shadow. 'Before she was your mother, she was my friend, my wife. Everything that one person can be for another. I knew the stories were lies.' He sighs again. 'For a long time, there was no one who shared my knowledge, my reality. It was as if the world had suddenly gone mad around me. If I started to think that maybe it was I who was mad, I was still happy to be that way. I always suspected that there was more to the horror of her death, Mira, but the fact that she was gone was horrible enough. It seemed easier to avoid the people who talked of her, and told me lies.'

He reaches out in the darkness and pats my face. 'I don't need pictures either. Not when I have you to look at every day.'

We sit in silence a little longer, and when I think our conversation has ended, Appa says again, 'She has been part of me for so long, for years before she died. She continues to be so. I always know what she would think, whether it was choosing a school for you, or a shirt to wear in the morning. She has never left me.'

He smiles, and I see the flash of his teeth suddenly white in the increasing darkness. 'Celia calls it my only harmless eccentricity.'

Vimala aunty smiles too, at that.

When he turns his head to the light again, I see his eyes. Despite the lightness of his tone, there is sadness there, silent and unremitting. Perhaps it is the sadness I have always seen and failed to recognise.

And then, suddenly, I remember. Ajji and I had a bedtime ritual when I had just started school. She lay down on the mat next to me, and together we imagined a trip to far-off America, a first airplane journey for both of us. It was a collage pieced together from stories we had heard, magazines and books that Ajji read, a movie a neighbour had seen. Ajji catalogued the details as obsessively as I did, and each day our imaginings got a little more specific. Here, Mira, here is your bag. This is your passport. Remember to hand it in at the immigration desk.

We stopped each other when a detail was skipped—you forgot that the air hostess will offer us juice, you forgot that we need to pick up our luggage before we see Appa. We imagined the send-off, the airplane rising into the sky, the magical trip that began with strapping on a seat belt, and ended with Appa waiting to gather me up in his arms at the end, stretching out every detail in delicious anticipation of the trip that we were to take in a few months.

The flight, when it did happen, could not match our imaginings.

Appa's apartment in Chicago, which he lived in as a doctoral candidate working on his thesis, was small. It sat midway up a tall building. Appa hoisted me up on his shoulders so I could see the street better. There were children on the street, even though there was a light April flurry of snow, waiting for a school bus that morning. Ajji hovered in the background, irritable.

Behind us was his tiny appliance-laden kitchen, where madi seemed impossible. She had her back turned to it, and she glared at the snow as if it were a malicious relative, and my fascination with it and impending school bus arrivals, a personal and specific insult.

'You will take that bus to school, soon,' Appa said. His voice vibrated through the back of his neck and into my chest, and I giggled from my perch on his shoulders.

'That's all very well,' Ajji said from behind us, 'if only good intentions were everything.'

Appa turned around to face her, even as I twisted my body to watch the children on the street below. 'I can take care of her,' Appa said, 'we'll survive.'

'Oh yes, you will, on eggs and meat and God knows what else. But who will feed her and bathe her and teach her our ways? Or take care of her when you are gone all day at that lab of yours?'

'Amma, other people have children here. She doesn't have to be in Bangalore to be taken care of. She can go to Murali's house. Seetha will take care of her during the day until I get back.'

'Oh, yes, of course, strangers will take care of her better than her own grandmother, all for the privilege of seeing you for two hours in a day before she sleeps.' The words were torpedoes out of Ajji's mouth, flying fast, just sliding past the edge of my attention. 'Because of course, you've raised children before, and know all about bringing up a girl all by yourself, in this—this alien place.'

'You could stay with us here too,' Appa said, but even I could see that the conclusion was foregone and he was just being polite to offer.

Ajji drew herself up. '*I* have no need to leave my home and my family.' After a beat, she said, 'But if Mira had a ... Gowri's daughter is also educated. They are looking for a match for her. You have seen her. She is better looking even than ... than anyone that I have seen.'

I twisted myself back to look, feeling the tensing of Appa's muscles in my loose, incidental embrace. The words had fallen with a studied carelessness, but a glance at Ajji's face was all I needed to know otherwise. They were circling, like animal adversaries over contested turf, around the thin politeness of their conversation.

'You can take Mira, and go back,' Appa said, and the anger in his voice seared, sudden, straight through my chest, all the way to my back. 'I will not be blackmailed into marrying again.'

Appa turned back to the window, the conversation at its end. I looked at the street again. The school bus had come and gone without my noticing it. The street was empty. The light snow that dusted it was already vanished by the sun. My chest ached.

In the days that came, I turned the words over in my mind, you-can-take-Mira-and-go-back, casual as the toss of a used paper towel into an American trash can, as I clung to Ajji at every opportunity. I cried when they left me with Murali's wife, Seetha. I refused to eat the sandwiches that Appa made, and waited for Ajji to bring me curd rice. Our visit ended early.

'She has never cried as much as she has this week,' Ajji said on the taxi ride to the airport. Appa was silent, but the load she set on his shoulders caused him to sag just a little bit more into his seat next to the driver at that remark.

'I will come and see you in India,' he said at the airport, hugging me as I twisted away. 'You will like it better here when you are older. I'll move somewhere warmer. It will be all right.'

It is that image that stays with me when I watch my father in the half lit veranda of my childhood home all these years later. For the first time, my heart goes out to the parent who was always there, even if he was locked in a struggle with his own demons and so seldom in my thoughts.

I step over to Appa and take his face in my hands, turning it to the light. 'Don't explain anymore.'

31
Mira

Celia has called me every day over the last fortnight.

'Come home,' she tells me over an Affenpinscher's excited barking, 'you don't have to stay behind just to sell the house.'

I can see her shaking her head when she says this, knotting the telephone cord over her index finger, pacing the kitchen floor as she usually does when she talks on the phone. It is true, what she says. That is my home and my life. There is my beloved Soldier. I should return.

Vimala aunty asked me a final time this afternoon if I would go with her to Malehalli. She leant out of her window in the train at the railway station. 'You can still get a ticket, Mira,' she said, tucking back the wayward grey strands that flew despite the multiple hair pins she had used. Her saree carefully pleated, she seemed a different person than the Vimala aunty I had known all my life. 'Come with me,' she said, 'before you leave for America. Don't worry about that house, of all things.'

But the house, bought with my uncle's ill-gotten gains, that no one wants to touch, is one I have wholeheartedly called home in happiness. I feel a stubborn responsibility to see it sold to someone will love it as it deserves. There are many who would buy it and tear it down to make way for a block of flats, a newer version of the one Anisa used to live in across the street. I am not sure if that is entirely a bad thing, but I hope for someone who might keep the garden path and tulsi in her pedestal for a few years more. The money will go to charity, perhaps to the orphanage in Malehalli where I will visit my aunt once the house is sold. Perhaps we will walk together then to the places my mother knew and loved. I say this in hope more than certainty. I could have gone this morning with my aunt, as she asked. But the years that I believed the ugly rumours about my mother hold me back, in embarrassment or shame.

Rehana aunty rings the doorbell almost as soon as I return from the railway station. She has visited every day, only leaving late in the evening just before dusk. Every day, her smile seems brighter than it was the day before, and there is less of the kernel of sorrow or resentment that I sometimes see in her eyes. Though she is careful to maintain her namaaz at its schedule, even if it means leaving mid-conversation, there are fewer arguments between her and Farid uncle. Today, she brings me clothes. One is a bright sleeveless tunic that I try on and find is more form-fitting than anything I own. It is a dusky red that complements my darker skin. 'I saw one in a light green, that Anisa could have worn,' she says. 'It was always the lighter colours that looked good on her, and darker ones on you.

'Maybe now you can stop wearing those shapeless things. They may be fashionable in America,' she sniffs momentarily, and it is remarkable in so many ways. She still wears her burkha, but announces her opposition to mine, and can finally mention Anisa without anger, or tears.

After Rehana aunty smiles her approval at my new outfit, she makes another of the oblique references to a possible marriage in the family. This is not the first time, either. 'It is high time Adil gets married,' she says, looking at me carefully out of the corner of her eyes. I see Farid uncle smile at his wife's nonchalance. For just that instant, it is the unshadowed smile of our past. It is in that minute that we see the world the way it would have been if Anisa had lived. Had she not died in that botched act of violence at Devidas's behest.

'Devidas was never found guilty for the theatre fire,' Adil had said on one of his early visits over the last fortnight. 'Can you believe how they let him get away with it?'

These are visits where we do not discuss his broken engagement or my seven year silence, where he is careful to time his arrival with Farid uncle and Rehana aunty's. We have avoided the awkwardness by pretending it does not exist, that we are bound only by the friendship I once had with Anisa. It is a decision that seemed easiest after I had made my first visit to their new house. It is on a street where every house has a name in Urdu on the door, or by the gate, in a tiny enclave where I am conscious of being different. Inside the house, I found verses from the Quran copied in a familiar hand that once copied Neruda or Ghalib, taped to the wall at eye level. Prayers for leaving, they say by the door or, prayer before eating, by the dining table.

'Adil,' Farid uncle confirmed for me, avoiding my eyes for just a minute. 'The praying is okay, but he also ran with a rough crowd for a while, soon after you left. I was lucky to talk Adil out of the mess before any violence happened. Not now, though,' he hastened to add. 'This is all from a few years back.'

Adil's small beard explains itself, as does the absence of the boy I once kissed. Austerity where there once was joyous banter, piety in place of his aspiration to poetry. There may be no way to bridge the years that have changed us from the people we used to be. Adil and I talk instead of other, more practical things.

'Devidas should pay for what he did. Maybe Vinay will testify,' Adil had said. But Vinay disappeared shortly after

Girish uncle's funeral. Without my uncle's protection, Vinay had found he was suddenly accountable for the laws he had broken in my uncle's employ. Lakshmi professed to not know his whereabouts, dabbing at her eyes with her saree. 'His life is worth nothing now, Mira-amma, let him be,' she said.

So it is that Devidas continues to ascend the ladder to divinity, his benedictions far-reaching, and his reach all-encompassing.

'For now,' Adil consoles us, 'for now. Vinay cannot hide forever. Devidas cannot fool the world for long.'

There will still be elections soon, and somebody will win. Not Surendra or Girish, but perhaps someone better at harnessing divisions of language, or caste, or religion, better at nurturing hate by rhetoric and careful organisation, more generously funded by bribes or misguided devotion. Having won, they will fatten their coffers by continuing to barter the things that do not belong to them, finding more conflicts to distract us from their emptiness, their insatiable appetites, and their greed. A sleight of hand, a prestidigitation perfected by repetition. Nothing changes, that was what they had all told me, Appa, Vimala aunty, Rehana aunty and Farid uncle. One leaves, another takes his place, they are all the same. Nothing will ever change.

And yet. In Malehalli, Ajji leaves behind an orphanage in the home she held as hallowed, named for a woman whose low birth she once detested. A Christian God hangs on his cross beside the Hindu Gods she adored and scolded in her pooja room there, while children whose caste no one cares to know play outside.

I cast my mind back, and I see Ajji in the temple again, asking Anisa to step up, so she can see Ganesha better. That was a different woman than the one who fought her husband over the rituals of caste. My grandfather would have smiled at her journey, but perhaps he always knew he would win over Ajji in the end. He had shared his mahatma's arrogance, after all, that they could change the things even the Lord Krishna failed at.

Perhaps my grandfather's eventual day of victory, of change in the world beyond, will still come. Perhaps it is his quixotic idealism in my blood makes it plausible, or maybe it is because the Bangalore that I have arrived into feels different, younger and new. There is furious construction all over the city and roads full of impatient traffic. There are young people everywhere.

'It's the Y2K influx,' Farid uncle jokes with me. 'Your American friends are afraid the computers will all stop in a few months when the calendar rolls into 2000, and these youngsters are here from all over India to save the world.'

They look so confident, I think. Perhaps they will save us all.

Adil arrives late in the evening, just as Rehana aunty and Farid uncle are about to leave.

Rehana aunty knots her face veil carefully under her chin, and Farid uncle grumbles, 'Must you still wear that thing? Everyone on this street has seen your face. No one will faint in surprise if they see it again today.'

Rehana aunty ignores him as seamlessly as she once did Anisa.

'I think I'll walk to the temple,' I say to Rehana aunty, because in her manner and that moment I both see and miss Anisa, my sister who was my friend.

'I'll walk you there,' Adil says.

Rehana aunty concurs as she steps into her sandals in the veranda. 'Yes, Mira, take Adil. It will be dark soon.'

Adil and I walk along our street, now more crowded with shops and people. We weave together in silence through the crowds, the noise of the evening all around us. I catch a glimpse of myself in a passing shop window, in the sleeveless red tunic worn over light, slim-fitting trousers that are a relic of my teenage years. My gaze stops for a moment instead of flitting away as it usually does. Do I look like my mother? She was a woman who stood up not just for herself, but for others who sought her help. Anisa was my other and better, self. Ajji, proud and flawed, yet brave in the admission of her faults, and in her gift of truth. I see them all in my reflection, and the red seems a fitting standard for our womanhood and our strength.

On we walk, past a new shopping mall that has come up where a theatre was once burnt; the still standing ration shop whose resident ghost might have witnessed my uncle's death. We pass young couples holding hands in the street, not exclaimed upon now as they once might have been, and others that flirt at street corners with the surreptitious air of new and secret attraction. We walk by old and familiar homes that are now tall blocks of apartments; pass magazine stalls, clothes shops and vegetable vendors. We mingle with grandparents and grandchildren making evening trips to the temple.

Adil waits below while I climb the steps alone. Inside, the pooja seems shorter and more hurried than in my memories. There is soon the rising crescendo of Sanskrit for the final prayer, to the clamour of ringing bells where Ganesha's face is illumined for us to see. A splash of holy water with tulsi into cupped hand, my solitary pradakshina around the temple without Ajji to steer me along, and a final prostration before the priest hands me the blessed offering. I recognise no one. All that is left is to sit in the temple for a minute as recommended by ritual, and I find the spot that Anisa and I always had.

I stand up an instant later and step outside to the broad open yard that fronts the temple. People leave after the evening pooja as Ajji did every day, with fruit and flowers that Ganesha has blessed. Beside the tall dwjasthamba, the flagstaff, is the small pedestal with Ganesha's footprints smoothed by decades of caressing hands in prayer, and His dominion stretches as wide as the eye can see. The vacant spot next to the temple where Anisa and I saw our last yakshagana, if only in part, is gone. The space has been eaten up by a tall building with offices and stores.

One of the offices catches my eye, its exterior walls and door a careful saffron that delineates it from the adjacent shop for small electric appliances. Swami Devidas smiles down from over the saffron door, the artist's rendering faithful and adoring. Devidas's saffron minions no longer stand along the steps to the temple, separate and distinct from the crowds that visit. Instead, there are his lay devotees, upstanding men and women, who stand at the door and down by the entrance, handing out saffron wrist bands, pressing them with gentle, insistent smiles to anyone who does not have one. Mother, brother, or sister, they say, wide-eyed and sincere, please, it is for a good cause. The ease with which his divisiveness is growing, weaving itself into the fabric of my city and faith is astonishing, if not frightening. But I remember the optimism of the young and impatient around me, who have the means to achieve their dreams. Not everyone is within the reach of his bluster, or his ilk. There is still hope.

Down Ganesha's hill, the wide stone steps are more worn but the rangoli patterns they bear carefully repeated and faithful. Lakshmi still sells her flowers halfway down the hill, older, perhaps wiser and more adept. Further down the steps, Adil waits, his face turned away from the temple and into the street, a faint embarrassment evident in the set of his shoulders. The walls beyond him are covered with posters as always, advertisements for movies interspersed with those for elections, every hue in the world represented in their spread.

The market, now without wood stalls and squatting vendors, without sparrows, stands modern and bright across the street made more narrow by parked vehicles. Despite the people, the vehicles and the adults' displeasure, there are still children playing cricket on the street, shouting to each other in Kannada, and laughing. The trees that stand around them and beyond are older, taller and more sweeping, their crowding branches a leafy canopy that stretches wide and green. Neon lights flare, announcing dusk along the street below and the next, pinpricks of light between branch and tree that stretch in an endless chain. Sampige Road, Malleshwaram, Bangalore and the world beyond lighting up in sequence as I watch. Homes and shops light up in succession, as if linked together by more than place and happenstance. It is a world at once imperfect and hopeful, and it beckons and beguiles me into belonging. The crowd thins. Adil chances to look up, and smiles. And still I tarry at Ganesha's feet carved into stone, reluctant to return.

Even as I wonder at what it is that I wait for, evening sounds rise up in the cooling air of dusk, melding conversations and commerce, bustle and traffic, crows and cricket balls all into an unexpected harmony. The remnants of burdens carried so long lift away in a gust of evening breeze. In moments, the sky darkens above to an indigo so deeply blue with the sparkle of appearing stars, that it is a beloved sequined saree, unfurling itself above the earth.

Acknowledgements

I came to writing at the most inopportune of times, impelled by an insistent image that came often and with increasing frequency—of an older white saree clad woman and a young girl who clung to her little finger. To think that a novel would grow out of that single glimpse seems improbable, even (or perhaps especially) to me. It would not have been possible without the generosity and support of so many.

My agent in the US, Emma Parry at Janklow & Nesbit, provided invaluable early encouragement with her faith in this novel. Jayapriya Vasudevan at Jacaranda Literary Agency has been tireless in her enthusiasm for this book in India. It is fitting and fortunate that this book found a home at Westland Publications, and with Deepthi Talwar, gentlest of editors—the novel is better for her wisdom and vision. My thanks also to Gautam Padmanabhan, Krishna Kumar Nair, Arunima Mazumdar, Neha Khanna, Shweta Bhagat, Rashi Mall Bhambri and Vishwanath Ghosh at Westland.

Every writer has a tribe. Mine includes the many wonderful writers who critiqued bits and pieces of this novel at Tomales Bay, The Breadloaf Writers Conference, Sirenland and the One Story writers workshop, as well as at the recurring Sacramento Master Teacher workshops closer to home. Many remain friends years after, and all were integral to helping me feel, and think, like a writer. Special thanks to the writers in

Sacramento at whose homes I've indulged in much talking and tea; you are my sisters. My gratitude to Julie Lekstrom Himes and Robert Anthony for their encouragement with the earliest rough-sketch version of this book, Madhava Chippali for his insights into all things Havyaka, Stephanie Siciarz and Sharon Van Epps who provided long-distance support and commiseration at critical junctures, and Coby Hoffman who read not only the first draft but every successive one with undiminished enthusiasm. My journey was made easier by the extraordinary generosity of writers who were my teachers: Vikram Chandra, in whose workshop at Tomales Bay I first began to see how a novel might take shape from the early chapter I brought; Dani Shapiro at Sirenland whose advice on leaving lily-pads made all the difference; Hannah Tinti who opened a door; Will Allison, Percival Everett, Kevin McIlvoy, Karen Bender and Peter Ho Davies whose insights into writing made this novel better; Melanie Abrams, whose advice on successive drafts was key, as was her optimism, and her ability to wave a wand and make my troubles disappear, every time. And finally: Mrs Hilda Peacock. But for a single and critical misunderstanding, our paths might have never crossed; I might never have seen, or loved, how sentences could be acrobats.

I'm grateful for my family who surround me with love and support my writing even at its most inconvenient. My parents and parents-in-law have stepped into parenting breaches without complaint; I choose to believe that both grandparents and grandchildren are happier for this. My extended family and friends who have treated my children and my writing as their own—your encouragement has meant the world to me. Everyone should have the kind of childhood I did in Bangalore, where neighbours took me into their hearts and homes. It was here that I first saw that being family was about more than being related—and there is no alchemy without you all. My parents, Jayashantha and K. Balasubramanian, my brother Deepak, my children, Nikhilesh and Samhita, and most of all, Nanda, my partner in all things, cheerleader, confidant and better human than I will ever be—your love has shaped my world, and this book.

All author proceeds benefit two charities: The Alumni Distress Fund at Christian Medical College, Vellore and CEG 90 Knowledge Foundation (www.aaceg1990.com) at Anna University, Chennai.